"Terry McMillan is not only a gifted fiction writer but a social critic as clear-eyed as Mark Twain, Zora Neale Hurston, or Edith Wharton."
—*New York Newsday*

"Terry McMillan stands...as a literary Bessie Smith."
—*The Toronto Star*

continued . . .

"Great storytelling with . . . McMillan's trademark earthiness and wonderful dialogue. This bestselling author has a rare gift for creating living, breathing people on the page."
—*Kirkus Reviews*

"An ambitious, redemptive novel. The story of the Price family transcends race. *A Day Late and a Dollar Short* is about family, its power to build us up and at the same time, as Mama would say, 'get on our last nerve.'" —*The Arizona Republic*

"Nobody does it better . . . sassy, inventive, humorous, and wise. She can make me laugh out loud, but she is just as capable of moving me to tears. As in *Waiting to Exhale*, *A Day Late and a Dollar Short* embodies McMillan's belief in romantic love as the most profound expression of one's humanity."
—*The Toronto Star*

"[McMillan] knows how to write with honesty, insight, and humor about love, family, and relationships. Live with the Price family for a day or two. You will learn some important life lessons as you read a novel that defines the essence of this author's work." —*Tulsa World*

"A page-turner . . . even better than *Waiting to Exhale*."
—*The Post and Courier* (Charleston, NC)

"A portrayal of African-American family life that could only be told by Terry McMillan. *A Day Late and a Dollar Short* is a phenomenal book . . . both entertaining and in your face. I loved it." —*The Tennessean*

"[A] hope-filled and uplifting novel of a black American family trying to find and hold on to the American dream."
—*Calgary Herald*

continued . . .

Praise for *Disappearing Acts*

"A love story ready to explode."
—*The New York Times Book Review*

"Unflinchingly realistic . . . warm, natural . . . *Disappearing Acts* is a get-out-your-handkerchiefs love story."
—*USA Today*

"Beautiful and easy to get lost in. . . . A stunning achievement."
—*Cosmopolitan*

"If Ntozake Shange, Jane Austen, and Danielle Steel collaborated on a novel of manners, this . . . entertaining book might be the result."
—*The New Yorker*

"With *Disappearing Acts,* McMillan firmly places herself in the same league as . . . Alice Walker, Gloria Naylor, and . . . Zora Neale Hurston."
—*Pittsburgh Post-Gazette*

"A strong story that readers won't want to put down. . . . McMillan has molded a moving winner."
—*Detroit Free Press*

"A down-to-earth portrayal of love, yearning, and self-preservation . . . *Disappearing Acts* is brimming with energy and the hard facts of life. McMillan's people are so real they make the floors and ceiling shake."
—*The Kansas City Star*

"Gripping and moving . . . intensely realistic."
—*The Cleveland Plain Dealer*

"An authentic portrayal. . . . McMillan has written a book that speaks not harshly of one sex, but honestly of the often-strained bond between men and women."
—*The Baltimore Sun*

"Ribaldly realistic . . . but touchingly lyrical. With eloquence and style, McMillan gives her work a voice that is her own, one tough enough to speak across class and color lines, daring enough to make a statement about our country and our times."
—*Newsday*

Praise for *How Stella Got Her Groove Back*

"A cast of likable characters, funny lines, smart repartee, and a warm . . . ending. Irreverent, mischievous, diverting . . . will make you laugh out loud."
—*The New York Times Book Review*

"Terry McMillan is the only novelist I have ever read who makes me glad to be a woman."
—*The Washington Post Book World*

"Rich in detail . . . leaves you feeling like you've just had a good gossip with your best girlfriend." —*Mademoiselle*

"A down-and-dirty, romantic and brave story told to you by this smart, good-hearted woman as if she were your best friend."
—*Newsday*

"A liberating love story . . . tells women it's okay to let go, follow your heart, take a chance, and fall in love."
—*The Orlando Sentinel*

Praise for *Waiting to Exhale*

"With relationships between African-American men and women in the spotlight as never before, here comes McMillan's report from the front . . . bawdy, vibrant, deliciously readable. A novel that hits so many exposed nerves is sure to be a conversation piece. It has heart and pizzazz and even, yes, the sweet smell of a breakthrough book." —*Kirkus Reviews*

Also by Terry McMillan

A Day Late and a Dollar Short

Terry McMillan

A SIGNET BOOK

SIGNET
Published by New American Library, a division of
Penguin Putnam Inc., 375 Hudson Street,
New York, New York 10014, U.S.A.
Penguin Books Ltd, 80 Strand,
London WC2R ORL, England
Penguin Books Australia Ltd, Ringwood,
Victoria, Australia
Penguin Books Canada Ltd, 10 Alcorn Avenue,
Toronto, Ontario, Canada M4V 3B2
Penguin Books (N.Z.) Ltd, 182–190 Wairau Road,
Auckland 10, New Zealand

Penguin Books Ltd, Registered Offices:
Harmondsworth, Middlesex, England

Published by Signet, an imprint of New American Library, a division of Penguin Putnam
Inc. Previously published in a Viking edition.

First Signet Printing, January 2002
10 9 8 7 6 5 4 3 2 1

PUBLISHER'S NOTE
This is a work of fiction. Names, characters, places, and incidents either are the product
of the author's imagination or are used fictitiously, and any resemblance to actual
persons, living or dead, business establishments, events, or locales is entirely
coincidental.

Contents

For my sisters and brother

Rosalyn, Crystal, Vicky, and Edwin

with much love and respect

and in memory of our mother

Madeline Tillman (1933–1993)

"who never missed a beat"

Acknowledgments

I'm grateful to the following people for taking time to provide me with technical advice: Dr. Elizabeth Whelchel, Gary Mahlberg, Denise Portuesi, Carol Carrillo, Dr. Michelle Clarke, Chef Mario Garcia, Lisa Crites, and Margaret Muller; for their legal expertise: the Hon. Theresa Sanchez and Walter L. Gordon III, Esq.; for all the athletic info: my nephew, Terrence Zenno; for writing space: Bob and Doralee Rae; for a listening ear: Blanche Richardson; for their administrative help: Judi Fates and Lorena Smith; for tolerating me and being so understanding in the length of time it took to complete this novel: my agent, Molly Friedrich, and my judicious editor, Carole DeSanti, as well as the astute editorial eyes of Beena Kamlani; for printing and getting the finished manuscript to my editor and agent: my cousin, Jacqueline Dixon; for her time and her friendship: Lynda Drummer; and last but not least, for their patience in general but their love in particular: my son, Solomon, and my husband, Jonathan.

Author's Note

This is a work of fiction inspired by my emotions and personal responses to issues that have arisen for many families, and in some instances, perhaps even in my own. However, neither the characters portrayed here nor any of the events that take place in this story should in any way be understood or construed as real. Rather, they are the product of my imagination.

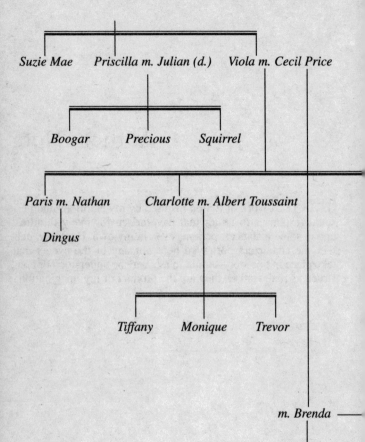

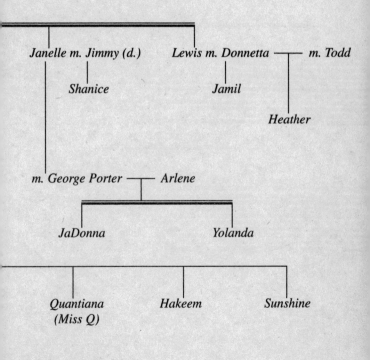

Janelle m. Jimmy (d.)   Lewis m. Donnetta ——— m. Todd

Shanice   Jamil

Heather

m. George Porter ——— Arlene

JaDonna   Yolanda

Quantiana   Hakeem   Sunshine
(Miss Q)

The Way
I See It

Can't nobody tell me nothing I don't already know. At least not when it comes to my kids. They all grown, but in a whole lotta ways they still act like children. I *know* I get on their nerves—but they get on mine, too—and they always accusing me of meddling in their business, but, hell, I'm their mother. It's my job to meddle. What I really do is worry. About all four of 'em. Out loud. If I didn't love 'em, I wouldn't care two cents about what they did or be the least bit concerned about what happens to 'em. But I do. Most of the time they can't see what they doing, so I just tell 'em what *I* see. They don't listen to me half the time no way, but as their mother, I've always felt that if *I* don't point out the things they doing that seem to be causing 'em problems and pain, who will?

Which is exactly how I ended up in this damn hospital: worrying about kids. I don't even want to think about Cecil right now, because it might just bring on another attack. He's a bad habit I've had for thirty-eight years, which would make him my husband. Between him and these kids, I'm worn out. It's a miracle I can breathe at all.

I had 'em so fast they felt more like a litter, except each one turned out to be a different animal. Paris is a female lion who don't roar loud enough. Lewis is a horse who don't pull his own weight. Charlotte is definitely a bull, and Janelle would have to be a sheep—a lamb is closer to it—'cause she always being led out to some pasture and don't know how she got there.

As a mother, you have high hopes for your kids. Big dreams. You want the best for them. Want 'em to get the rewards from life that you didn't get for one reason or another. You want them to be smarter than you. Make better choices. Wiser moves. You don't want them to be foolish or act like fools.

Which is why I could strangle Lewis my damnself. He is one big ball of confusion. Always has had an excuse for every-thing, and in thirty-six years, he ain't changed a lick. In 1974, he did not steal them air conditioners from the Lucky Lady Motel that the police just happened to find stacked up in the back seat of our LeSabre way out there in East L.A. Lewis said his buddy told him they belonged to his uncle. And why shouldn't he believe him? All of a sudden he got allergies. Was always sneezing and sniffling. He said it was the smog. But I wasn't born yesterday. He just kept at it. Said he couldn't help it if folks was always giving him stuff to fix or things he didn't even ask for. Like that stereo that didn't work. Or them old tools that turned out to be from Miss Beulah's garage. Was I ac-cusing him of stealing from Miss Beulah? Yes I was. Lewis was always at the wrong place at the wrong time, like in 1978 while he waited for Dukey and Lucky to come out of a dry cleaner's with no dry cleaning and they asked him to "Floor it!" and like a fool he did and the police chased their black asses all the way to the county jail.

For the next three years, Lewis made quite a few trips back and forth to that same gray building, and then spent eighteen months in a much bigger place. But he wasn't a good criminal, because, number one, he always got caught; and, number two, he only stole shit nobody needed: rusty lawnmowers, shovels and rakes, dead batteries, bald tires, saddles, and so on and so forth. Every time he got caught, all I did was try to figure out how could somebody with an IQ of 146 be so stupid? His teachers said he was a genius. Especially when it came to math. His brain was like a calculator. But what good did it do? I'm still waiting for the day to come when all them numbers add up to something.

Something musta happened to him behind them bars, 'cause ever since then—and we talking twelve, thirteen years ago—Lewis ain't been right. In the head. He can't finish nothing he start. Sometime he don't even start. Fortunately, he ain't been back to jail except for a couple of DUIs, and he did have sense enough to stop fooling around with that dope after so many of his friends OD'd. Now all he do is smoke reefa, sit in that dreary one-bedroom apartment drinking a million ounces of Old English, and play chess with the Mexicans. When ain't nobody there but him (which ain't often 'cause he can't stand being by hisself more than a few hours), he do crossword puzzles. Hard ones. And he good at it. These he *do* finish. And from what I gather, he done let hundreds of women walk through his revolving door for a day or two but then all he do is complain about Donnetta, his ex-wife, who he ain't been married to now going on six years, so most of 'em don't come back.

And don't let him get a buzz going. Every other word outta his mouth is Donnetta. He talk about her like they just got divorced yesterday. "She wanted a perfect man," he claimed, or, "I almost killed myself trying to please that woman." But even though Donnetta was a little slow, she was nice, decent. After I'd left Cecil for the third time, I stayed with 'em for close to a month. By the second week, I was almost ready for the loony bin. First off, Donnetta couldn't cook nothing worth eating; she wasn't exactly Oprah when it came to having a two-way conversation; cleaning house was at the bottom of her things-to-do list; and that boy needed his ass beat at least twice a day but she only believed in that white folks' "time-out" mess. She didn't have as much sense as a Christmas turkey, and how you supposed to lead a child down a path when you lost your damnself? I understood completely when that chile turned to God, got saved, and finally stopped giving Lewis dessert at night. A few months ago she sent me a pink postcard from some motel in San Diego saying she got married, is seven months pregnant and they already know it's a girl, and her new husband's name is Todd and he wants to adopt Jamil, and what do I think about all this? And then: P.S. Not that it should matter, but Todd is white. First of all, who she marry is her business, even though Lewis'll probably have a stroke when he find out. But one thing I do know: kids love whoever take care of 'em.

Lewis been lost since she left. And he blames everybody except Lewis for his personal misery. Can't find no job: "I'm a threat to the white man," he says. "How?" I ask. "You more of a threat to yourself, Lewis." He huffs and puffs. "I'm a victim." And I say, "I agree. Of poor-assed planning!" And then he goes off and explains the history of the human race, and then black people, and then finally we get to the twentieth century and the castration of the black man that's still going on in society today because just look at how successful the black woman is compared to us! This is when I'd usually hand him another beer, which finally either shut his ass up, or he'd nod off into a coma.

Tragedy is his middle name.

For years I fell for his mess. Would lend him my Mary Kay money. My insurance-bill money. Even pawned my wedding ring once so he could pay his child support. But then it started to dawn on me that the only time he call is when he want something, so I stopped accepting the charges. Last week he come calling me to say another one of his little raggedy cars broke down on the side of the freeway, way out in redneck country, where Rodney King got beat up, and I guess I was supposed to feel sorry for him, which I did for a hot minute, but then I remembered he ain't had no driver's license for close to a year, and then he asked could I wire him $350 till his disability check came, and this time, this was my answer: "Hell, no!"

He got mad. "You don't care what happens to me, do you, Ma?"

"Don't start that mess with me, Lewis."

"You don't understand what I'm going through. Not one bit. Do you?"

"It don't matter whether I understand or not. I'm your mother. Not your wife. Not your woman. And I ain't no psychiatrist neither. What happened to Conchita?"

"It's Carlita."

"Comosita, Consuela, Conleche . . . whatever."

"We broke up."

"I'm shocked."

"I need your help, Ma. For real."

"So what else is new? You ain't even supposed to be driving, Lewis."

"Then how am I supposed to look for work or get to work?"

I decided to just pretend like I didn't hear him say the word "work." "I don't know. Call one of your friends, Lewis."

"I ain't got no friends with that kind of money. It's tough out here for black men, Ma, and especially if you handicapped. Don't you know that?"

"I didn't know you was handicapped."

"I got arthritis."

"Uh-huh. And I'm three months pregnant with triplets."

"How come don't nobody ever believe me when I tell the truth? I can't hardly ball up my fist, my knuckles is so swollen. And on my right wrist, the bone is sticking out. . . . Oh, never mind. Ma, please?"

"I have to go now, Lewis. I ain't got no three hundred and fifty dollars."

"Yes, you do."

"You calling me a lie?"

"No."

"I'm telling you. All my money is spent."

"Where's Daddy?"

"Barbecuing. Where you think?" I say, lying my butt off.

"Could you ask him? And tell him it's for you?"

I just started laughing. First of all, I ain't seen Cecil in over a month, but I didn't feel like getting into it right then.

He groaned. "How about two hundred dollars, then?"

That's when I slammed the receiver down, because I couldn't stand hearing him beg. My hands was shaking so bad and my heart was beating a mile a minute, so I reached in the kitchen drawer, grabbed my spray, and took two or three quick puffs. Seem like he ain't gon' be satisfied till he use me up. That thought alone made me start crying, and I don't like to cry, 'cause it always do me right in. I couldn't get no air to come through my nose or mouth, and I clenched my fist and said in my head, "God give me strength," as I made my way to my room and sat on the edge of the bed, turned on my machine, grabbed that plastic tube, and sucked and sucked until my palms got slippery and my forehead was so full of sweat that I snatched my wig off and threw it on the floor.

I love Lewis. Would give him my last breath. Lord knows I don't want nothing bad to happen to him, but Lewis got problems I can't solve. It's some things love *can* do. And it's some things it can't do. I can't save him. Hell, I'm trying to figure out how to save myself.

Now, Charlotte. She a bull, all right. And I wish I didn't feel like this but I do: half the time I can't stand her. I don't know how her husband can tolerate her ass either. I feel sorry for Al, really. He's one of them pussy-whipped, henpecked kinda husbands but try to pretend like he Superman in front of company. *Everybody* know Charlotte is a bossy wench from the word go. We ain't spoke this time going on four months. I think the record is five or six. I can't remember. But, hell, all I did was tell her she need to spend more time at home with them kids and she went off.

"When was the last time you worked full-time, took care of three kids and a husband, ran a household *and* three Laundromats, Mama, huh?"

"Never," I said.

"So how can you sit there on your high horse telling me what you think I *should* be doing?"

"Get some help and stop trying to do it all yourself."

"Do you know how expensive housekeepers is these days?"

"Oh, stop being so damn cheap, Charlotte. You don't have no trouble spending it."

"Cheap? Let me . . ."

"I heard Tiffany got expelled and Monique is running her mouth so much in class that she might be next."

"Who told you this—Janelle? With *her* big mouth? I know it, I just know it. Well, first of all, it ain't true."

"It is true, and it's your fault for not being there to keep their behinds in line."

"I'ma pretend like I didn't hear that. But let me tell you something, *Mother*. Tiffany did *not* get expelled. She got sent home for wearing too much perfume, 'cause half the class— including the teacher—started getting nauseous. And for your information, Monique just told a joke that made everybody laugh."

I knew she was lying through her teeth, but I didn't dare say it, so I just said, "Un-huh."

"And since Janelle's running her mouth so much, did she bother to tell you that Monique is also having a tough time 'cause we regulating her medication?"

"I *got* her medicine, all right."

"Mama, you know what? I'm so tired of your sarcastic remarks I don't know what to do. Sick of 'em! You never have nothing nice to say about my kids!"

"That's bullshit, and you know it!"

"It ain't bullshit!"

"When they do something good, then I'll have a reason to say something nice."

"See, that's what I mean! Has Dingus thrown a touchdown pass lately? And what about your darling Shanice: did she get straight A's again? Go ahead and throw it in my face. I could use some more good goddamn news today!"

"You better watch your mouth. I'm still your mother."

"Then don't call me until you start acting like a mother and a grandmother to *my* kids!" And—bam!—she hung up.

The truth always hurts. This ain't the first time she done slammed the phone down in my face or talked to me in that nasty tone: like I'm somebody in the street. I ain't gon' lie: it hurts and cuts into me deep, but I refuse to give her the satisfaction of knowing how bad she makes me feel. To be honest, Charlotte just likes people to kiss her ass, but I kissed their daddy's behind for thirty-eight years. I ain't here to pacify my kids. No, Lordy. Them days is over, especially since they're all damn near middle age.

Charlotte came too quick. Ten months after Paris. I did not need another baby so soon, and I think she knew it. She wanted all my attention then. And still do. She ain't never forgiven me for having Lewis and Janelle, and she made sure I knew it. I had to snatch a knot in her behind once for putting furniture polish in their milk. Made 'em take a nap in the doghouse with the dog and fed 'em Alpo while I went downtown to pay some bills. Had 'em practice drowning in a bathtub full of cold water. How many steps could they jump down with their eyes closed without falling. The list goes on.

Now, all my kids is taller than average, as good-looking as they come and as dark as you can get, and I spent what I felt was a whole lotta unnecessary time and energy teaching 'em to appreciate the color of their skin. To not be ashamed of it. I used to tell 'em that the blacker the berry the sweeter the juice, 'cause everybody know that back then being yellow with long wavy hair meant you was automatically fine, which was bullshit, but here it is 1994 and there's millions of homely yellow women with long straggly hair running around still believing that lie. Anyway, no matter what I did or said to make my kids feel proud, Charlotte was the only one who despised her color.

Never mind that she was the prettiest of the bunch. Never mind that she had the longest, thickest, shiniest hair of all the black girls in the whole school. And nothing upset that chile more than when Paris started getting breasts and learned how to do the splits and Charlotte couldn't. She was the type of child you couldn't praise enough. Always wanted more. But, hell, I had three other kids and I had to work overtime to divide up my energy and time. What was left, I gave to Cecil.

Where's my lunch? I know this ain't no hotel, but a person could starve to death in this hospital. Would you look at that: it's raining like cats and dogs and here it is March. This weather in Vegas done sure changed over the years. It sound like bullets hitting these windows. I wish they would turn that damn air conditioning down. My nose is froze and I can't even feel my toes no more. I hope I ain't dead and just don't know it.

Anyway, it ain't my fault that right after we left Chicago and moved to California, Charlotte didn't like it and put up such a fuss that we sent her ass back there to live with my dinghy sister, Suzie Mae. She forgot to tell me and Suzie Mae she was damn near four months pregnant when I put her on the train. Young girls know how to hide a baby when they want to, and I'm a hard person to fool. I pay attention. Don't miss too much of nothing. But Charlotte is good at hiding a whole lot of stuff. She snuck and got married, and wasn't until another two months had passed when Suzie Mae come calling me saying, "You could send your daughter a wedding present or at least a package of diapers for the baby." What baby? Did I miss something? But I was not about to ask. I sent her a his-and-her set of beige towels from J. C. Penney, even though I didn't know nothing about the boy except his name was Al and he was a truck driver whose people was from Baton Rouge, so I couldn't get no initials put on 'em. I bought a mint-green booty set for the baby, 'cause they say it's bad luck to plan so far ahead, and right after her honeymoon (they didn't go nowhere except to spend the night at the Holiday Inn two exits off the freeway from where they live), Charlotte woke up in the middle of the night in a puddle of blood. She was having terrible cramps and thought she was in labor, except later on she tells us that the baby hadn't moved in two or three days. The doctors had to induce labor, and the baby was stillborn—a boy. I asked if she wanted me to come there to be with her, and she told me no. Her husband would take care of her. And *that* he did.

With so much going on, college slipped her mind altogether. She got that job at the post office and worked so much overtime I don't know when they found time to make anything except money, but somehow they managed to generate three more kids.

Now, Tiffany—that's her oldest daughter—got those big gray eyes and that high-yellow skin and that wavy plantation hair from her daddy's side of the family—they Louisiana Creoles—which is why she walk around with her ass on her shoulders thinking she the finest thing this side of heaven. She is. Ain't big as a minute, and prettier than a chile is supposed to be. But folks been telling her for so long that sometimes I can't hardly stand her behind either. She thirteen going on twenty. Can have a nasty attitude. Just like her mama. Ask her to do something she don't wanna do and she'll roll them eyes at you like a grown woman. I threw a shoe at her the last time I was there and accidentally hit her in the eye, which is probably one more reason why me and her mama ain't speaking. The child stays in the mirror. Change her hairstyle at least two or three times before she leave for school, which is apparently the reason she don't have no time left to do her homework. Every time I see her she washing and rolling a ponytail or cascade and putting it in the microwave to dry, which is why the whole upstairs smell like burnt hair. I told her, Being pretty and dumb won't get you nowhere in this day and age. There's *millions* of pretty girls in the world. You just one. Put something else with it.

Now, Monique is on the verge of being sweet but something

stops her. She supposed to have some kind of learning disorder they giving out to every other child who don't pay attention, but let one of those music videos come on BET and she'll drop whatever she doing and go into a trance. Know the words to every rap record and hippity-hop song that come on the radio. And can move her behind so smooth she look like a pint-size woman practicing what she gon' do to her man the next chance she get. But I give her this much credit. She can play the flute so sweet it make you close your eyes and see blue. She know how to read all the notes, too. She taught herself how to play the piano. But once she get up off that bench, she too grown. I bought some videos for both of 'em when I was visiting last year and just slap me for buying PG-13s. "Granny, don't you know that all the best movies are rated R?" she asked me. Monique had her hands on what one day might be hips. "If ain't no sex, blood, or don't nobody get killed, it's boring, huh, Tiff?" And Miss Thang put the glue down and started blowing on her $1.99 Fancy Nails and said, "Yep." I couldn't say shit. At the rate they going, if these two make it outta high school without a baby, it'll be a miracle. This ain't wishful thinking on my part, it's what I see coming.

Now, Trevor is the only one in the house with a ounce of sense, but it's hard to tell what he's gon' do with it. He smart as hell—get straight A's and everything—but he don't seem to be interested in too much of nothing except his sewing machine and other boys, and not necessarily in that order. His mama refuse to believe that he's like that, but I saw it in him when he was little. He was always a little soft. Did everything lightly. But he can't help it. And even though I don't like it, Oprah has helped me understand it. He has a right to be who he is, and I'll love him no matter where he put his business. I just hope he don't grow up and catch no AIDS. He dance better than both of the girls, like ain't a bone in his body, and he been blessed with more than one talent. Besides clothes designing, the boy can also cook his ass off. It wouldn't kill his mama to take a long hard look in his room to get a few decorating ideas either, 'cause her mix-and-match taste ain't saying nothing. One minute she Chinese and the next she Southern Gothic or French Provincial. Some rules ain't supposed to be broken. Class is one more thing Charlotte think she can buy.

Trevor call me collect from time to time. "I can't wait to get out of here, Granny," he say each and every time we talk: "But it's okay. Two more years, Granny. And I'll be free."

Is that a real-live nurse coming in here carrying a tray? Yum yum yum. More babyfood? Who can swallow when you got a tube going down your throat and through your nose? I done already had two breathing treatments since this morning, what she want now? Nothing. All she do is look up at the numbers on those machines and then smile at me. "Comfortable?" she ask, and I shake my head no, since she know good and damn well I can't hardly mumble, but she just kinda curtsy and say, "Good," then turn around and walk out! If I was able to open my mouth I'd say, "Huzzy! I'm hungry as hell, cold as hell, and I could sure use a stiff drink." But I can't talk. And Lord knows I'm scared, 'cause I'm still here in ICU and I'm bored and I wanna go home, even though I know ain't nobody there waiting for me. Cecil been gone since the first of the year, but I don't feel like thinking about his old ass right now. That's another reason why I'm glad I got kids.

Now, Paris is the oldest. And just the opposite of Charlotte. Probably too much. Never gave me no trouble to speak of. And even though you love the ones that come afterwards, that first one'll always be something special. It's when you learn to think about somebody besides yourself. At the time, I was sixteen and watched too many movies, which is how I got it in my mind that one day I was going to Paris and become a movie star like Dorothy Dandridge or Lena Horne and I'd wear long flowing evening gowns and sleep in satin pajamas. I wanted to speak French, because Paris, France, seemed like the most romantic place in the world, and back then I craved romance something fierce. But I didn't expect it to come in the form it came in: Cecil. I used to close my eyes, laying right between my sisters: Suzie Mae on one side and Priscilla on the other. I'd smell bread baking and see red wine being poured in my glass and pale-yellow cheese being sliced and I could see the mist through those lace curtains and feel the cobblestone beneath my spiked heels. I heard accordions. Saw small wooden boats in dark-green water. But by the time I married Cecil and got pregnant—or, I should say, by the time I got pregnant and married Cecil—I knew the chances of me ever getting on a airplane going anywhere was slim to zero, so I named my daughter after the place I'd probably never see.

I made two mistakes: married the first man who was nice to me, who showed me some unfiltered attention and gave me endless pleasure in bed. But because of my particular kind of ignorance, my second major mistake was dropping outta high school at sixteen to have a baby. It wasn't until five or six years down the road, when I was watching *Casablanca* on TV one night—alone—that I had to ask myself if I really loved Cecil. Would I go this far for him? Long before Humphrey and Ingrid even made it to the airport I knew the answer to that question was no. What I felt back then was comfortable—not comfort—just comfortable. There was no guesswork to our lives. But over the years all of it melted and turned into some kind of love, that much I do know.

Speaking of heat. All my kids are too hot in the ass—which they got from their daddy's side of the family—and Paris ain't no exception. It's probably the reason they all been divorced at least once (except for Charlotte, of course, but that's only 'cause she just too stubborn to admit defeat). All four of 'em married the wrong person for the wrong reasons. They married people who only lit up their bodies and hearts and forgot all about their minds and souls. To this day I still don't think they know that orgasms and love ain't hardly the same thing.

Paris sure don't know how to pick no man. Every one she

ever loved had something wrong with him. Nathan—that's my grandson's daddy—scores very high on this test. I don't know why, but she seem to pick the ones that's got major wiring problems. They should've been wearing giant signs that said: "Defective" or "Lazy" or "Retarded" or "Not Father Material" or "Yeah, I'm Good-looking but I Ain't Worth Shit." I guess she think her love can fill in their blank spots, 'cause for some strange reason she gravitate to these types. The kind of men that drain you, drag you down, take more from you than they give, and by the time they done used you up, got what they want, they bored, you on empty, and they ready to move on to greener pastures.

She love too hard. Her heart is way too big and she's too generous. To put it another way: she's a fool. Ain't nothing worse than a smart fool. And she's smart all right. Got her own catering company. Well, it's more to it than just cooking and dropping the stuff off in those silver trays with little flames underneath. No sirree. This ain't no rinky-dink kind of operation. First of all, you need some real money if you want to eat Paris's food, 'cause she's expensive as hell. Say you having a big party—not just your regular weekend type of bash, I mean the kind you see in movies: like *The Godfather Part I*, for example, when the food don't look real, or too good to eat, and you too scared to touch it. Give her a theme: she'll cook around it. Give her a country: she'll transform your house. Make it look like you in Africa or Brazil or Spain or, hell, Compton. All you gotta do is tell her. She make all the arrangements: from the forks and tablecloths, to the palm trees, hedges, and flowers, to the jazz band or DJ. One of her assistants, and she's got a few of 'em, will even make hotel arrangements for the guests and have folks picked up in limousines at the airport.

Anyway, she got class, and she got it from my side of the family. She been in the San Francisco newspaper, and I think the *L.A. Times*, too. Been on a few of them morning talk shows, where she pretended to cook something in a minute that she really made the night before. One of the local TV stations asked her about doing her own cooking show, but like a fool she said no, because she said she had enough on her plate. Like what?

Food must run in our family. Me and her daddy opened our first barbecue joint, which we named the Shack, fifteen years ago. But Vegas ain't the same no more. With all the violence and gangs and drugs and kids not caring one way or the other that you the same color as them while they robbing you at gunpoint and can't look you in the eye 'cause you probably favor somebody they know, we had to close two down and ain't got but one left. It's been a struggle trying to make ends meet. Paris stopped cooking like us years ago. She think our kinda food kill folks. She right, but it's hard for black people to live without barbecue and potato salad and collard greens with a touch of salt pork, a slice of cornbread soaked in the juice, a spoonful of candied yams, and every now and then a plateful of chitterlings. Her food is so pretty that half the time you don't never know what you eating until you put it in your mouth, and even then you gotta ask.

In spite of all the money she make and that big house her and my favorite grandson, Dingus, live in—yes, I said favorite—she ain't happy. What Paris need ain't in no cookbook, no house, or no garage. She need a man quick and in a hurry, and Dingus need a daddy he can touch. Another baby wouldn't be a bad idea. She ain't but thirty-eight but swears up and down she's too old to be thinking about a baby. I said bullshit. "As long as you still bleed, you able." She rolled her eyes up inside her head. "And just where am I supposed to find a father?" Sometimes she make things harder than they really are. "Pick one!" I said.

I don't know how she's survived over there all by herself. Hell, it's been six years since her divorce. To my knowledge, Paris don't love nobody and don't nobody love her. She put up a good front, like everything just so damn hunky-dory. Only she ain't fooling me. I know when something wrong with any of my kids. They don't have to open their mouth. I can sense it. Paris spend so much energy trying to be perfect, trying too hard to be Superwoman, that I don't think she know how lonely she really is. I guess she think if she stay busy she won't have to think about it. But I can hear what's missing. She too damn peppy all the time.

I'm here to testify: ain't no time limit on heartache. Cecil done broke mine so many times I'm surprised it still know how to tick. But forget about me. Paris been grieving so long now for Nathan that she done pretty much turned to stone. I think she so scared of getting her heart broke again that now she's like the Ice Queen. Can't nobody get close to her. They say time heals all wounds. But I ain't so sure. I think they run around inside you till they find the old ones, jump on top until they form a little stack, and they don't go nowhere until something come along that make you so happy you forget about past pain. Sorta like labor.

What time is it? I know my stories is off. I watch *Restless* and *Lives* and occasionally *World*, but some days they piss me off so bad that I can't hardly stand to watch none of their simple asses. Ha ha ha. I'm "trippin' " as Dingus would say, laying in a hospital bed in intensive care thinking about some damn soap operas when what I should be doing is thanking the Lord for giving me another shot: Thank you, Jesus.

To be honest, I didn't trust Nathan from the get-go. Paris hadn't known him but two months when they got married. He was in law school for seven of the eight years they was married. Even I know it only take three. I just bit my tongue and gritted my teeth when she told me she wasn't taking him to court for no child support. "I don't want the hassle," she said. That was what, 1987? Here it is 1994 and I can count on one hand how many times he done seen his son since he went back to Atlanta. He don't hardly call. I guess he forgot how to write, and ain't sent nary a birthday card and not a single solitary Christmas present in the last three years that I know of. I ain't heard her mention nothing about no surprise checks either—not that she need 'em—but that ain't the point. She handled this all wrong. If a man ain't gon' be there for his kids then he should at least help pay for 'em. It's the reason we got so many juvenile delinquents and criminals and gangs running through our neighborhoods. Where was they damn daddies when they needed one? Mamas can't do everything.

The one good thing that came out of that marriage was my grandson Dingus. He's turning out to be one fine specimen. Just made the varsity football team. The first black quarterback in the history of his high school. He in the eleventh grade and I ain't never seen a C on his report card. He ain't never come home drunk and he told me drugs scare him. He say he gets his high from exercising and eating vegetables and drinking that protein stuff everyday. I got my money on him. That he gon' grow up and be something one day. Putting the boy in that Christian school all them years was the smartest thing Paris could've done. Going to church at least one Sunday a month wouldn't kill her though. I just hope I live long enough to see him in college. And mark my words: if he wins a scholarship or goes on any kind of TV, watch and see if his daddy don't come rushing out of nowhere to claim him then.

The day before I got here, Paris had called the house and after leaving three messages on my answering machine and she didn't hear from me, she called emergency and they told her I'd been admitted, that I was in ICU, and of course she was all set to hop on a airplane but I grabbed that doctor's arm and shook my head back and forth so many times I got the spins. He told her I'd probably be home in three to four days. That I was almost out of the danger zone. That if I kept improving they would move me to a regular room on Thursday, which is tomorrow, and if my breathing test is at least 70 percent I can probably go home Saturday morning. It don't make no sense for Paris to spend unnecessary money to come see me when

I'm still breathing and she can take that very same money and slide it inside my birthday card in three weeks.

Sometimes I feel like they made a mistake in the hospital when they handed Janelle to me. She a case study in and of herself. Been going to college off and on for the past fifteen years and still don't have no degree in nothing. Hell, she should *be* the professor by now. Every time I turn around she taking another class. One minute it's stained glass. The next it's drapes and valances. But I think she was tired of being creative and now she wanna be a professional. Did she tell me she switched over to real estate? Who knows? Maybe all them years of comparing one child to another messed her up. Treating her like a baby is probably why she still act like one. Me or her daddy didn't have such high expectations of her like we did with the first ones, and maybe this is what made her not have too many for herself. I don't know. But I have to blame Cecil for the chile being so wishy-washy. He lived and breathed for that girl. Spoiled her. Janelle couldn't do no wrong. But back then neither one of us knew we was doing it.

Even still, Janelle is as sweet as she wants to be, a little dense, but the most affectionate child of the whole bunch. She even go to psychics and palm readers and the people that read them big cards. I don't know what lies they telling her, but she believe in that mess. And she say some of the dumbest shit sometime that you can't even twist your mouth to say nothing. The chile live from one holiday to the next. If you don't know which one is coming up, just drive by her house. For Groundhog Day, you can bet a groundhog'll be peeking up from somewhere in her front yard. On St. Patrick's Day: four-leaf clovers everywhere. On Valentine's Day: red and pink hearts plastered on everything. She had seven Christmas trees one Christmas, in every room in the damn house, and a giant one in the front yard! And now here come Easter.

Ever since Jimmy got killed back in '85, Janelle been a little off. He was her second husband. She wasn't married but twenty-two days the first time. He beat her up once and that was enough. But Jimmy is Shanice's daddy. Once Janelle finally got back into the dating game—the last few men she dealt with was all married. I told her it was wrong, but she said this way she didn't have to worry about getting too serious.

Well, guess what? She married this last one. He left his wife of a million years for her. His name is George. He's ugly and old enough to be her daddy. But his money is long and green and he don't mind spending it on Janelle. That's her whole problem: she always want somebody to take care of her. Ain't this the nineties? Even I know this kind of attitude is ridiculous in this day and age and I'm almost a senior citizen. This is the reason so many of us became slaves to our husbands in the first place, and why so many women don't have no marketable skills to speak of now. Can't no man take better care of you than you can take of yourself. Janelle is thirty-five years old and still ain't figured this out yet.

I have tried my damnedest to like George, be nice, act civilized toward him, but I can't pretend no more. He's head of security at LAX, but work for the LAPD. Janelle brag that he got over six hundred people working under him. I ain't impressed in the least. Now, Shanice, she's my granddaughter who's all of twelve, came to spend last Christmas with me and Cecil. That was three months ago. I knew something was different about her but I couldn't put my finger on it. First of all, she wouldn't take off that stupid baseball cap, but I know it's the style these days, so I didn't say nothing. She wasn't here but two days before I noticed how strange she was acting. Not her usual talkative self. She seemed nervous. Downright fidgety. Like her mind was somewhere else. Almost burnt up my kitchen frying a hamburger. Forgot all about it. Dropped three eggs on the floor and sliced off a chunk of her finger helping me chop up the celery for the dressing. When she wasn't the least bit excited after she opened her presents—some ugly clothes she asked for—I said, "Hold it a minute, sugar. Take that hat off and look at me." She shook her head no. "I know you're not saying no to me—your granny—are you?" She shook her head no again. I walked over and snatched that cap off her head, and when I looked down I could not believe my eyes. All I saw was big beige circles of scalp and strands of hair here and there. "Cecil, get my spray for me, would you?" But I forgot he went down to Harrah's right after the game, and I looked around till I saw one on the table next to the couch and I grabbed it and took two deep puffs. Shanice didn't move and I didn't take my eyes off her. "Why is your hair falling out?" She didn't answer. Just had this blank look on her face. "Is it from a bad perm?" She shook her head no. Shit. Then what? I looked at her hand moving up toward a strand and she started twirling it tight. "You pulling it out?" She nodded yes. "Why?" I'm waiting and trying not to cry, 'cause I want to know what the hell is going on here, but that's when the chile crumpled over all that wrapping paper like somebody had stuck her with a knife. "Tell Granny what's wrong, baby." She just kept crying. "You scared?" She shook her head yes. "Scared of what? Who?" She wouldn't say nothing. "Is it somebody we know?" She shook her head no, then yes. "Talk to me, Shanice. Sit your butt up and talk to me." She sat up but looked over at the Christmas tree. "Is it George?" She nodded her head yes. "Has he been putting his hands on you?" When she shook her head no, I wasn't sure if she understood what I meant. I put my arms around her and rocked her. When she finally stopped, she said that George is mean and sometimes he hits her and she's scared of him. "You got any marks on you?" She shook her head no. "You sure that's all he's done is hit you?" She nodded yes, but for some reason I didn't believe her. "Have you told your mama?" She shook her head yes. "And?" She started crying again, but by now I grabbed my spray and snatched that phone out the cradle and got Janelle on the phone. "Shanice just told me George been hitting her and she tried to tell you and you don't believe her. Tell me this ain't true."

"Mama, George has never hit Shanice. She's been lying about a lot of things lately. She's just being dramatic."

"Oh, really. What about her hair? How dramatic is that?"

"The doctor said some kids do this."

"Have you at least confronted George?"

"Of course I have. Mama, look. George is a good man. He loves Shanice like she was his own daughter. He's done everything to get in her good graces, but she has never really cared for him, so this is just another desperation move on her part to get him out of the house once and for all."

"What makes you so sure?"

"Look. Why don't you send her on home?"

I took a few more puffs off my inhaler, then slammed it down on the counter. I changed ears. "I'll tell you something. A home is where a child is supposed to feel safe, protected."

"I know this, Mama, and she should . . ."

"Apparently, your daughter don't feel this way."

"Are you about finished?"

"No. I'm just getting started. I'll say this. You better watch that motherfucker like a hawk, 'cause he doing more than hitting her. You may be blind, but I ain't. And I'll send her home when I'm good and damn ready!" And I hung up.

My granddaughter ain't no actress, and them tears was real. Since she run track and had a big meet coming up, I sent her home, but promised her I would look into this. I told her to dial 911 the next time he so much as bump into her. I just been patting my feet, trying to figure out what to do about this mess. Cecil told me to mind my own business. I told Cecil to kiss my black ass. This chile got my blood in her veins.

The more I think about it, I'm beginning to wonder if we ain't one of them dysfunctional families I've seen on TV. A whole lotta weird shit been going on in the Price family for years. But, then again, I know some folks got some stuff that can top ours. Hell, look at the Kennedys. Maybe *everybody* is dysfunctional and God put us all in this mess so we can learn

how to function. To test us. See what we can tolerate. I don't
know, but we don't seem to be doing such a hot job of it. I
guess we need to work harder at getting rid of that d-y-s part. I
just wish I had a clue where to start.

I won't lie: none of my kids turned out the way I hoped they
would, but I'm still proud to be their mother. I did the best I
could with what I had. Cecil worked two jobs back in those
days, which meant I had to do everything: like raise 'em. I tried
to teach 'em the difference between right and wrong, good and
bad, being honest, having good manners, and what I knew
about dignity, pride, and respect. What I left out they shoulda
learned in Sunday school. Common sense is something you
can't teach, which is why there's some things kids should
blame their parents for and some shit they just have to take responsibility for on their own.

I still can't believe they all came out of my body. Grew up
in the same house. I tried my best to spread my love around so
none of 'em would feel left out. Even lied to 'em so each one
would feel special. I've tried to steer 'em in the right direction,
but sometimes they just didn't wanna go that way. They had
their own destiny in mind, which was okay, except when ain't
no clear path in front of 'em you kinda wonder where they
headed.

I've watched 'em make all kinda mistakes over the years.
Been scared for 'em. Worried myself gray. Prayed like a beg-
gar. But I done finally learned that you can't carry the weight
for everything that happen to your kids. For the longest time I
have. But not no more. I'm letting go of the coulda-woulda-
shouldas and admit that I was not the perfect mother, but I
broke my neck trying to be a good one. I'm tired of mothering
'em. It's time for them to mother themselves. I can't do no
more than I already have. And from now on I'm standing on the
sidelines. I've made too many trips to this hospital from worrying about husbands and kids, which is why from now on the
only person I'm worrying about is Viola Price.

That's me.

I'm pushing fifty-five. Twenty-three more days and I'll finally qualify as a senior citizen. I can't wait! April 15. A day don't nobody want to remember but can't nobody forget. Hard to believe that me and Charlotte was born on the same day. Them astrologers don't know *what* they talking about. We different as night and day. All I know is when I get outta here this time, things gon' be different. I'm about to start living. I can't wait to start doing some of the things I've been meaning to do but never have for one reason or another. The day after my birthday, I'm going straight to Jenny Craig so I can lose these thirty or forty pounds once and for all. When I look good, maybe I'll feel good. By then, maybe I can figure out what I'm gon' do with the rest of my life. Selling Mary Kay ain't exactly been getting it. I just did it to get away from barbecue and smoke—to stop myself from going completely crazy being home. As hard as I tried, I couldn't take the smell of all that perfume they put in their products, and at the rate I was going it woulda took me about twenty years before I ever sold enough to get me one of them pink cars.

That phone could ring. Paris shoulda told Charlotte's evil ass by now, and I know she called Janelle first, and somebody shoulda put out a SOS to Lewis, and Cecil of all people should know I'm in here. I just heard it through the grapevine that he over there living with some welfare huzzy who got three kids. He must really think he John Travolta or somebody. But his midlife crisis done lasted about twenty years now. Hell, he pushing fifty-seven years old. I can't lie. Cecil was driving me nuts after he took early retirement from bus driving for the school district, and on top of that, he had to quit putting in time at the Shack altogether, 'cause his sinuses took a turn for the worse. We had to hire strangers to run it, and we didn't need no bookkeeper to see that they'd been robbing us blind. Cecil didn't know what to do with so much free time on his hands. Vegas being a desert, and where our little stucco house is, ain't no grass to cut, no hedges to trim, no weeds to pull, no pool to clean, so this is when he started hanging around the crap tables and at the same time discovered he could still drive his truck: ram it into some little dumb cunt who probably thought she'd found herself a genuine sugardaddy. Unfortunately, Cecil's truck ain't had no pickup in years so what this chile is getting I don't know.

In all honesty, I really ain't missed him *personally,* but what I do miss is his presence. That raggedy house feel even smaller without him in it. Like all the moisture been sucked out. I can't even smell him no more. Ain't nothing to pick up. Or hang. Ain't washed but once this past week, but even that was only a half a load. And plenty of leftovers. Never learned how to cook for just two people, let alone one. If I thought about him long enough, I guess I *could* miss him.

He stopped by last month to pick up his little pension check, looking all embarrassed, and, boy, was he surprised when he saw all his stuff stuffed in old pillowcases and balled up in old sheets and stacked on top of each other in the storage closet right off the carport. The spiderwebs was already starting to do their business. I only did it to impress him. I wanted him to think I can live without him. I'm sure I can, I just ain't figured out if I want to or not yet. He didn't mention nothing about coming home, and I didn't bring up the subject either. I can't lie: right after he left, I was relieved, like I was getting a much-needed vacation. It was like the part of me that used to love him had been shot up with novocaine. I didn't shed a single tear. I been numb too long. Even still, another part of me is scared, 'cause I ain't never lived by myself. Always had him or the kids here: somebody.

"How you feeling, Vy?"

Well, look who's here: Cecil! At first I pretend like I'm already dead. I want the guilt to eat his ass up. But he can see the oxygen coming through this mask, hear me breathing through these tubes, see that monitor zigzagging with my life in green. He take my hand and I snatch it back. When I open my eyes, he look like a bear. He smell like curl activator. Cecil will not cut off his Jheri Curl to save his life. I told him a thousand times to look around: this "do" ain't been in style for years. But he don't care. He think, 'cause he dye it black, it makes him look younger, which ain't hardly true. He think he still "got it going on," as Dingus would say. To set the record straight, Cecil look like he about four months pregnant. He wearing his exciting uniform: them black polyester pants that don't need no belt, his Sammy Davis, Jr.–pink shirt without the ruffles (thank the Lord), and those lizard shoes he bought at the turn of the century, when we still lived in Chicago. He look like a lounge singer who just got off work. But other than this, I'd say he still might be handsome, all things considered.

"I was worried about you," he say like he mean it. "You doing all right?" If I ain't mistaken, them look like tears in his eyes. I know how to do this, too, which is why I ain't the least bit moved by this little show of—what should I call it, emotion? I open my eyes wide—like a woman who done had too many face lifts—grab the little notepad from my tray, write, "Take a wild guess," and hand it to him. He look somewhat hurt and sit down at the foot of my bed. The heat from his body is warming my right foot. I feel like sliding both feet under his big butt but I don't. He might get the wrong impression.

"Is everythang all right at the house?"

I nod.

"You want me to bring you anythang?"

I want to point to my mouth but I don't. I shake my head no. My friend Loretta promised to bring me my teeth, which I know is somewhere on the dining-room floor, 'cause I heard 'em slide across the wood when the paramedics picked me up and slung me onto that stretcher. But her car's been in the shop. Loretta is my next-door neighbor. She's white and nice and a brand-new widow. She even trying to teach me how to play bridge. I just hope she watering my plants and got the rest of that stuff out the refrigerator, 'cause I was cleaning it when I first felt my chest go tight.

"You looking good," he say. If I had the strength, I'd slap him. I look like hell froze over and he know it. My hair is still in these cellophaned burgundy cornrows, 'cause they won't let me put my wig on. Cecil just sit there for a few minutes, looking like a complete fool, like he trying to remember something only he can't. I guess the silence was starting to get to him, 'cause he take a deep breath and finally say, "So—when you get to come home?"

I hold up three, then four fingers.

He stand up. "You need a ride?"

I shake my head no.

"I can come back and see you tomorrow."

I shake my head no. He shake his head yes. "After I get off work."

My eyes say: "Work?"

"Just a little security job. Part-time. It's something."

I'm wondering if it's at Harrah's or Circus Circus or Mirage: his second homes. I write the word "SHACK" down.

"Shaquan got robbed again, so we boarded the place up. I can't take the stress no more."

No more barbecue.

"I'll stop by the house to check on things," he say and bend over and give me a kiss on my forehead. Either he still love me and don't know it or he feel sorry for me. I don't much care right now, but all I know is that his lips is the warmest thing I've felt touch my body since I was greasing Shanice's scalp and she fell asleep in my lap. I hate to admit it, but Cecil's lips sure felt good.

I turn my face toward the window and close my eyes. I'm hoping these tears can hold off a few more minutes. I hear the soles of his shoes squish against the tile floor. The door opens. A shot of cold air comes in, and then the click of that door. I look at the clock. Cecil was here for all of eight minutes. When that door pops back open, I turn, thinking he done come to his senses, done had a change of heart, wanna say something mushy to me like they do on *All My Children*: something that gon' make me feel like I got wings and can fly outta this hospital bed straight into his arms, where I can sink against his soft chest and he'll hold me, rock me like he used to, and I'll be able to take one deep breath after another.

But it ain't Cecil. It's a nurse. Finally bringing me my lunch. Some thick green soup and mashed potatoes and it hurts when I swallow, but I don't care: I'm starving. I eat every drop of my tapioca, even though I can't usually stomach smooth-and-creamy nothing. I drink my apple juice, wishing all the time it was a beer. When I push the call button so they can take my tray, something metal hits the floor. They're Cecil's keys. Ha ha ha.

I musta dozed off for a few minutes after they picked up my tray and the doctors checked my numbers. I know I'm in bad shape. I hate having asthma. I wasn't even born with this shit. I was forty-two when Suzie Mae called me at four-thirty in the morning to tell me that Daddy's sixteen-year-old grandson by his first wife, who he had took in, had stabbed him thirty-six times and killed him 'cause Daddy wouldn't let his girlfriend spend the night. I had a anxiety attack and couldn't catch my breath. The doctors treated me for asthma, and I been on this medication ever since. Each time I try to stop taking it, I have a attack, so my feeling is the doctors gave me this damn disease. I can't win.

And I can't lie. This attack scared me. In the back of my mind, I'm thinking: Is *this* gon' be the one? In a split second you remember everybody you love, and in the next one you ask yourself: Did I do this thing right? Did I do everything I wanted to? What would I change if I could do it all over? Did I hurt anybody so much that they won't be able to forgive me? Will they forgive me for not being perfect? I forgive myself. And I forgive God. But then you feel your eyes open and you realize you ain't dead. You got tubes coming outta you. Lights is bright. Your heart is thumping. You say a long thank-you prayer. And you lay here thinking about everything and everybody, 'cause you got another chance to live. You ask yourself what you gon' do now. My answer is plain and simple: I'ma start doing things differently, 'cause, like they say, if you keep doing what you've always done, you'll keep getting what you've always gotten. Ain't that the truth, and who don't know it?

So this is the deal, Viola. First of all, if I don't do nothing else, I'ma get this asthma under control, 'cause I'm tired of it running my life. Tired of grown kids and husbands running my life. Tired of being smart but ain't got no evidence to prove it. I wanna get my GED. I don't see why not. It ain't never too late to learn. I just hope what they say about the brain being a muscle is true. The way I see it, I figure I owe myself a cruise to *somewhere* before I hit sixty, especially since I took Paris, France, outta my dreams a million years ago. Hell, I ain't been *nowhere*. How I'ma get the money is a mystery to me, but I'll get it. If it's meant to be, it'll be. I should try to get some decent dentures: the kind that fit and don't look false. But if me or my kids ever hit the lottery, I'ma get the kind that don't come out. Paris and Janelle think playing is a waste of time and money. Paris say only emigrants and legitimate senior citizens ever seem to win. But Charlotte play Little Lotto three times a week, and Lewis, whenever he get a extra dollar, which ain't all that often. Both of 'em promised that if they ever hit, they would split the winnings with me. I told 'em I'd divide mine three ways if I didn't win but twenty dollars, and I would.

The first thing I would do is buy myself a house that don't need no repairs, and walk around barefoot, 'cause the carpet would be just that thick. Hell, a condo would do the trick, as long as I had a patch of dirt big enough to plant some collards, a few ears of corn, some cherry tomatoes, and hot peppers to pickle for the winter. And I'd like to know what it feel like to drive a brand-new anything. I know I'm dreaming, but deep down inside, when you know your life is at least 80 percent over, you ain't got nothing left to live for but dreams.

More than anything, if something *was* to happen to me, I pray that each one of my kids find happiness. I want 'em to feel good. Live good. Do what's right. I just hope I live long enough to see Lewis get hisself together and start acting like the man I know he is. Lord knows I'd love to see Paris marry somebody worthy of her and I'd pay cash money to be there when my grandson throw a touchdown pass on nationwide TV. And Charlotte. I hope she stop getting so mad with me for every little thing and realize that she ain't no stepchild of mine, that I love her just as much as the other kids. I want the day to come when Janelle stand on her own two feet and get rid of that rapist she married. And if I don't get my old husband back, hell, I'll settle for a new one. One thing I do know about men and kids is that they always come back. They may be a day late and a dollar short, but they always come back.

Cold
Keys

Viola makes me sick. Sometimes I honestly thank she make herself have these attacks. She'll do anything to get some attention, but this woman is aging me by the minute. Under all these layers of black dye, my head is full of gray hair, and I won't be fifty-seven till come September. My daddy didn't go all the way gray till he was almost seventy, and he spent his whole life in the fields. I ain't had it half that bad, and look at me: a middle-age old man.

I can't believe it's still raining so hard. I'm getting soaked. Doggone it! Who can remember where they parked in such a big parking lot? If my Lincoln wasn't red it'd be a whole lot easier, but there's thousands of red cars in Vegas, and most of 'em seem to be at this hospital today. I know I must look like a fool walking around in circles out here, if anybody's watching. I thank that's her window, right up there. Wait. There it is! Four rows over and two back. But my keys ain't in my back pocket. Not in the side ones either. Wait a minute. Retrace your steps, Cecil. Damn it! They at the foot of Viola's bed.

I shoulda stayed a little longer. I know I shoulda. But Viola acted like she wasn't all that glad to see me. Seemed like she wanted me to hurry up and leave. At least that's my thanking on it. She said no to everythang I asked her. I was trying to be nice. Yesterday, I called the house just to check on her, 'cause, even though I don't live at home no more, I still like to see how she doing, see how she holding up over there all by herself and everythang. But I didn't get no answer. So I stopped by on my way to work. Her car was right there under the carport. Viola don't walk nowhere. And ain't but so many places she could be. I knocked at least ten times and didn't get no answer. I knew Loretta was at her volunteer job, so she couldn't be over there. When I tried my key it didn't work. I guess she finally changed the locks on me. I went on to work, but I had a feeling that something was wrong. Soon as I punched in, I called the hospital. My heart was burning the whole time I dialed that number, which I knew by heart, and since don't nobody know how to find me, if something hada happened to Viola ain't no way I woulda known. The whole time they had me on hold I was praying that, if she was there, this was just another mild attack, that she was breathing any kinda way she could, even if she was hooked up to *something*. And, sure enough, as soon as I heard that nurse say, "She's in ICU," even though I'm new and still hourly and the casino don't pay me when I ain't there, I punched out.

I thank I see her peeking out the window but I can't be sure. I don't thank she can get up, but that look like her hand pulling the curtain back. I could be wrong. I don't know what else to say to Viola right now. I don't feel none too good inside. It ain't been right between us for a long time. Barbecue is what started our problems. I guess it would be fair to say that the crap tables ain't helped us out none neither.

Way back when, a whole bunch of my people had hightailed it from Texarkana up to Chicago looking for decent work during the Depression and the rest of 'em boxcarred it over to Los Angeles. Daddy sent me up to the Windy City to live with his brother when I was sixteen, so I could finish school. He said one farmer in the family was plenty. Try to find a job where I don't get dirty. If possible, try to find one where I get to wear a uniform. Protect something. Anythang.

Which is how I met Viola. I was a crossing guard for the elementary school right down the street from where we lived.

She was fine and fourteen. Sassy. I fell in love. She was my chocolate rose. Next thang I know, we married and got four kids and we'd had about enough of them icy winds, that crunchy snow, them mean winter rats, and them blood-sucking mosquitoes every thick, sticky summer. I guess that was back in '73.

It was her bright idea to leave Chicago and move to Los Angeles. I just went along with the program. I didn't particularly care for L.A., even though I got on with the school district driving a bus. But since neither one of us wanted to be movie stars and Viola wasn't too crazy about most of my people 'cause she said they was too country, too loud, uncouth, and just plain nasty (she had a point), and being around 'em was embarrassing as hell, so, when Daddy died in '78 and left me a little something from the farm, we couldn't thank of enough good reasons to stay in California. The kids was grown and gone and I heard we still had a handful of decent kinfolk left in Vegas, so we took a chance on the desert and bought us a little tract house here. All five of them relatives was dead before we opened the first Shack, 'cause that's the same year Viola made me take her bowling, that much I do remember.

Everybody, including me, always thought Vegas was all bright blinking lights and casinos. Strip joints and the Strip. But real people live here. In regular neighborhoods. And it wasn't all that pretty. It was dry and flat and bare and mostly brown. Now, with all the building going on, it's new housing developments everywhere you turn. It's still dry and flat and bare, but some people got grass and shrubs and flowers, and quite a few trees done managed to grow. But not in our yard.

The first year after we got here, Viola convinced me to take all our savings and put it with Daddy's money and we opened up our first barbecue joint. They grew to three, 'cause we knew how to smoke the meat just right (like they do in Texas), and my barbecue sauce was a family secret. Everybody said I shoulda bottled it up and sold it, but I didn't feel like being bothered. Hell, between loving Viola, driving a school bus for another thirteen years, and running the Shacks, when I took early retirement almost two years ago, I was tired. Tired of living like I was waiting for something else to happen. That's what it was beginning to feel like. Like I was missing something. Like *this* ain't it. Like my life should add up to more. Every day was starting to feel like it do when I call a professional business and they put you on hold for a long time and you forget who you called but you know you shouldn't hang up, so you just hold the line, listen to that recorded music, and wait. When they come back on the line you pray that you remember why you called and that they have the answers to all your questions. But they never do. So then you start thanking if you just look a little further ahead you might find them missing pieces. But how far can a man see? And what if you don't know exactly what it is you looking for?

Viola didn't understand why or just how long I'd been feeling bad inside. Years. It was hard to explain and she didn't seem all that interested when I tried. Between the two of us, she thank she the one who got the right to get scared. Ain't nobody else supposed to worry except her. She thank she got all the answers to everybody's problems even when she ain't sure what the problem is. She just said if I didn't start feeling better no time soon then go to the doctor. I ain't never liked going to the doctor. I ain't got no physical problems except this arthritis, but I know what to do about that. How is a doctor supposed to fix head feelings? And what about your heart? What can he do to make it feel good again, to make it feel passion and excitement? Can a doctor give you a prescription to feel all that again? I don't believe he can.

When we started getting robbed and had to close up all but one of the joints, Viola got mad with *me*. She blamed me for everything that went wrong but didn't give me no credit when thangs went right. That's why I got me a new street address. 'Cause if it weren't for her I'd still be home. It's only so much a man can take after years of being told what to do, how to do it, when to do it, how to be a man, or how much man you used to be. What you ain't up to no more. A woman can wear a man down. Viola is and always have been one bossy woman. I accepted that. She didn't use to be so pushy, but she knew how to push my buttons. She'd say "Jump" and I'd ask, "How high, baby?" That's the kind of power she had. Still got, but I finally had to take my finger off the plug and let the air come on out. 'Cause I got tired. Tired of fussing. Tired of explaining. Tired of lying 'cause it was safer than the truth. But mostly I was tired of apologizing for being Cecil.

I used to didn't thank it was possible to ever stop loving somebody once you started, but I was wrong. Well, maybe I should get this right. I do *love* Viola, but I guess the point I'm trying to make is that I just don't like her ass no more. She's mean. A old broad who used to purr but now all she do is roar. I wish there was a nice way to tell your wife she's a royal bitch and a major pain in the ass, but I ain't been able to come up with one. Lord knows I woulda told her a long time ago. I never wanted to hurt her feelings, not like she hurt mine.

I don't mind getting wet. It ain't that cold out here. This is March. Our winter ain't no real winter. It must be sixty-five or seventy degrees. As a matter of fact, these raindrops feel good. I could stand out here all day if I just had to, but I don't have to. Do I? I done forgot all about my hair. Lord knows I don't want no activator dripping on my good shirt. I wore it just for Viola.

When she moved out the bedroom last year, that was the last straw for me. Sex was like some kind of reward anyway. I had to earn it, then beg for it. Sometimes I have trouble in that department, but sometimes I don't. And I can't lie, Viola still got some of the best stuff I've ever had, but after living like you been sentenced to solitary confinement for so many years, good pussy ain't enough no more. Plus. I found out it's plenty of good pussy in Vegas, and most of it is cheap. You ain't gotta look her in the face, don't need to know no last names or how-comes and where-you-beens or what-time-you-coming-backs. They don't care if all you good for is five or ten minutes. Just get it, leave your money where they can see it, and ease on down the road.

Viola used to be my friend. I could trust her. Tell her anythang. But here lately, you can't be too sure what she gon' do with the information you give her. Mostly she hoist it right back at you like some kind of weapon. She got a big mouth and she makes me feel bad about myself. She used to thank I was everythang: Handsome. Sexy. Smart. Strong. Now all she do is criticize me. Hell, I know I'm country, and I don't mind it. She knew how I was when I married her. People don't change they ways just 'cause they get married. When you been brought up a certain way, you *that* way. Unless you go to one of them head doctors who can talk you into being somebody else. Viola stayed on me anyway. "When you gon' get rid of that Jheri Curl, Cecil?" Or: "You need to do some situps, your gut is growing by the minute." And if I forgot something, anythang: "Where's your mind going, Cecil? Is Alzheimer's creeping up on you already?" We'd be ready to go somewhere: "You ain't going nowhere with me in that getup." It mighta been a old suit, but she the one who picked it out in the first place. And we always watched what she wanted to see on TV, 'cause she held the remote in our house. But the worse one of all was: "You finished already?"

She don't take nobody's feelings into account except her own. Say the first thang that come out her mouth, which is why she ain't got but a roomful of friends. Loretta ain't no threat, that's why she's so nice to her. Plus she white. I thank Viola is either scared of white people or feel like she gotta prove she just as good as they are. But Loretta don't want nothing. She just downright friendly. Decent. She came with offerings, her palms turned up. Viola loved that. Somebody doing something for her.

If you was to count her sisters, them being the only family she got left, it's a doggone shame, 'cause both of 'em is dizzy as all hell. Priscilla is a fifty-year-old gangster. Been in and out of the penitentiary for the last twenty-some-odd years for petty crimes. I thank she out now. But you never know. Blink and she locked up again. She even had one of those thangs they stick in your ankle and she still messed up. Plus, she a drug addict, which is probably why it's hard for her to stop robbing folks and business establishments and what have you. Everybody in the family call her Bonnie.

Suzie Mae is sixty-five. She always was missing a few links and now it seem like her bulb just keep getting dimmer and dimmer. I thank she got a touch of that Alzheimer's but don't nobody wanna fess up to it, 'cause she always been a few nuts shy of a fruitcake, as Viola herself used to say. I thank it's 'cause she ain't never gave birth. But then Suzie Mae's husband died from some kinda cancer back in '71, and according to Viola, she still sleep with his picture like she waiting for him to come back from a war. Suzie Mae always have been a religious fanatic, going to church four and five nights a week, and giving almost all her Social Security money to the church. But two years ago after her pastor talked her into having what she told Viola was a healing fling, Suzie Mae found out just how big his flock was and that's when she decided to study the Bible at home. After that incident, she wouldn't let nobody in her house. Talked to you through the door. I heard her kitchen pipes froze right before last Christmas and her sink got backed up, so she washed dishes in the bathtub. From what Charlotte told Viola, it still ain't fixed. But Suzie Mae said she don't want no help, 'cause she don't need no help.

Speaking of lost. I done lost touch with my own kids. Outta touch is probably what I mean. I don't know 'em too good. Not on a personal level. I do know they good kids. Got good souls. The girls done turned into real women, which is kinda hard to believe when I thank about it. First of all, they grew like weeds.

All three of 'em gotta be between five seven and five nine. Being the only boy, Lewis surprised me and didn't turn out to be no more than six one or two. I don't know how that happened. But my little girls. One minute you rubbing Vaseline on they ashy faces and watching they long thick braids swing back and forth when they jumping rope, and the next thang you know, they got breasts and wearing pantyhose and heads full of soft black curls and eye shadow on top of they eyes and they lips is some kind of creamy red or pink. Seem like all I did was blink and I was taking the training wheels off my baby girl's bicycle and when I looked at her again she was driving, had caught up with the rest of the kids.

As for Lewis, me and him ain't never seen eye to eye. He stay pretty much out my way and I stay outta his. Ever since he got arrested the first time and wouldn't listen to nothing I had to say—swung his fist in my face like he wanted to hit me—we ain't had too much to say to one another since. He feel like he always been a man, and you can't tell him nothing. In that way, we just alike. But I stopped trying to talk to him son to father a long time ago. I'm hoping, the next time I see him, maybe we can just talk man to man. See if time make a difference. I love all my kids, I do, but, working so doggone hard all them years, I missed 'em growing up. Viola was always there and I thought I was doing my part by paying for the roof over they head and putting food on the table. But a man can work too hard. I see that now. He can miss a lot: years. They just go by. You look down at your hands and they full of fat green veins, knuckles knotty from arthritis, knees bad, white of your eyes is brown, and you wonder where was you when you was supposed to be doing all this living? At work. I missed the prime of my life. That's what I did.

Well, they all grown now, and from what I understand, or what Viola been telling me, each one got they own share of problems—but no more than most folks. I been trying to get Viola to keep her nose outta they business and let 'em run their own lives, but she don't pay me no mind. None whatsoever. This is another reason why I had to leave. Viola don't listen to me. She don't listen to nobody. She always right. But she *ain't* right all the time, and she gon' have to learn the hard way.

She been accusing me of cheating on her for years. But it's all in her head. Well, maybe once or twice I slipped up, but that's 'cause I was working late at the joints. I bent over backwards trying to show her how sorry I was, but my back broke. Apologizing. Now it's her turn to say she sorry, 'cause I ain't done nothing more than be myself.

What did I do? It was New Year's Eve. She didn't wanna go nowhere, so we stayed home and watched them young kids in New York City on TV. Stood outside in the front yard and watched the fireworks from the Strip and counted twenty-six gunshots and toasted with some Scott's champagne and then went on back in the house and went to sleep. I wanted to brang in the New Year with a bang, but Viola wasn't having it. She went on into her room, and I went into mine. First thang that next morning, I went over to Howie's house. We in his garage. I'm helping him fix some old air conditioners. We have a little taste we pass back and forth. We get tired and clean up enough to look like we ain't dirty and decide to stop by Harrah's for a hot minute. I'm hitting left and right, and when I get around to looking at my watch it's pushing close to two-thirty in the morning. That's what them tables can do to you. Make you forget about everythang, especially time. I felt like Cinderella. I ran to the cashier and cashed in all my chips and told Howie I'd catch him later.

When I pulled up to our little blue house the lights was still on. I turned into the driveway but didn't get out, 'cause I couldn't get out. The thought of being cussed out again was making my teeth grind all by theyself. I couldn't lift my hand up to open that door to save my life. Next thang I know I heard my name, "Cecil!" She yelling it. I'm hoping the neighbors don't wake up. I'm already embarrassed. Why she have to be so loud? "Cecil!" I rolled the window down. "Yeah," I mumbled. "Why you sitting out there in the car like that?" I didn't know how to tell her the truth, so I didn't say nothing. "How much did you lose this time?" I didn't say nothing. I wanted to tell her that tonight I got lucky—I got over four thousand dollars in my pocket, and you can have it to do something to the house. "What's her name? Did you take a shower before you left?" I just looked at her, standing under the porch light, her hair looking like a silver blaze, and the silhouette of her big hips blocked some of the light trying to get through her nightgown. Viola was so mad she bent down and picked up a flowerpot and threw it toward the car, then she put her hands on those hips and I saw 'em swivel back and forth and saw her mouth moving a mile a minute and that's when I felt my right hand push that gear shift in reverse and, looking straight ahead, I backed out the driveway real slow. When I got out in the street I rolled up all the windows and just looked at her. Viola looked like a statue. Frozen. All except for her head following me. But I didn't care one way or the other what she felt. I turned on the air conditioner and then pushed "play" on my cassette. B. B. King helped me step on the gas and drive. I didn't know where I was going and I didn't have no place to go. I drove up and down the Strip until the brightest lights was coming from the sun.

I'm through with Viola.

Which is why I'm over there with Brenda and her kids. She used to come in the Shack all the time, mostly around the first and fifteenth. I realize now how much I looked forward to seeing her. I got a rise out of her on more than one occasion. Nice to know you can still get excited standing up. Brenda ain't no beauty queen, but she can be pretty good-looking on a good day. She's very clean. Always smell good. She got the longest fingernails I ever seen on any woman. With little designs on 'em. When me and Viola broke up, Brenda was so nice and sweet to me that one thang led to another. She always did flirt with me. She said she found me attractive, but I am attractive. I'm blacker than Evander Holyfield. We could be cousins. If you looked at me real hard and long and pretended like I'm thirty, you might could see some resemblance. But maybe not. I ain't no big man, but I ain't short neither. I used to be five eleven, but they say you shrink as you age. Viola got a little Amazon in her, 'cause she just a inch or two shorter than me which is why she stayed on me about my posture so I could look taller than her. Even now, I can be anywhere and I bolt right up. Even though I don't wanna thank about Viola right now, she always find her way into my head, and I been standing out here in this rain like a damn fool for I don't know how long trying to get the nerve to go back up in that hospital room and get my keys. I'ma have pneumonia in a minute. Might need a bed myself. But I need another minute or two. To drum up some courage. What I'ma say this time.

Last time I checked, I was tipping the scales at 225. I'm thanking about doing some kind of exercise this year, since they say it can extend your life, make you feel better, something about some metamorphins get in your brain and make you feel like you on dope. I ain't never wanted to know what dope feel like, but I know I could stand to drop a few pounds. Brenda said she never even noticed how big my stomach was, and when she did, said it didn't bother her none. She said it made a nice cushion. Plus, she said I'm a good man. Not many of us around. She been looking in the wrong places. But she said, "I ain't been looking nowhere. I wanted to be found." Well, I found her. And she *love* my Jheri Curl. She got one, too. Sorta. Hers is long. But sometime Brenda's cousin who wanna be a hairdresser one day practice doing fancy stuff on her even though Brenda say she just really wanna get her hair braided when she get enough money 'cause braids cost a lot more than a curl. I'ma see what I can do about that.

She ain't got no father over there for them kids, which is why she on welfare. She don't like living in the projects (I don't either) and she been trying to find work, but what she really wanna do is go back to school to get her GED. She said she wanna do better for herself. And her kids. I'ma help her. But first she trying to figure out if she should go to AA. First thangs first. She have trouble realizing when she drunk. I like a little taste myself, but I ain't crazy about that drunk feeling: spinning and not knowing what I'm saying, or being confused about my whereabouts and what have you. This is another reason why Brenda likes me. She say I know how to control myself. But that ain't completely true. I got a continuing weakness for them tables. To be honest, we both need help. I thank we can probably push each other in the right direction, but not until we get serious. I ain't quite threw the dice away yet. Even still, she appreciates me. And when I win, I brang it home to her. Everythang I do for her, she always say thank you. Viola could learn something from this woman.

Her kids is still kids. Africa, who they call Sunshine, is eighteen months. Hakeem is three. And Quantiana's five. I call her Miss Q. Why do young black folks give their kids names can't nobody hardly remember let alone spell or pronounce? And why would you name a child after a country instead of a relative? These kids is bad, but I like 'em. And they like me. They thank I'm they granddaddy, but it don't bother me none. Miss Q and Hakeem's daddy might be dead, Brenda ain't sure, but she heard somebody shot him last year. Sunshine's daddy is somewhere running around Vegas. I know him. Took his money in a crap game once. He ain't worth nothing. Somebody gotta take care of these kids, why not me? I don't mind one bit. It's nice to feel needed.

Get out the rain, Cecil. Go on up there and face the woman. She ain't gon' *do* nothing to you. Hell, she can't even talk, thank the Lord, and, Lord, please forgive me for thanking it. But those eyes of hers. She can cut glass with 'em. Ain't gotta say a single word. Do it, Cecil. Stop acting like such a chump. Besides, I need to hurry up and get home. I forgot. Brenda asked me to stop by the store and pick up some hamburger meat and ketchup. She making Sloppy Joes. Her kids is greedy. Don't eat nothing but junk, and that baby eat like a grown man. I don't know how they growing, and I told Brenda they should really be getting more vegetables. She said the only kind they'll eat come in a can: them waxed yellow string beans or creamed-style corn. This ain't exactly what I had in mind, but it's a start. When she do get around to cooking, Brenda is something in the kitchen. She say she wish she could afford a housekeeper. She sure could use one. But it's okay. I ain't been there long enough to make no changes, but I will. As soon as I get settled in. When it feel like I live there and not just on a long vacation.

I like Brenda. I like the way she make me feel. Like I'm something. She say she thirty-one, but I thank she lying about her age. She look older than that. But I don't care. She was born and raised right here in West Vegas. Her people live right down the street and around the corner, but they ain't no help to her. They worse off than she is, depending on how you look at it.

Move your feet, Cecil. And I do. This time I run toward the hospital entrance, and when I get inside I go over to the front desk. "I forgot my keys up in my wife's room. Her name is Viola Price and . . ."

The lady holds up her hand and dangles my keys in front of me. "She figured you'd be back for them."

"Thank you," I say. I take them from her real slow. The keys is cold. And I feel bad. I feel real bad. I walk out the hard way, through those revolving doors, and head toward my car. It stopped raining. This time I don't bother to look up toward Viola's window, 'cause she might be looking at me. She might be thanking that she still got the power over me. But she don't. When I get to my car, I know I should let it run for a few minutes, since it's fifteen years old, but I don't. I gotta hurry up and get to the store. I got some hungry kids at home. Maybe I'll get Brenda a forty. But, then again, maybe I won't.

Clearing House
Sweepstakes

I don't care what nobody say, ain't nothing wrong with me. In fact, I'm fine. Perfectly fine. My life is going along better than I expected. It ain't perfect, but it ain't as messed up as Mama and everybody else in my family seem to think it is either. To be perfectly honest, sometimes I wish there was a way I could start my life over. And sometimes I wish I'da been born white. Things probably woulda been a helluva lot easier. More like a straight line to some-damn-where instead of this S-curve to no-fucking-where.

But I ain't stupid. I know I was supposed to go to college instead of prison. Back then, I *was* stupid. Which is one reason why I read a newspaper and do a crossword puzzle every single day, and it's the main reason why I been taking college classes off and on for the last ten years. Mostly business and marketing. Computers. Entrepreneurial-type courses. Plus, I try to take some kind of philosophy class whenever I can, because I pride myself on thinking on more than one level. It's hard talking to people half the time, and these classes give me the opportunity to exchange ideas without feeling ridiculous. I like being able to interpret shit. To look at life from a whole lotta different angles, not just the most obvious. Except this time I couldn't afford the inductive-and-deductive-logic class, so this semester I'm gon' have to do all my thinking by myself.

I got a job. But it's on hold. I'm on disability right now. Don't nobody in my family believe I got rheumatoid arthritis.

Just like me, they thought only old people get it. Hell, I'm only thirty-six. It blew my mind when that doctor told me what was happening to my body. I don't know what I'm gon' have to do to prove it to everybody. When I told Mama, she acted like I made it up. Like I invented the disease itself. But I'm at the point now where I can't even hardly hammer. Not all day. Not no more. For years, I pretended like wasn't nothing wrong with me, but the pain started messing up my income. Off and on, for the last six months I been putting in hardwood floors in these upscale housing developments for this guy Woolery who wants me to maybe be his partner if I could come up with about five or ten grand, but where would I get that kind of money? Opportunities like this don't knock a whole lot in my world, and even though I got two sisters with a little money, you think I could ask either one of 'em to lend it to me? No fuckin' way. They'd probably laugh in my face. They think I'm full of shit. Shaky. 'Cause it's been hard to finish things I've started. But it ain't always my fault. And they don't give me no credit for trying. Hell, I *could* be a crackhead. I *could* be out here breaking and entering. But I'm trying to be an upstanding citizen. It's a slow process, but I'm doing it the only way I know how and the best way I can. If they could see me without my clothes on they'd be shocked. Shit, I got knots on my wrists that look like acorns. Bones in my elbows that look like they trying to push through my skin. Some mornings they're so puffed up I can't hardly straighten out my arm. And I don't even wanna mention my knees and ankles. I'm on my way to deformity. Most of the time my right knee look like it's got elephantiasis. And ain't no cure for this shit. I live on Tylenol Extra Strength. Sometimes I eat ten of 'em a day. The doctor said it's only gon' get worse. But I ain't complaining. I been through more, much more pain than this.

The truth of the matter is, I wanna start my own business one day, 'cause I got some 100 percent guaranteed invention ideas which—if I do it right—could make me some real money. Hell,

I got a garageful of ideas but I have to keep my mouth shut, 'cause people in a better position will steal your shit right from under you and call it theirs. I know how to go about getting stuff patented, but it cost money. And of course don't nobody in my family wanna hear about *my* ideas. They think I'm talking off the top of my head again. "Get a job first," Paris always says. "And try keeping it long enough to get some health insurance," Charlotte is guaranteed to throw in. Shit, when you got a pre-existing condition, it's kind of hard to get insurance. "I hope you're not getting high or drinking that hard stuff again, Lewis," because Janelle thinks everybody who takes a sip is a alcoholic, or if you smoke a joint every now and then you're on the road to being a drug addict. Mama seems to be the only one who wants to believe in me: "You got good sense, Lewis. I'll just be glad when you start using it." And Daddy, the man who don't never like to take a stand: "Do whatever you can, Lewis. As long as you stay outta trouble, it's fine with me."

They don't even *know* me. They *remember* me. They look at old pictures and think I'm the same person I was twenty years ago. Well, I'm not. My family don't have a single solitary clue who I am *today,* what I'm going through, what I'm feeling in-side, and I don't think they care all that much. They don't re-spect me, because I ain't doing as good as they are. This shit hurts. But they oughtta take a long hard look at their own damn lives and stop wasting so much time trying to solve the equa-tions of mine.

I'll be frank. Paris—even though she's the oldest and I love and respect her and everything and she's got a successful food business going and her life is on track—she sees life like it's a straight line. Ain't no room for no detours in her world. You ei-ther are or you ain't. It's hard talking to her on the phone. It's like getting a pop quiz when I call her. Plus, she don't have no patience. She don't like to listen, and she think she know ev-erything. Yeah, she smart, she got degrees from two colleges, but she don't know *everything*. Just 'cause you a success don't mean you perfect. It don't make you flawless. She doing a good job with Dingus and everything, but she likes to put me down 'cause I ain't the kind of father she thinks I *should* be. You think I need her to remind me? She the one up there in the Bay Area in a big house with nobody to love. I don't have *no* problems finding somebody to love me. I can get just about any woman I want. Well, maybe not *any*, but most of 'em. It's some desperate women out here, all you gotta do is learn how to spot 'em. And, believe me, it ain't all that hard to do.

Which brings me to Janelle. She lives in a dream world. Like she on some Fantasy Island kinda trip. She simple, really, and don't understand that life is like a jigsaw puzzle. That you have to see the whole picture and then put it together piece by piece. Janelle want it all in one lump. That's why she's always trying to latch on to somebody to give it to her. Her husband that died spoiled her, gave her too much of everything. I liked him, though. I ain't so sure if this dude George is the answer.

My other sister Charlotte don't do nothing unless she positive she can get something out of it. She don't like to make no big investments, just little ones, but she want big returns. Them Laundromats is in shambles, but she too cheap to fix 'em up. I can't count how many businesses she done tried but quit because the money wasn't coming fast enough. Plus, she thinks the whole world is suppose to revolve around her. She was the same way when she was little. She missing the point like a motherfucker.

All of 'em remind me year in and year out that if I had acted like a *real* man I'd probably still be married to Donnetta, probably be wearing a suit and tie (which to this day I do not own), working nine to five, picking Jamil up after school and taking him to soccer and Little League practice. But that ain't the way the shit worked out. I'm divorced. And I'm glad. That girl had problems much deeper than mine, but my family made me feel like she was the one who got the booby prize. Donnetta put on a nice innocent act, which was how I fell for her in the first place. There was a softness to her I hadn't seen in none of the black women I'd been out with. She pretended to have ambition just like she pretended to believe in me. But she was lazy. Didn't know what she wanted. Just what she didn't want. Our marriage ended up being a process of elimination, and then the shit just changed up completely after she found God. She wasn't never all that crazy about sex, but after she got saved, if we did it once or twice a month, that was almost too much. To this day I don't know if Donnetta ever even had an orgasm or not. She claimed she did, but for some reason I just never believed her. Patience is what I mostly got outta this marriage, 'cause I was hoping to have a few more kids, but after nine years and nothing never happened, she just said maybe she was finished, and that one was enough. I went through all them years of hell for nothing. But, then again, it was only because I ended up loving my son more than I did her.

Jamil: I wish I was in a better position to do for him, but since I'm not—at least for the time being—I just pretend like I don't have a kid, otherwise I'd be eaten alive inside every day, which I already am, and it's probably why I drink the way I do. If it wasn't for Donnetta, I'd be in much better shape financially. She's the reason I have to work under the table half the time, because right after we split up she insisted on taking me to court, knowing I wasn't making nothing but two dollars over minimum wage. She didn't care. She wanted *that*. And she *got* it.

As a man, it makes you feel small when you know what your limitations are. When you know you ain't lived up to your potential, when you ain't sure if you ever will. It can fuck your head up big-time when you know how you wish you *could* be living versus how you *are*. I guess the space in between is a big-ass blank you have to learn how to fill in.

At least I know Jamil ain't over there suffering. He ain't wanting for too much. I know he ain't deprived. Donnetta may not be the brightest person in the world, but she's a good mother. That much I give her credit for. They only forty-seven miles away from here, and I know for a fact that it won't be long before I'm able to pull up in front of the house—or maybe meet 'em at the corner 'cause no way am I going into that house—and take Jamil somewhere. Plus, I heard she got another man coming over there on a regular basis. He supposed to be a religious fanatic like she is. But I don't care who he is or what he is, as long as he don't abuse my son. I do not under any circumstances ever want to meet the motherfucker. No way.

If everybody only knew. It has taken a lot of work just to get where I am. Considering. I mean, I don't hold no grudges. Well, maybe a few. 'Cause it's some people who've done some unspeakable, despicable shit to me. One thing I have learned to be true is this: relatives can do more harm to you than a total fucking stranger. They got statistics to prove that most homicides happen within the family, and believe me, I can understand why. As much as I would like to, I've tried hard to forget the fact that my sixteen- and seventeen-year-old cousins—Boogar and Squirrel—pushed me inside the trap door of our fallout shelter when I was ten years old and made me suck their penises. I couldn't believe they was making me do it and I didn't understand why. We were boys. Plus, we was cousins. I ain't never felt so humiliated and confused in my life as I did that day. When I threw up afterwards, they just laughed and told me if I *ever* told anybody about this they would kill me. To this day, I ain't never told a soul.

But I ain't completely stupid. Just like I know what the gross national product is, I know that this incident has probably had some effect on my personality and everything, but I don't think it's been the deciding factor in what kinda man I am today. Hell, when I was locked up, to maintain my sanity, all I did was read encyclopedias and that's where I started doing crossword puzzles. Plus I read all those psychology books by Freud and Jung and the rest of them motherfuckers who think they can psychoanalyze everything and everybody. But, like they say on the street: shit happens. And some shit don't always fit so nice and neat into no textbook. Even if it could, so the fuck what? This is the reason why I never told nobody. People always want to analyze you. Figure out what slot you fit in. What if you don't fit? If something traumatic happened to you as a child, they automatically think you'll be fucked up or affected by it the rest of your life. Hell, look at me. I'm a perfect example of somebody that turned out okay. That's why I don't buy the shit. And I ain't in no fucking denial either. If you smart, you can teach yourself to forget anything, put it in a little compartment in your brain that you know you won't need, lock it, and throw away the key. This is particularly helpful when you're dealing with shit that hurts. So what if it creep in every now and then? You still gotta live.

Plus. Payback is a bitch. I was only locked up for a hot minute. I didn't do no hard time or no bending over in the joint neither. I stuck mostly to myself. Spent most of my time reading. Educating myself. Boogar and Squirrel was doing five to ten when I got there. Armed robbery and assault with a deadly weapon. I stole some damn lawnmowers. Garden tools. I get out. Six years go by. They get out. I move back to California to be closer to my family, to get away from the thugs and drugs that's on every other corner on the South Side of Chicago, and to dodge all forms of criminal activity, including loose bullets. One more year goes by. It's 1981: Boogar get shot in the head on Lake Shore Drive for something, and almost a year to the day later Squirrel OD's on heroin. Nobody understands why I don't go to either one of their funerals. Especially Mama. "Your own cousins, Lewis? Y'all used to play together when you was little."

"We didn't play all that good together," was all I said.

I ain't hung up on the past. I'm trying to live in the here and now. And right now I'm all twisted up between the bottom sheet, the mattress, and this woman. A very plump woman. I need a cigarette bad but I know I ain't got none. That much I do remember. I'm almost scared to roll over and see who she is, but I blink a few times, straining to put yesterday and right now together. Luisa. That's her name. What a fucking relief. I push her to the side and roll out the bed. The telephone comes out of the cradle and crashes to the floor, but it don't matter, 'cause it don't work. Shit. My head is killing me. This tiny-ass room is dark and it smells like cigarette ashes, warm beer, and stale reefa. But I'm used to it. Still, opening a window wouldn't be such a bad idea. Kids are playing outside.

Before I make it out to the bathroom, I hear a knock on the front door. Who in the hell could that be this time of morning? I wrap a towel around me, walk over, and look through the peephole, but I don't recognize the middle-aged black dude's face. I crack the door open a little bit.

"Yeah?"

"Are you Lewis Price?"

"Who wants to know?"

"The Clearing House Sweepstakes, sir, but if you're not Lewis Price . . ."

"Wait a minute," I say. My heart is pounding like a galloping horse, because by the time he hands me that white envelope through the crack of the door I know that, number one, there is a God; number two, one day my luck was bound to change; and, three, it do pay to gamble sometimes. I let out a long sigh after I take the envelope.

"Sir, this might be important, too," he says, handing me a piece of paper. "It was taped to the screen. Have a nice day." I close the door, wishing I had at least a half a cigarette to inhale, to help me take this all in. I don't know how much I won, but it's gotta be enough to buy that Ford pickup I been looking at. Burgundy. That's my color. Whew! I can pay all my back child support—blow Donnetta's mind once and for all. And I can maybe build my own ranch house even further away from all these crazy motherfuckers out here in the High Desert. I can start my own business. More than one! Get some of my ideas patented. Take some harder classes. "Slow the fuck down," I say out loud. I got time to figure it all out, so I take a deep breath, trying to humble myself, but my fingers are tingling from the envelope in one hand and the piece of paper in the other. I read the paper first, sorta like prolonging an orgasm: "Lewis: Mama's in the hospital. Do something. Get to a phone. She's getting out of ICU today, but don't let that stop you from worrying. Janelle." This is the third time in two years Mama's been rushed to the hospital. I'm just glad that Daddy's there. But, since I'm off work, I should go spend a few days with her. Help out, 'cause Daddy's probably busy running the Shack.

I gotta get to Vegas. But no way am I riding for four hours inside a car with Janelle. No way. First of all, she can't drive. Her mind ain't on the road. She don't read signs, and she drives too damn slow. Plus, she won't let you smoke and she likes that weird New Age music. Hell, no. I'll take a bus. This way I can get some thinking in without no distractions.

As soon as I cash this check. No. First I need to open up a bank account. But I forgot. I don't have no driver's license. Can't even get 'em for another eight months. They suspended. Two DUIs in five months. This is exactly why no more drinking and driving for me. But maybe I can get one of them California IDs. No. I got other proof that I'm who I'm supposed to be. I got bills. Maybe I can convince the bank lady that I am who I say I am when she sees how big this check is. That I got other mail with the same name and address on it. Plus, I got some Polaroids around here somewhere.

A half-empty bottle of Schlitz is sitting on the kitchen counter and I gulp it down. Then I scrounge through an ashtray till I find a decent butt, and light it. It's burning a hole in my throat when I feel somebody's eyes staring at me. As I turn to see if it's Luisa, my towel falls to the floor and the brown face of a five- or six-year-old Mexican kid is peering at me from the back of the couch. He looks like he don't know where he is.

"Hi," I say, dropping the hot-boxed butt back in the ashtray, picking up the towel, and wrapping it tighter around me. I'm grinning wide, but the little boy just sits there like I'm some kind of wind-up toy, which is pretty much how I'm feeling. Those days of being ashamed to see my son on Christmas are over. Now I'll go out there sober as a preacher, with boxes and boxes of presents. And I'll drive my new truck. That 1994 F-250 with the stretch cab. And I think I'll talk to Woolery about that hardwood-floor offer, see if the white boy was really serious. If not, fuck him. I got a real partner, my homeboy Silas. Everybody call him Simple Sam, and we been talking about buying a big rig. It's mucho money to be made in trucks. And I'll give Mama and Daddy a hand, 'cause it don't take no rocket scientist to see that the last Shack ain't doing as good as it used to. People don't eat that much barbecue no more. They need to fix up that house, at least get a new roof, make a Arizona room in the back or something. They could also use a vacation. Hell, I could use one, too. But where would I go? Acapulco. Naw. Half of Mexico live right here in southern California. We'll see. And then there's my wonderful sisters. I think I'll do something nice for the three of 'em. Blow their little minds. I don't know what it'll be, but whatever it is, they'll get a charge out of it.

"I'm Lewis," I finally say to the little boy. "And I'm rich!" I decide now would be a good time to open this envelope, since I've gotten used to the idea of being loaded, but as soon as I flip it over to slide my index finger under the flap, I recognize the logo for Family Court from the County of Santa Rita. "Kiss my black ass!" I say, then catch myself when I look at that little boy. "I'm sorry." We both look like we about to cry. He slides down behind the brown plaid couch so I can't see his eyes, just the crown of his head.

I don't need to finish tearing this fucking envelope open but I figure I might as well see how much I owe. It's a summons all right. To appear in court for delinquent child support. The figure is humiliating and embarrassing: $3,268. Half of it's interest.

"Where's my mommy?"

What a bitch Donnetta is. She know I ain't working. She

know I been living off disability, and I told her I'd send what I could when I could. The problem was, I couldn't. And I haven't. Shit, after I pay my rent and electricity, squeeze in a meal here and there, that's it. This is why I don't have no phone.

"Where's my mommy?" the kid asks again.

"I'll get her," I say, turning toward the bedroom, and then I stop dead in my tracks. "What's your name?"

"Miguel. And I'm hungry. You have Cocoa Puffs?"

"Naw, but we'll get you something in a minute."

When I walk into the bedroom, Luisa is still sleep. I want her and her son outta here as quickly as possible, but I know I need to be nice. My car ain't running—I blew a head gasket over a month ago—and in order to go see Mama, I gotta catch a Greyhound. I know they got a 1:35 to Vegas. My only glitch is I gotta borrow the money from Luisa to catch it. I bend down to kiss her on the lips, but her breath stinks so bad from last night that I let my mouth press against her cheek instead. She kinda stirs. "Wake up, baby," I say. "Your son wants you and I ain't got nothing in here for him to eat."

She struggles to sit up. Her long black hair floats over her shoulders. Her skin looks like gold. She's a pretty woman—about twenty-something—but her body looks much older than she is. She's built like a round square. I met her at a bar a few weeks ago. She asked me to dance, but I don't dance, so we had a few beers and by the fifth or sixth one she asked if she could go home with me. Hell, I was relieved. I don't like sleeping by myself if I don't have to. My mind is too active, and no matter what kind of mood I start out in, I can think or drink myself straight into being depressed. A lot of times when I'm by myself, drunk, I cry. Sometimes I cry in front of women, too. Not on purpose. All I want is a little empathy, somebody to feel my pain, somebody to listen, to understand my disappointments, my desires—hell, my dreams. Women love men who cry, which is why I've cried in front of a whole lotta different ones. They feel closer to you after you let 'em see you like this. But it ain't no act I'm putting on. It ain't no performance, and most of the time I don't want nothing except their undivided attention, or maybe some pussy to finish off the evening.

I won't lie. I miss being married. I miss being a father. I miss my son. And I wish I had more than one. I know it's been almost a year since I seen him. And I can't blame nobody but myself for not going out there, but I can't stand the sight of Donnetta these days. It's true I was a little drunk the last time I went out there and I did cuss her out in front of Jamil, but that's only 'cause she wouldn't let me in since I forgot to call first, and she sent Chuckaluck—her big brother who makes my six-one ass look like a dwarf—to the door and I did not feel like fucking with him. But I was still fuming, so I broke the windshield outta her car, and she went and got that restraining order and I ain't been back since.

Sometimes I hate women. Maybe "hate" is too strong a word. I resent their power. Growing up in a house full of nothing but girls helped me see just how manipulative and slick they can be. How far they're willing to go to get their way. How we fall for the okey-doke every single time. My only problem is, they're also my weakness. They're necessary for my survival, which is why I'm rarely without one. I don't care what color they are, except I ain't never slept with a white woman, but that's mostly because Mexican and black women been keeping me pretty busy. I know how to make women surrender, can talk 'em into just about anything, because I guess I'm handsome, been told I got sex appeal—whatever that shit means—but I'm also intelligent, and on top of everything: I'm a good lay.

Little Miguel charges into the bedroom and Luisa pulls the covers up to hide her long breasts. "Hi, sweetie," she says as he jumps on top of the bed. "We're going to get you some breakfast and then we go home, okay?"

He looks at her like he don't believe her.

"Now, go, go, go, so Mommy can get dressed. Watch cartoons for a few minutes and I'll be right out."

"He's a nice little boy," I say.

"Thanks," she says, and gets up. When I look at her in broad daylight with no clothes on, I realize that her body is jacked up. But who am I to complain? Shit, she's still nice. She ain't no crackhead (like a lot of 'em I've run into at the bar). She ain't no diehard alcoholic. And she ain't on welfare. Wait a minute. Yes she is. But she definitely ain't married, and she ain't vulgar or nasty or some ignorant high-school dropout. She takes night classes in continuing ed, too; besides, she likes me. She kept me company last night, fucked me good—at least I think she did—and I'll keep her around until I get bored or find somebody better, whichever happen first.

In a way, what I'm hoping to do is stumble upon a wife. I been trying to replace Donnetta for years, but it ain't easy to fall in love. It ain't something you should have to work at. I think I'm still making the transition from being married to being divorced. It's only been six years. If I tell the truth, on some days, when Donnetta might be washing clothes or drinking iced tea with her BLT or sitting in rush hour traffic, I pray that she'll come to her senses and realize she still love me as much as she love God, that she'll beg me to come home and we can be a family again. I can make myself remember how much I *used* to love her, when her faith was in me instead of just God, when she made me feel like a king. I'm sure I could love her again. It would be so nice to have my life back. But this is all bullshit, and I know it.

I follow Luisa to the bathroom and close the door behind us. "I need to ask you a favor, baby."

"What's that?" she asks while turning on the shower. She's looking for the soap, but there's only three white curled-up slivers left, which she's gotta settle for. The blue towel she's gon' have to use already been used by Melody three or four days ago. I need to go to the Laundromat, that much I do know.

"Did I tell you my mama's in the hospital?"

"No, you didn't. Is she all right?"

"Well, sorta. She lives in Vegas, and I need to go see her today. She's got asthma real bad." I let out a long sigh. "Anyway, I had to pay my child support last week, and you know my car ain't running, and all I got is $4.52 to my name and I was wondering if you could lend me forty or fifty bucks so I can catch the bus up there this afternoon. I'll pay you back next week, I swear it. I got a little job loading furniture for a few weeks, so I'll have some cash."

"Don't worry. Since it's for a good reason, I'll lend it to you, Lewis. But just remember, Easter's coming up, and I've got things in layaway at Kmart, and if I don't get them out by the seventh, they'll put them back. *Comprende?*"

"*Comprende.* And don't worry. I wouldn't do that to your kid."

"Kids. Did you forget about Elesia and little Rocky?"

I had. But, hell, most of the women I deal with got at least one, so why should I be so surprised? "Naw, I didn't forget," I say. "I just ain't met 'em yet, that's all."

"Don't worry," she says, stepping into the bathtub and pulling the shower curtain closed. "You will."

"I can't wait," I say. I leave the steamy bathroom and go sit on the edge of the bed, praying she'll be quick. My head is tight. Burning. Like I got a baseball cap on too tight. I look down at the floor and spot her black vinyl purse. I would love to go in it and get the money and walk to the corner to get her kid a box of cereal, buy a newspaper, a new crossword book to do on the bus, a pack of Kools, and just one forty-ounce to get my day started. But that wouldn't be too cool. And, besides, I ain't that desperate. So I just fold my hands. And sit here. And wait.

Track

"Why're you so quiet?" Shanice is sitting in the backseat of the Jaguar with a book up to her face, which is also pressed snugly against the window. She's already cracked and devoured at least two hundred sunflower seeds on the drive here. The bulk of the shells are piled on top of the plastic bag in her lap. I keep telling her these things are full of fat and high in sodium, but she doesn't care. For somebody who runs track, she eats way too many of them. It's a nervous habit. Like a chain smoker. But I can't stop her. She sneaks and buys them. Sits up in her room and reads book after book and cracks and sucks on those nasty things until her trash can is full of crumpled-up paper towels.

She's not talking today, and when Shanice doesn't feel like talking, nothing I say or do can make her. She can be an evil little wench, just like her Granny Vy at times. They're cut from the same cloth. Stubborn as hell.

George, who is sitting on the passenger side, dare not say anything to her when she's like this. He knows better. She's been so short with him that I had to ask him not to question, criticize, or chastise her outside of my presence. The reasons stem from that time Shanice went and told that lie on him to Mama, and ever since then I've been watching his every move—much too close for George's comfort—which has also created a circle of constant tension in our household. He doesn't have two words to say to Mama when she calls, but this of course is because he claimed she threatened him. Knowing

Mama, she probably did, but he wouldn't tell me what she said. Whatever it was, George doesn't answer the phone anymore when it rings.

"If you eat too many of those things you won't want your lunch," George is saying to Shanice.

"She's fine," I say, as we turn in to the Sizzler. We're treating Shanice to her favorite restaurant, since today and tomorrow are some sort of in-service days for teachers and she gets out at twelve-thirty.

When we get out of the car, my daughter walks up ahead. She's filling out too fast. If I'm not mistaken, the cheeks of her behind are peeking out where her jeans are slit. She's in a tight tube top, but thank God she's not filling a B-cup yet. At least I don't think she is. She could be me, twenty years ago. At thirteen, I was dangerous, and at fifteen, according to Mama, lethal. I had the body of a grown woman. At thirty-five, I don't look too shabby. A lot of people swear I'm twenty-eight or twenty-nine.

Of the three girls in my family, I'm the smallest. I should say, the most fit. I'm the only one who works out, but I got the habit being married to Jimmy. He was not only a high-school track coach but, in his day, a decathlete. He believed in taking care of his body, and it certainly rubbed off on me. I've been trying to persuade Mama and my sisters—particularly Charlotte's big butt—to at least try walking. But they're too lazy. Paris has been lucky. She looks good in her clothes, but I know she must be getting soft under those jeans, because she doesn't do anything with any consistency except cook. Her mind's on it but her heart isn't, otherwise she'd find time to fit it in. I don't care what's going on, I make sure I get to the gym. I'm even entertaining the thought of becoming a personal trainer, but under the circumstances, of course, I wouldn't dream of doing it right now. We'll see how things evolve over the next few weeks. Regardless, I still might take some certification classes if this real-estate thing doesn't work out. I believe it's best to leave the door for options open.

I tend to give George—the human incinerator—the evil eye every time I see him inhale a Twinkie or watch him slurp up a bowl of Dreyer's Butter Pecan or devour a chunk of carrot cake. This would be every night before bed. He eats teriyaki anything, and if he can't watch the butter drip onto his plate, it means it's not enough. He doesn't believe in exercise. Says we were given the bodies we were destined to have. I have a hard time accepting this, especially since he's got a little inner tube forming around his waist, and pectorals that sag worse than mine. I told him this is called fat. It can be burned off. A few crunches and handheld weights could help get rid of it. He thinks he looks good, which must be the reason why he always wears pajamas to bed. I can count how many times I've seen him naked. We bathe separately. I have to leave the bathroom when it's his turn. He says it's about privacy. I can respect that most of the time. When we make love—if you can call it that— he takes everything off under the covers. He's quick about his business, too, but sometimes I can beat him, depending on how tired I am. He doesn't even like to put it in very often, and when he does, it's not for very long, which is why I was so shocked when I found out yesterday that I'm seven weeks pregnant. I have not told George, because I don't know how to tell him. Or when. He's the first man I've ever met that can get off just by rubbing up against me. He says it's about friction. I just say whatever works. Other times he likes me to pretend it's an ice-cream cone or begs me to use my hands like I'm trying to start a fire by stroking up and down. It's been like this for a while, but I figure every man has pet things he likes, and these are George's. One thing he refuses to do, however, is put his mouth down there. I've pleaded with him to try, but he said he just can't do it. It's unsanitary. He can't stand the smell. But we have a ritual: I bathe every single night at nine o'clock, because I read at least an hour before I go to bed. He goes in right after me. I've tried everything, but all he'll do is use his finger, and sometimes, when we're sitting in bed watching a video—not necessarily a porno—and both of our hands are working, I feel really stupid. *Really* stupid.

To be on the safe side, when Shanice came home from Mama's after the New Year, I sat her and George down in a room together so we could get all this ugly business cleared up and behind us.

"George, have you ever raised your hand to Shanice without my knowledge?"

"I'm not even going to dignify that with an answer."

"Please, just tell me."

"Why don't you ask her?" he said, and quite loudly.

I turned to Shanice. "Has he?"

"Not really."

"Is that a yes or a no?"

"No."

"Then why'd you lie, Shanice?"

"Because Granny was looking at my hair and she kept bugging me about why and how it had come out, and when she finally asked me if George had anything to do with it, I just said yes to shut her up."

"And that's it?"

She just nodded.

"Then I think you owe George an apology."

She didn't say anything.

"Forget it," he said.

"Shanice?"

"Sorry," she said to the wall or the door, but it definitely wasn't to him. "Can I go now?"

"Go," I said. George looked like he always did: preoccupied with something else. And that was it. We've never talked about it since, and things seem as close to normal as we can get.

Now I'm watching Shanice swing those two hundred or so braids dangling over her shoulders like they're hers. I let George's niece do it a few weeks ago. You can't see the bald spots all that much, and it seems as if she's slowed down some on pulling it out. I never knew why she started doing it in the first place. The doctor said sometimes it means something traumatic has happened and this could be her reaction to it. I asked Shanice about that. She said the only thing that had terrified her was that earthquake we had back in January. But she'd been doing this long before then. Sometimes kids keep secrets, and if they don't want to tell, they won't tell. She knows I'm here for her, I've made that perfectly clear.

As much as Shanice tries to pretend as if she doesn't like George, she really does. He spoils her like she were his. Buys her just about anything she wants, and she certainly knows how to ask. He doesn't know how to say no to her, and I chide him about this all the time. For some reason, he acts like he's indebted to her for even being here. But this is his house. Technically. My name still isn't on the deed, but that's just one more thing on a long list we have yet to iron out. Luckily, we're in California, a community-property state, so I'm not all that worried about what's mine and what's his. Push comes to shove, I would not have to walk out of here with nothing.

George holds the door to the restaurant open for us. At twelve and three-quarters, as she puts it, Shanice is five six: almost as tall as me. I'm five nine. All the girls on Jimmy's side of the family are lanky with narrow hips. I'm still waiting for more of the Price blood to come to the surface. Jimmy's skin looked like red clay, but Shanice got both of our coloring and turned out deep bronze.

She walks past George clutching her book. He's only about an inch taller than her. I'm barely speaking to him today myself, as he just announced this morning that he is not paying to send her to boarding school like he promised he would. She wants to go. As a matter of fact, she's been begging to go, which I think is a little strange, considering she's got all the comforts a girl could ask for at home. Her room is full of everything, which is probably why she rarely comes out of it.

I walk past George, and once we're inside and seated, Shanice turns her attention to the traffic outside. We bore her.

"What do you feel like having today?" he asks her.

"I'm not hungry."

"I told you those seeds would ruin your appetite."

"It's not the seeds. It's you. You make me sick."

"Stop it, Shanice. Right now!" I yell, and then try lowering my voice. "Not today, please."

"Look, we can't afford to send you to boarding school, if that's what this is about."

"You *can* afford it. You know I want to go, that's the reason you're not doing it. Both of you just want to keep me prisoner for the next five years, that's all."

"You should watch the tone of your voice," I say. "Look. I can try asking the insurance company to reconsider releasing more of your trust, but your father's lawyer set it up so that it's paid out in specific increments until you turn eighteen."

"Private school is already costing us a small fortune," George says. "Do you have any idea how expensive boarding school is?"

"No, I don't," Shanice says.

"Can we not get into this right now?"

"Whatever," she sighs.

"Look. I've got two midterms this week, Mama just got out of intensive care, and I'd like to drive up there on Saturday to see her. Make sure she's doing all right."

"Can I go, too?" Shanice asks.

"We'll see."

"You can't go," George says.

Shanice cuts her eyes at him. "Why not?"

"Because your first league meet is this weekend."

"But it's not a qualifying meet, and, plus, I want to see my granny."

"I'd like her to come with me, George."

"I thought you said Viola was going home on Saturday."

"That's right."

"Don't you think she needs a few days to fully recover at home?"

"I'm going there to *help* her recovery, George. There'll be a lot of things she can't do."

"I thought you said Lewis was headed over there to be with her?"

"He's just the welcoming committee she needs, George. Be serious."

"I understand all this, but it just seems like next weekend would make more sense."

"Is there something you need me to do for you?"

"So you did forget about the banquet on Saturday. It's an important dinner. And you know that. Everybody's wives will be there. Except mine, of course."

"George, I'm not sure just how bad Mama's attack was, but . . ."

"She's still in the *hospital;* that should give you a clue," Shanice says.

"You should really watch the tone of your voice," George says. "Look, we only have this awards dinner once a year. It's been on the calendar for eight months. Your mother's illness is somewhat of an inconvenience, wouldn't you say?"

Self-restraint is something I pride myself on, and it's rare that I even raise my voice at George, but he was taking this much too far. "Well, it's sad when your mother gets sick and has to be rushed to the hospital and may very well have died, but, then, that's not half as important as, say, some dry-ass chicken or overcooked roast beef, and do you think I really want to miss rubbing shoulders with a tableful of phony women who can't even remember my name, just to go to my mother's aid? What a tough decision."

"So this is how you value my colleagues?"

"Colleagues? They're cops, George."

"So—am I supposed to go alone?"

"If I could be in two places at once I would. Please don't make me feel guilty about this."

"So you're going to Vegas, then?"

"I don't have a choice. She's my mother."

"That's so touching."

"Ma, can you take me to track practice today?"

"No, I can't. The only time I could reserve a computer at the library was from five to seven, and I wanted to go to the gym for an hour. I should be home by eight-thirty. I can take you tomorrow."

"I don't mind taking her," George says.

"I don't want you to take me," she says.

"Well, you really don't have much of a choice, now, do you?" He smirks and heads for the salad bar. I know he means well, but Shanice has gotten too grown and her mouth is like sour candy. Sometimes I wish she *was* going somewhere.

————————

When we get home, it's almost two-thirty. Shanice goes straight up to her room and closes the door. As usual. The music comes on almost automatically. I go out to the garage to look for my Easter stuff, and of course George follows me.

"What are we going to do about her attitude, Janelle? I can't take much more of this."

I see the big blue bunny. He's leaning against the wall in a corner, covered in plastic. "Look. She's going through puberty. This is the time when most young girls are difficult. Just try to be a little more patient with her, please?"

"She's got it in for me and you know it."

"I think you're misreading her, I really do." I pull the stepladder below the shelves where I keep all my boxes. They're pretty much in holiday order and each box is labeled— "Xmas Decorations," "Fourth of July," "Valentine's Day," "St. Patrick's Day," etc., and there's "Easter."

"She wants me to apologize for not being her father."

"Well, there's not much we can do about that, now, can we?"

I get up on the ladder and look down at George. "Can you help me do this, please?"

"Sure," he says, and we trade places. He hands me all four boxes but then accidentally gives me one marked "Fourth of July." "Not that one!" I yell, and he puts it back like I just screamed "Fire!" or something. I walk over to where all the flags are rolled up, lift the plastic, and flip through them one by one until I find the Easter-egg flag. All holidays deserve to be acknowledged, as far as I'm concerned. It adds a measure of excitement to otherwise boring weeks and gives me something to do.

"I'm doing everything I can to be a good father to that girl, but she shuts me out."

I start opening the boxes one by one, looking for the papier-mâché eggs. They're almost twelve inches round. I made them in a papier-mâché class. I didn't like it. It was too messy. "Well," I say after I find the yellow and pink ones, "you'll have another chance."

"Another chance, how?"

"To be a good father. To the next one. Where's the nest? I don't think you got the one with the nest in it."

"What next one?"

"The one in here," I say, tapping my stomach. I spot the box marked "Nest/Baby Chicks/Baskets," and point to it. George leans back against the big blue bunny and it almost tips over. He catches it. "You're *not* pregnant?"

"I am."

"Janelle, I thought we talked about this."

"We did talk about it. Can you pull my car out into the driveway so I can spread all my things in here?"

"I told you I didn't want any more kids. I've had enough of kids. I've already raised two, and they're finally grown and paid for. I'm fifty-one years old. I don't need to start over. I'm too damn old to start over."

"No, you're not." I hand him the keys from the hook on the wall next to the door leading to the kitchen.

"I thought you were using protection," he says as he presses the garage-door opener and opens the door of my Volvo.

"Protection from what, George? I can hardly believe it even found its way up there, considering."

He starts the engine, then sticks his head out the window. "Are you complaining?"

"No."

"Well, something managed to find its way," he says, and backs the car out into the driveway.

Cars dart by. I just watch. There's far too much traffic on this street. One day I'd like to find a quieter one to live on. A cul-de-sac, even. When he gets out of the car, he comes back in and pushes the garage-door button. As it lowers, I blurt out: "I'm having it." The tarp is always in the same place. I spread it out in the spot where my car was and, one by one, place every single item on top of it.

"Look, don't sound so defensive, Janelle. I'm not saying I don't want it. It's not like something you pick up for me at the store."

"I'm thirty-five years old, George. My days are so very numbered. Besides, Shanice has always wanted a brother or sister, and now she can get her wish. Look at Hugh Hefner."

"I'm not Hugh Hefner."

"Well . . ."

"How far gone are you?"

"Seven weeks." There's the pink egg. Thank the Lord. Now. Tomorrow, right after my exams, I can put them all out in the front yard. It'll be lovely.

"Anything could happen," George says.

"What do you mean: *anything?*"

"There's still time to change our minds."

"I'm not changing my mind," I say, and walk past him toward the kitchen door.

"Sometimes you remind me of my ex-wife, you know that?"

"Don't you *dare* compare me to her," I say. "I've been compared enough in my life."

"I'm not comparing per se, but she loved to push me into a corner to get what she wanted, too. This feels pretty damn familiar."

"Look, I've got studying to do."

"I'm sorry," he says apologetically. "I just wasn't expecting this. I've got lots of other things on my mind. You know the two duplexes off Western and Forty-seventh?"

"Yes."

"Well, the crackheads are taking over the whole damn street, and black people are moving out of there left and right. Between them, the Koreans buying up everything, and the Crips and Bloods destroying it all, the neighborhood's turning into a war zone. I might have to sell both units."

"And what fool do you think would buy those dumps?"

"Those 'dumps' provide almost half of my annual income, which you don't seem to mind one bit."

"I'm sorry." But I don't mean it.

"It's all right. I just have to get used to this whole idea. Give me a few days. At least. But right now I better get Shanice over to the track."

"Are you going to wait for her?"

"Yes."

"Please don't say anything to her about this. I want to wait until I'm at least ten weeks."

"Why?"

"Because I want to get an amnio and that'll tell me if everything's okay."

"Whatever."

"And, plus, *I* want to be the one to tell her," I say, and hold the door open for him to enter.

"Your secret's safe with me," he says.

After they leave I walk into the kitchen to get a banana. I love my kitchen. It's spotless. Just the way I like it. I can't stand for things to be out of place or in disarray. It drives me crazy. Every open shelf in here is filled with black knickknacks I've collected over the years: Daddy Long Legs, All God's Children, Aunt Sarah's Attic—and any other kind I could find.

My house is pretty. Soft. Clean. All lace and pastels. Parquet floors, except the foyer is a creamy marble. It's imitation, but it looks real. I guess my taste is modern with a traditional twist. I bought the entire living-room set from Scandinavian Designs and my dining-room table from Ikea. They've got nice things at reasonable prices. I live for one-stop shopping. One day I hope to be able to afford some real artwork instead of the prints they sell at the mall.

Once in the study, I sit in my beige leather reading chair. It reclines, and has a matching ottoman. To tell the truth, I don't feel like going to the library today, but I'm going. I don't feel like studying either, but I will. I'm trying to teach myself to finish what I start. To follow through. The book on contracts is in my briefcase, but so is my romance novel. Oh, why not? I'm addicted to love stories. They relax me. Help me escape the ho-humdrummedness of my own uneventful, inconsequential world. Everything that's missing in my life I find in these books. Some nights I thank God for Danielle Steel, Nora Roberts, and Janet Dailey alone.

The only reason I'm taking this real-estate course is because a psychic once told me I was a "people person," and, plus, I'm trying to find something I like to do. Something I enjoy. No doubt, it's been hard. But I give myself credit for trying. Nobody else seems to. Yes, I've been going to college off and on for what seems like forever, but I've gained more knowledge and insight than I ever would working at the DMV or the post office, or, say, Nordstrom's. I'm no prodigy, and I'm not all that creative either—this much I do know about myself. But I like people. And I like houses. And I'm sure I can sell them. Especially out here in Palmdale and Lancaster, where they're building them faster than you can blink. If I do it right, I might even go for my broker's license later on. But these classes are harder than I thought they'd be—very technical—and you need to be good in math, which was always my worst subject, so, if I don't end up doing so hot, I'm seriously going to look into becoming a personal trainer or a nutritionist.

I'm also very much aware that my family makes fun of me behind my back. I know they refer to me as the slow one in the family. I've been called "Loose Brains," "Dinghy," "Miss Space Cadet," and a host of other endearing names. I'm also known as the Professional Student in search of a major. Lewis told me all of them one morning when he was drunk and I'd taken him to IHOP for French toast and coffee, trying to sober him up. I know they don't mean any harm by these little innuendos and they don't say this stuff with any malice—at least I don't think they do. They're just my family.

I make myself get out of this chair. I even go to the library with twenty minutes to spare. I'm proud of myself, since I'm notorious for being late. But guess what? The computers are down. Some kind of power outage caused them to go off-line or something, and it'll take at least an hour or two before they come back up. It could be as late as tomorrow. At first I don't know what to do, but then I realize there's a six o'clock low-impact class that I'm sure won't hurt the baby. I'll shower and shampoo at the gym, then study at home.

When I pull into the driveway, it's almost seven-thirty. I am just about to press the garage-door opener when I remember that all my Easter things are still on the floor. George would have a fit if I took his spot and he had to park his Jag outside in the elements all night. I guess it doesn't matter that it's ten years old. A Jag is still a Jag to him. I leave my car in the driveway and go through the front door, something I don't think I've ever done before. It feels strange, walking in your own house like you're a guest. I take my sneakers off, since I usually ask everybody else to remove their shoes. I look up at the stairwell; it could use another coat of white satin gloss. Oh, no! There's a humongous spiderweb hanging from the chandelier. I didn't see it there this morning. This thing has to go. I take my attaché case into the study and drop it on the floor. It is so quiet in here. George and Shanice should be home soon, within a half-hour or so. He usually takes her to get something to eat after practice.

I go upstairs to change into some clean sweats, and when I step outside my bedroom, I walk out to the landing with a towel to see if I can reach that spiderweb, but I can't. That's when I notice Shanice's backpack down on the hall table by the kitchen. I didn't hear them come in. I walk down the hall to her room, and as usual, her door is closed. Because she's not allowed to lock it, out of courtesy and respect for her privacy I always knock. For some reason, tonight I ease it open. I don't know why I'm not shocked when I see George sitting on the edge of Shanice's bed with his hand pressed on top of hers pushing up and down inside his black pants. His eyes are closed peacefully, but Shanice is scrunching hers so tight I can tell it hurts, because she's biting her bottom lip the same way I am. An inferno invades my whole body, and then, suddenly, feels like a block of ice. George's eyes open wide and he looks frightened. Shanice drops her head. In a split second, I look at these walls, which I can't even tell are yellow because they're plastered with magazine photos of probably every hip-hop singer and rapper on the planet. Four pair of sneakers are lined up under her bed. They should be in the closet. Why aren't they? I'm tempted to do it, but now I'm sinking in water so deep I can't move. I shake my head back and forth, trying to get to the surface, but it's sealed tight. I try to take a deep breath and leap, push, but I'm stuck. This fucking room is too small. Stuffy. And suffocating. Why'd we put her in here anyway?

And why's it so noisy? Why's that stupid music blasting so loud all of a sudden? Who turned it on? I wish those kids on the walls would stop singing and rapping. "Shut the hell up!"

George is trying to zip his pants and stand up at the same time, but it doesn't matter. He has to get past me. I have been spared. I have thawed out. I don't need air to stop him. Which is why I grab the halogen lamp from the desk near the doorway and walk toward him and stop. We are eye to eye. He opens his mouth to say something, and maybe he does, but I don't hear a word of it. I start pounding him over the head with this lamp until the sight of blood and Shanice's screaming stops me.

"I'm sorry," he screams, trying to flee from the room, holding his head.

"You get back here, you sick motherfucker!"

"Mama, stop it!" Shanice yells.

"I'm really sorry," George says again, and runs out the door. I hear him heading downstairs.

I follow him. He's putting a dish towel up to his head when I catch up to him. He's not hurt that bad. Not bad enough. He looks at me. Pitifullike.

"I've never done any more than this."

"Fuck you, George."

"I swear it."

"She's my *baby*."

"But I never hurt her."

"You should leave now."

"But this is *my* house."

"Fuck you and this house!"

"I want to explain."

"I said get out! Now!"

"Can I at least take something with me?"

"You've already taken more than enough. Now, get out of here before I call the police! Oh. I forgot. You *are* the fucking police!"

Now I'm shivering and can't stop. There's blood on my

hands and wrists, and I realize I'm still gripping the lamp as he heads toward the garage. I could kill him. I should kill him. But I don't move. I listen as he starts up the car and the Genie lifts and then the garage door closes shut. I stand in the kitchen for the longest time until, finally, I open the door to make sure he's gone. My Easter stuff looks stupid out there. I should stop doing this silly shit. I really should. Nobody cares anyway.

Shanice's cleats are on the top step. They look worn out. All she ever wanted to do was run track. Break records. Fly. Like they say on those Nike and Reebok ads. She pushes herself so hard. Harder than I've ever pushed myself to do anything. Maybe that's why he wanted her. Because she's young and beautiful and can still fly. But I used to be her. Stop lying, Janelle. You wish you were her. She *knows* what she likes. What she's good at. She's more focused at twelve than you are at thirty-five.

Why didn't I see the signs? When she stopped giving us both good-night kisses? That was over a year ago. Now I'm confused. I have to think back. I have to replay the last year or two in my mind. But now I'm wondering just how long he's been doing this shit to my baby. And what if he's lying? What if he's touched her the same way he's touched me? Why didn't I see it? Why wasn't I paying closer attention? And why in the hell did I believe him when he said he hadn't harmed her in any way? I blot my eyes. Because you wanted to believe him, that's why. Admit it, Janelle. Because harm equals abuse, and that meant I'd lose everything. We would be on our own. And I've never been on my own. I don't even know if I can make it without someone holding me up.

I close the door, walk over, and look up at the stairs. I will put a fresh coat of paint on that railing tomorrow. I will. I know I have to walk all the way over there and then up those steps, but I can't. Not yet. She lied because she was probably afraid. And I believed *him*. I set the lamp on the counter and force my feet to move. I don't know how I'm going to make it to that top step. But I have to. There's no one here to help me. But there's no one up there helping my daughter either. My legs weigh a ton. All I can do is pretend to be in step class and lift one foot after the other until I find myself standing here, outside her bedroom door, which is closed. I knock. Listening for her voice. It cracks when she tells me to come in. She's in there waiting for me. I touch the doorknob, but don't have the strength to turn it. I try again, but it won't turn. I'm afraid. Afraid I won't know what to say to her when this door finally opens, but even more afraid of what she's going to say to me.

Nothing
in Common
Except Blood

I'm trying to drum up the courage to call Mama, but I don't know what to say. She picks the worst times to get sick. When I got a million other things on my mind. We running to the mailbox every day hoping our income-tax checks gon' be in there. But we ain't getting back half as much as we did last year, which was close to eight thousand. Me and Al both put in too much overtime, but it ain't worth it. You kill yourself and still can't get ahead. This house look good on the outside, but on the inside, it's falling apart, little by little, and it need some work or we need to sell this sucker. We might have to take out a second mortgage just to make it sellable, but I really don't wanna go that route: double debt is what I call it.

And then there's the kids. Tiffany's having problems at school. Boys pestering her so much she can't keep her mind on nothing. That phone rings off the damn hook. She used to make a tent outta her covers and sit under there with a flashlight writing her little poetry, but lately I done caught her under there running her mouth on the portable with no pen and nothing but a blank piece of paper in her lap. I just finished picking Monique up from basketball practice three times a week and since she done got so good on that flute, her teacher is trying to get her to try out for band next year, so now I gotta take her to band practice four frigging days a week. It don't make no difference one way or the other, 'cause I still gotta clock in at the post office Monday through Friday, supervise twenty-six dim-witted mail carriers, listen to the rich folks in Hyde Park complain 'cause their mail was late or the carrier won't deliver to their house 'cause their dog tried to bite him, and then come home and try to scrape up something to eat, and the weekend is just as hectic 'cause this is when I try to iron and go to the grocery store and pay bills and plus every single Sunday since we been married I gotta bake Al something sweet and cook him a damn southern feast, and last but not least, there's still the upkeep of two losing-money-by-the-minute Laundromats over in Englewood, where half the time I'm scared to get out the car while Al is in his rig on the road sometimes two and three days at a time.

Where I live, dirty clothes come outta nowhere. I do at least one or two loads a day, 'cause people in my house think they rich and don't wear nothing twice. I been told I should get a housekeeper, but that's why I got kids. Even still, by the time I remind 'em, day in and day out, what they supposed to do, I could do the shit myself. But I can't do everything, which is why I'm probably always so stressed out. It's times like this when I wish I hadda went to college. Hell, if I could ever find the time, I'd like to go back to school: at least take a few classes. Not necessarily for no degree. Shit. Why shouldn't I try to get a degree? People on *Oprah* and *Sally* in their fifties and sixties is just learning how to read or getting their GED. They say it ain't never too late.

Speaking of late. This morning I get two messages from my lovely sisters, trying to lay a guilt trip on me for not rushing out to see Mama, knowing I don't get on nobody's airplanes. I mean, what am I supposed to do, just drop everything, jump in my Suburban, and drive to Vegas? This household would fall apart if I was gone for more than twenty-four hours. Besides, they can afford to go see her, 'cause they all live out there on the coast. I don't. And I can't. Money don't grow on trees in Chicago.

Plus, I'll be honest, when we all under one roof, they get on my nerves. Seem like everybody gotta compare notes: Who's doing better or worse than the last time we saw each other? Did you ever get new mattresses for the girls' rooms or are you still spending it on stuff you don't need? That's Mama. And who done gained too much weight and need to lose some? That's Janelle. Who's looking older than they should? Whose shit is raggedy? And so on and so forth. So I ain't exactly in no big hurry to see all of 'em at one time.

Deep down inside I know Mama probably don't mind my not coming. She ain't all that crazy about me no way. Everybody know it. She dropped me when I was a baby. Everybody know that, too. She was supposed to be giving me a bath, but the story goes that Paris had slammed her finger in the door and was screaming so loud that Mama forgot all about me, and when she went to check on her, I fell off the counter and hit the linoleum. Had to be rushed to the hospital. At first they thought I might have brain damage, but Aunt Suzie Mae told me that by some kind of miracle I broke my own fall and just ended up with a big knot on my head. If things hadda happened differently, I coulda died. But they said I was all right and sent me home a few hours later. To this day, Mama ain't never apologized to me for that.

She always have favored Paris, and I don't think it's 'cause Paris was the oldest either. Paris couldn't do no wrong. She was so perfect. So smart. So this. So that. And Janelle, being the baby, got her way all the time. Daddy spoiled her rotten, which is probably why she turned out to be such a leech. And my one-and-only brother. Lewis. What a poor excuse for a man he turned out to be. But that's Cecil's fault.

I love my family. I do. But I resent the hell out of 'em, too. Most of the time I feel like a outsider, 'cause I'm here in Chicago and they all out there. I didn't like California for two reasons: I thought it looked better on television, and my boyfriend, who ended up being my husband, wasn't there. I ain't been to Vegas yet. We might go this summer, if I can get

Al to switch our plans around. We been to see his people in Baton Rouge for the past six years, and I told him point-blank: this time we going to visit mine.

The only time I see all of 'em at one time is when somebody die, get married, or we have a so-called family reunion—which we ain't had since '91. I ain't been out to visit nobody going on seven years, but that's only 'cause my cash flow's been tied up in these Laundromats and I had to remodel the kitchen. It seem like it's always something going on around here that slurps up all my time, and we don't even wanna mention money.

Which is something we could use a lot more of. This is one reason why I'm investigating certain mail-order businesses. There's thousands of low-cost start-up opportunities out here, all you gotta do is take a little time, do your homework, and figure out how to get one going. It ain't no reason why we gotta settle for being middle-class when we can move into a whole 'nother income bracket if we just picked up the pace. But I got more energy in my big toe than Al got in his whole body, except of course when it come to sex. Most of the time he's downright sluggish when it come to getting off his ass and thinking fast on his feet. He don't miss work, I'll give him that much credit. But I done told him a million times: I'm not gon' be living in this imitation house when I retire. No sirree. We can do better than this. Much better than this.

The portable phone is just there, staring at me. On one hand, I feel bad for not calling Mama before now. Yeah, it was me who slammed the phone down in her face, but she was yelling at me like I was somebody in the street.

And so what if I didn't go to college. Janelle and Lewis never finished neither. I'm the only one who ain't been divorced. I ain't never slept with nobody's husband. I didn't marry no lowlife pretending to be no lawyer. I ain't never done no kinda drugs and don't have no bad habits worth mentioning. I ain't never had to call her collect or ask her for no money—

for nothing, really—except maybe to watch the kids when they was little, and even then, I paid her.

I've done everything in my power to prove to Mama that I'm just as smart and just as capable as Paris, but she just gotta put her on a pedestal, like her shit don't stink. Paris ain't no saint. And she ain't hardly perfect. Yeah, she can cook. But so what? I can burn, too. She ain't the only one in this family who can read a damn recipe. The only reason she in the position she in is 'cause she know people who know people. These ones I heard buy her fancy food. But, hell, anybody can start a catering business. If I just wanted to, I could, too. But food don't mean all that much to me.

Now, Janelle is the one Mama *should* be handing out advice to by the plateful, 'cause she's the one with no damn sense, no scruples, and no major ambitions whatsoever. They got books out about women like her, being codependent and shit. She screwed her way to middle-class. She sent me pictures of where she live. Didn't look like nobody even lived in the damn house. It looked like one of those model homes, only Janelle got weird taste. No class. No taste. No pizzazz.

But let's face it, Lewis is the real victim in this family. He got some emotional problems. It would help if he stopped drinking so much of that crack-in-a-bottle otherwise known as Schlitz Malt Liquor or Old English. Lewis is a alcoholic, but he seem to be the only one who don't know it. If he could get some help, maybe he'd be able to help Donnetta pay for his damn son.

And speaking of kids. Mama ain't never got nothing nice to say about mine, except maybe Trevor, but then she went and accused him of being gay. Janelle told me she said it. Well, my son ain't nobody's faggot. I know this for a fact. He's girl-shy, and he'll grow out of it. Every time I look around I gotta hear about Dingus did this or Shanice did that in the two-hundred meter and how many books she read a month and even Lewis's son, Jamil, who's around Tiffany's age, and who don't nobody even hardly see no more, made that all-star soccer team that travel all over (she done sent me the newspaper clippings three years in a row) and broke her neck telling me all the details of how he got accepted to the junior ROTC program and that he been skipped a grade. Shit, Monique can play the flute like ain't no tomorrow and she the leading rebounder on her basketball team, but all Mama seem to remember is that she got ADD—like they don't have it out there in Vegas. And so what if Tiffany can't grasp math or science? She write poetry as good as Maya Angelou, but have Mama ever bragged about her? It's common knowledge that both my daughters got good sense, they just going through growing pains—waiting for their periods to get here—and things should turn around and quiet down in this house once they do. Trevor's *my* bright star. He gets damn near straight A's, but do I ever hear about Mama bragging on him?

Shit. Here I go again. I need to stop this before the kids see me getting all worked up. I take a sip of my Asti Spumanti and push the lever on the recliner so it go back as far as it'll go. I'm sick of this blue shag. It shows when you spill anything. And I'm getting rid of this plaid couch and get one of those leather sectionals, since leather's supposed to be so "in." I wipe my eyes on my sleeve. Why do I always have to cry when I think about Mama? Probably 'cause I know that, no matter what I do, it ain't never good enough. Sometimes, when I really think about my family, it feel like we ain't got nothing in common except blood.

The girls is out there in the backyard playing in the last of the snow. The wall clock says it's 5:46. That means it's almost four o'clock in Vegas. She probably taking a nap. Mama always nod off after her stories go off. I hear Al coming from the garage. I ain't speaking to him either.

He got a lotta nerve. Last night, right after we did it, he says, "Oh, baby, I forgot to tell you. Me and Smitty going ice fishing for three days. I took a vacation day. We leave Friday." And that was it. I pushed him all the way over to the edge of the bed and put a pillow in between us in case he didn't get the point. He told me I was being childish. "You can go to hell," was all I said, and this morning, when he did not get his grits and eggs and bacon and wasn't no coffee waiting for him, he knew what the deal was. And now he's home, and, like always, he probably in there making hisself a gin and tonic, then he'll take it upstairs and sip on it while he take his shower. I sit here and pat my feet till I hear the water come on, and then, before I know it, I'm standing up in that bathroom, watching him undress.

"If I came home from work one day and just told you I was taking a few days off to go gallivanting with one of my girlfriends, can you stand there and tell me you wouldn't be mad?"

"First of all, Charlotte, you don't have no girlfriends," he says, getting out of his clothes. He don't know what he talking about.

"I do have some girlfriends. But that ain't the point. Why you gotta go ice fishing with Smitty all of a sudden? Why's it so important?"

"First of all, it ain't that it's important, Charlotte. I wanna go. It don't hurt to do something with your friends every now and then. Smitty's wife ain't mad. And I can't for the life of me see why you making such a big to-do about this."

At first, I don't say a word. I know he just trying to make me feel guilty. Well, just fuck you, Al, I'm thinking as I look at his long hard body through the shower door. His skin is the color of straw, his eyes a piercing gray-green, his lips thick, he's got good hair—thick and wavy—and a quarter-inch gap between his two front teeth. He's still pretty, a luscious Louisiana Bayou man, and sometimes I wish to hell I didn't love him as much as I do, which is exactly why I don't want nobody else to have no part of him. "How do I know you going with Smitty and not meeting some woman at a motel for three days?"

"You really ought to quit it. Right now. I'm going fishing. When I get back I should have some fish. If I really wanted to go off with some other woman I think I could come up with a much better lie. So stop it, would you? Could we just not have the melodrama for once?"

"Why didn't you ask me to go?"

"I just told you! It's a man thing. As a matter of fact, it's a whole group of us going. Union guys. And since you already mad, I might as well tell you, next month we going hunting, so get it all out your system now."

"You got a lot of nerve, Albert Toussaint. A whole lotta nerve."

"You the one being selfish and foolish. Now, if you don't mind, could I take my shower in peace?" He stands there wet and naked, all six feet of him, with his hands gripping both sides of his waist. I wish I could drown him for a few minutes, but I just slam the bathroom door in his face. I don't really care about him going fishing. It's the way he did it. He just *told* me he was going. He didn't ask if I minded and didn't bother to ask if I wanted to go with him. We do everything together. I can't remember us ever going somewhere without the other. And, plus, deep down inside, I don't trust Al. No man can be trusted. Period. Given a opportunity to get some free coochie, they'll take it every single time.

I got my reasons for feeling this way, and he know it. A few years ago—but I guess it was more like ten—I was cleaning out the garage and, like a fool, tried to lift his toolbox to put it back on the workbench, but I dropped it. Screwdrivers, pliers, hammers, nails, and nuts—everything—fell out and clanged against the cement floor. I started putting the stuff back in and came across a dirty piece of crumpled-up notebook paper. I flattened it out and noticed it had writing on it, and then, as soon as I started reading, realized it was a love letter to Al from some woman who didn't sign it. She was telling him how tired she was of doing this. That it's been going on too long and it's clear he ain't getting no divorce. And then, "I love you too much but I love myself more. Call me when you've made your move."

Call me when you've made your move? I threw every single tool, including that toolbox, at his Thunderbird, 'cause I couldn't believe this shit. I wasn't hurt. I felt betrayed. Double-crossed. Deceived. And as much as I loved Al, and as good as he was in bed and all the freaky shit we did together, and he's fucking somebody else? He always swore I was the best piece he ever had. He lied. And what else did he lie about? That can't nobody outcook me. Can't nobody starch and iron his shirts the way I do. Can't nobody cut his corns without making him bleed the way I do. Hell, I should have at least a hundred gold medals for all the things I'm so damn good at. And what else did I do to please Mr. Man? Made sure I looked good all the time. One thing he claimed he loved about me most was looking at me: how black and smooth and tender my skin was, and how he loved it that men was always trying to hit on me and everybody thought my hair was a weave or a wig and nobody ever thought I was thirty-four-five-six-or-seven years old and had had three kids. Shit, back then I still wore a ten, and Al always told me how proud he was to have me for his wife. How proud. And here he was fucking somebody else? He was obviously confused, so I packed a bag and took the kids over to Aunt Suzie Mae's house for three days. Al was frantic when he came home and we was gone. And as soon as he found out that I found out, he was worried sick I would leave him. But I *had* left him. That's why I was over to Aunt Suzie's. I was trying to figure out my next move. But he just had to come over there. Wanted to talk.

"It's not what you think it is, Charlotte."

"Oh, so I must just be crazy. I didn't really read no letter from no woman talking about how much she love you, and by the way, did you want a divorce, Al? 'Cause, according to her letter, you been promising to get one. Where's the papers?

Bring 'em over here and I'll sign the goddamn things right now! Or, better yet, I'll get my own!"

"I don't want no divorce. This was a mistake I made, and it was so long ago I had forgot all about it."

"A mistake? And you forgot about it?"

"It was more than five years ago, Charlotte. When you was pregnant with Monique. You was having a rough time those last four months, remember?"

"So. If every husband went off and had a affair 'cause his wife is having a hard pregnancy, where would that leave us? This is so tacky, Al, I swear it is."

"I'm sorry, Charlotte. I'm very, very sorry. It wasn't about nothing. I was just feeling lonely, and I broke it off right after Monique was born, 'cause I got the woman I married back. I don't even know what happened to her. I'm sorry."

"Why should I believe you?"

"Because I'm telling you the truth. I love you, Charlotte, and if I wasn't happy, I wouldn't be here. I'da been gone."

"Oh, really. How decent of you. I need to stop by the house and get the kids some clothes. Please don't be there when I get there. They wanna come home, and I'd appreciate it if you would make arrangements to find yourself someplace to live."

"Don't do this, Charlotte," he pleaded, but I slammed the door in his face. Right afterwards, I couldn't believe that my marriage was over. Just like that. That it could end with a few words in a few seconds. I was messed up. I told Aunt Suzie Mae everything. "Sit down, baby," she said to me, tapping the top of the kitchen counter with her fingers. Thank goodness, this was before she lost her scruples. "And let me tell you something."

"I don't wanna hear it, Aunt Suzie."

"You gon' hear it," she said, and adjusted her wig. She looked just like a older black version of Roseanne Barr. She was standing in front of the stove, adding tomato paste to a giant pot of chili. "You acting foolish. Now, I know you hurt and everythang, and this ain't something a wife likes to go through, but at some point all men cheat. Most of the time, if they good, they don't get caught, which makes it easier on everybody. But when they do, and they act truly pitiful and say they sorry, sometimes they mean it. If you still love that man, drop your pride and give him another chance. God asks us to learn to forgive."

"But how can I ever trust him again, knowing he did something like this to me?"

"He didn't do it to *you,* baby. He did it for hisself. It wasn't meant to hurt you. That's why he snuck and did it. But you can't pretend it don't hurt. You won't forget this business either. But what you can do is put it in a corner of your mind you can do without and get on with your lives. Women do it every day."

"But what if he do it again, Aunt Suzie?"

"Then that would leave you with one of three choices: divorce his ass; get *you* somebody; or blow his brains out." Then she started laughing so hard I could see her gray edges.

Two days later, I went home. But only after hours of crying and negotiations and threats and promises of never-will-I-cheat-agains. Al went out of his way to show me how happy he was to have us back. He took me shopping, took me to the movies, let me get on top, and swore that this was the only time during all our years of marriage that he'd ever messed around. I decided it was easier to take him back than it was to leave.

So here we are. A little more than ten years later. I guess we still in love, but we got more problems than fish. That much I do know.

"Ma, what's for dinner?" Trevor is asking me.

I look over at him, looking just like his daddy—except Trevor got my Maxwell House color, but those green eyes from them Toussaints. He's much taller than Al—almost six four—and the doctor say he still growing. How I don't know. I get on up out this chair. "Order a pizza," I say. "I don't feel like cooking. Go tell the girls to come on in and get started on their homework. And I don't wanna hear no whining today."

"Can I go get the pizza?" This means he wants to drive. He just got his license a few months ago. How, I'll never know. As Mama would say: His mind ain't long as a toothpick. He so busy watching what everybody else is doing that he don't pay enough attention to what he doing. He can't parallel park to save his life, and the way he change lanes scares me, but what the hell. It's only down the street.

"Go," I hear myself say. "And pick up my lottery ticket, would you? I forgot."

"What about some money? Who should I get it from, you or Daddy?" He standing right next to me and I gotta look up to him. He's not only taller than Al, but better-looking. Even though I didn't think that was possible.

"Ask me what?" Al says, standing in the doorway.

"For pizza money," Trevor says, as he heads toward the sliding glass door to go yell to the girls.

"Did you hear the messages on the machine from Paris and Janelle about your mama?"

"Yes."

"So—she's all right, then, ain't she?"

"I haven't talked to her yet."

"Why not?"

"I was gon' call her later."

Al just look down toward the floor, then back at me. "Later? One day it might just *be* too late, Charlotte. You oughtta stop acting so childish."

Next thing I know, Al is reaching for the phone, but I go over and snatch it from him. "She's my mama, not yours!" I yell, and start crying again.

"What's wrong with Ma, Daddy?" Tiffany's asking. Her and Monique are standing in the foyer, unzipping their ski jackets. Looking at them, you'd swear Monique was older, since she's taller. Both of 'em are prettier than any of those girls that be in them music videos on BET. Run circles around a whole lot of Miss Americas, too. People forever telling me that Tiffany is Vanessa Williams's double.

"Your Granny Vy is in the hospital, but she's gon' be all right," Al says.

Tiffany walks around to see if she can get a better look at me. My eyes must be red and shiny, 'cause she looks at me like she can't believe I been crying. The kids ain't used to seeing me act weak and stuff. I usually cry when I'm mad, not hurt. I straighten up. Crack a smile. Tiffany cracks one, too.

"You guys go do your homework. Trevor's going to get a pizza."

"Yeah!" Monique yells.

"Anybody wanna come with me?" he asks.

"Nope," Monique says.

"Not me," Tiffany says. They don't like his driving either.

"Just order the thing, go, and come right back," I say. Al reaches in his pocket and gives him a twenty. After the girls go upstairs and Trevor heads toward the garage, Al stands there and looks at me with the phone in my hand.

I'm thinking: I wanna call, but what am I gon' say? Sorry for hanging up on you and not calling for four months? Why you have to be so stubborn, Mama? You coulda called me, too, after all, you the one who was yelling at me.

"Well?" he says, shaking his head, then goes on back upstairs and turns on the TV. I look down at the *Essence* magazine I wrote the number to the hospital on, but for some reason I find myself dialing Smitty's number instead. When his wife answers, I'm tempted to hang up, since we ain't never been close except sitting next to each other at company dinners or in the same row at church and what have you, but I figure she might get suspicious and accuse Smitty of something stupid if I do, so I say, "Hi, Lela, how you doing?"

"Charlotte?"

"Yep. It's me."

"What a surprise. How's everything?"

"Fine, Lela. Look. Can I ask you something, woman to woman?"

"I guess so. Like what?"

"You ain't mad about Smitty going fishing?"

"Going where?"

"Fishing."

"When?"

"This weekend. With Al."

"Smitty ain't going nowhere this weekend except in the backyard. He's been promising to build us a shed, and unless we have another snowstorm, that's exactly what he's gon' be doing. Plus, his uncle died and the funeral's on Saturday. You sure he said this weekend?"

"I thought he did, but maybe I got the dates mixed up."

"It don't make no sense to me. Smitty's scared of water unless it's in a bathtub," she says, and chuckles a little. "So—how's everything else, Charlotte?"

"Well, my mama's in the hospital."

"Is she gon' be all right?"

"I think so. I'm about to call her now."

"I'll pray for her," Lela says.

"Thank you, Lela. Take care. And do me a favor?"

"What's that?"

"Don't even bother mentioning this to Al. It ain't important."

"Okay. Hope to see you in church real soon."

"You will. You definitely will." I'm trying hard not to bite my tongue, I'm gritting my teeth so hard. Fishing, huh? Now I know exactly what kind of pole he plan on using. Well, good luck, Al. I hope you catch more than you bargained for. I do. I really, really do.

I dial the hospital numbers so fast they blur. Everything in here is a blue blur. Wrong number. Try again. I wish I had a good girlfriend I could call. But I don't. Al was right. Wish I could talk to my sisters. But I can't. They worse than two-faced friends. Tell 'em your business and they talk about you like a dog behind your back. To each other. To *their* friends. Which is one reason why I keep my business to myself. I only tell people what I want them to know. You can't hardly trust nobody. Can't give out personal information. They just like a employer. Put everything in your file, then use it against you later.

That's why I need to talk to my mama. I shoulda called her before now. Before she got sick. Long before she got sick. I shoulda called months ago. Never shoulda hung up in her face. Fishing. And my mama's in the hospital 'cause she can't breathe. Well, I can't hardly breathe either. Call her, Charlotte. Right now. She'll tell you what to do. She been in this situation before herself. First, I need a glass of Asti Spumanti. No you don't. Dial the number. And this time be honest. Tell her about the first time. And now this. Tell her you was wrong. For hanging up. Can you do that? Admit you was wrong? No I can't. Because I wasn't wrong, was I? Yes you was, Charlotte. But what difference do it make? By calling, she'll know I'm sorry. By dialing this number, she'll know. She'll hear it in my voice. I ain't gotta say the words. Plus, they words she ain't never said to me. Regardless: call. Listen to the sound of her voice. Pray she ain't wheezing. You know she gon' try to act like ain't nothing wrong with her. Like she ain't in no hospital. Like she can breathe. So you pretend, too. Pretend you don't hear that rattle in her chest, and when she ask if you been doing all right, try to tell the truth. And this time listen to her. Listen to every word that comes out of her mouth, whether you agree with what she says or not. Keep your mouth shut. And just listen. And whatever she tell you to do, Charlotte, just do it. Even if you have to pretend.

Behind My Back

I heard I might be a lesbian. If I was I certainly wouldn't try to hide it. But, then again, I also heard I have terrible taste in men. I'm confused. Which is it? Or could I possibly be both? I understand the source of the first lie stems all the way from Chicago. This is where my used-to-be-favorite sister, Charlotte, hails from. The second untruth comes directly from none other than my mama, who thinks she's a good judge of character, but if that was the case, why has she stuck with Daddy all these years?

I also heard I'm a perfectionist. Which I will admit to: and proud of it. They make it sound like a dirty word. All I have to say is: don't hate me because I'm organized. Which is exactly why I'm sitting in front of my computer at five-thirty in the morning, lamenting over another episode of the Price Family's Continuing Saga, when in fact I should be finishing up the final details for a Moroccan birthday party a client is throwing in three weeks for her future husband. I just had to open my big mouth and suggest that she make it exotic, and of course she got so excited picturing her forty guests sitting on the floor, eating with their fingers, then washing them with warm rose-scented towels while two belly dancers swish and swirl their way around them, that now I have exactly four hours to fax the proposed menu and budget.

I'll make my deadline, because I believe when you make someone a promise you should keep it. Even if you have to break your neck to do it. When people depend on you, you should be reliable. That's how I run my business. It's how I try to run my life. Business is often much easier, but, then, who's complaining?

Right now, I suppose I am. Mama's in the hospital. In Las Vegas. And my so-called siblings have taken their sweet time calling to let me know what their plans are. She's just getting out of ICU, which is reason enough for me to hop on a plane to go see her. I'll bet that Hello Sweet Charlotte won't be coming—she'll use that lame-ass excuse about being afraid to fly. But Charlotte's just cheap. You'd think your mama would be worth more than some new wallpaper.

Lewis, on the other hand, probably doesn't even know Mama's in the hospital. He has trouble keeping a phone. He has trouble keeping apartments. He has trouble keeping cars, at least the kind that run. He went out and bought a bike. But then he claimed his so-called arthritis was bothering him so much that he couldn't ride it, and then somebody stole it, and what was he supposed to do then? Somebody's always stealing something from Lewis. Last time it was a mattress. How in the world do you steal a damn mattress?

And how about that daddy of ours? He's the one who *should've* called all four of us in the first damn place. I left three messages and he never bothered to return my calls, which is when my instincts told me to try the hospital. Daddy is not my most favorite person. In fact, I might as well admit it: I don't like him, mostly because of the high heartbreak rate he has going against Mama. I've known about his girlfriends probably longer than she has, but for some reason she's either blocked it out or—as they say here in California—she's in denial.

The baby in our family certainly behaves like one, but who can blame her? Daddy did everything for her, gave her every-thing she wanted. Now she's into her drama with what's-his-name. But I do not trust short men who dye their hair, wear pin-striped socks, smoke cheap cigars, and drive big cars. I don't care if he is a cop.

For starters: How about an Exotic Fruit & Mediterranean Vegetable Platter; Madagascar Coconut Prawns seasoned with a hint of curry and browned to perfection; Cape Verde Island Crab Cakes served alongside cilantro-lime rémoulade; Salat Cashmere, a lavish platter of tabouli and hummus with steamed prawns and served with an olive-oil-and-fresh-lemon dressing, garnished with Roma tomatoes, feta cheese, and fresh mint, accompanied by fresh-baked garlic-butter pita bread; and Bastia, a classic North African pastry course of delicate, flaky filo pastry filled with layers of shredded chicken, cottage cheese, ricotta, and black walnuts with a touch of cinnamon and a host of aromatic spices.

What else have they been saying about me? That I think I know everything; that I feel like I'm always right. Well, I can't help it if I'm resourceful, know more than some folks about some things, but never have I acted like I know everything about everything, and I don't make assertions unless I can back them up. I do not consider this a form of arrogance, and if certain people in my family would allow themselves to be enlightened by something other than *Melrose Place*, *The Young and the Restless*, or *Rikki*, *Jerry*, *Jenny*, and *Oprah* (even though I love Oprah), maybe they'd be better informed, too. I *can* say this for Lewis: he reads books that make a point, but I think he's read too many, because he's bursting at the seams with information that he hasn't found an outlet for, but, then, that's where family comes in handy.

I've gotten used to dealing with all of their criticism and accusations. Wait. That's a lie. I haven't. Well, maybe from Mama, but I expect it from her, because, number one, she's my mama and, two, she hardly ever has anything nice to say about any of us, which just means she loves us. If I didn't know better, I'd swear that Charlotte either doesn't like me anymore, or is holding some kind of grudge against me for something I don't have a clue about. Deep down, I know she has a good heart, but I think being soft scares her. She sees it as a weakness. Janelle is just sweet and simple. I wish there was a way I could intravenously dispense some confidence into her while she sleeps, because she doesn't know that self-doubt can ruin a genius; and, plus, Janelle's a whole lot smarter than she gives herself credit for.

The long-held consensus among the Grown Price Children is that, because I was the oldest, I always got my way. Maybe they're confusing me with somebody else. If I remember correctly, we all got our behinds beat when we did something wrong; but because I was the oldest, I was the one who usually got punished when they screwed up. Mama and Daddy held me accountable, which I never did think was fair. Like that time Lewis lit a fire in the dryer. I couldn't leave the house for two weekends in a row. "You shoulda kept a closer eye on him. I left you in charge." And then that time he put the car in neutral and it rolled out into the street and blocked traffic and we couldn't find the key or push it back uphill and Mama and Daddy got on my case even though I was in the bathroom washing my hair when it happened. "Lewis don't know how to drive. He ain't but eight years old. So what was he doing in the damn car anyway?" I wanted to scream back: "Am I supposed to have eyes out the back of my goddamn head?" But I wish I *would've* acted like I wanted to raise my voice and talk back. I wouldn't be here now. And how about that time Charlotte fed Lewis and Janelle dog food and put them in the doghouse? Who had to swallow a teaspoon of Alpo and then get on my knees and mop and wax every inch of hardwood flooring in the whole house? Charlotte told Mama I made her do it.

For entrées, please consider starting with: Grilled Curry Chicken Brochettes lightly marinated in exotic spices and cooked on the grill; your guests have a choice of: Filet Mignon Brochettes seasoned with sea salt, garlic, and fresh herbs and grilled on an open fire, or Fire Roasted Lamb Alibaba, bro-

*chettes of tender marinated lamb. To accompany these entrées,
my chefs will prepare: Butter and Herb Seasoned Couscous,
garnished with French petits pois and chickpeas; and, for
dessert: West African Bread Pudding, flavored with cinnamon,
cardamom, and saffron, complemented by brandy crème
anglaise. And if you'd like, I can make a luscious Pistachio
Birthday Cake that might make him marry you in the morning.*

Anyway, I'm flying to Vegas tomorrow, I don't care what
Mama says. Asthma *is* serious. People die from it. I don't even
want to think about what I'd do—what we'd all do—if one of
these times Mama didn't make it to ICU. Thank God, Lewis
won't be there. It means there'll be less drama. Unless somehow by Morse code he found out. Then again, maybe he got his
disability check, or got one of his dumb women to lend him
some money, and he's on a Greyhound right now. Lewis loves
buses. As for Charlotte, although I'm not convinced that her
lesbian comments weren't said out of malice, I can forgive her.
Mama tried to clean it up by saying that Charlotte said it like
she was joking. But Charlotte doesn't joke about anything.
Everybody knows that. I still hope she comes.

I also heard that Lewis told Janelle that I think I'm hot shit
because I bought a house without a husband. Mama made a big
mistake of telling Charlotte it was a mansion—which it is not.
It's a five-hundred-thousand-dollar, four-thousand-square-foot
semicustom home in a typical northern-California middle-class
subdivision. We don't even have a pool. Every sixth house
looks pretty much like mine. Apparently, I'm one of the last
ones to landscape my backyard. I'll get to it when I can.

When I get to Mama and Daddy's, I'm telling them, once
and for all, to cut me some slack; to give me a break. I'm tired
of apologizing for who I am. I *like* who I am. I like what I'm
doing with my life. I love to cook, which is why I cater for a
living. And have a lot of fun doing it. I love the power of food:
The beauty of it. I want people to enjoy the entire experience—
using all five of their senses—I try to create an environment

that is visually intoxicating—full of color, scents, and aromas that seduce you until you leave. I see what I do as art, and I offer it like a gift. I also meet tons of interesting people and get to travel all over the world. Folks seem to appreciate my culinary talents, and it makes me feel good when they do. That's all I want: is to be appreciated for what I do. Doesn't everybody?

The budget. Oh, forget the budget for now. The schedule is easier: 3:00: I arrive to start preparing the food; 5:00: service staff arrives to set up bar and service area and assist; 6:45: all hors d'oeuvres service begins; 7:00: guests begin arriving; 8:00: guests seated on floor at round tables (guests should bring their own cushions); 8:15: belly dancers perform at beginning, during salad course; 8:30: second course, belly dancers finish; 8:45: main course served; 9:15: champagne service; 9:30: men and women separate for strippers, and show begins; 10:00: dessert; 10:30: music and more partying. Staff (not me!) stays until last guests leave, for cleanup.

On second thought, maybe I *should* just go there and apologize, because I grew up and did what Mama and Daddy encouraged all of us to do: went to college, graduated, and found my place in the world. I can't help it if Charlotte opted to make her mark at the post office. Or that Lewis got his bachelor's in Jail 101 and is now working on his master's in progressive alcohol. Janelle is apparently still on the lookout, but how many Tarot cards does it take?

My sisters and brother think that I think my life is perfect because it looks good on paper. They're the ones who don't want to accept the fact that I have problems just like they do. But since I have a little extra cash in the bank, they assume I can buy my way. If they didn't watch so much TV, they'd know the cliché that most intelligent people understand: that *money* does not guarantee happiness or peace of mind. It can take your mind off of things, distract you, but it can't replace the generic stuff a person needs. If I could go to Neiman Marcus and put some love on my charge card, I would. If I could get a prescription for good health from my local drugstore, I would. If I could walk down the Feminine Needs aisle at the grocery store and pick a husband from the shelf that would complement me, my lifestyle, and my son, I'd have done it by now.

Mama, on the other hand, has a tendency to confuse stress with misery. I'm also not *I Dream of Jeannie*, so I can't exactly twitch my nose and drum up husband number two the way she keeps hoping I will. Yes, it *would* be nice to have a man that could fulfill all my fantasies, but in all honesty, I don't even know what they are anymore. Three years after my divorce, I was in an emotional funk. It felt like the person I'd loved the hardest had died and I was mourning his loss. His name was Nathan. He is my son's father. I can't stand his ass now. For eight long years I gave him the benefit of the doubt. He said one thing, but did another. He could've passed the bar the first time, but deep down inside I don't think he felt worthy. He sabotaged his own greatness by succumbing to failure, because failure was easier. But it wasn't attractive. I got tired of pumping up his ego when he never reciprocated. My business was flourishing and he couldn't even pretend to be happy for me. In fact, he resented it. But somebody had to wear some kind of pants in the family, or we would've been up shit's creek. It got harder and harder to love Nathan. He was no longer the politically charged idealist, that spontaneous male engine that kept me up nights describing outrageous court cases in one breath and making love to me the next. He lost interest in the law, and I guess I was next in line. I didn't really think he'd leave, or run back home to his family in Atlanta. But that's exactly what he did. I doubt if I'll ever love another man with the same intensity and conviction, but I also hate Nathan for disappointing me and our son. I hate him for not fighting harder for what he wanted—for not living up to his own expectations. I hate him for not being happy for me because I was living up to mine. I wanted him to feel good about my accomplishments. Wanted him to be proud of me. Is that so hard for a husband to do? In

Nathan's case, I suppose it was, because he bailed out of the airplane before he even knew if it was going to crash.

But Nathan did give me one gift he couldn't take back: Dingus. My son gives my life a sense of purpose. He's almost seventeen, and I still like him. He shows me respect. Doesn't have a smart mouth. I'm grateful I didn't have a daughter. If I had've, I'd probably be going crazy about now, just like Charlotte and Janelle.

Budget breakdown. Just look at an old invoice and prorate it based on the number of guests. If I remember correctly, for 40 people it should be in the neighborhood of about $4,000. Who had the last Moroccan party? Check the files. And don't forget to give Mariah a break on the price for being such a loyal client.

Is that the phone already? I'm afraid to answer it. Other than Mama, nobody calls me this early, because I sent out a directive years ago that this is the only quiet time I have to myself to get organized and jump-start all the things I have to do in a day. It could be Miss Ordelle, the lady who irons for me once a week. If it's her, then it means she's got another toothache, a cold, or pains in her chest. She never calls this early. Somebody's been calling here all week and hanging up. I assume it's one of those ditzy girls trying to catch Dingus before he leaves for school, hoping she'll get a chance to make some kind of pathetic offering to get her name on his list, but that won't be happening anytime soon, because he is totally enthralled with Jade: smart, tall, as black as she is pretty, goes to Sunday school and church every Sunday because her daddy's a preacher and sings in the junior choir, power forward for her high school's team, and is not giving it up to my son as far as I can tell. For a while there, I was worried because he was strung out on this trashy little white girl—Meagan Somebody—who was as dumb as they come. But I kept my mouth shut, hoping she would run her course and he'd get her out of his system, which he did, after finding out she was also sleeping with one of his homies. Then

I told myself to take a chill pill, let my son choose whomever he likes, to stop being such a racist and show the girl at least an ounce of respect. Which I did. By not saying more than a friendly hello and a relieved goodbye whenever he brought her over here. I offered her some chips and dip once, and that took all the strength I had. She flunked seventh grade, for God's sake. My son has always been on the honor roll. What Mama and Dingus fail to understand is that I don't have a problem with white people. I like a whole lot of white people. And I don't have a problem with my son liking a white girl. That's not it either. I don't care what color she is. But dumb is one color I don't like and have a hard time tolerating. It's a slow mind that tests my patience.

I pick up the phone, but apparently Dingus has already gotten it from the kitchen.

"Hello," he says. My Lord, the boy's voice seems to get deeper by the day.

"I didn't get my period," Meagan says.

Oh, no, she didn't just say that. I hold my breath back.

"You said you were taking the pill," Dingus says.

Yeah, you little bitch. I knew this was going to happen. I just knew it. Ever since Dingus got his letterman jacket and his picture in the local newspaper and the college scouts started watching him, not to mention older girls swarming around him after the games like flies, this heifer's been on a mission to put a stop to his extracurricular activities. But this is a very weak trick to pull. And so old: like 1950s old. But not to worry. There's no fucking way my son is going to forfeit his future. Didn't your mama teach you anything? I should cut a few inches off Dingus's little immature dick, since he has obviously not been using the condoms I put in his drawer and backpack.

"Remember when I told you I had to stop taking them for a few weeks because they were making me nauseous?"

"Look, Meagan. This is jacked. My moms would *kill* me if she found out about this. What are you thinking about doing?"

"Doing? I don't know. What do you want me to do, Dingus?"

What does he want you to do? Is the girl on drugs? He's not even seventeen fucking years old. She's eighteen. Ask your mama, girl—not my son—what the hell you should do.

"Look," he says, "can you meet me at the mall after school? In front of Mrs. Field's?"

"Yeah," she says, and hangs up.

I do, too. But first I reach inside my desk drawer and look for one of my prescription bottles. They're pain pills I got when I had my boobs done and dental surgery. I discovered that they also work well for tension headaches, which I'm definitely getting right now. I pop one, and gulp it down with a few sips of hot coffee. By the time Dingus knocks on my door, it's working.

"Good morning, Ma," he says, sluggishly, but walks over and gives me his regular kiss and taps me on the head.

"Good morning. Who was that on the phone?"

"Asokah. He forgot what the math assignment was, so I had to give it to him."

"Oh." He sure can lie fast.

"So, what's on your agenda today, Mother Dear?"

"The usual."

"Break it down to me, why don'tcha?"

"You better get out of my face."

"What's wrong with you this morning?"

"I had a nightmare last night."

"Tell your loving son what's bothering you." I look up at this boy. All six foot three inches of him. Wasn't he just in his bassinet last week? And didn't I just take him to peewee Little League practice the other day? And now he's shaving? Time is moving too fast. Mama was right. I should've had another one. But too late now.

"I dreamed that you had a blast from the past."

"And?" he asks, futzing with my phone-pad pages that hold

the twenty-three calls I have to make and return today in order
to make sure the Louisville Barbecue scheduled for this weekend will go smoothly in my absence.

"Some little girl claimed she was pregnant by you."

He looks down at me without the least bit of surprise in his
eyes and flashes his metal teeth. "You worry too much over
nothing, Ma. It was just a bad dream. Get over it."

"Dingus?"

"Yes, Ma." He's at the door now. Obviously feeling the pressure.

"I hope you're using a condom when you do your business."

"Of course I do," he says. "Is it okay if I stop by the mall for
about a half-hour after school?"

"For what?"

"They've got some new Jordans coming in today at Foot-
locker, and me and my homies wanna check 'em out."

"You don't have any Jordan money."

"We're just window-shopping."

"I don't care. Just be home by five-thirty."

"No problem," he says, turning away, then stops. "Oh. I
wanna call my granny later on to see if she wants me to bring
her anything."

"Okay," I say.

"I gotta cheer her up. You know I have that power."

"Yes, you do," I say. "Love you."

"I love you more," he says.

I watch him walk away. My baby. On his way to manhood.
I like the effect of this pill. Now I feel like I can say exactly
what I mean without biting my tongue. I wish I could feel like
this all the time, is what I'm thinking as I dial Meagan's phone
number, and she answers. "May I speak to your mother,
please?"

"She's not home, Paris."

"She doesn't work. Why isn't she at home?"

"Because she's at the grocery store."

"At seven o'clock in the morning?"

"It's a twenty-four-hour."

"Would you ask her to call me as soon as she gets in?"

"Would you mind if I ask why?"

"You figure it out," I say, and hang up.

Simple bitch. Be nice, Paris. But right now I don't feel like being nice. I'm nice all the time. To every-fucking-body. I need a break from niceness. So what do I do? Dial Nathan. He deserves a little blast from the past, too. Of course I get his machine, but that's quite all right. "Nathan, this is Paris. How've you been? Good, I hope. The reason I'm calling is just to give you your annual reminder that YOU STILL HAVE A GOD-DAMN SON, who'll be turning seventeen any minute, and if you are so moved, perhaps you might consider acknowledging his birthday by way of, say, a FUCKING BIRTHDAY CARD or a phone call. Something. That is, if it's not too much of an inconvenience, or is your shit still raggedy, Mr. Sports Agent? Do you represent any ATHLETES yet? And did you ever pass the Georgia bar, or did you forget to take it again?"

The machine cuts me off, even though I was just getting started, but it's okay. I've got another call coming in. I can't imagine who this could be. "Hello."

"Paris, are you there? Pick up. It's me," Mama says.

"It *is* me, Mama."

"Oh. You sound just like your machine."

"How're you feeling? You're not home yet, are you? Dingus and I are flying over tomorrow whether you like it or not."

"Slow down, girl, damn. I go home in the morning. Thank the Lord. I done lost seven pounds I did not intend to lose so fast, being in this place. But I'm feeling much better."

"Good. Where's Daddy?"

"Me and your daddy ain't been getting along."

"What else is new, Mama? You two never get along."

"He's gone."

"Gone where?"

"Living with some young girl with three kids on welfare in the projects."

I reach in the desk drawer looking for my pills, but then I realize I don't have a headache, so I push it shut. "What did you just say?"

"You heard me. Don't act so surprised. This ain't the first time, but it's damn sure the last. It's been a long time coming. I *been* sick of him."

"Daddy moved out?"

"That's what I just said, didn't I?"

"When?"

"Around New Year's."

"What?"

"Stop yelling in my damn ears, girl."

"Why didn't you tell any of us before now?"

" 'Cause it ain't no big deal."

"No big deal? The man you've been married to for almost a half-century is gone and it's not a big deal? Come on, Mama."

"I just had a damn asthma attack, what you want me to do, have a heart attack and drop dead over your stupid-ass daddy?"

"No, Mama."

"I do not miss him."

I don't believe her, not for one minute. "So, then, you're there all by yourself, Mama?"

"Not exactly. Lewis just got here."

"You're kidding."

"I wish I was."

"Did you ask him to come?"

"Do birds fly north for the winter?"

"How long is he staying?"

"Not long. Lord willing."

"Is he standing right there?"

"Yep."

"Has he been drinking?"

"Yep."

"Is he getting on your nerves yet?"

"Yep."

"Is he moaning and groaning about Donnetta?"

"Yep."

"Does he know she got married?"

"Yep."

"Did you tell him everything, Mama?"

"Yep."

"Did he get mad?"

"Yep."

"Why'd you tell him?"

"He made me mad."

"How? What did he do?"

"Guess."

"He came with no money and now can't get home."

"You guessed it. Plus, he was gon' find out sooner or later. Anyway, you all set for Easter?"

"Easter? I'm not thinking about anybody's Easter right now, Mama. You're getting me confused with your other daughter."

"You going to church or not?"

"Easter's a tough one for me, Mama. Too many hats and new clothes, like a Paris runway or something . . ."

"Okay! You made your damn point!"

"Anyway, would you like to come and spend it with me and Dingus?"

"It depends on how I'm feeling. That's too close to my birthday. Unless of course you planning something special."

Does she think she's slick or what?

"First of all, I put a three-hundred-dollar deposit down on this cruise that Loretta talked me into. It's in June, late June, but I just did it to be doing something."

"A cruise?"

"Yeah, they go to about five or six islands all over the Caribbean. Don't ask me where. And don't ask me how much. Not right now. Plus, me and your daddy gotta get our taxes in order before I do anything, or we gon' be in big trouble. Anyway, I'll let you know. Hold on a minute. Your brother wanna say hi."

"Hello there, sis."

I switch ears. "Hi, Lewis."

"I'm fine," he says, but did I ask him how he was doing? He always does this. "How's Dingus?"

"He's fine. How long're you staying in Las Vegas?"

"Just a few more days, even though I think I like it here. If I could find a decent job, I'd consider staying."

"Don't even think about it, Lewis."

"Well, most of my business ties are in L.A. anyway," he says, sighing.

I have to stop myself from saying: "What business ties?"

"So, I guess Mama told you about Daddy, then, huh?"

"Yep. But he'll be back."

"How can you say that when you don't even know what's going on here?"

"You know how long they've been doing this, Lewis? Please."

"But this is serious."

"I'm glad he's gone."

"How can you say that? You know, you women can be . . ."

"Don't start with me, Lewis."

"Start what? I was just saying . . ."

"Look, I'll say it again: I'm glad he's gone. It should've happened about twenty years ago. Just do me a favor, Lewis. Don't get on Mama's nerves, okay? She's not even home yet."

He lets out yet another exasperating sigh. "I came here to help. How could I possibly get on her nerves?"

"Never mind."

"So I guess you and everybody else but me knew about my ex, then, huh?"

"What's to know? So she's got married. She has a right."

"He must be a chump, that's all I have to say. Anybody who'd want her?"

"Yeah, well Todd's a chump with a job and . . ."

"How'd she find a black dude with a name like Todd?"

"He's white. I thought Mama told you."

"He's *what?*"

"Oh, get over it, Lewis. This is America. 1994."

"She went and married a fucking cracker?"

"Yep, by-golly she did, and she just had his baby, too. A little girl named Heather. Mama said she told you."

"She just said the bitch got married and the dude wanted to adopt Jamil. That's all."

"She's not a bitch and don't ever let me hear you use that word when referring to a woman, do you hear me, Lewis?"

"Yeah, sorry. But . . ."

"But anyway, as I was saying, that 'cracker's' been taking pretty damn good care of *your* black son."

"Donnetta done completely lost her fucking mind. What kinda church is it she go to?"

"You better watch your damn mouth, boy!" That's Mama in the background.

"How should I know? Besides, it's irrelevant."

"That cracker better not even think he's gon' be my son's father. And he better not ever lay a hand on him either or I'll kick his pale ass."

"Okay. Stop, Lewis. I'm not about to listen to you . . ."

"How do you think this makes me feel? First hearing from my very own mama that my ex-wife has married some stranger I don't even know, and then a few hours later I find out he's white and he wants to adopt my son?"

"Somebody needs to be a father to the boy. When was the last time you saw Jamil?"

"It ain't been that lo—"

"When was the last time you did anything for him, Lewis?

You need to get a fucking grip and join the real world. I'm so sick of men like you I don't know what to do."

"You know, all you women think alike. . . ."

"Put Mama back on the phone, would you?"

"I'm not finished."

"I'm hanging up this phone if you don't put her back on."

"Hold on a minute. A man can't even get his own sister to listen to him anymore. Hear what I feel. Anyway, I guess I'll see you tomorrow."

"Can't wait."

Mama gets back on the phone. "Yes indeedy," she says.

"He's pathetic, isn't he, Mama?"

"Worse."

"I thought you said you told him everything?"

"Everything I wanted to. But what's done is done."

"Have you talked to Janelle or Charlotte?"

"Janelle and Shanice are driving here tomorrow sometime. And, no, I have not heard from Charlotte, and don't even think about calling her to ask her to come. I don't want to see her ass."

"I won't."

"I mean it, Paris. For once in your life, don't try to play the referee. Just come and bring me some of that sour bread from Fisherman's Wharf and a box of those little oyster crackers to put in my soup—could you do that?"

"No problem, Mama. Love you."

"You ain't said nothing but a word," she says, and hangs up.

I look down at my phone list. Then over at the budget sheet. I don't feel like facing any of these folks. Do not feel like chitchatting, hearing their voices. I don't feel like thinking about fire-roasted anything or Moroccan-this or Moroccan-that. Don't care what kind of salad they eat, or where in the house a band will fit, or the difference in cost for the strippers who go all the way or those who show only breasts. My daddy's gone. I wonder if Mama really is glad. People say one thing but feel another. Oh shit! I forgot about that stupid interview with the producers who want me to host a cooking show preparing meals from start to finish! From start to fucking finish. Look at this desk! It's covered with every kind of paper you can think of: pictures of food, recipes I've been altering and saving for years which will one day go into my cookbook—if I ever find the time for *that*.

What I do know is, I've got a budget to write, a soon-to-be-seventeen-year-old son who may or may not be on his way to fatherhood, my mama's in the hospital, I do not feel like meeting with anybody today, and my head is getting tight again. I take a few deep breaths, but this doesn't quite cut it, so I reach inside the drawer and take out the prescription bottle. I dump one white pill into my palm, but then I think two should probably do the trick.

Every Shut Eye
Ain't Closed

Shanice jerks the door open.

Before I can decide whether to walk in or not, she appears from behind the doorway. It looks as if she's trying to block the entrance by her presence alone. I feel a sheath of heat jut out from her body that creates an invisible shield I know I can't penetrate right now. I look at my daughter. She does not look like my little girl. She's too tall for her age. Her shoulders are erect, her chest up too high, like some runway model. Her hands are pressed deeply into her hips, as if she's trying to stop herself from leaping on me. I could be wrong. I hope I'm wrong. She does not look scared or frightened, the way I imagined she would. She looks more annoyed than anything.

"Can I come in?"

She looks me dead in the eye. "For what?"

"I think we should talk, Shanice."

"What's to talk about?"

"I'm so sorry, baby," I say, reaching out to touch her, but she jumps back.

"I'm sure you are." She says this in a sarcastic manner, then flops down on the edge of her bed, the very same spot she was sitting in minutes ago. There are drops of blood on her pink comforter that look like burgundy stars coming out of her fingertips. She leans back even farther and looks at me. "So where is he?"

"Gone."

"Gone where?"

"I don't know."

"He'll be back," she says matter-of-factly.

"No, he won't."

"Yes, he will."

"He *can't* come back."

She looks at me again as if she doesn't believe me. "Who's going to stop him?"

"The police."

"Don't call them, Ma. Please. Don't."

"Why not?"

"Because then the whole world will know."

"The whole world won't have to know. Shanice, baby," I say slowly, "why didn't you tell me?"

"Because you wouldn't have believed me anyway."

I bite my lip and flip the light switch on and off, but luckily the bulb has been blown out for some time. George promised to fix it weeks ago. Now I know why he hasn't. "What would make you think that?"

"Because you believe everything he tells you."

"That's not true."

"It is true. Even Granny said you're a fool when it comes to men."

"Did she really?"

"I agree with her," she says, crossing her arms.

I feel like strangling her. Why on earth would Mama be discussing my relationships with my twelve-year-old daughter? "Your granny is not in a position to judge how I've handled myself."

"But I am. I know how many of your boyfriends were already married, even the pervert who finally married you."

"Let me tell you something to set the record straight, Shanice. After your father was killed, I was afraid to get too attached to any man, which is why I did things the way I did. I wasn't trying to hurt anybody."

"I don't really care. All I know is, if you'd done what you were supposed to do with your husband, I wouldn't have had to do it for you."

"What did you just say?"

"You heard me."

I want to slap her into next week. How *dare* she talk to me this way, in this tone of voice. Besides, she doesn't know what the hell she's talking about. She's probably in shock. Traumatized. Because this entire conversation isn't even close to what I imagined. I came in here to comfort her. To try to understand what has happened. Which is why I decide to overlook the nasty things she's saying. "Maybe you're right."

She looks genuinely surprised. As if she was ready and prepared for battle. "You're getting fat."

I want to tell her about the baby. The baby. What about the baby? What am I going to do with *his* baby? Don't want anything of his. Nothing. But too much to think about right now. Forget this baby. Help that one over there. "Has he hurt you?" I ask.

"What do you mean?"

"What all has he done to you?"

"I don't want to talk about this right now."

She reaches over and picks a book up from a pile—clearly one she's already read—and puts it in her lap, then opens to a page at random and starts twirling those braids around her fingers. "I need to know, Shanice."

"He did enough."

"How long has he been touching you?"

"Touching me?" She lets out a sarcastic chuckle.

"Yes."

"He's done more than touch me."

"How much more?"

"How about right after you married him? When I was seven. You were always asleep when he came in to say good night to me. He would flip that light switch off right over there, but then he didn't leave. He would walk over here and lay down next to me and give me a good-night kiss. But then he didn't get up."

I feel nauseous. I know he hasn't been doing this to my daughter for five fucking years. Where was I? How in the world could I not notice something like this? And how in God's name could she have gone all this time without telling me? "He's been doing this to you for five years?"

"Six is closer to it. I'll be thirteen soon, remember?"

"Shanice," I moan.

"It's cool, Ma. But I cleaned up."

"What are you talking about?"

"Look at all the shit in here. Why do you think he bought it?"

I don't want to look. I know what's in here. Too many stuffed animals. Too many dolls. Too many video games and gadgets. Hundreds of trinkets. I blink and blink and blink until all of it disappears. "But, Shanice, you never gave me any sign that anything was wrong."

"My granny noticed," she says tartly.

Is this the daughter I've got to live with from now on? Is her sweetness gone? Has that son-of-a-bitch destroyed it? I have never heard my daughter swear. Nor has she ever used this tone of voice when talking to me. Her head is down and I see her shoulders droop and she starts shaking her head back and forth and then she sits back up slowly.

"I'm standing here going over and over in my head why I didn't see any signs that something was wrong."

"Because, instead of being a cop, he should've been an actor, that's why. I mean, he was this whole different person in the morning. At night he came in here. He said things. Did things. At breakfast, he was my stepdad again. He was two people."

"This is a sickness."

"Yeah yeah yeah. He's sick all right. Why do you think I never wanted him to take me to track practice, Ma?"

"Because I knew you didn't care for George."

"Didn't you ever wonder why?"

"I thought it was because he wasn't your real dad."

"I don't even remember him, Ma! I was four years old when he died."

"Oh," is about all I can say. I want to go sit next to her. I want to put my hand on her head the way I used to when she was little and pull her face between my breasts until I feel her breathe. I want to slide her head down my belly until it rests in my lap and stroke her hair until she falls asleep. The way we used to.

"What do you do in there at night?"

"What?" I'm startled not only by the question but by the fact that she's still over on the bed and I'm still standing by the door. She is not in my lap. And she's not my baby anymore. But I'm still her mother. "That's none of your business."

"He *made* it my business."

"I read."

"I do, too. See, here's a book to prove it." She holds it up, then drops it back in her lap.

"And then I sleep."

"Well, I learned how to sleep with my eyes open and stay awake even when they were closed."

I cover my mouth and feel tears rolling down my cheeks. She knows I'm crying. But she doesn't care. She's not even looking at me. And why isn't she crying?

"What else did you do in there?" she asks.

"What normal grown-ups do."

"Normal?" Now she gives me a cutting look. You'd think she hated my guts. "He's not normal," she says.

"I know that now."

"Granny says you read too many romance novels."

"How does your granny know what I read?"

"Because I told her."

"I read what I like to read."

"She said you're living in a dream world. And you know what? She's right."

"Stop it!"

"You stop it."

"Okay," I say, and blow my nose on my sweatshirt. I look at her again, still sitting there. I'm going to get her a new bed. This one's out of here. Tomorrow, in the trash it goes, along with anything and everything else he's ever bought her. I cross my arms and watch her read. "Shanice?"

"What?" she asks, still not looking up.

"Why couldn't you just tell me this was going on?"

"I've already told you."

"No, you didn't. You said I wouldn't have believed you, but that's not good enough. There has to be another reason. Why?"

"Because he said that if I ever told he would do more than what he'd been doing, and it would hurt worse."

Something thick is moving up into my throat. I reach down and grab the white trash basket and let whatever needs to come up, out. Shanice doesn't budge. She just keeps right on reading. I set the basket outside the door. I'm hot. And I'm even more confused. Since she was seven years old? My baby. That sick son-of-a-bitch. When I met George he was in the process of divorcing his second wife, a woman I'd never met, but I knew she had two daughters about Shanice's age. Had he done the same thing to them? And what about his grown daughters by his first wife? I think I have the first one's number somewhere. I need to know. I have to know. But how could he have been so clever? I'm not that stupid. And for so long? And why on earth would a grown man want to mess with a little girl? *My* little girl? "I'm sorry," I hear myself say again.

"I heard you the first time. Can you go now? I just got the new Goosebumps and I really want to finish it tonight. It's called *Why I'm Afraid of Bees*. Hey, this should be cool, and I can relate, because I've already been stung at least a hundred times. Get it?"

"Shanice?"

"What?" she says in a clearly irritated tone now.

"This isn't the end of this."

"Probably isn't."

"No. I mean I should have you checked out."

"I've *been* checked out. Like they say in my dance class: I've already had my rite of passage."

I wish she would stop this. But I know why she's doing it. I don't blame her. But she's my daughter. I love her. And I need to take steps to let her know that I have her best interests at heart regardless of what she thinks or how it looks. "I should probably get some kind of counseling for you."

"I already have a counselor at school."

"I don't mean that kind."

"Oh, you mean a shrink?"

"Maybe."

"I don't need to see any shrink. There's nothing wrong with me. It's your husband who's the freak. He's the one who needs to see a doctor. Not me."

"I'll tell you what. We can think about this for a while and see what happens. How's that sound?"

"I know I'm gonna feel the same way next week, next month, and probably even next year, too."

"You don't know how you're going to feel."

"You don't either."

"You're right. But I want to know."

"Well, right now I'm just glad he finally got caught and thankful he's gone. I hate his ugly guts."

"I know."

"No, you don't."

"I hate him, too," I say, leaning against the molding because I need something to support me.

"You don't hate him."

"Yes, I do."

"You hate what he's done to me. But you can't hate him, because you love the ground he walks on."

"There's a very thin line between love and hate, and he crossed over it."

"But what are you gonna do without him?"

"What do you mean?"

"What are you going to do without him?"

"Do?"

"I'm not repeating it."

"We'll be fine."

"We'll see, won't we?" She tosses the book onto the pile, grabs another one, opens it to the first page, and looks as if she's already totally engrossed. "Would you close the door behind you?" she asks, not looking up.

"Are you sure you're all right?"

"I'm fine," she says, flipping what looks like five or ten pages.

"You think you'll be up for the drive to see your granny?"

"Of course I will." She sighs. "Why wouldn't I?"

I'm sorry for asking. I close the door slowly and stand outside it, listening for some sign, a sound, anything that might let me know she's feeling something besides anger. I hear more pages turn. And more still. And although I know my daughter is the real victim here, the sad thing is, I feel quite wounded, too.

Hives

The portable falls out my lap and hits the floor. I bend over the arm of the recliner to get it and all the blood rushes straight to my head, 'cause when I come back up I get the spins and then feel lightheaded. I let the phone rest in my lap until I get my bearings. What am I gon' say to her? "Hi, Mama, heard you had a asthma attack and sorry you had to be rushed to the hospital but I'm glad you didn't die and I'm sorry for not calling before now and I wish I could fly out there to help you get well but I can't 'cause I just found out my husband is cheating on me for the second time in ten years and when I get up out this chair most likely I'ma go upstairs and tell him to get out. I don't wanna hear none of his weak-ass explanations this time. He can't talk his way outta this divorce. Mama, please tell me if you think this is the right way to handle it? I got these kids and so many responsibilities; I don't know how I can handle all this without no help. But I won't let him, or nobody, use me. What did you do when Daddy did this? Why didn't you make him leave? Why didn't you divorce him? Ain't it hard pretending you don't care? Ain't it hard acting like it don't hurt? How do you get brave enough to face the pain and hold your head up and get on with your life? How do you do it, Mama?"

I could start there. But I better hurry up before I forget everything I'm thinking in the order I'm thinking it, and then it won't make sense and she'll think I'm having a nervous breakdown, like she always think as soon as any of us kids get in a fix and ain't quite sure how to deal with it. But I ain't having nobody's nervous nothing. I wouldn't let no man drive me that damn crazy. Ain't no man worth losing your fucking mind over. He done got your heart. That's enough.

I finally press the talk button, but as soon as I do, I hear Tiffany on the other end. "I need to use the phone," I say.

"Ma, it's my tutor. Did you forget? I've got a big math test tomorrow and we got a lot to cover in forty-five minutes."

"Sorry," I say, and hang up.

Now what? I recline the recliner and press the remote for the TV. My mind ain't hardly ready for nobody's sitcoms and I think I got enough news for one day. I gotta get outta here. Go somewhere. Anywhere. I flip the lever forward and come up so fast it almost don't take nothing for me to keep going and end up standing. I look around for my purse. It's over by the door. I grab it and head for the garage. I hope the keys is in it. They should be. I hear 'em jingle, and I'm so glad Trevor didn't close the garage door I don't know what to do. This way Al won't have to hear me leave. All he'll hear is me burning rubber.

I grab my burgundy ski jacket off the hook, and when I slide my arms in, my white ski cap falls on the floor. I pick it up and pull it down on my head and then put on my brown snow boots that roll down so the creamy knots of fur show. My blue jeans ain't wide enough to go over it, so I tuck 'em inside. Now my knees is sagging low and look three times their normal size, but I don't care. I ain't trying to win no fashion contest tonight.

I get in the Suburban. I hate this truck. It's too big and too blue, even though blue is my favorite color. But not this shade of blue. Too much green is in it, and as soon as Al is gone, I'm trading it in for a black Tahoe, which is what I wanted to get in the first place. See what happens when you compromise? If it wasn't so late I'd head straight for the dealership and trade this bitch in right now. Tomorrow won't be too soon. I back the truck out into the street without knowing where I'm going and just start driving. Before I get to the first stop sign, I slow down, pull over to the curb, reach in the glove compartment, and get a little bottle of Beefeater's. A friend of mine at work, her husband works for a company that supply the booze for a lot of airlines, and she brings us grocery bags full of all different kinds. We just take our pick, but I ain't picky. Free is free. And, besides, at times like this, it's nice to have a stash for the road. I break the paper around the neck and twist the top, swallowing this nasty stuff in one gulp, then I drop the empty bottle in my purse. I'm feeling warm. Mellow. Better. That son-of-a-bitch.

I jerk the gear into drive, and that's exactly what I do until I find myself turning into the parking lot of the mall twenty minutes later. This makes sense. Being away from him and the kids. It's nice and bright in here. Full of strangers who don't know that my husband is cheating on me for the second time in ten years. I try to smile as I walk in Zales Jewelers and find myself standing at one of the ring counters, where I spot a diamond that looks like it's got my name on it.

"May I show you something?" The saleswoman is black, and her hair is parted down the middle in two thick silver braids.

"Yes, that one right there," I say, pointing.

"This is a gem. Half a carat. Pricey. But. Well, is it for you?"

"Yes," I say, as she hands it to me.

"Engagement?"

I cut my eyes at her. "Not quite."

She says a soft and embarrassing, "Oh." The ring fits perfectly, which I take as a sign that I'm supposed to buy it.

"Would you like to know the price?"

"Is it in under a thousand?" I know I'm close to or up to my limit on my Zales charge, so I cross my fingers.

"Just a smidgen over."

"I'll take it." I hand her my card and notice red welts on my right hand. The lady goes over to the cash register. I scratch my hand, which all of a sudden is itching.

"Shall I wrap this for you?"

"No. I think I'll wear it. You can put the box in a little bag, if you don't mind."

"Don't mind at all," she says. I can't stand the sound of her voice. It's too soft. Like she thinks she's doing a commercial or something. When she hands me the credit slip, I sign and head back out into the mall. I feel better. I did something for Charlotte. Something extravagant. Now. The kids need some things, too. But what?

I head down toward all them new hip-hop stores that seem to be side by side. I'ma divorce him. I ain't letting him get away with this shit. Not this time. There ain't enough apologizing in the world he can do to weasel his way outta this. Fishing. Me and the kids'll be just fine.

Tiffany and Monique get two pair of blue jeans and some turtlenecks that's on sale, and since their ski jackets'll be too small next year, I buy one for both of 'em. Trevor don't never like nothing I buy him, so I just get him a few of them "No Fear" T-shirts, a bag of socks, and some Jockey underwear. I wonder how fast Al can pack his stuff and get out? Leave. Go. Anywhere. He don't deserve me. Or the kids. I work my ass off trying to be a good wife and mother, and this is the thanks I get? I don't think so.

Now my left hand is itching, and these bags is heavy, so I sit on a bench, but realize I have to go to the bathroom. I look in both directions to see where the closest one is, and my eyes stop on a telephone. The next thing I know, I'm standing at it dialing the hospital, since I know the number by heart now. Maybe she's watching TV. Or maybe she's just laying there in the dark waiting for one of her kids to call to say good night or something. When the operator comes on, I'm a little stunned at first. "Yes, Viola Price's room, please?"

"I'm sorry, dear, but your mother's sound asleep and she asked that she not be disturbed. She could use a solid night's sleep. I can take a message if you'd like."

"Okay. Would you just ask her to call her answering machine at home? This is her daughter Charlotte."

"I sure will," the nurse says. "She'll get this message first thing in the morning."

I say thank you and then call her house. I hope Cecil ain't home. Good. He's not there. I get that computer voice that says Mama's name and not Cecil's, and after the beep I say: "Hi, Mama. I know you ain't home yet. This is Charlotte. I keep missing you and just wanted to see how you was feeling. I hope you doing okay. Me and the kids is good. Al ain't in the best of spirits. He's going on a long trip. Don't know for how long. Anyway, I would really love to come out there if you need me to, but I'd have to take a train, and right now I don't have no-body to watch the kids, but just let me know what you want me to do. I love you, Mama. You take care, and let me know when you gon' be home. I wish I could send you some flowers, but remember what happened last time? You were allergic to 'em. Anyway, you take care. Get well. And don't worry about me. I'm fine. Couldn't be better. Love you again. I'll call you back tomorrow."

I go in the bathroom, and when I look down at my hands they're covered with more than just red splotches. I take my coat off and pull the sleeves of my sweatshirt up and can't be-lieve when I see at least a thousand tiny bumps covering my arms. What the hell is this shit? Nerves. That's all. Nerves. I look in the mirror. My face is clear but my neck is getting red. I lift my pants up but my legs is so dark I can't hardly see these bumps. I feel 'em. Calamine lotion should do the trick. I shake my head back and forth in the mirror: See what men can do? Make you break out in fucking hives!

I pretend like there ain't no bumps on my body when I come out of that bathroom and head toward the parking lot, but then I see this purple velvet hat staring me in the face that would go perfect with a purple-and-orange suit I been wanting to wear to church. I buy it. But I can't carry no hatbox, so I take off my white ski cap, stuff it in my purse, and put the other one on my head. I know I must look like a damn fool, but I don't care.

I throw the bags in the backseat of the truck and get another bottle out. This one is Stolichnaya. They all do the trick. I finish it, take my red leather gloves outta my pockets, and put 'em on. On the way home, I take 'em off, 'cause they're irritating my skin, even though I keep telling myself I don't itch, and at the same time I'm trying to figure out the best way to tell Al he's gotta go:

"You can take more than your fishing pole with you on Friday when you leave. Take all your shit. And I hope you catch more than you bargained for. I've had it, Al. In damn near twenty years of marriage, I ain't never even thought about cheating on you. Even when we been pissed off at each other the thought never even crossed my mind. Why do men have to cheat? Why ain't one woman enough?"

And I'll walk away, 'cause I know he ain't gon' have no answer. But, then again, maybe I just shouldn't say nothing. No. Gotta say something. Oh. I know:

"Talked to Smitty's wife and looks like he's not doing any fishing this weekend. Did you know that?"

And he'll play dumb. And I'll say: "Turns out, Smitty's uncle died and he's building a shed in the backyard this weekend, so looks like he ain't never had no plans to do no fishing. What you think about that, Albert Toussaint? Who you gon' go fishing with now? Tell me that."

And he'll stand there looking like the Creole he is, and I'll have to stop myself from picking up something and hurting him.

When I pull into the garage, he's standing in the doorway, waiting for me. This is good. Perfect. 'Cause the kids won't have to hear. I hope he comes out to the truck. That would be even better. My hands grip the steering wheel. As a matter of fact, I have to stop myself from squeezing it. Here he is.

"Roll the window down, Charlotte."

I do. But I look straight ahead at the skis stacked against the wall and the bikes hanging from the ceiling. I count 'em. One two three. One two three four.

"Where'd you go?"

"To the mall."

"Why didn't you tell somebody you was going?"

"Who cares where I go?"

"I do. You scared me. And the kids."

"My heart goes out to all y'all."

"What's wrong?"

"You know what's wrong."

"No, I do not."

"Think about it for a minute or two."

"Hold on, now. Smitty called a half-hour ago cussing me out."

Now I look at him. "Go on. You getting warmer."

"Why'd you call over there?"

"Because."

"Because why?"

"I felt like it."

"Charlotte, you done got Smitty in a heap of trouble."

"How'd I get Smitty in trouble?"

"First of all, I didn't know he hadn't told his wife he was going fishing, but he said you told her."

"I thought she knew."

"Well, apparently she didn't know, and it wasn't your place to tell her."

"It wasn't my intention to. When she told me about Smitty's uncle's funeral, I thought you was lying to me."

"Smitty said he didn't even know his uncle that good, and, besides, he's sick of funerals. This would make his fourth one this year and it ain't even April."

"So what are you telling me, Al?"

"I'm telling you that Smitty lied to his wife."

"So—you saying you *are* going fishing?"

"I told you that's where I was going. Oh, so you didn't believe me?"

"No."

"I said it was gon' be me and Smitty, and a group of other guys."

"Yeah, but what other guys?"

"Bill Carson, Willie, and Buffalo."

"For real?"

"Well, we can forget about Smitty. He ain't going nowhere now. He's grounded."

"How can he be 'grounded'?"

"You know how his wife is, Charlotte."

"I'm sorry, Al."

"Don't apologize to me. Smitty's the one who's mad. You can take it up with him."

I open the car door and he backs away to make room. "What's that on your finger?"

Shit. I didn't want him to see this. I'll take it back. Tomorrow. Didn't need it. Got enough diamonds. "Nothing."

"Let me see." He takes my hand but I don't want him to see the splotches. It's too late. Now I feel stupid for spending all this money on a ring I didn't need, not to mention this hat. Which apparently he ain't noticed. "It's pretty."

"What?" He must not be able to see in this light. Good.

"So—was this a revenge ring?"

"Kinda. But I can take it back."

"Why?"

" 'Cause I don't need it."

"We got a house full of stuff we don't need, don't we, Charlotte?"

"Yep."

"So you still don't trust the old man?"

"I want to, Al."

"You should. You really should."

I get out the truck, and since the windows are tinted he don't even see the bags in the backseat and I don't bother to get 'em. When we get inside, the kids have left the pizza boxes on the kitchen counter and a few dried-up slices for me, I guess. But I don't eat nobody's pizza.

"Come on," I say to Al, and lead him upstairs to our room.

"Don't get no ideas," he says.

"I'm full of ideas," I say.

When we get to our room, I go in the bathroom to find the calamine lotion, and decide to take a shower. Al gets in the bed. "I called Mama," I yell.

"And how she doing?"

"I didn't get to talk to her. But I left a message."

"That's good. I'm glad to hear it, Charlotte. Now, didn't it feel good?"

"Yep," I say, and stand in front of the mirror butt naked. I hold out my hands and arms and they're completely smooth. No welts. No redness. No bumps. Just a 180-pound dark-brown body. After lathering all over, I'm wondering if I'm feeling good because I made the call or because I know my husband ain't cheating on me. I don't really care right now. I feel so good I decide not only to wash my hair, but shave my legs and underarms, too. I splash St. Ives Apricot Splash all over my body, then sprinkle a little talcum powder between my breasts and the inside of my thighs and slip on my light-pink gown hanging behind the door. When I prance out to the bedroom to give my husband the best part of me, he's sleep. But it's all right. I ease on in the bed and slide under the covers next to him. I kiss his warm hands and am staring at him when the phone rings. I know I should trust him. He's a good man. The phone rings again. I'm wondering why nobody's getting it. I look over at the clock. It's ten to ten. The kids are already in bed, and, besides, they don't have a phone in their rooms. I kiss Al's thick eyebrows and then pick up the phone.

"Yeah," I say, in a voice that will make the person feel like they woke me up.

"Is Al there?" Loretha asks.

This bitch was his first wife. It's been seventy-two whole hours since she last called. She must be trying to break her own record. "He's sleep, Loretha."

"It's important."

"Isn't it always?"

"Look, Charlotte. It's late. I don't wanna go through this tonight. Just tell him Birdie's tuition for summer school is still due next week, and for him not to forget it."

"I thought she was graduating from that beauty school?"

"She is, after this summer. She needs a few more courses."

"I bet. Didn't she go last summer?"

"Don't you remember when she took sick and couldn't finish?"

"No, I don't."

"Look, Charlotte, Birdie is Al's daughter, too, just like Tiffany and Monique, okay? Except she got here first, so don't hold it against her."

"I ain't got no problems with Birdie, so don't try to twist this shit around, Loretha. It's you that irk the hell out of me."

"Well, get over it. We been going through this too long, and we only got one more year left to tolerate each other. You sure Al is sleep?"

"I won't dignify that with a answer, and for your information, I don't need you to remind me when and for how long Birdie been Al's daughter. I'm very much aware of it. All I'm saying is that I ain't never seen nobody go to a two-year program and it takes three. You shoulda never let her drop outta high school in the first place."

"That really ain't none of your business, now, is it?"

"I'm making it my business. Al's money is my money."

"Since when?"

"How much is the deposit, Loretha?"

"Three hundred and sixty-two."

"Dollars?"

"That's what I just said. Please make sure he gets this message, would you?"

"I guess child support don't cover tuition, then, huh?"

"Don't seem like it, do it?"

"I'm hanging up now, Loretha."

"Good night, Charlotte. Sleep tight."

I hang up. I hate that bitch. It never fucking fails: as soon as I start feeling good, can't ten seconds go by without some bull- shit popping up. Why can't she just disappear? Birdie! Birdie is getting on my last nerve, too. I prayed for the day to come when that girl graduated from high school, turned eighteen, and them child support payments would finally stop. Loretha been nickel-and-diming Al to death, and it seem like Birdie been seventeen for the last three years. Loretha didn't get pregnant till she found out Al was divorcing her. Loretha always was a sneaky whore, everybody knew it except Al, and once he found out she'd been sleeping with his so-called friend Scratch, he cut him loose, and to this day Al still don't know for sure if Birdie is even his. She didn't use to look nothing like him, but he been paying for her so long that she done finally started to favor him.

My head falls into the middle of my pillow. It's cool when I turn my face toward Al. A few minutes ago, I wanted to wrap my arms around him so tight until wasn't no space between his body and mine, but now all I wanna do is go to sleep.

In the morning I make him some cheese grits, hard-fried eggs, bacon, and biscuits. When he walks in the kitchen, I'm just fin- ishing up the gravy. He comes over and gives me a wet kiss. "Good morning, baby," he says.

"Good morning yourself, sweetheart," I say.

"Who was that you was talking to on the phone so late?" he asks, dipping his finger in the hot grits.

"It was just Janelle," I hear myself say.

"Well, is everything all right?"

"Yeah, same old, same old."

"Then why she call so late if everything is all right?"

"Shanice and George is at it again."

"Yeah? I don't trust that old guy," he says, pouring me and him a cup of coffee. "Something's missing in him. I can't put my finger on it, but the few times we been around him, he seem like he two different people: the one he want us to see, and the one he don't. You know what I mean?"

"No, I don't. But it ain't our business and it ain't our problem: it's Janelle's. Now, come on and sit your butt down and let's eat."

"I'm coming, I'm coming. And since you ain't mad with me no more, what do I get for dessert on Sunday?"

"Me with a raspberry glaze."

"Oh yeah? Well, I guess it don't never hurt to try something new," he say. And we leave it at that.

Hot Links

"What woulda happened if she'da died?" Brenda asks me.

"What you mean, 'What woulda happened'?" I'm buttering six slices of white bread. The kids like white bread with butter on it, even though this is margarine. They don't know the difference and they eat it every single day. Sometimes Miss Q even put salt on hers.

Brenda's frying some hot links in a big skillet with no handle. They was half-price, 'cause the expiration date to sell 'em was today. She done already cussed me out for taking too long to get back. She said the kids was so hungry they was having conniptions waiting for me and the Sloppy Joe meat, which was why she left 'em in here for ten quick minutes to run to the corner and get something on credit. I told Brenda I didn't thank it was such a good idea leaving them kids in here by theyself. For no amount of time. She just said Quantiana got good sense. But Miss Q ain't but five years old. How much sense could she have? I told Brenda that this is how kids end up on the six o'clock news, but she swore up and down that this was the first and last time she ever done it. All it take is one time, don't it?

They all huddled in the living room, waiting. That room must be at least three or four colors: one wall is lime green, another look like a very ripe tangerine, and I guess she got tired and just made the last two black. The ceiling ain't no shade of blue I ever seen in my life. It'a hold your interest, that's for sure. Miss Q and Hakeem is sitting on the floor with their heads sideways on the cocktail table. The baby—Sunshine—is underneath it on that dirty rug, sucking her thumb. They watching TV. But that's all they do is watch TV.

"Who would get the house?" she's asking me, while she take another sip off her beer, which she also musta got on credit, 'cause wasn't none in the icebox when I left. When I put the ketchup and hamburger meat inside it there was three more loose bottles making a circle around a empty Kool-Aid jug. I guess these is her dinner. But I don't say nothing.

Hot grease is popping everywhere, even on the front of her light-blue top, but it don't seem like Brenda's fazed by it. In a saucepan right next to the hot links is some cream-styled corn, bubbling. "That house ain't worth nothing," I say. "You should turn the fire down on that corn before it stick, baby."

"It's a house. Better than this," she says, turning the dial on the stove from five to two. "This" is the projects, but if Brenda was to go back forty or fifty years to the backwoods of Texas and see what and where me and my eleven sisters and brothers was brought up, she wouldn't be complaining. She got running water. A bathroom with a toilet that flush. A phone that work since I been here. And two whole bedrooms for three little kids. That's all we had, too. She ain't got to worry about no rats. Nothing but a few straggly roaches every now and then. So. "This" ain't so bad, is what I'm thinking as I look around. It all depends on your frame of reference.

We had to take turns working on the farm, so some of us went to school and some of us didn't. After two of my other brothers got killed fooling around with a forklift, Daddy sent me up to Chicago to live with his brother. I was only in the tenth grade. He wanted me to graduate. I liked school. Wanted to finish. Did, too. When I left Texas, I already knew how most things worked. I'd watched my daddy operate machinery and run the farm. I knew how to cook. Knew how to put two and two together. Even figured out how to make a living without a good education. Sometimes it was hard. Sometimes it was easy. I still thank college woulda been the best way to go. If I had my druthers. But. It's almost April. It's 1994. I'm on the other side of middle age. Supposed to be retired. And here I am. Starting over.

"The IRS got a lien against the house," I say. "So you *could* say I don't even own it."

"What's a lien?" Brenda asks, setting some paper plates on the table with clean plastic spoons she gets out the silverware drawer. She got two or three real forks and case knives in there too, which me and her usually eat with. I been meaning to stop in Target and buy two sets. They ain't but $19.99 each, and the handles come in different colors.

"A lien is when the IRS get mad 'cause you didn't pay your taxes and they let everybody in the world know it. You can't get no credit nowhere, and you can't sell the house till you pay them first. If you don't pay nothing for a long time, they charge you so much interest and then penalties on top of the interest, that it add up to ten times more than you owed in the first place. If you can't keep up the payments, they do not feel sorry for you at all. They can and will take everything you own to get their money, even if it mean taking your house, your car, your wedding ring, anything you got that's worth something. This is what happened to Redd Foxx."

"Who?"

"Never mind."

"But what you supposed to do if they take your house and car and stuff?"

"What you mean, 'what you supposed to do'?"

"Well, it wouldn't make no sense to me to pay for something you ain't even got no more."

"It don't work like that, Brenda. It means I couldn't never buy another house until I paid the government they money."

"Then you better go on and pay them folks. Cecil, would you make some Kool-Aid for the kids right quick?"

"Sure, where's the pitcher?" But then I remembered.

"Where it always is. In the refrigerator. Why didn't you pay your taxes, Cecil?"

"That's a dumb question, Brenda."

"What's so dumb about it?" she asks, getting a real fork out the drawer and jabbing it deep into them crunchy hot links two at a time. Grease is dripping all over the stove, and dark-brown drops fall right on top of that yellow corn. I can't eat this mess.

"What's usually the reason why people don't pay their bills on time, Brenda?"

" 'Cause they ain't got the money, I guess."

"All right, then."

"But you had them barbecue places."

"Had, is right."

"QUANTIANA! Y'all come on in here and eat! Well, what happened to 'em?"

"You been listening to me, gal?"

"Yeah," she says, "but you ain't told me nothing, really."

Here come the kids. One by one. Like little soldiers. Miss Q is beautiful. Her hair is wild and curly. Her skin is the color of a brand-new copper penny. I thank her and Hakeem's daddy is, or I should say was, Mexican. I can't be sure. They mixed with something. Hakeem is a handsome little dude. Already got the face of a grown man. You can see what he gon' look like twenty years from now. Small for his age, seem like to me. He three, but ain't much bigger than Sunshine, and she won't be two till Labor Day. Now, this child is 100 percent black. Ain't no guessing game necessary here. Her daddy like to throw dice, but his luck was always low when he come up against me. I won that gold cap in his mouth once, but I couldn't take the man's tooth. And if memory serves me correctly, he still owes me the value of one gold crown.

Brenda leans against the sink while the kids sit down at the table. Ain't but three chairs, so even if we all wanted to eat at the same time, we couldn't.

"Mama, Hakeem is in my chair."

"I ain't in your chair."

"You is!"

"I ain't!"

Miss Q, who is standing behind Hakeem, puts both hands on his chair and flips it backwards so fast that, before anybody can say a word, that boy is on the floor screaming out the top of his lungs. Then Sunshine start crying, and Miss Q just gets in that chair and start eating like ain't nothing going on. I wanna say something, but it ain't my place. These kids like me. And if I start chastising 'em like they mine, feelings have a tendency to change.

Brenda takes another sip of her beer before she even open her mouth. "You want me to go get my belt?"

I don't know which one she talking to, and I don't thank she do either, but all three of 'em shake they head no.

"Get up off that floor, Hakeem. You know Quantiana sit in the same chair every day, so why you have to aggravate her like this?"

He is not crying like I thought he was. He was just making a lot of noise. Being dramatic, as Viola would say.

But he already in the other chair, slurping up that corn. Miss Q rolls her eyes at him, like she done won another round, and the baby is sucking on a hot link. Brenda should know that that girl too little to be eating this kind of spicy food, but she don't seem to be having no problems.

"Y'all gon' be okay, then?" she asks them.

They all nod yes. "Then me and Cecil gon' go on and sit in the living room, 'cause we got some important thangs to talk about. Don't come in there till I tell you it's all right, understand?"

Miss Q and Hakeem nod yes, and then the baby imitates them. Me and Brenda walk in the living room and sit down on the couch. It's a sad couch. I couldn't tell you what color it is. These kids destroy everything. All I know is there's a dip in the middle cushion, so, to keep from sliding into each other, we have to sit at opposite ends. I gave her five hundred dollars last week and I thought she said she was gon' buy one since they was having a big inventory sale at Levitz. But I don't see no new couch.

Brenda got her beer in her hand, which, after she take a long squig, she set on the cocktail table. It's sticky from something. I don't even wanna know what. And the rug under it is tore in one place, so, to keep it together, I lift the leg of the table and push this end of the rug against the other. You can't hardly tell it's split, but I know it.

Brenda picks up the remote control and press it until she get BET. It's some music videos on. She lean back on the couch and her bra strap done fell down on her left shoulder, but I don't thank she realize it, 'cause she don't do nothin' about it. I thank Brenda got a buzz going. She cocks her head to one side and look at me and smile. I smile back. If she could just stay in that pose, she could almost pass for pretty right now. But of course she move back to her position and then look down at the floor.

"You like me, don't you, Cecil?"

That is a dumb question to ask a man who living with you, who give you all his money, and is helping to take care of somebody else's kids, but I just say, "Of course I do."

"How much?" she asks.

"What you mean by how much?"

She must feel her bra strap, 'cause now she makes a hook outta her index finger and pull it back up on her shoulder. I just noticed that she changed her nail polish. It's a bubble-gum pink with green palm trees on each finger. She got some kinda imagination. "Okay. You know how they measure earthquakes, right?"

"Yeah, on a Richter scale," I say, even though I thank she about to lose me, but, then again, I don't usually have no trouble following Brenda's line of thanking, so why should I thank she about to get all philosophical on me now?

"Okay. So how high was that last one in L.A.?"

"I don't know. But it was a big one."

"Of course it was, Cecil! It had to be at least a eight-something to kill folks and do the kinda damage it did, am I right?"

"You right."

"Okay, so let's say a nine is like the very highest earthquake, and say like a three ain't nothin' but a little tremor. Where do your feelings for me fall on the Richter scale, Cecil?"

That's all she getting at? "It's a easy eight, Brenda."

"Don't lie to me, Cecil."

"I ain't lying, girl. You the best thang that's done happened to me in a long time. I ache for you. My feet don't hardly touch the ground when I walk, and when I do I can't even hardly feel my bunions no more. What about your feelings?"

She take a sip of her beer, then decide to go on and finish it. She set the bottle down and stands up. She do some kind of sexy stretch so her breasts rise up and then fall. Then she cup her hands over both of 'em and squeeze. "You could be on your way to being a eight, too."

"What is that supposed to mean: 'on my way'?"

"Well, we got some decisions we gotta make."

"Like what?"

"Well, tell me something. Since your wife didn't die, was you planning on getting a divorce any time soon?"

"Of course I am. We over here living in sin. It ain't right. I know that. Your kids is little now, but not for long."

"How soon?"

"Well, I gotta let the woman get back on her feet, and I just told you, we got some financial problems we have to straighten out first. It ain't as easy as one two three, Brenda. Why you wanna know all this today, when we done talked about it before?"

" 'Cause things is different."

"What's different?"

"Something done happened and I can't do nothin' about it."

"Something like what?"

Next thang I know, she look toward the kitchen to see if the kids is looking, and they ain't, so she lift up her light-blue top and pull both her breasts out from under her bra. "Do they look bigger?"

"I can't say. I ain't never really looked at 'em with no ruler in mind."

She puts 'em back and pull her top back down. "Well, they gon' be bigger than this in a few months."

"You don't need no surgery, Brenda, if that's what this is about."

She shakes her head back and forth. "How old is your youngest child, Cecil?"

"Thirty-five."

"And the oldest?"

"I thank she thirty-eight. Why?"

"Well, you might wanna let 'em know that they gon' have a brand-new little sister or brother sometime in September."

"You playing with me, ain't you now, Brenda?"

"Why would I joke about something like this?"

"You sitting here telling me that right this minute you got a baby growing in your belly that's got my blood?"

"That's exactly what I'm telling you," she says, and walks toward me. My heart is skipping every other beat. I feel hot. I feel young. I feel blessed. Like I'm being given another chance. A baby. A real live baby. Hot damn, Cecil. Didn't even know the old fella still had the power.

"So," Brenda whispers in my ear and then licks my earlobe. She know this drive me crazy and I can't hardly tolerate myself. "Do you wanna be the father of my baby?"

"I certainly do," I say. "I certainly do."

"Then we gon' have to make some changes."

"I know we do."

"We need to move."

"I know."

"Someplace decent."

"I know."

"Where the kids can go to good schools."

"Yeah."

"Closer to white folks, is what I'm getting at."

"We ain't gotta move with no white folks for that. They can go to private school."

"Private school?"

"They got some good Christian schools around here. It wouldn't hurt these kids none to get closer to God and get a good education at the same time, since don't nobody seem to go to church around here."

"We can start doing that, too, you'll see."

"I thank that's a very good idea, Brenda."

"Okay, but I ain't finished."

"I'm all ears, baby. You got my undivided attention. Do my ear again, though, please?"

"I can't be doing too much more cleaning in my condition."

"Don't even worry about that, Brenda."

She makes one long stroke with her tongue on the side of my neck up to my ear, and then she blows inside it. Hot-diggety dog.

"And my car need more than a transmission."

"We can trade that sucker in."

Now she do her nibbling thang on my earlobe. I like this one, too. I do.

"I need to get this Curl outta my hair and get some braids, so I won't have to be worrying about lifting my arms up over my head when I get too big to fix it."

"Okay."

"And you might wanna get yours trimmed some, too, Cecil. Or maybe by the summer you might see a new style you like. We ain't got but a few pillowcases, and between the two of us, they all getting stained. And pillowcases ain't cheap."

"I'll certainly look into it, Brenda."

"Oh. Last thing," she says, and then she kiss me on my cheek, which makes me feel all squishy, and I squirm when I feel her lips cover my mouth. She sucks on 'em like they tangerines or something, and then she gives 'em back to me, I guess. "Hakeem and Sunshine need to go to a good preschool, 'cause I can't get no studying done with two kids in the house all day long."

"Studying for what, Brenda?"

"My GED. Remember I told you I wanna get it?"

"Yeah, I do remember. It wouldn't hurt me to look at them books neither."

"I told you we needed to make some changes, didn't I?" she say, so proud. I do like this girl. She ambitious. Everything she wanna do is about improving herself, her kids, and, I guess now, us. This is all new to me. But it feel good. And it feel right.

"Yep. You sure did, Brenda. But we need to add one more thing to this list."

"What?" she asks, looking a little worried—that is, if I'm seeing her right.

"Pour them beers in the icebox down the drain. You don't need 'em, and neither do the baby."

"I will, Cecil. Don't even worry about it."

"A baby," I say.

"Yep. But it ain't coming today," she say, turning toward the kitchen. "Did you want a hot link or not?"

"Naw. You go on and help yourself."

I'm so happy right now I feel like I could run down the street screaming at the top of my lungs. I feel like calling Viola to tell her my good news. Woman, I can still make a baby! After all this time. Lord knows I can't let her know nothing about no baby. Can't tell my kids neither. Not yet. But hell, I need to do something to celebrate. What?

Brenda's in the kitchen doorway, looking at the kids. They paper plates is clean. They drinking they Kool-Aid. I stand behind her and put my hands on her belly and rub in a circle. "What?" she asks.

"I gotta go celebrate," I say.

"Just bring me back something green, okay?"

"Broccoli or collard greens, baby? Take your pick!"

She stomps on my toe, right on my corn, but I refuse to feel it. "Okay!" I say, and head for the door.

"Would you bring the kids back something sweet?"

"Y'all want something?" I ask.

"Yeah!" they all say.

"Vanilla Wafers!" Miss Q says.

"Cookie Dough ice cream!" Hakeem says.

The baby just grins. She'll take whatever they having. When I get outside the door, I just stand there and look out at the black desert. All I see is the flashing lights of the Mirage and Excalibur and Caesar's Palace. I feel lucky. Like I done already hit the jackpot and I need to tell somebody. I run on my tiptoes all the way to the bottom of them steps. Before I put the key in my Lincoln, it hit me: Howie! That's who I can tell. He the one person in the world I can trust. Howie won't pass judgment on me. He'll be happy for me.

I get in the car and start it up, but before I put it in gear, I push in my B. B. King tape and don't hear a word he sanging 'cause I'm grinning so hard. I can't wait to tell Howie. I know he ain't gon' hardly believe this. But, hell, he ain't the only one.

Fish
Dreams

"I can walk!" I yell at the nurse who just insist I ride out of here in this damn wheelchair. I know the rules. I been through this before. But, hell, some rules was made to be broken.

"I'm sure you can, Mrs. Price, but you know hospital regulations: we have to assist you out in a wheelchair regardless if you're able to walk or not. Is that your son over there?"

Lewis is sitting in one of those lookalike chairs with his hands clasped together like he's praying hard for something he know he don't deserve. His face is shiny in a dull kinda way from perspiring and look like he need a hot shower. Why do he have to come out in public looking like he homeless or something? "Yeah, that's my son," I mumble, and Lewis looks at me like he's apologizing for it. Sometimes I wish God had made me a witch, or at least given me some magic powers. I'd start by rewiring my son, give him a clean start, put him on a wholesome path: one that lead somewhere.

"Is he going to drive you home?"

I look at him, hard. He ain't got no driver's license, but I let him drive my Sentra down here to bring me my dentures since Loretta's been a little under the weather herself these past few days and ain't been able to get up here. I asked him to bring me some clean underwear and something decent to wear home—anything hanging in my closet that stretch, and please: no zippers, or buttons, or hooks and eyes. I told Lewis I better not smell a drop of liquor on his breath either, even though it'll probably be oozing out his pores, and if he even thought about driving my car anywhere but here, he best forget all about the whole idea. I'd know it, 'cause I keep track of my mileage, and if I found out he had, I'd make him walk his ass all the way down to the Strip to find his daddy. He could stay with Cecil and his young girlfriend and her kids in the luxurious projects till he wore out his welcome. Lewis promised he'd be up here by twelve even though they wasn't releasing me till one. Two of the nurses told me he been here since ten-thirty.

I get on in the wheelchair and nod yes to the nurse. Lewis gets up and follows us to the counter, where they hand me a plastic bag with my personal things in it. I put it in my lap. The nurse hands me a stack of papers—a million instructions on how to keep breathing, and then a pile of tiny ones. I know what they are.

"You have seven prescriptions that need to be filled as soon as possible. Can your son do that for you?"

"Yes, I can," Lewis says.

"Okay, okay. Get me outta here. I wanna go home."

I hear him let out one of his long sighs, and I don't hardly say two words to him till we pull in my driveway.

I can't believe it. The house is clean. Spotless. "Who did this?"

"Me. Wasn't much to do."

I go in the kitchen and open the refrigerator real slow. It's been cleaned out, too, with the exception of some French's mustard packages, a jar of Folger's coffee crystals, and two big bottles of Schlitz Malt Liquor. These ain't hardly mine. All of a sudden I smell the disinfectant he used, so I slam that door. The fumes alone can do me in. All I need is to go rushing back to that hospital the same damn day I get home. Wouldn't that be a kicker?

"I fixed your car," he says, heading straight for the refrigerator. I try to guess what he's going in there to get. A fix. But, hell, I could use one, too.

"Wasn't nothing wrong with my car," I say, as I head for my bedroom. I can see in the room where Cecil slept that Lewis done made hisself right at home. I hope he don't think he moving in. I got news for him if that's what all this fixing and cleaning is about. He should really think of my house like it's a motel.

"Ma, when was the last time you changed the oil?"

"What you mean, the last time? I ain't *never* changed the oil. That was your daddy's job, not mine."

Lewis comes in the living room with one of my Classico spaghetti jars full of beer and sits down on my off-white couch. "No, you don't!" I yell.

"What's wrong?" he asks, looking scared.

"Please don't sit on my good couch with them dirty clothes on, Lewis."

"Okay," he moans, and gets up, looks around the room at two gold chairs I just had re-covered, then down at his pants, and decides to stand. "Anyway, your spark plugs were shot, and you needed a new starter, so I basically talked the man into letting me barter in exchange for some work, which is one reason why I'm so dirty."

He looks down the hallway at me, waiting for me to praise him, I guess, so I do: "Thank you, Lewis. Glad you still use the good sense you was born with. At least some of the time." I should've left that last part off, but it just slipped off my tongue. "Work?"

"Yep. He said he'd hire me if I wanted a job."

"That'd be one helluva commute, Lewis."

"I'm thinking about making some changes."

"Well, don't think too fast. Do you realize how hot it gets here?"

"Ma, please. You need anything?"

"Yeah, let me have a sip of that beer." Then I stop and think about it. "Never mind, pour me a glass, would you?" I say. "Do you know when Paris and Janelle supposed to be getting here?"

"I don't know. I think there's quite a few messages on your answering machine."

I get up from the edge of the bed, and lean over to see a orange "4" blinking. "Why didn't you listen to 'em?"

" 'Cause it's not my phone."

"Well, what if it was something urgent? I've been in the damn hospital, Lewis."

"Sorry," he says. "Anyway. What about those prescriptions? You want me to take 'em down to the pharmacy to get filled?"

"Yeah, but I ain't got but about seventy-something dollars to my name, so ask 'em how much they gon' cost. Ain't nothin' to eat in here, is it? I'm starving."

"Me, too."

"I bet you are," I say. "I hate that I'm even thinking it, but what I wouldn't pay for some of your daddy's hot links and some baked beans and potato salad and a side of collard greens. Just a teaspoonful."

"I can stop by the Shack."

"Where you been? Ain't no more Shacks," I blurt out and then start flipping through a pile of mail next to the phone. Lewis just shakes his head, and guzzles up the last of his beer. All this is too much for him to digest, I guess, but that's what he get for always thinking everybody except him is always doing so good. That everybody else are so goddamn happy. I don't know no really happy people. Not the kind that makes you walk around humming. Maybe a short verse every now and then, but that's about it. So—could be this family news flash might snatch him out of this fantasy world he been living in. "Just get me a Big Mac and some large fries and two hot apple pies. No. No apple pies. And make that a small fry. I forgot. I'm on a diet."

"Should I drive or walk?"

I feel like throwing something at him for asking such a

dumb-ass question. He was smarter when he was a teenager. "Get there whatever way you think makes the most sense, Lewis."

He thinks about it for a minute. Sighs. Takes a couple of steps toward the front door, then says, "I guess I'll drive, then. Would it be okay to get a pack of cigarettes?"

"Add it to your tab and go straight there and come straight back, and Lewis, don't even think about smoking in my car *or* this house, you got that?"

"I don't consider it an option," he says.

After the door slams shut, I realize I forgot something important: "Lewis, get me two quick-pick lottery tickets!" Sometimes he's just as smart as I hoped he would be, but then other times I can't figure out how he graduated from high school.

The first message is from my dizzy sister Suzie Mae, wondering if I'm still in the hospital. If she wanted to know so damn bad, why didn't she call one of my kids to find out? Then I can't hardly believe my ears when I hear Charlotte's voice. At first it don't even sound like her, she sound so mellow, and I can tell she was calling from a pay phone, 'cause I hear that mall music and a lot of noise in the background. Something must be going on at home, otherwise she wouldn'ta called me like this. At least she called. I ain't exactly shocked that she ain't coming out here. I wonder what kind of vacation Al's going on. Maybe he got a big job on his rig or something. Oh hell, not Cecil? Says he found out I was coming home today and he'll stop by later to make sure I'm okay. Plus, he say he got some news. I hope he paid the IRS. This would mean I can move when I want to, not 'cause I have to. It just dawned on me, where in the hell will I go if I have to move? I'm living on a fixed income, which seems to keep me in one fix after another all right. I'm meditating on this when I hear Essex, the head of our bowling league, saying they ain't heard hide nor hair from me, and "We lagging behind without you, Vy. You better hurry up and get your big butt down to the alley. Where you been hiding? You still alive, ain't you? Don't die on us before the tournament next month, gal. Chuckle. Chuckle." Is that a knock at the front door? I do not feel like getting up to answer it, especially if it's Cecil, or Loretta, 'cause I just barely walked in the house long enough to catch my breath. I ain't hardly in no mood to be chitchatting yet. I peek through the curtains and, sure enough, it's Loretta. She done dyed her hair again. Now it look lavender. She ought to stop. You can see her pink scalp straight through her hair 'cause it's so thin, but she got enough mousse and hairspray on it that it look like cotton candy spinning on over her head.

"Viola, are you in there, sweetie?"

Oh shoot. I can't lie to Loretta like this. I knock on the window to get her attention and she walks over and stands there. "Hi, Loretta. Thanks for stopping by, honey, but I just got home and I'm supposed to stay in bed at least until tomorrow."

"Okay. But do you need anything? I'm on my way to the supermarket and I could get you something if you want."

"Thanks, but my son already went for me."

"Oh, your son is here. That's nice."

"Yep. My other kids will be here today, too."

She looks hurt. Like what is she supposed to do now. "Who did your hair, Loretta?"

"Got it done down at Vivacious."

"It looks fabulous, honey."

"Thank you, Vy. Well, I'll head on home, but you call if you need anything. And let me know when you're up for bridge."

"I will. And you're feeling okay?"

"Depending on what day it is. Diabetes can play havoc with you. But I'm thankful to the Almighty just to be here."

"Join the club. See you later, sweetie."

She smiles and waves, turns, and leaves the porch. Loretta is so frail and pale. Hard to believe she lives in Las Vegas. She don't have no family to speak of, but, from the looks of things, I guess that would be me.

———

"Mama, wake up," Janelle is saying. But that's impossible, 'cause I ain't sleep. But my body is being shook, and I realize my eyes is closed, been closed for a few minutes, I guess. The mail I was opening laying next to me look like a fan of white envelopes except for that brown one from the IRS threatening for the last time to take this house. They can have this raggedy hole. I ain't losing no more sleep over this dump. Let Cecil worry about it. Let him figure it out.

"Granny, how are you feeling?"

"Shanice?"

I try to sit up, and when I do, she helps me, while Janelle stands at the foot of the bed putting on rubber gloves. "When did y'all get here? Is Lewis back yet?"

"No, thank the Lord. We got here about fifteen minutes ago, Mama. You were out like a light, and we wanted you to rest, but your nosy granddaughter here insisted on sitting next to you until you woke up. Did she wake you?"

"No, I didn't," Shanice snaps.

"You better watch the tone of your voice when you talking to your mama, girl."

"Sorry, Granny. Sorry, Ma."

"So are you feeling close to normal yet, Ma?"

"Fair to middlin', but I'm alive, so I can't do too much complaining. How about you? I know you tired. Y'all drove all the way here?"

"We sure did. It was a nice drive. We needed the time together."

I look at Shanice. Her eyes ain't got no glaze, like she trying not to show no feelings one way or the other. She's good at it, too. Then I glance up at Janelle, whose eyes is doing just the opposite: straining to hold back something. Not tears. Something way past that. What in Lord's name could it be? I hope it ain't what I think it is. She'll tell it when she wants to. And I'll wait. "You putting on weight?" I ask Janelle.

"A couple of pounds, maybe."

"I thought you liked being a anorexic," I say with a smirk.

"I don't like being fat," she says.

"Well, for what it's worth, I dreamt about fish last night."

"And?"

"It usually means somebody's pregnant. How you feel about that?"

"Old wives' tales haven't stood the test of time, Ma, and you know it."

"Oh, but you'll spend ten dollars going to a psychic and consider it money well spent?"

"It's another way to gain self-knowledge, insight, and an opportunity to get to know yourself better."

"Spare me, would you? Who in the world would know you better than you know yourself, besides me? Have any of them psychics mentioned when you might graduate from college or get a real job?"

"I have a job."

"No, you don't," Shanice blurts out.

"I run a household and I'm raising a child. Look, Mama, I just got here, so don't start yet, please?"

She rolls her eyes at her daughter, so I decide to cut in. "Shanice, go get Granny's glass that your Uncle Lewis left sitting in the living room, would you, baby?"

"I poured it down the drain," Janelle says.

"What? Why?"

"Because the last thing you need right now is beer. Paris was just telling me about this article she read in a holistic magazine about hops—which is the stuff they use to make beer—and a lot of other things asthmatics should stay away from."

"Paris believe everything she read. Where is she, by the way? Did she change her mind?"

"She and Dingus should be here any minute. Their plane

was supposed to land a half-hour or so ago. She didn't want anybody to pick her up. She's renting a car. You know how she is."

"Yeah, I know how she is. Shanice, stand up and let your granny look at you!"

She gets up. All legs. Not a drop of meat on them thighs.

"How come those shorts is cut so high?"

"They're Daisy Dukes," she says.

"Daisy who? I don't care what her name is. You can't bend over to get nothin' in those things without your behind hanging out."

"So?" she says, about as sarcastic as it gets.

I reach over and get my inhaler and take a few puffs. "I don't wanna see you wearing 'em in my presence or out in public so go take 'em off and put on something decent."

"It's all right, Ma?"

"It ain't all right," I say. And if I could jump out this bed and slap the taste out of my granddaughter I would, but when I look at her eyes, I realize something is missing. That little smart remark she just made is not the way *my* granddaughter talks to me. Not using that tone. Something ain't right. So let it go, Vy. Let it pass. "All right."

"So—where's Daddy?" Janelle asks.

I hear engines in the driveway. "Go see if that's him," I say, before catching myself. Both of 'em head out toward the living room and I force myself to get up. At first, I feel dizzy, then a little lightheaded, but I'm okay. By the time I get out to the living room, we're at the beginning of what looks like a Price family reunion, minus two.

Okay. So everybody hugs everybody but don't nobody act like they really mean it, except for when I wrap my arms around my grandson, who is now some kind of giant. Dingus kisses me on my forehead, then takes me by the elbow and leads me over to the couch. He's wearing blue jeans and a long red sweatshirt. This boy look good in red. "Should you be up, Granny?"

"I'm out the hospital, baby. And I ain't about to become nobody's invalid. I just had a little asthma attack. I swear, you looking more and more like your daddy by the minute. And what you doing, growing a inch a month or what?"

"Nope. Can I get you anything?"

He's grinning, showing off those braces. I hope they work out, 'cause the boy's teeth was two deep in some places. Before I can answer him, here come Paris and Lewis from outside. They're already arguing about something.

"Ma, would you tell her that you asked me to get you McDonald's?" Lewis is looking like he's on trial for a crime he didn't commit. Poor thing.

"I did. And give it here, I'm starving."

"Mama, you know you shouldn't be eating this junk," Paris says, standing with her hands on her hips. If she don't look like me twenty years ago, I ain't sitting here. Them blue jeans look like twelves, and she filling out every inch of 'em, too. But them ain't my breasts on her chest. No, Lordy. The other girls been calling her Tiny Tits for years. I snatch the bag from Lewis and take out a few fries. "Is there anything to eat around here?" Paris asks heading toward the kitchen. I hear the refrigerator door open and close. Shanice done fell asleep across Cecil's bed with a book in her hand. Her mama's running water in the bathroom. I know she ain't in there bathing 'cause she took the portable phone, and, plus, she's wearing rubber gloves.

"What happened with my prescriptions, Lewis?"

He's back outside, sitting on the steps doing one of them crossword puzzles and smoking a cigarette. He probably deep in thought 'cause he don't answer me.

"Uncle Lewis, Granny wants to know what happened to her prescriptions?" Dingus asks from the doorway and then goes over and turns on the TV. Like some kind of magic, a basketball game is on.

"Oh, yeah," I hear him grunt and open the screen door and limp in. "You won't wanna hear this."

"What?" I ask. "It's way more than seventy dollars—that much I do know."

"All together, the total came to $497.83."

"What did you just say?"

"I have it written down right here, because I couldn't believe it either."

I put my hand across my chest and just watch one of them Utah Jazz guys make a three-pointer.

"Where's the pharmacy, Lewis?" Paris is asking.

"Just a few blocks from here."

"What about the grocery store?"

"They're one and the same," he says.

"Then let's go," she says. "We'll be back in a half-hour or so. Anything in particular you need or want, Mama?"

I just shake my head. She always coming to my rescue. I wonder who comes to hers.

Dingus waves his long arm in the air. "Mom, would you bring back some Diet Pepsi, please?"

"Wait a minute!" I say. "Some Velveeta cheese and tortilla chips would sure be nice. We could have us some nachos while we watch the game—right, Dingus?"

He winks at me. But his mama is shaking her head like it's about to fly off. "No dairy products for you, Mama. If you want to start feeling better, forget about cheese, milk, and eggs altogether. I have a list of things for you to avoid. Anything else you can think of?"

"Why don't you just tell me what I need?"

"Granny, I forgot," Dingus says. "I can't eat that cheese either. It gets stuck between my braces and it's too hard to get out."

"We'll be right back," Paris says, turning. "And, Lewis, I'm warning you. If you so much as mention Donnetta I'll stop the car and you'll walk back. Got it?"

He looks confused. "You're the one who just brought her up. I wasn't even thinking about that woman."

"Just a minute," she says, and reaches inside her purse, and sprinkles out a white pill into her palm.

"What's that?" I ask.

"An Advil. I feel a headache coming on."

"I ain't never seen no white Advil," I say. "What strength are they?"

"Strong," she says. "Lewis, are you ready?"

"I've been ready. And just for the record, my mind is so far away from my ex-wife I can't even begin to get you to understand."

"Then don't try," Paris says, and I just slide my hand from my chest to cover my mouth so nobody will see me laughing.

I guess we all musta dozed off again during halftime, 'cause the next thing I know, Paris and Lewis is back and it seem like they just left. Dingus is laid out on the floor, his red arms spread out like wings of a hawk. He taking up most of my living space, so that his mama have to step over him in order to get to the kitchen, but first she gives him a little kick, and he looks up. "Would you help us get some things out of the car, and bring our bags in?"

"Sure, Mom. Where's my granny?" he asks, looking around.

"Right here," I say from behind him. He looks up at me, nods, and smiles.

"Where's your bowling ball, Granny? I dreamed we were all bowling."

"In there, under the bed, I guess. I can't think about no bowling for at least another couple of weeks."

He stops to watch a play. Shanice walks out the bedroom wiping sleep from her eyes. She still ain't changed them shorts. She waves hi to Dingus. "Where's my mom?" she asks me.

"On the phone with George, I guess. She's been talking to somebody since we starting watching the game."

Shanice rolls her eyes 360 degrees.

"Why you trippin' so hard, Niecie?" Dingus asks, pushing the door open when he sees Paris coming to get him.

"I ain't trippin'," she says in a nasty voice.

"I believe you are. And you best to watch the direction of those eyes," he says, and out he goes.

"Come sit over here next to your granny," I say, motioning to her. She sits down at the end of the couch. I pat the cushion in between. "Come down here and sit close to me."

"Why?"

"Shanice, are you talking to me, your granny, or to somebody else?"

Seems like she comes to or something, and then eases down close enough where her arm touches mine. She looks straight ahead at the TV but I know she don't watch no basketball. "Shanice?"

"Yes," she says without turning to look at me.

"Look at me."

She turns her face toward mine in slow motion, and when she's facing me, now I can see that something done happened to this child again. That's what's in her eyes. Sadness, and some kind of hurt. Right now they red and glassy, like she been crying or slept real hard. But wait a minute. If I ain't mistaken, is that beer I smell coming from her breath? This can't be right. Her mama poured that beer down the drain. Even still, I know beer when I smell it. "You okay?"

"I'm fine. Just tired and hungry. Aunt Paris, did you get anything fun to eat or only healthy stuff?"

"I got some halibut," she says.

"I talked her into buying some pork chops," Lewis says with a little chuckle. He's standing at the screen door, puffing on another cigarette and sipping on a bottle of something. He always sounds cheery after his first couple of drinks, but his happy thermometer drops to depressing in a matter of minutes after that third one.

"What are you drinking now?" I ask.

"Just a cooler. It's only seven percent."

"But this is the third one. You forgot to mention that," Paris yells from the kitchen. "Ma, have you heard from Charlotte?"

"I can hold my liquor, Paris, thank you very much. I'm not a child, so you don't have to spill the beans on me to Mama like you used to. I think we've all grown up, if I'm in the right house."

"Shut up, Lewis," she says.

"She ain't coming," I say. "She still scared to fly. Said she'd have to take a train or something. I don't care. She said Al might be going on some kinda vacation. I don't know what she talking about."

"Janelle! Hurry up and get off the phone. I need to use it!" Paris yells.

"Where's my prescriptions?" I ask.

"In here," Paris says in a much lower voice from the kitchen. "I'll make dinner. And trust me. It'll be something everybody can recognize and eat."

"I'll get them for you, Granny," Shanice says, apparently looking for any excuse to get up. Janelle finally comes out the bathroom with the portable in her hand. She looks like she just lost something. She hands it to Paris.

"What's wrong with you, girlfriend?"

Janelle just shakes her head. "Nothing."

"Well, do something besides look pitiful. Help me. Make the salad."

"Ma, Daddy just pulled up," Lewis says.

I pop five of the seven pills with a sip of Diet Pepsi, which I cannot stand the taste of, that Dingus set on the cocktail table. I hope one in particular works fast. "Shit," I grumble.

"Why'd you say that, Ma?" Janelle asks.

"None of your business."

"I haven't seen Gramps since last year," Dingus says, and gets up from the floor. I see Lewis shake his daddy's hand from the top step, and then Cecil pats him on the shoulder while he moves toward the door. When he comes inside, you'd swear he was Santa Claus or something, the way his grandkids rush over and give him big burly hugs. Dingus is taller than Cecil, of course, and Shanice ain't too far behind.

"Hello there, everybody," he says.

"Hi, Daddy," Janelle says, and gives him a kiss.

Here come Paris. She stands on a spot and don't move. "Hi, Daddy. Glad you found time to stop by."

"Stop by?" Janelle says.

I forgot she don't know.

"I wanted to make sure the old gal was all right, and not over here by herself."

"By herself?" Janelle says.

"I told you Lewis was here, didn't I, Cecil?"

"No, you didn't."

"Did I miss something?" Janelle asks.

"You didn't tell the kids?" Cecil asks me.

"Not all of 'em."

"Tell us what?" Janelle says.

"Isn't it obvious, Ma?" Shanice says. "Gramps doesn't live here anymore. Hel-lo."

"Since when?"

Poor thang. She looks so confused. "Around New Year's."

I don't think this house ever been this quiet. Everybody just kinda don't move, and Cecil look like he wish he could disappear. But ain't nowhere to run. Serve his ass right.

"Daddy, did Ma put you out, or you left?"

Cecil just kinda look Southern pitiful and say, "Talk to your mama about that."

"Well, when are you coming back home?" Janelle still don't get it.

This time he don't even bother to answer.

"Why don't you tell them when George is coming back?" Shanice blurts out.

"Where's George?" I ask.

"Where's Charlotte?" Cecil asks.

Paris grabs the phone and starts dialing her number. This is getting too deep for me. "Where's my inhaler?"

"I'll get it, Granny," Dingus says, and heads for the bedroom. Cecil still don't know what to do: you can see he trying to decide if he should sit or keep standing. "And bring me that brown envelope from off the bed, too, would you, baby?"

"The one that says IRS on it?"

"That's the one," I say and eyeball Cecil. It's easy to see now that he wished he hadda come another time.

"Charlotte?" Paris says. "Yes. We're all here. At Mama's. She got home today, but I guess the fact that she almost died doesn't seem to faze you all that much, does it?"

This is a big mistake: calling her, and using that tone of voice. She ain't gon' like it. Knowing we her audience, too?

"Yes. And what kind of vacation is Al going on? I figured as much. You don't have to raise your voice, Charlotte. I did not. And stop swearing at me. All I'm saying is that Mama could've died and you should have your selfish ass here like the rest of us!"

Paris takes the phone away from her ear and just looks at it. "She hung up in my face."

"Surprise, surprise," Janelle says.

"Bitch," Paris says.

"Where is George?" I ask Janelle.

"He's gone."

"Gone where?"

"I don't know, and don't care."

"Well, look. How long you all gon' be in town?" Cecil asks.

"Just for the weekend. Why? Do you want to invite us over to your place?" Paris asks.

"Can't you stay for dinner, Daddy?" Janelle asks.

"No, he can't," I say.

"I can't, sugar," Cecil says. "I gotta get to work."

"Work?" Janelle says.

"You might not be too familiar with the term: work," Paris says to her in a sarcastic way. She really is just trying to be funny. I think.

Dingus is back down on the floor, just listening, his head moving back and forth like he at a tennis match. He's got a smirk on his face, like this shit is better than *The Young and the Restless*. He's about right. Shanice done disappeared into the kitchen. I hear the refrigerator open. Ain't nobody thinking about it but me. Gotta watch her. It's beer today, scotch tomorrow. Gotta talk to my granddaughter. Get her to understand. Get Janelle to do something.

"Go straight to hell, Paris," Janelle says. "Daddy?"

"I work security at Harrah's."

"You think that's smart, being inside a casino for all those hours?" Paris asks. She should stop.

"I manage okay."

"Paris," I say, "is your pill working yet?"

"Not quite."

"Maybe you should take another one."

"Why?"

"Because you still seem a little testy."

"Testy?"

"That's what I just said."

"Then maybe I should just cook and not say a word."

"No, wait. Cecil, didn't you say you had some good news?" I ask.

"Me?"

"No, your uncle."

"It can wait," he says.

"No, come on, Daddy," Paris says, "we would love to hear some good news, wouldn't we, you guys?" She looks around at everybody until it seems like they all agree.

"Good news is always worth sharing," Janelle says.

"I could sure use some," I say.

"Me, too," Lewis says from the front porch. I'm beginning to wonder if he gon' sleep out there.

Cecil looks nervous, worried, scared. Maybe his news ain't good. He just said he had some news. He didn't exactly say it was good news, now, did he? Hell, I didn't mean to put him on the spot. Maybe it's private business. Between me and him. "Tell me later and then I'll tell the kids," I say. He looks relieved. Good, I think, 'cause things was getting a little too thick around here. All I know is that I'm home. I'm alive. And happy to see my kids and grandbabies. We need to break this up some. Lighten up. "Hey, did I mention that I dreamt about fish last night?"

"No," Paris says, her hands pressed hard on her hips, like she can't wait for Cecil to leave so she can go on in the kitchen and do her business.

"Yes, you did," Janelle says.

"Well, I gotta be going," Cecil says.

"What's up with dreaming about fish?" Dingus asks.

"It means somebody supposed to be pregnant or something like that, doesn't it?" Lewis asks, standing at the screen door again.

"It most certainly does," I say, and if I wasn't on so much medication right now, I'd swear that Janelle and Cecil, and even Paris and Dingus, all look like they just seen God or a goddamn ghost.

Ten Thousand Things

"Did you like the halibut, Mama?"

"It was different, that much I can say. Seem like it had kind of a vinegary taste. I ain't complaining, but I was sure in the mood for some fried pork chops smothered in gravy."

"I don't fry anything, Mama."

"Of course you don't, Paris. Anyway, what I really liked was the dressing on that salad and that crumbilay stuff you made for dessert."

I chuckle. "It's called crème brûlée, Mama."

I'm lying next to her in her bed. I'm surprised she's still up. After all, it's almost one o'clock in the morning. We've been playing Trivial Pursuit since right after dinner. Lewis won. Mama just watched. She abandoned us a little after eleven. The TV is on with no sound. We're half under the covers and half out. Everybody else is asleep, except Lewis. I hear the TV out there and the ice in his glass clinking. His mind is probably flitting from one thing to another, because he hasn't learned to compartmentalize like the rest of us. I feel sorry for my brother, really. He's so smart he's dumb. Sometimes I feel like I've got too many circuits going at once, too, but I unplug a few in order to get the pace down to a manageable level so I can do one thing without thinking about the ten thousand other things I still have to do. I often wonder, will I ever have a day with nothing on my "to-do" list?

"Paris?" Mama's over near the edge, and I can just barely

feel her body heat. I slide closer to her, which I can tell makes her somewhat uncomfortable, but I take hold of her arm so she can't squirm away.

"Yes, Mama."

"Is the mattress all right?"

"It's very comfortable," I say.

"I had it on layaway for the longest. It's a Sealy, you know."

"It's nice."

"I got a bed and dresser on layaway at Thomasville. You ever bought anything from them?"

"Nope."

"For my money, they got the best layaway plan in town. You can take your time and pay 'em twenty dollars a month, they don't care. And their furniture ain't cheap. It's good quality and very sophisticated. I love that store."

"I'm glad you do, Mama."

"I need to do *something* in here, but it might not be worth my time and energy."

"What do you mean by that?"

"I don't feel like talking about it right now."

"Okay," I say. The bed, chest of drawers, and dresser in this room are clearly from the seventies but everything in here is well kept. The sheer cream curtains have been starched and ironed. I know she did them herself. Mama's always been clean and neat. I like that about her. Her perfume bottles are all lined up on the dresser, even though some are thirty years old and only full of fumes; there are round containers of dusting powder with various paisley prints and flowers with mint-green vines swirling around the curves; tons of lipsticks, some of them I know are at least five or six years old because I can spot about ten pink Fashion Fair tubes that Janelle, Charlotte, and I gave her for her fiftieth birthday. There's no sign of jewelry, because, even though most of it's costume, Mama still keeps it hidden in her drawers, between all her "raggedy" underwear (and she's got stacks of them), because that's where a thief probably wouldn't look. Daddy gave her a diamond so small that when it fell out she didn't even notice. It's in the box with the fake stuff.

The walls are an old eggshell color that's yellowing by the minute, and on top of that they're bare except for two identical seascape prints she got from a garage sale. The carpet is an atrocious rusty brown. Always been ugly, but she works around it. I wish I could buy her a new house, full of brand-new furniture, with shiny hardwood floors, area rugs from some other country, and at least one original piece of art.

"Thank you for coming," she says.

"You don't have to thank me."

"I know. But I already feel better, knowing y'all are here."

"That's what kids are for, Mama. To give you some degree of comfort."

"I wish Charlotte felt that way."

"She does, Mama."

"Who you kidding? I think she like adding to my misery, but it's okay. Three out of four ain't bad."

"Charlotte's always been jealous of anybody you show some attention to besides her. In your heart, you should know she doesn't really want to hurt you, Mama."

"All kids don't like their parents, you know. And ain't no rule that say you gotta like your kids either. Anyway, I don't wanna talk about her. I want you to listen to me and listen to me good, you understand?"

"Okay."

"And take everything at face value."

"Mama, please don't let this be one of those if-I-die-today-or-tomorrow speeches. Please?"

"Be quiet, Paris. You can call it anything you wanna call it, I don't care. Just pay attention, would you, Miss Know-It-All?"

"Okay, I'm listening."

"This attack scared the hell out of me."

"They all should, Mama."

"No, baby. This one was a doozy."

"But you're still here," I say, trying my damnedest to sound positive even though my cheery voice is fake.

"Yeah, but I can't keep doing this."

"Doing what?"

"Fighting."

"What do you mean, 'fighting'?"

"Every time I feel one of these things coming on, I panic, and that's what makes it harder and harder to breathe, and it's taking all the strength I have to keep doing it."

"So what are you saying, Mama?"

"I'm saying that, if the day should come when I can't fight no more, I wanna make sure you see to it that the other kids don't completely fuck up their lives. They need guidance, Paris, and you might have to be the one to give it to 'em."

"Me?"

"Yes, you."

"Just because I'm the oldest?"

"Naw, that ain't the only reason. You got good sense. And you using it the way I always prayed all of you would, and you also doing something the rest of us ain't."

"What's that?"

"Making money."

"Oh, really. Well, first of all, Mama, you might want to consider giving up this gloomy notion of dying altogether, because, as soon as you get on this new diet—if you can force yourself to give up that stupid beer, among other things—and you go see a holistic doctor instead of these pill pushers, you'll see how you can learn to manage this disease."

She's shaking her head like I don't get it and is squeezing my hand hard. Too hard.

"Lots of people are leading productive, active lives who have asthma. Look at Jackie Joyner-Kersee. She's a heptathlete, a gold-medalist, an Olympian."

"Yeah, well, she's also young."

"Mama, you're not old. You're only fifty-five."

"I won't be fifty-five for two and a half more weeks. Anyway, I don't wanna run or jump no-damn-where. So more power to that girl. I would just like to walk up a flight of stairs or to the corner and back without getting short of breath."

"I know."

"No, you don't know."

"Okay," I say, not sure what to say next, but this is what comes out of my mouth: "Well, Mama, let's just say that, hypothetically speaking, if something were to happen to you and I became the so-called guide, as you say, my question to you is this: who's going to be there to help guide me?"

"Me," she says, matter-of-factly. And then releases her grip.

I'm not enjoying this conversation. Don't like the topic or the tone, and especially the direction it's going, so I decide to change it. "What's the real deal with Daddy, Mama?"

"We ain't talking about Cecil right now, are we?"

I shake my head.

"Look, Paris. I ain't trying to scare you. I could live another two years or another twenty. You just never know. I been meaning to get some things out in the open in case something was to happen to me, so somebody would be prepared."

"I feel lucky. Okay, Mama. I get it. Now, can we talk about living for a few minutes?"

"Okay," she says. "What do *you* want?"

"What do you mean, what do I want?"

"For yourself."

"I've got just about everything I need."

"I beg to differ with you, baby."

"What's that supposed to mean?"

"You got blessed with Dingus. We both know that. But, Paris, it's written all over your face: something's missing in your life. Food and money ain't quite cutting it, can't you see that?"

Why does she have to go here? I said I was going to put

everybody in their place when I got here, didn't I? But this doesn't exactly feel like the wisest time to chastise my mother, so I just say: "I'm doing the best I can."

"That's not true. You trying too hard to do all the right things, to fill up all your blank spaces. But you filling up them holes with bullshit. Stuff that don't make you feel good inside. It look good from the outside, and that's why you getting headaches and taking pills. But ain't no pill in the world can cure what you got."

"And what is it that I've got?"

"Heartache."

"Heart what?"

"You can spell it any way you want to, but it still boils down to plain old loneliness."

She does not know what she's talking about. "I'm not lonely, Mama. And when was my heart supposed to have been broken?"

She looks at me like I'm crazy. I guess she would be referring to Nathan.

"You can't fool me, Paris. I brought you into this world. I can see right through you. What you need to do is drop your guard and let somebody find the latch that opens the gate to your heart. You'll feel a whole lot better."

"What makes you think it's *not* open?"

" 'Cause you shooting out radar that screams: 'Don't talk to me, don't bother me, I'm fine, I can manage all by myself. I don't need nobody!' "

"I think you're overstating the point, Mama. But what's bad about managing on my own?"

"Nothing, Paris. But stop focusing so much on Dingus. That boy's already on his way. You've done a good job raising him, and he's gon' be all right. Now put some of that energy into you."

"How?"

"Go out. Do something stupid sometime. Something silly,

something that tickle you—hell, something that don't make no damn sense."

"Could you be more specific, Oprah?"

"Join a club."

"What kind of club?"

"Hell, I don't know! They got clubs for everything."

"What about you, Mama?"

"We ain't talking about me now, is we, or are we?"

"No. So let's make this a two-way session. Try this on: I'm not the one who's fifty-four and seven-eighths years old with a husband who has moved in with some welfare hoochie and left me in a tacky little house by myself that from what I gather the IRS has a lien against, and I didn't just get out of the hospital after having a severe asthma attack, and I'm not the one who doesn't have a major source of income except Social Security. So—what kind of changes do *you* have in store, Miss V?"

"Well, first of all, if you gon' tell it, get the shit right. This house got more than a lien against it, baby. They gon' take this hellhole in a hot minute."

I get a lump in my throat. "Take it?"

"You heard me."

"Well, what do we need to do to stop it?"

"We ain't doing nothing. I don't wanna live in this dump no more."

"But what about Daddy, Mama? Are you sure he's not coming back?"

"I don't want him back."

"We've heard this before."

"Anyway, do you wanna hear some of the things I wanna do or not?"

"Yes, I do."

"Okay," she says, her tone softening. "I would love to go on that cruise with Loretta."

"Sounds good."

"I wanna get some decent dentures. A tight fit, so they don't click when I talk."

"You should have only the best teeth, Mama."

"I'm serious, Paris! I hate these damn things. They make my gums sore."

"Sorry," I say, smirking and glad it's dark in here.

"And I'm gon' lose some weight. At Jenny Craig."

I want to laugh when I think of Mama doing a commercial for Jenny or starving on those miniature meals, but I know she's serious, so I just say, "Uh-huh."

"And I wanna live in a real house with a garage-door opener, but a condo would be just fine, as long as I can have enough yard to plant a handful of something."

"Sounds like a plan to me."

"Now, this last one might seem outlandish," she says. I assume because the others haven't.

"What's that?"

"I want a brand-new car. I don't care what kind it is. Did you know that me and your daddy ain't never had a new car?"

"Nope. But, Mama, I don't mean to put a hole in your balloon, but how are you planning to get all this stuff?"

"I don't know."

"You have to have some idea."

"I might start a day care."

"A what?"

"You heard me."

"I thought kids got on your nerves."

"They do. I could just run it. I wouldn't necessarily have to take care of 'em."

"Good idea. But you have to get a license."

"So I'll get one."

"You have to take classes."

"I can read."

"I know that."

"Plus, I been playing the lottery and been hitting for four

numbers off and on this past year, and my palm keep itching which means something's gon' happen in the very near future. I just feel it."

"So—I'm assuming you'll be alive when you hit the lottery?"

"You go to hell, Paris."

"I'll keep my fingers crossed for you, Mama. But, in all seriousness, I might have a few extra dollars to spare. After my taxes are paid this quarter I'll check with my accountant and see what I can do to help you out in a few of those areas."

"That would be nice, but don't strain yourself."

"Well, I have to do something."

"You ain't *gotta* do nothing."

"But I *can,* Mama."

"Okay, can I ask you something else?"

"No, Mama."

"Why don't you wanna do that television program?"

"Because it would be too time-consuming."

"What ain't? It sounds like a whole lotta money."

"That's why so many people are miserable as it is, doing it just for the money. And it's not as much money as you think."

"Well, what about that cookbook idea?"

"I'm working on it. I just need time to develop the proposal. It's more to it than handing over a bunch of recipes, Ma."

She rolls over and, out of habit, reaches for her inhaler and takes a few puffs, then rolls back over and looks up at the ceiling. She's quiet for a few minutes. I'm listening to the silence. "Janelle is going through something. I think she done found out that George been doing what I suspected he was doing all along."

"What makes you say that?"

"Can't you see how grown Shanice is looking, not to mention acting?"

"I didn't notice one way or the other."

"She's different."

"She's going through puberty, Mama."

"Puberty, my ass. Somebody done messed her puberty all up, and his name is George or my name ain't Viola Price."

"So what should we do?"

"I don't know. But if I tell you something, I want you to keep it to yourself."

"All right."

"I smelled liquor on Shanice's breath today."

This makes me sit up. "What?"

"You heard me. I *know* it was beer."

"Mama, she's only twelve years old."

"Wake up, Paris. Something is bothering that child. My instincts is telling me that things ain't right in their house. I just wanna make sure you watch out for her, 'cause if Janelle's too goddamn stupid and put that man before her own daughter—if and when the shit do hit the fan—promise me, before anybody else gets her, you'll take care of Shanice."

"I thought Janelle said George was gone?"

Mama just sucks on her teeth, then takes them out and sets them on the table. I think I *will* get her a decent set.

"How far could he go?" Mama says. "It's his house."

"Well, I'll ask her about it in the morning."

Mama grabs my arm. "I just asked you not to say nothing about Shanice and no drinking."

"I won't. I'll ask her why George is gone and if she's planning to take him back, if he comes back."

"He'll be back," she says, and rolls over on her side. "I'm going to sleep now. So, if you got something else to say, you'll be talking to yourself. Good night."

It's hard to get to sleep. I toss and turn and then slide off the bed, reach for my purse, and feel inside until I find my pills. I almost step on Dingus when I go out to the living room. He's rolled up inside a few sheets and a small flannel blanket Mama must've taken from an airplane. Lewis is conked out on the couch. From the kitchen, I hear a glass clink against the inside of the sink. Shanice appears, in the same shorts she had on earlier and a light-pink tank top. "What are you doing up so late?" I ask. She of course is surprised to see me.

"I was thirsty. Needed some water," she mumbles fast.

I walk over to her and she beelines it toward the room she and Janelle are sharing. "Wait a minute," I say.

"What is it, Aunt Paris?" Her back is toward me.

"Why are you in such a hurry?"

"I have to go to the bathroom."

"All right, then. Good night."

" 'Night," she says, and dashes into the hall bathroom. I hear the faucet come on and, a few minutes later, the toilet flush. In the kitchen I see a clear blue glass lying on its side in the middle of the stainless-steel basin. I place the pill on my tongue while I pick up the glass and take a whiff. It hurts when I smell that Tropical Breeze cooler, but I swallow the pill dry and go on back to bed.

I wake up to the smell of bacon and loud rap music. Mama's already up. I don't feel like moving, really. There's a tap tap tap at the door. "I'm up," I say.

"Can I come in?" Janelle asks.

"No, stay out there and talk to me through the door."

She eases it open and the phone rings at the same time. I hear Mama yell, "I got it!" from the kitchen. I look at the clock. It's just barely eight-thirty.

"What's up?" I ask. Janelle looks sullen, despite the white sweatsuit. Her hair is in a ponytail and she's got on dark-pink lipstick. With that against her dark skin, she looks like a Somalian Barbie. If I'm not mistaken, it also looks like she could stand to lose a few pounds. I dare not say anything or she'll freak out. "Sit," I say. "No, wait. Come on into the bathroom while I brush my teeth."

"Dingus!" Mama yells. "A girl name Meagan is calling you!"

I stop dead in my tracks and Janelle bumps into me from behind. Her boobs feel bigger.

"Paris, can I talk to you for a minute?"

"Just a second." I go over to the door to see if Dingus is still asleep. He is. Lewis is nowhere in sight. If I didn't have an audience I'd get on that phone and put this little bitch in her place and then maybe kick the hell out of my son for putting us both in such a precarious situation. On the ride here I was too busy worrying about Mama to bring the subject up, and even though it was taking up a big chunk of my mind, I decided to wait until we leave to deal with this issue. Now is not the time or the right circumstances to mention it, because not only would Mama be heartbroken, but this kind of news could put her back in the hospital. I still give him a stiff kick in his ass. "Ouch! Ma, dag! What's wrong?"

"What's so important that this girl has to call you here?"

"Who?"

"Meagan. That's who."

"I don't know."

"You and I both know you know. And I suggest you handle it now or suffer the consequences."

"I don't have a clue about what you're talking about, Ma. Granny, would you ask her if I can call her back later, please?"

"You ain't making no long-distance calls on *this* phone. Period. Paris, come talk to this girl, would you?"

"No!" Dingus says. "Never mind. I'll talk to her."

"What we doing today, Paris? Wanna go to the mall?"

"Mama, are you supposed to be walking and doing stuff already?"

"I feel good. I don't wanna sit in here all day looking stupid. We need to do something. What time y'all leaving?"

"My plane leaves early tomorrow morning."

"Please get a seat on it for your brother."

"Where is he, by the way?"

"Said he went to work. And don't ask."

I shake my head and head back toward the bedroom, but stop at the door when I hear Mama say, "All I know is, he better bring my damn car back in one piece."

"You shouldn't let him drive it, Mama."

"I know. But it's too far and too frigging hot to walk anywhere, and with his arthritis acting up and all."

"His what?"

"Maybe he ain't been lying about it. His right knee is all puffed up, and you should see his elbows and wrists, Paris. They look like big knots. Even two of his fingers is getting crooked."

"Really? I just thought he's been faking these past couple of years. That he's just been complaining to get some sympathy and using it as an excuse so he wouldn't have to work."

"I saw it with my own eyes."

"Then why doesn't he go to a doctor?"

"He said he's been to three or four, but all they do is give him this medicine that messes up his stomach. He said Tylenol works, sometimes. And he took four of 'em at one time. Why don't you give him one or two of your *Advils*?"

Is she trying to be funny? "I'll ask him if he wants to try one when he gets back. Where's Shanice?"

"Still sleep!" Janelle screams from the bathroom. She's sitting on the edge of the bathtub when I get back, fidgeting with Mama's shower curtain with tropical fish swimming behind her. "I guess she was beat."

"I *know* she was," I say, and get out a brand-new toothbrush from under the sink.

"What are we going to do for Mama's birthday?"

"That's what you wanted to talk to me about?"

"Yes."

"That's it?"

"Well, not exactly."

"Then what?" I ask.

"First, do you have any ideas what we could do?"

"Well, I was thinking about asking if she wanted to come up for a few weeks, which we know the answer to that already. Plus, I might have to go to London for four or five days. She could hang out with Dingus, maybe spend a week with you."

"I'm not sure what my situation is going to be like yet."

"Don't worry about it. Anyway, what's the deal with George? Have you guys really split up?"

"Probably."

"What happened?"

"I don't want to talk about it."

"Why not?"

"Because I'm still far too pissed."

"He didn't touch Shanice, did he?"

"No," she says, dryly.

"You wouldn't lie about some shit like this, would you, Janelle, seriously?"

"No, I wouldn't. But I don't feel like talking about George right now, Paris, okay?"

"Are you pregnant?" She looks shocked by my question.

"What would make you ask that?" Her eyes are black and glassy. Like she's going to break down any minute.

"Well, you look like you've gained weight and your boobs are bigger."

"So what? Yours are, too."

"Yeah, but I bought mine."

"What?"

"I got implants."

"When? Why didn't you tell me? Let me see!"

I lift up my pajama top and show these beauties off.

"Damn," she says, staring. "They're humongous!"

"They are not. I'm a 34-D. That's it." I cup them with both hands, then let them go. They don't move.

Janelle's hands are over her mouth. "How come you didn't tell me?"

"You don't tell me all your business, now, do you?"

"The important stuff."

"So are you or aren't you?" I say, dropping my top.

"I don't believe this, Paris. How much did it cost?"

"About five thousand, and it was worth every penny. I can actually wear tank tops again without a bra."

The phone rings. "Somebody get that!" Mama yells from the kitchen.

"I'll get it," I say, and walk over to the bedside table and answer it. "Hello," I say.

"Yeah, Paris. This is Lewis. I had a little mishap. Nothing to be too worried about, but . . ."

"Where are you, Lewis?"

When I hear him sigh, I know immediately something's wrong. "Where are you?"

"In jail."

I switch the phone to my other ear. "What are you doing in jail?"

"Driving without a license."

"That's all?"

"And being under the influence."

"The influence of what?"

"Alcohol."

"It's only eleven o'clock in the morning, Lewis!"

"I know what time it is. I just went down to the place where the guy said he was gon' hire me, and he wasn't there, and this other guy was waiting on him, too, and he had a taste, and I started sipping with him, and then he decided not to wait and asked me for a lift home, and I gave him one, and we got stopped."

"Where's Mama's car?"

"They impounded it."

"She's going to be pissed."

"I know, but could you or somebody come bail me out, please?"

"Shit, Lewis. Mama just got home yesterday and look what you're doing."

"I don't need a lecture right now, Paris. Can you or can you not come and get me out?"

"How much is bail?"

"Two thousand."

"Dollars?"

"All you have to do is put up two hundred. I'll pay you back, don't worry."

"Yeah, sure. I'll hold my breath. Give me an hour."

"Make it two. I have to stay here for at least four hours. They wanna make sure I'm sober, which, believe me, I am. Thanks, sis."

"And I've got nothing but love for you, too," I say and hang up.

"I heard," Janelle said. "Don't tell Mama, just go get him."

"So?" I say, looking at her stomach.

"No, I am not pregnant," she says.

"Come with me," I say.

"Okay," she says, but doesn't move.

"Can I ask you another question?"

"I'm listening," she says.

"Have you noticed anything different about Shanice's behavior?"

"I certainly have," she says. "And I'm going to get her some counseling."

"So you've caught her doing it?"

"Doing what?"

"Drinking."

"Drinking what?" Janelle asks, stunned.

Uh-oh, Paris. You and your big fucking mouth. "Well, maybe I'm mistaken, but I think she was enjoying a wine cooler last night."

"You must be crazy, Paris."

"Janelle, Mama smelled beer on her breath yesterday."

"And what the hell is this supposed to mean? Mama's been giving all of her grandkids a sip off her beer for years. So maybe she took a little sip. All kids experiment. Big deal."

"Is something going on at home that could be bothering her?"

"Well, her dad's gone."

"George is not her *dad,* and everybody knows she can't stand him, Janelle, so I doubt if his leaving would throw her off kilter."

"Well, it's nothing the two of us can't handle," she says. "I'll be ready in fifteen minutes." When she gets up, Mama's shower curtain pops out from three of the loops. I guess I just must look stupid to her.

"Ma, can I go with you to get Uncle Lewis out of jail?" Dingus asks from the living room.

"Shut up," I whisper loudly.

"Where y'all going?" Mama asks.

"To get something at the mall."

"I said I wanted to go, too."

Shit. Shit. Shit. I look at Dingus and make a motion like I'm slicing his neck off. "Okay, Mama, but first Janelle and I need to make a quick stop, and you can't come with us because it's a surprise."

"What kind of surprise?" she asks, coming into the living room, wiping her hands on a yellow dish towel. She's already dressed, in her pink cotton slacks and pink polo shirt, white leather Keds. Her hair is a mess. Square patches of dry braids fill her head, and she doesn't have on any makeup. She's probably been waiting for me or Janelle to do it.

"If we told you, it wouldn't be one, now, would it?"

"I love surprises," she says.

"We all do, Mama," I say, "we all do." And on that note, I decide that we will rush to get our stupid brother out of jail and get her car out of hock and then find out where that Thomasville furniture store is and get her stuff out of layaway and hope they can deliver it sometime today, and then maybe we can look for a black beauty shop that will deep-condition and maybe cut and perm her hair, and we can come back and take her to Red Lobster for lunch before we hit the mall, and who knows, if we have any time left, maybe we can take her to test-drive something new.

Liquid Jesus

Okay. So I messed up. I shouldn'ta never took a squig off Kirk's bottle. Plus, I didn't even know the dude. He could have a disease. Many diseases. What the hell. Now I gotta get ready for my sisters to lecture me all the way back to Mama's. They don't understand. And ain't no way for me to get them to understand. I don't want to have to drink, but while I was out here waiting for this dude all I was thinking was that here's an opportunity for me to make some money, I don't care how much or how little, but enough so that I won't have to ask nobody for nothing. Especially my family.

I don't like to beg. Which is all borrowing really is, when you get right down to it. 'Cause I ain't got it, and somebody else do. The way it usually goes down is that the chances of you ever getting an opportunity to pay it back are slim, 'cause once you start borrowing it's like getting behind in your bills: you hardly ever catch up. First you have to keep track of who lent you some money and how much. But just say one day you get lucky and run into a few extra dollars (which ain't likely). Shit, by that time you've probably forgot how much you even borrowed and who you still owe (unless the person won't let you forget, especially if it was some *real* money, like over a hundred dollars), and if that's the case, since you can't in good conscience decide who to pay first, you just avoid all of 'em for however long it takes you to pay everybody back: never. Of course this means your relationship is damaged forever, because in the back of their mind, you fucked them, showed no respect, took them for granted, or just can't be trusted or depended on. Which also means that when you get into another jam, you can't even twist your mouth to ask for so much as a quarter. This is the reason why I try not to borrow. I'll go to the pawn shop first. But I've done that so many times that I don't have nothing left worth pawning.

As a man, I don't care if I am handicapped, I still want to maintain some level of dignity. Have to set standards for myself, even if I don't live up to 'em. Which is all I'm trying to do. It's just hard. A part of my mind knows exactly what I need to do to get on track, and another part *wants* to do it. Just the way the first part's laying it out. I mean, it's crystal fucking clear. But. There's another part—and, sadly enough, a very small part but it's the piece that seems to have the most power—that says: It's too hard. You're too scared. You ain't never going to amount to nothing no matter how hard you try, no matter what you do. You ain't never going to know what real success feels like. Won't be able to inhale it. Exhale it. Puff on it. No. That little section screams the loudest: You're fucked up, Lewis. Twisted. Far from crazy, but just got too many ideas and not enough of what it takes to execute them. You don't even really know where Point A is any-fucking-way. And how do you know when you reach Point B? Sometimes you don't even realize that one step ain't even a whole step. You just thought you was moving, but you been standing still. I know I ain't been making much progress, so, to stop all them red-hot wires from short-circuiting my whole mind, I shut it up with a drink.

I didn't come all the way to Vegas to go to jail. I just wanted to see if Mama was all right. Say hi to Daddy. Shit, I'm facing a court date here, and possibly more time when I get back to California. I'ma have to stay here with Mama to see when I have to appear and if they put me on probation or make me do a few months in the county jail, but fuck me if they find out about those other DUIs, in California. Shit. This technological

age is good for some things but not when you've got a record.
They can find out the history of your entire life in a matter of
minutes.

I need to send Donnetta a little something. A token. Enough
to be symbolic. But she won't understand what being a little
short represents. She could care less what it means to a man's
ego when he can't take care of his kid. It's too hard trying to get
her—or other people—to understand. So you stop trying.

Damn, there they are. Why did Paris have to bring Dingus?
I don't want him to see me anywhere near this kinda place. It
don't matter whether I'm a criminal or not. It's still jail, any
way you look at it. But, sadly enough, most of these dudes in
here ain't criminals. They're just stupid. Like me. Behind bars
for committing crimes against machines, businesses that rip
people off, or ourselves. Hell, I didn't *do* nothing to nobody. I
was just driving under the influence. I wasn't even close to
being drunk, but I'm glad I didn't hurt nobody, even though I
don't ever get so drunk I can't drive. I'm not that stupid.

The redheaded guy with steel-blue eyes hands me my stuff
in a plastic bag: my beat-up black wallet; my Casio watch that's
got a memory and a calculator; a high-school class ring with a
red stone that this girl gave me as proof of her love; a crushed-
up pack of Kools with three bent cigarettes in it; two red-and-
yellow Tylenol Extra Strength; and ninety-two cents in change.
The dude that gives me the bag look like he's waiting for me to
thank him, but I don't. He ain't doing me no favor.

There's a long buzz, and I push the beige metal door open,
which I take my time doing. Paris got her hands on her hips, but
she lets one side drop. I guess she's trying to act like she ain't
too pissed. Janelle looks like her mind is somewhere else and
she just came along for the ride. I could be anybody. Dingus
walks over to me and puts his arm over my shoulder. "What up,
Uncle Lewis?" He breaks into a smile, showing off those silver
braces. Handsome boy. Smart. Not sure if he knows what the
real deal is, living in the world he lives in, but regardless, he's

a good kid. He's got the rest of his life to learn what's happening in the streets, or avoid 'em altogether.

"I'm all right. Glad to be outta there."

"I hear you," he says.

"Well, at least it's a nice building," Janelle says, looking around at this sterile-ass place. "It doesn't look anything like I thought it would."

I don't bother to respond. I just follow behind them. Paris doesn't say a single solitary word until we're outside, standing next to her blue rental car. It's a Cutlass. I ain't drove one of these in years. "How far away is Mama's car?" she asks.

"Don't worry, Paris," I say. "I'ma pay back all your money. Don't even worry about it."

"I'm not worried, Lewis. I never worry about when you're going to pay me back. Who's keeping tabs? Answer my question, please."

"I don't know. But it can't be that far," I say, and light a cigarette.

"You know you can't smoke that thing in the car, so hurry up," she says. I take two more long drags and then get in the backseat, next to Dingus. Paris whips out her cellular phone and gets directions to the place. It's only a few blocks from here. As usual, she takes care of everything. Janelle follows us in Mama's car. I can see Paris's eyes in the rearview mirror. She is totally disgusted with me, but it ain't her I'm worried about, it's Mama. It's a for-sure lecture. In a few minutes, I'ma have to be fourteen all over again.

"When we get to Mama's," Paris says, "don't you say a solitary word about any jail or her car being impounded, do you understand, Lewis?"

"Yeah. I mean, no. Why not? You mean she don't know?"

"No, she doesn't know. Let me refresh your memory: she just got out of the damn hospital! This is all she needs on her second day home, wouldn't you think?"

Here we go. Rubbing it in my face. I'm the devil. The bad

seed, I guess. I just listen. No sense in arguing with her about nothing. Plus, she's right. Always right. "So—how's business?" I ask.

"What?"

"How's business?"

"Business is fine, Lewis. Stop trying to skip the damn subject."

"I'm not. You made your point. Now, tell me. What's the name of your outfit again? I forget."

"Wild Thyme," she blurts out. "Wild Thyme."

I fall asleep in the backseat. When I open my eyes, we're parked in front of a furniture store. I'm in here by myself. The engine is running. The air conditioner's on. When I see Paris and Janelle coming through the store doors, I close my eyes again, fast. I leave 'em like that, even after they get in. I wonder where Dingus is, but I ain't opening my eyes till we get home. Speaking of home, that's what I need to do: go home. But the big question is how?

"Y'all took long enough," Mama says when we walk in the front door.

"You ready?" Paris asks her.

"I *been* ready," she says, and gets her purse. "Who's going and where exactly are we going?"

"Not me," I say, raising my hand like I'm in school. Paris rolls her eyes at me.

"We're going to the mall. Come on, Shanice."

"I don't wanna go," she says, coming out of the bedroom. That girl got some long legs and she sure don't mind showing 'em off. Janelle oughtta watch that. The wrong eyes'll be on her.

"You're going," Paris says.

"You certainly are," Janelle says from the porch.

"Why don't you want to go to the mall, baby?" Mama asks.

"I don't have any money. Why go to the mall if you can't buy anything?"

Janelle holds up two twenty-dollar bills. Paris holds up two more. My mouth is watering, my palms are itching. They can just reach in their purses and get money like that. Life is good to some people.

Shanice scrunches her shoulders like she's trying to get excited, but anybody can see she ain't.

"Where's Dingus?" Mama asks.

"At a car dealership," Paris says.

"What in the world is he doing at a car dealership?"

"Looking at cars. We'll pick him up on the way," Paris says. "Mama, go on, I need to make a quick phone call."

"Okay," she says, and heads toward the front door. I sit on the couch, waiting for my orders.

"There's going to be a delivery," Paris says, pointing her finger down at me. "Don't drink anything. It's going to be furniture. Let them in and show them which room the stuff goes in."

"I don't know which room whatever is coming goes in."

"I'm about to tell you. It's a bed and dresser. It goes in Mama's room."

"Well, what about her old furniture?"

"Figure it out, Lewis."

"Well, how long do you think you'll be gone?"

"Why?"

"I'm just asking."

"Two or three hours."

"I was thinking about catching the bus home tonight."

"With what?"

I feel my teeth grinding. "What do you mean, with what?"

"You don't have any money. How are you going to catch a bus?"

Why does she have to get so technical? She don't know how much money I got, not really. "I've got almost enough," I say.

"Almost isn't enough, Lewis."

"I know that, Paris. I'm not stupid."

"Tell me something. Have you already forgotten about your court date?"

"No, I have not."

"Well, if you fail to show up, my two hundred dollars is gone."

"I wouldn't do that. Give me some credit."

"Anyway, Mama suggested you fly home with us in the morning."

"I don't like airplanes."

"Get over it," she says. "Besides, it's already done." She turns and leaves. It's already done. Already. Done. What would make her think I want to get on an airplane and sit next to her in close quarters where I have no escape route, and be forced to listen to what I should and shouldn't be doing? I don't think so. As soon as these furniture people get here, I'm outta here. I can figure out a way to get back for my court appearance, but I've got business I need to take care of at home.

I take a long shower, shave, brush my hair a thousand times, put my same clothes back on, go in the kitchen, and microwave myself some Campbell's potato-and-bacon soup. I eat it and then try to figure out what to wash it down with. My eyes zero in on one of those coolers. I decide against it, but before I know it my right hand is unscrewing the top and the cold rim is pressed against my lips. I consider pouring it down the drain, but it ain't but a couple of ounces and it's only 7 percent, so I polish it off, dig a hole in the bottom of the trash under the sink, and bury the bottle.

I get my cigarettes out of my shirt pocket and go sit out on the front porch to smoke it, when this white lady comes strolling up the sidewalk. I think I know who she is. "Hello," I say.

"Hello, son. And you must be Lewis."

"Good guess. And you must be Miss Loretta."

"I am indeed. Where's your mom?"

"Her and my sisters went to the mall."

"Well, she must be feeling much better."

"She is."

"What are you doing sitting out here all by yourself?"

"You want the honest-to-God's truth?"

"Of course."

"I'm in somewhat of a dilemma."

"What kind of a dilemma?" She looks interested, genuinely concerned.

"Well, I'm waiting for some furniture to be delivered for Mama, and I just received a phone call that's somewhat of an emergency and requires that I leave right away to go back to California, but I'm a little short on cash and not exactly sure how to handle this situation."

"Well, how much do you need, Lewis?"

"About forty or fifty dollars, but, Miss Loretta, I'd mail it back to you, I promise I will."

"Don't you worry about that. Is anybody hurt?"

"No, thank goodness."

"Well, I'll just run and get my purse and be right back." And off she goes.

Just then the furniture truck pulls up, and when they get out to ask me where the stuff goes, I realize that Mama's bed is all made up and her dresser is full of stuff and I don't know what to do with it, so I just tell the men to leave everything under the carport in front of Mama's car, where nobody can see it. While they're doing that, Miss Loretta comes back.

"Well, Vy finally got herself a new bedroom set, huh? She's been praying for one for years! See, prayers do get answered."

"Sometimes," I say.

"Here you go, Lewis," she says, handing me three twenties.

"I only needed forty or fifty."

"It's okay. You don't want to get there empty-handed, do you?"

"No, ma'am. Thank you."

"Can I give you a lift anywhere?"

"Would you mind dropping me off at the Greyhound station?"

"Of course not. Just let me get my keys."

On that note, I go in and write a quick note on the first thing I get my hands on, which happens to be a napkin, and place it under a magnet on the refrigerator. Then I lock the front door and pray we don't pass my family on the way.

Before
I Pop

I don't like eating in restaurants that have booths with shellacked wood and the tables have those Western chairs with plaid seat covers and one thick ruffle just to convince you that this is how serious they are. I feel sick. Like I could barf. Mama's chili fries are soaking through that thin white paper and oozing between each red square of the plastic basket they're threatening me from. I lift my chin high enough so I'm looking out past the wooden wall of this dark booth where me, Dingus, Shanice, Paris, and Mama are having what I assume has to be dinner.

Paris outdid herself this time by handing over her Neiman Marcus card to Mama, who refused to look anywhere but the clearance racks. She needed help carrying the bags through the mall out to the parking lot. Then, when we pulled into the Acura dealership, Mama said, "And just what are we doing here?"

"Auntie Paris wants to buy you a car," Shanice blurted out with her big mouth.

"Lord have mercy. I can't take so much excitement in one day. Paris," Mama said, turning to her while reaching in her purse to get out her spray, "I don't need no expensive Acura. But if you just wanna spend this kind of money, then drive down a few more blocks to that Mitsubishi place. I saw a snazzy Galant on that lot that I swear got my name on it. But we ain't gotta do it today. I'm tired and I'm hungry. So can we please stop somewhere and get something to eat?"

"Whatever you want to do, Mama. But keep in mind that we're leaving in the morning, remember?"

"I know, I know. But I ain't had a decent car in ten years; a few more weeks won't kill me. Besides, I don't wanna leave Lewis in my house for too long by hisself."

So we came here. This was Mama's bright idea. I don't even know the name of the place. But I'm sure it's a chain. My chef salad was disgusting and everybody else just had cheeseburgers and fries. Mama and Dingus were the only ones who said yes to the chili.

"I need to go to the bathroom." I'm hoping Mama can hurry to get up, but she seems to be taking her time. I feel a lump of chili at the base of my throat, and pushing it down are pieces of straw chicken, and then, under them, are the Eggo waffles I had for breakfast. All of it's racing to get out. When Mama finally slides off the edge of the seat I can't hold it anymore and there, all over the table and floor, comes my breakfast, lunch, and dinner. Shit.

"What is wrong with you, girl?" Mama asks, while Dingus helps me stand.

"Are you okay, Janelle?" Paris asks. "What all did you eat today?"

But I'm not finished. This time I aim for the floor. Other people are now spectators. My face is hot and throbbing. My stomach hurts. My head aches. I am embarrassed and hope I can explain it away. By the time I feel like I'm finished, I realize that Shanice hasn't moved. She's still sitting in the corner of the booth, leaning her head against the padded plaid wall, looking bored.

"I betcha it's food poisoning," Mama says. "It's a terrible feeling, ain't it, Janelle?"

I just look at her. "I need to find the bathroom," I say.

"I'll take you," Paris says.

"And, Dingus," Mama orders, "call the house and check on your uncle. Tell him we'll be home in ten or fifteen minutes, so whatever he doing that he ain't supposed to be doing, he got time to stop."

"You got it, Granny."

"And, Shanice, is something wrong with you, girl? You better get your behind up and make sure ain't nothing wrong with your mama." I watch my daughter uncross her tightly folded arms and act like it's killing her to come to my aid.

When we get inside the ladies' room, she goes directly into a stall. She does not unzip her denim shorts. She doesn't even sit down. I can see the toes of her platform sneakers pointing toward the toilet; her brown calves pressed against the gray metal door. She's getting on my nerves with this huffy attitude of hers. She thinks the world revolves around her, but it does not. I rinse my mouth out with tap water and lean against the sink. Paris looks me dead in the eye and just says, "Janelle, you can fool Mama, but you can't fool me. You have not been poisoned. You're pregnant or my name isn't Paris. Now, spit it out."

I stand up too fast, holding my right index finger up to my mouth to shush her, shaking my head so fervently I get the spins. Before I know it, she's knocking on Shanice's stall door, and now I see her toes pointing in our direction. "Shanice! Is your mother pregnant or not?"

When that door opens, I'm afraid of what she might say, how she'll look, what she might do. But she just looks at her aunt and says, "I have no idea. Do you need me in here, or are you okay?"

"Go," I say, pointing to the door.

"Hold it a minute," Paris says. "What the hell is going on here?"

"What?" Shanice moans.

"You better watch the tone of your voice," Paris says, and then: "You act like you don't even care."

"I'm just not interested."

"Okay, *stop it!*" I yell. "I might be pregnant, but, then again, I might not be. What difference does it make? I'm a married woman. Would it be a crime if I was?"

"Why don't you ask your husband, the policeman? He knows a lot about crime," Shanice says, and prances out the door.

"Don't ask another question," I say, brushing past Paris.

From behind, I hear her say, "Curious minds just want to know, is this Part Two of *Guiding Light* or *As the World Turns*? All I do know is something ain't right in Kansas."

I can't even muster up a response.

Lewis isn't there when we get back. Mama's car is, because she has the keys. All of us walk around the house as if he might appear, but it's obvious he's gone. Then Dingus says, "Check this out," leaning against the refrigerator. " 'I had to go home. Don't worry about me, please. Glad you feeling better, Ma. Didn't know what to do with all your stuff, so your furniture is under the carport in front of your car. Love, Lewis.' "

"What furniture?" Mama asks.

"He must be crazy!" Paris blurts out. "What about his court date?"

"His what?" Mama yells from the bedroom. "And what furniture is he talking about? I ain't bought no new furniture!" She heads straight for the side door that leads to the carport. Shanice follows her.

"He had a court appearance he forgot about," I yell, giving Paris a shut-your-big-mouth finger for the second time today.

"It's always something with that boy," Mama says. I hear her give out a big yelp and then an "Oooo" and then a "Y'all too much!" and in she comes, with a humongous grin on her face.

"Who did this?"

Paris lies, and points to me. "It was her idea."

"Y'all too good to me, but I love it, I love it, I love it! Thank you, Janelle."

"You're quite welcome," I say, and smile a thank you to Paris. She knows if I could I would.

"And I'll be damned if I'm putting it in this lean-to. Remind me to get some tarp to cover it up. Won't nobody suspect anybody would be stupid enough to leave a brand-new bedroom set outside." She goes back into her bedroom. "Shanice, come unhook Granny's brassiere before I pop. Anyway, Lord only knows how Lewis got home. By hook or by crook, I'll betcha. Dingus, come in here and check your granny's jewelry, would you, baby? Lewis don't know that I put the fake stuff out just for thieves. Look in my middle dresser drawer, under my underwear, and lift the middle stack until you feel a plastic bag with a sock in it. Just tell me if it's still there. And, Janelle, your loving husband left a message for you to call him at home."

"Home?"

"Are you deaf?"

"Are you sure he said 'home'?"

"Come listen for yourself. Nat King Cole also left a message. He wanna know if he can take y'all out to dinner—which is a new one on me—or if y'all wanna do some gambling while you here. He didn't leave no number. Said he'd call back around seven, which is fifteen minutes from now."

"Mama, aren't you the least bit upset about Daddy being gone?"

"Do I look upset?" she says with a smile. I know this is all just part of a façade. She's hiding her pain, just like me. I hate this. All of it. Standing here pretending, as if nothing has happened. That me and my daughter are members of a healthy, loving, tight-knit family unit. That my husband is really a good man. That I couldn't have asked for a better person to share my life with. And what about my daddy? What made him just pack up and leave Mama after almost a half-century? Why do men always seem to do what the hell they want to do when they feel like doing it, without any regard for others, at least not us, the women who do everything for them? And what is the reward for that? Desertion? Cheating? No child support? Abuse of your child?

———

Shanice has flopped down on the sofa next to Dingus. Her head is resting on his shoulder, as if she's tired, but I know she's not. She's wearing makeup. Cinnamon-colored lipstick and a dark, dusty line on her lower lid. I hadn't even noticed it until now. When did she start wearing makeup? And who gave her permission? "Shanice, sit up."

She frowns and then bolts straight up. "What?" she asks, clearly annoyed.

"What's your problem?" Paris asks, from the kitchen. She's fixing something that smells foreign. Lord only knows what it might be.

"Leave that girl alone!" Mama yells from her bedroom.

I walk into her room and sit down next to her on the bed. She has to scoot over. "Mama, I need to ask you a big favor."

"You won't be the first. What is it?"

"Could Shanice stay here with you for a few weeks until I can make some decisions? George and I have been having a few problems and I don't want her subjected to them any more than she has been already."

"What kind of problems y'all having?" she asks, looking out the corner of her eye.

"Not the kind you think, Mama. It's complicated, and Shanice could be a big help to you around here, you know, with Daddy being gone. And that school down the street isn't so bad, is it?"

"You mean you want her to go to school here?"

"She can't just sit around the house all day."

"What Shanice think about this?"

"I haven't asked her yet."

"Asked or told: which is it, Janelle?"

She just has to make this difficult. "Shanice? Would you come here for a minute, please?"

We both sit there and wait for her to appear in the doorway. "Yes?" she says. Her braids are getting frizzy around her hairline, and her roots are looking like tiny black radishes. She needs a touch-up bad.

Before I can even figure out how to frame the question, Mama says, "I understand your mama and George is having some troubles and she thinks it would be better if you stayed here with me for a few weeks, until she can get things worked out. What you think about that?"

Shanice's face lights up. I haven't seen her look this excited in ages. "You mean I don't have to go home with you tomorrow?"

"No," I say.

"Yes!" she exclaims, pushing her elbow down to her knee like Arsenio Hall does on his talk show. "How long can I stay with my granny?"

"I don't know. A few weeks or so."

"That's all? That's not even fair. You want to take me out of school and put me in another one for a few weeks and then go back to my old school? How'm I supposed to know what's going on?"

"Wait a minute! I'm thinking. Just trying to figure this out. It's all happening too fast."

"Can't I stay until the end of the school term?"

"I can't agree to that," I say. "How about until after spring break?"

"You can stay until you start getting on my nerves," Mama says, smiling.

"Thanks, Granny. Can I get you anything?"

"Yeah, a beer," she says, then abruptly, "No. There will be no more beer or booze in this house after today. I'm tired of drinking. You got that?"

"Yes," she says.

"You can make me some tea. That should about do it."

"Ma, what about my stuff?"

"Don't worry. I'll send whatever you need."

"She gon' need some spending money, I can tell you that much, 'cause I'm getting ready to start eating Jenny Craig. And I ain't gon' be doing too much cooking around here."

"I don't mind eating Jenny Craig, Granny."

"Marie Callender's is what you need."

"I'll leave you a check, Mama."

"I can't use no check. The IRS know too much of my business as it is. Just send me a money order when you get home."

"Ma, can you send some of my books?"

"Look, don't go getting too excited, Shanice. This is not permanent by any stretch of the imagination."

"Any amount of time away from him is fine with me."

Mama just picks up the remote control and starts punching. She doesn't want to think she heard what she knows she heard, and I don't want to acknowledge it. "Well, you gon' call him or not?"

"I will when I feel like it, Mama, but right now I don't really have anything to say to him."

Just then the phone rings and I jump off the bed at least five or ten inches. "You get it," Mama says. "It's Tarzan, and right now I'm feeling the same toward him that you claim to be feeling toward old George."

But by the time I pick up the line, Paris has beaten me to the punch in the kitchen. I dread what she might say to Daddy. I just listen. "This is Paris, Daddy. What can we do for you?"

"I was thanking about trying to take y'all out to get something to eat before you all leave."

"That's sweet, but I'm almost finished with dinner; maybe next time."

"Well, y'all don't want to spend a hour or two at the casinos?"

"I'm not big on gambling."

"I'm not much up for it either," I hear myself say.

"Is Lewis there?"

"He went home already," I say.

"Why don't we meet for a drink, Daddy?" Paris asks.

I'm shocked to hear her say this, which I know means she's got something up her sleeve. And I don't know if I want to be there for it.

"I ain't doing much drinking these days, but we can sit at the bar, if that's what you wanna do."

"How about eight, then? I'll meet you right out front of your place of employment. It's Harrah's, right?"

"Yes, it is. I work in security," he says proudly. "That sounds good, baby. Janelle, you coming, too?"

"I'm too tired, Daddy, and, plus, I have to get up early and drive home."

"Then why don't you talk to him now?" Paris says and hangs up. I feel like a fool. I have nothing to say to him. Well, I do, but I don't exactly know how to put it, so I just ask something I never got an answer for: "When are you coming home, Daddy?"

Mama hits me on my shoulder with her fist so hard I feel a lump forming, so I get off the bed and pull the cord out of her reach. She's shaking her head back and forth, and at the same time listening carefully to the introduction of all three *Jeopardy!* contestants as if she's going to be quizzed about their biographical information one day.

"We might have to talk about this another time," he says. "I just wanted to spend a little time with you all while you was here."

"Where do you live?"

"In an apartment."

"What kind of an apartment?"

"It's the projects," Mama interjects, her eyes still glued to the TV.

"A everyday apartment."

"Do you live alone?"

"Not exactly."

"What does that mean?"

"I live with a friend."

"Male or female?"

He clears his throat. "Female."

"She on welfare and I heard she some kinda alcoholic," Mama says, switching the channel to *Wheel of Fortune*, where she will never in a million years guess a puzzle. We've played together too many times.

"Are those kids I hear in the background?"

"Yeah, sure is. Three of 'em."

"You're living with somebody who has kids?"

"What's wrong with that?"

"Nothing, Daddy. Nothing. I have to go."

"Wait a minute. I've got some good news, but you gotta promise not to tell your mama. Not yet."

"What is it?"

"I'm gon' be a daddy!"

"A what?"

"A father."

"You can't be serious, Daddy."

"I am very, very serious. The ole man ain't lost his touch after all, huh?"

"Who was ever concerned about that?"

"I don't want to answer that one right now. How's your mama doing?"

"She's doing just fine. And don't you dare stop by here without calling first, getting her all worked up so she ends up back in the hospital. You got that, Daddy?"

"Buy a vowel, dummy. Buy a vowel. Thank you!" Mama says in a loud whisper.

"You sound mad, baby girl. What's wrong?"

"Apparently, I'm not your baby, Daddy. And what difference does it make if I sound mad or not? You can't do anything about it. You're part of the reason I'm pissed, but right now I don't think I want to hear the sound of your voice another minute. Goodbye," I say and hang up.

" 'Taxpayers' Money'!" I hear Mama blurt out. She makes a loud clap with her hands. I look over at the TV. Another puzzle is about to be put on the board. Vanna White looks the same now as she did twelve years ago, when I was breastfeeding Shanice. That's what money can do. Mama presses the remote and we're back at *Jeopardy!* When the phone rings again, she says, "That's him again."

I answer it. "Yes?"

"Janelle," Daddy says, "I'm sorry you mad at me, and, the way things is looking, I don't think it's gon' be such a good idea for me to have that drink with Paris."

"You aren't scared, are you, Daddy?"

"He should be," Mama says. She's back to *Wheel of Fortune*. This is a hard puzzle. A place. Three lines. "Tell him there's another brown envelope in the mailbox waiting for him, if and when he in the neighborhood. It might hold his interest."

"I heard her, Janelle. And to answer your question, naw, I ain't scared: not of my own daughter. But I just get the feeling that y'all don't understand what's been going on over there for quite some time, and it's understandable that you would take your mama's side, but I ain't done nothing wrong and I didn't do nothing to hurt your mama on purpose. And she know that."

"So—what do you want me to tell Paris, Daddy?"

"Tell her I'll have that drink with her on the next trip," he says. "When things cool down some."

"I'll tell her," I say, and hang up without saying goodbye.

And, without taking her eyes off the screen, Mama utters: "He ain't shit."

"The answer is 'San Juan, Puerto Rico,' Mama. And he's certainly not alone."

Bingo

"What movie y'all going to see?" I ask the kids from the laundry room.

"We wanna see *Above the Rim* with Tupac and Leon," Tiffany yells, and then all three of 'em appear in the doorway. They wearing the ski jackets I got 'em that they ain't supposed to be wearing until next year, but I don't feel like saying nothing.

"There's no way I could sit through that," Trevor says.

"We're too shocked!" Monique says, rolling her eyes up in her head. One day they gon' get stuck up there.

"Well, which one *do* you wanna see, Trevor?" Tiffany asks.

"Actually, I was planning to drop you guys off and meet a friend at the fabric store and just hang out until your movie's over," he says, turning to me. "If that's okay with you, Ma."

"Why you need more fabric?" I ask. A whole corner of the basement ain't got nothing but stacks and stacks of material, just sitting there, dry-rotting, right next to my treadmill, which is doing the same thing. "Can't you think of something else you wanna do today?"

"This *is* what I want to do today."

"All we wanna know is when you ever gon' make me and Tiff a pair of them shiny Janet Jackson pants like you promised us for Christmas that wasn't nowhere to be found under the tree?"

"Soon, soon, soon," he says. "I've got a few other orders I have to finish first."

It's hard for me to even believe this conversation, but when you ask your one and only son what he wants for Christmas and he says just one thing, a Surger so he can finish off his seams like a professional, you shouldn't be shocked to hear this. I just keep separating what looks like two tons of dirty clothes into three or four piles: dark, medium, whites, and filthy.

Trevor done put some kind of perm in his hair, 'cause it's all wavy and brushed forward. Looking like a black Beatle. He's worse than the girls when it comes to fooling with his hair. And even though he's got the scoop on the fashion scene in Paris and New York, he dresses like what the kids call a "nerd." He's wearing navy-blue Dockers, a white turtleneck underneath his yellow, white, and blue Nautica jacket, and navy suede boots.

I haven't had the nerve to just come out and ask him, and Al says leave him alone, he ain't hurting nobody, and if he is you can't blame him for it, 'cause they say it's in their genes or something. But nobody on either side of our family's got these kind of genes, at least not that I know of. He even got the girls giving him manicures and pedicures. Made 'em swear they wouldn't tell, but I ain't blind. His nails look better than mine, his heels smoother than most women's. Just the thought of him kissing on some other boy—and Lord knows I don't wanna think of nothing else they might do—makes me wanna gag.

"Get out the mirror, Tiffany," I say, and pick up a pair of panties that smell too strong for girls their age, and when I look closer I see a dark-red stain where ain't supposed to be one. I ball 'em up and toss 'em on they own separate pile. How come she didn't say nothing to me? I'm her mama. I'm supposed to be the first to know this. Who told her what to do? And when did it happen? I certainly don't feel like embarrassing her right now, so I just keep my mouth shut.

Apparently, Miss Tiffany is on a Cindy Crawford kick today, 'cause she's wearing a blue "North Carolina" baseball cap turned backwards with a whole bunch of reddish-brown hair that ain't hardly hers flowing past her shoulders. Her jacket is powder blue; Monique's is cotton-candy pink. Tiffany's is zipped all the way up to the throat, which mean she ain't wearing nothing close to no turtleneck underneath it, but I ain't in the mood for arguing and I want all three of 'em to hurry up and get the hell outta here. Al left yesterday on his fishing trip, and even though I was mad at first, I was surprised at how relieved I felt not five minutes after he was gone. Now, when these kids leave, the whole house will be mine, something that hardly ever happens.

They should be gone at least three or four hours, which should give me plenty of time to look under beds, go through closets, and empty out overstuffed drawers. I do this two or three times a year to get rid of things they done either outgrown or just never got around to wearing. Some of the stuff needs to be thrown out, but these the clothes and shoes I usually look at twice, 'cause like they say, one person's trash is another person's treasure. I usually give some to the church and take the rest down to one of the shelters for them women with kids. I ain't chintzy when it comes to giving away me and Al's stuff either, but I already did him and me this morning.

It depresses me when I go into them shelters—there's two or three of 'em I take turns going to—but it do remind me how truly fortunate and blessed we are to have as much as we do. Every now and then, when I'm just bored and wanna get outta the house, I'll go through my credit cards and pick out one or two that's got real low balances and head for the mall, knowing ain't a damn thing me or the kids need, and I think about them kids at the shelter and go berserk. I pretend like they my kids, or at least my nieces and nephews, who can't help it that they got stuck with crackheads or alcoholics or dumb asses for parents, or whatever the reasons are that they ain't got no place to live.

Is that lipstick on Monique's lips? I hope it's just Vaseline.

When I look a little closer, I realize that's all it is. But Tiffany is a whole 'nother story: she got black pencil inside the bottom of her eye. Lip liner and a pretty pale-pink color inside. Who taught her how to do this? She looks nice, even though I don't know if this is the right time for her to be wearing makeup yet, but, what the hell, times have changed from when I was their age. Girls is doing all kinds of things at thirteen we didn't even think about until we was almost out of high school.

"Let's go," Trevor says, heading out the garage door. He's so impatient. I don't know how he sews as good and as much as he do. But he can make damn near anything he sees in those magazines he gets: that one with a "W" on it, and some European ones that ain't even in English. Half the time he don't even use no pattern. I sure can't fault him for having talent. If I ever lose these thirty pounds, I want him to make me a slinky dress, but not until I can get into a ten again.

"Hold up, Trevor!" Tiffany yells. "Ma, would it be okay if we went to the mall after?"

"For what? You don't have no money, do you?"

"Nope. We was just about to ask if we could get our allowance early?"

"For what?"

" 'Cause we wanted to look for your birthday present."

I'm shocked they even remembered, considering it's two whole weeks away.

"I don't want nothing."

"I'm getting you something anyway," Monique says. "But this time, it'll be something I know you like."

"Me, too, Ma," Tiffany says.

"My lips are sealed," Trevor says.

"I told y'all I don't want nothing and I meant it."

"We heard you the first time, Ma. What about Granny? What you think she might like?" Monique asks.

"I don't know! Call and ask her."

"It's weird you guys got the same birthday and y'all ain't nothing alike, huh, Ma?" Tiffany says.

"Yeah, it's a trip all right. Would somebody get my purse off the kitchen counter, please?"

Monique dashes off and is back before I take a breath. There's $132 in my wallet. I give them forty apiece. Their eyes light up.

"Thanks, Ma!" Monique says.

"Wow, yeah, thanks," Tiffany says.

"I'm covered," Trevor says, refusing his, and his sisters look at him like he's crazy, especially after I take it back.

"You're welcome. If I ain't here when y'all get back, I'll probably be making my rounds at the Laundromats. Now, go on, get out of here. And have fun." As soon as I hear that door slam and the car back out the driveway, I feel myself grinning. I'm so glad they're gone I don't know what to do. I don't care how much it cost to get rid of 'em. Sometimes I ask myself why I had to have three whole kids when one probably woulda been plenty. It's too much work, too many different personalities to deal with, and, hell, don't add a husband to the mix.

I pour a little Clorox in the water, add some Cheer and Biz, and then throw in three or four handfuls of white clothes. It must be about three o'clock. It's definitely Saturday, and I feel entitled to something that'll give me a little more enthusiasm, so I walk over to our little makeshift bar and pour myself a Tanqueray and tonic. When I get upstairs, the girls' room is a disaster of pastels: clothes, socks, towels, sheets, panties—all kinds of shit is everywhere except where it should be.

Trevor's door, as usual, is closed, and even though he's got a lock on it he don't know that I know where he hides the spare key. He always locking hisself out, and I saw him get it from under the cushion of this old fat chair he said he would re-cover one day. Sure enough, it's here. I set my drink down on the floor, but as soon as I do, the piling of the carpet is so high the glass tips over. Shit. I'll clean it up later.

I never knew there was so many different shades of blue. Trevor painted this room hisself, and ain't nothing out of place. Nothing. He makes his bed every morning, even if he's running late. He shares the bathroom with the girls but keeps his towel and washcloth on a hook he put right next to his closet. He made some kind of giant picture which ain't nothing but cutouts of men and women from them magazines and pasted 'em so close together you can't even see the corkboard. He calls this his "Fashion Collage" or something. I don't get the point, really. He's had that same dresser since he was ten, and it's looking like it. I don't even know if it's real wood or not, but he keeps it polished. His cologne bottles are on a swivel thing, and all his jewelry in a blue velvet box. I stand here for a minute wondering if this really looks like a boy's room. It do, sort of. Ain't nothing frilly about it. But, then again, there's all different kinds of homosexuals, from what I understand.

I open one of his dresser drawers real fast. Underwear stacked neat. Next drawer. Undershirts. Next. Socks. And then pajamas and T-shirts. I'm tempted to just slide my hand under some of 'em, like they do in the movies, but I'm too scared. Plus, everything is so organized, I can't see how he could hide anything.

His closet could pass for two racks at a department store. This is ridiculous. On the shoe boxes he done actually wrote the type and color of shoe in each box. His bed looks like nobody ever sleeps in it. Before I know it, I'm sliding my hands between the mattress and box spring and—bingo!—magazines. I pull one out and flip through it, and—Lord have mercy!—men doing all kinds of things to each other. Things I do to my husband. I close it fast. The next one is *Playgirl*. Mostly young white guys with big thick penises. It becomes very clear that the shit they been saying about white men having little ones ain't hardly true no more. I don't even realize I done got comfortable sitting on the floor, and taking my sweet time looking at these pictures, especially when I find myself reading about

Jim and Bill and how they're on some soap opera. These is some good-looking, sexy young men, I swear to God they are. But then I snap the magazine shut, slide both of 'em back where I found 'em, and smooth the bed back the way it was, and then get the hell outta here. After locking the door, I put that key right where I found it.

Okay. So it is true. What the fuck can I do about it? Nothing. Absolutely nothing. I can forget about my son getting a football or basketball scholarship; forget all those fantasies of seeing him play in the NFL or the NBA; forget about him ever giving us any grandbabies or, hell, what about his wedding? The part I hate the most about this whole affair is everybody in my family finding out that what they been saying about Trevor all along is true. I don't think I can handle it, really. So—I'ma just keep my mouth shut.

In the girls' room I just start throwing shit into piles, but it don't take me but a minute to realize that every single piece belong to Tiffany: clothes she don't fucking appreciate, 'cause if she did they wouldn't be on the goddamn floor. They just gotta have all this hip-hop shit these rappers who done all become designers overnight is selling and my kids and everybody else's kids is buying as fast as they can make it. Correction: I'm the one buying it. I open Monique's side of the dresser, and all of her things is folded. She always complaining that Tiffany is the slob, and she ain't never lied. And just look at all these sneakers: we should own some stock in Nike, 'cause that's all they wear. And if that Michael Jordan comes out with one more sneaker, I'ma kick his ass myself.

It takes me close to a hour to clean out this room, and some little kids gon' be happy as hell when they get all this stuff, some of which ain't never even been worn. I should have my own ass kicked for spending this kinda money on these kids. I fill up three of them big green trash bags that's made for leaves and grass and push 'em out in the hallway with my foot, and then kick 'em one by one down the steps till they in the middle of the entryway. I walk around 'em and go pour myself another drink. I wonder if Al caught any fish? I ain't calling him, that's for damn sure. I don't wanna get my feelings hurt if he ain't in his motel room. And I ain't in the mood for jumping to no conclusions. I shoulda told him Loretha called. I know it. But I didn't want him to be depressed while he was gone.

My recliner is waiting for me to bring my drink on over and sit down. It feel like somebody just took a vacuum cleaner and sucked all my get-up-and-go outta me. To hell with them Laundromats. They still as raggedy today as they was last week. Washers don't spin. Dryers don't dry. Everybody always want their money back. I don't know what we pay Popeye and Flozena for. They don't know what the word "upkeep" mean. And I sure don't feel like smiling at no drug dealers pretending I don't know they drug dealers who come inside to keep warm, 'cause whenever they see me—they know who I am by now— they always walk over and press their face against the window of a warm dryer, trying to act like they checking on they clothes. No. I think I've done enough for one day.

When the phone and doorbell ring at the same time, I damn near jump out this chair. "Hold on a minute," I grumble and stumble out to the front door. The mailman's truck: must be our checks. Probably too much mail to put in the box, so he's bringing it to the door. I open it. It ain't our normal guy, and this one just says, "Good afternoon, ma'am. Certified mail, if you would sign here, please."

And I do, and he hands me a brown envelope addressed to Albert Toussaint, and it's from the IRS. I want to open it, but my name ain't on it. Just his. I lay it down on the side table and go on back in the family room and pick up the portable. "Yeah," I say as I walk over to the sliding glass door and look out into the backyard. What a dreary day. Patches of gray snow look like dirty clouds on the ground.

"Did I wake you up, baby?"

"Aunt Suzie?"

"Yes, it's me. Was you sleeping?"

"Naw, I just dozed off for a minute. How you doing?"

"I'm blessed and highly favored, if I do say so myself, although everybody keep telling me they swear I got a touch of Alzheimer's. That may be, but I won a hundred and forty-six dollars at Bingo yesterday. Or maybe it was two days ago. It don't matter. I won it."

"That's nice."

"Yeah, it sho' is. I'm going to look for me a car."

I know I must be hearing things. "Aunt Suzie, where in the world would you get that kind of money?"

"I been saving."

"Hold it a minute. First of all, when was the last time you drove a car?"

"In 1978, I thank it was. Some thangs you don't never forget how to do, baby, if you get Aunt Suzie's drift." And she lets out a howl.

"I thought you could barely lift your leg ever since you had your hip surgery."

"I'll manage."

"But what about all that medication you take?"

"That's my business. Ain't it? I'm tired of sitting in this house waiting for the senior citizens' bus or my friends to take me everywhere. Shoot. Sometimes I don't feel like being bothered with old folks."

"Do you have any idea how much cars cost these days?"

"I got almost sixteen thousand dollars in the bank, baby; I should be able to find something that run for that, you thank?"

Did she say sixteen thousand? I just grunt a chuckle. No wonder she done lost so much weight. She ain't eating. But Aunt Suzie been losing it in the head for a long time; I don't know how she think she gon' get behind a wheel. "Aunt Suzie. Let me ask you something. Do you have a current driver's license?"

"It's in my wallet."

"But is it current?"

"I don't know. Stop worrying so much, Charlotte. So how you doing these days?"

"I'm fine."

"That's good. And Al?"

"He's at work. Just got back from his fishing trip."

"Did he catch anything?"

"Yes, he did."

"Then tell him to save me some for my Deepfreeze."

"I will."

"How the kids?"

"They fine. They at the movies."

"You still only got three of 'em, don't you?"

"Aunt Suzie, you know how many kids I got."

"It's too many to keep track of sometimes. How many?"

"Still three. Same as last week and last year."

"You know your Aunt Priscilla getting out of prison sometime this week."

"Don't give her my number, please, Aunt Suzie."

"I won't. She said she might wanna go spend some time with Viola, when she get back on her feet good."

I knew this call was really about Mama, she just getting around to it.

"At the rate she going, I betcha Viola gon' be dead before me."

"Stop talking like this, Aunt Suzie! I mean it!"

"I ain't said nothing that probably ain't true. I know it ain't what you wanna hear, but, hell, I may be losing my mind, but one thang fo' sure, I ain't got no problems breathing."

"Well, thanks for cheering me up, Aunt Suzie."

"You're welcome. We all getting old, Charlotte. You is, too, so don't go acting like you gon' live forever."

"You finished, Aunt Suzie?"

"Nope. How come you didn't take your ass out there to see your mama?"

Goddamn it! I don't need this from her, too. But. Say something. "Aunt Suzie?"

"I'm listening."

"First of all, sometimes people have reasons why they can't do certain things."

"That's why I'm asking, Miss Charlotte. I wanna know what kind of reasons you got that would stop you from going to see your own mama when she coulda died for all you know."

"But she didn't die!"

"She coulda. It ain't over till the fat lady sing. Ain't you heard that?"

"I couldn't afford it! There! You satisfied now?"

"Look, don't go raising your voice at me, missy. If you can whip out them damn credit cards to go to the mall when the spirit move you, how come you can't use one of 'em to get on a airplane?"

"I don't fly," I say.

"Then you need to learn," she says. "Goodbye, Charlotte. Have a nice day. And tell Al don't forget my fish. I ain't forgot."

Aunt Suzie always call at the wrong time. It never fail. I put the phone up and walk over and look at that envelope. Shit, I'm his wife. I got a right to open his mail. I do it so fast I get a paper cut. First of all, it definitely ain't no check. Not even close. It's a letter. I don't believe my fucking eyes, and my ears start ringing when I read that the IRS is keeping our income-tax checks in order to start paying off his back child support. But he's *paying* child support! Loretha been getting money taken outta his check for years. What is this shit about? This gotta be some kinda mistake. And when Al get home tomorrow, we gon' find out whose mistake it is.

Housecleaning

I never bothered to call. What would I have said to him over the phone, anyway? "Do you miss me, honey? Or do you miss my daughter more? Why aren't you gone? You were supposed to be gone." Even still, I knew he'd probably be there when I got home. I just knew it. In fact, the more I drove, the more I prayed that he would be. I needed to see him face-to-face. Look him in the eyes to see if I saw any remorse, any signs of regret or shame.

The drive from Las Vegas was long enough to help me sort out some things. Not everything, but enough. Even though I'm afraid, I'm going to pretend I'm not afraid of what will happen when I file for divorce Monday morning. I've been married to this man for six years. I shouldn't have to worry about how I'm going to manage once he's gone. After all, he adopted Shanice. She has his last name: Porter. He's legally responsible for her until she's eighteen. I'll get a real job. I don't care if it pays minimum wage. That's a lie. I need to make more than that. Right now, I almost don't care what I have to do.

When I turn onto our street, George has put all the Easter things in the front yard. But it's all wrong. First of all, the big blue bunny isn't supposed to be so far away from the eggs; the nest is supposed to be inside the basket. The flag shouldn't be stuck in the ground; it goes in the flagpole on the porch. I've only been hanging them at this house for the past five and a half years. And where are my baby chicks? Why didn't he put my miniature eggs out? They're the prettiest: all robin's-egg blue. The yard looks so amateurish and sparse. He should've left it alone if he didn't know what he was doing or couldn't do it the right way. I can't imagine what the neighbors are saying. I'll fix it later.

The garage door is opening before I even press the Genie. I get out of the car and George almost runs out to greet me. "Hello, Janelle," he says. "Let me get your bags for you."

"There's only one."

"Where's Shanice?" he asks.

"She disappeared," I say. "Can't you see that?" I walk past him into the kitchen, letting the door slam in his face.

"Seriously," I hear him say as he comes through the door.

"She's somewhere she'll be safe."

"Actually, she'll be safe here from now on."

"Spare me, would you, George?" This place is a mess. Soiled dishes piled in the sink. Something sticky's on the floor. Juice containers and a few empty wine bottles are all littering the counter. Two uneaten Marie Callender's veal and beef TV dinners sit on top of the microwave. Pots are on the stove. It stinks in here: like day-old broccoli. He disgusts me.

I walk into the dining room, and there, in the middle of the table, is probably the largest bouquet of spring flowers I've ever seen in my entire life. I hear him enter the room. Feel him standing behind me. When I turn to face him I realize that George is not handsome at all. I don't know when it was that I thought he was. And he's old. He looks much older than fifty-one. Now I see why people often mistake him for my father. But right now he just looks pitiful. Like a puppy. But I don't feel sorry for him one bit, because he is not a puppy. He is the man who molested my daughter.

"I start counseling tomorrow," he says.

"What did you say?"

"Counseling. For my behavior. To stop it. So it never happens again. I didn't mean to do what I've done, and I never really actually did anything to her, if that matters."

I feel like I need Mama's inhaler. "Are you packed?"

"I can't leave here," he says.

"You'll have to when I report this," I say.

"Please, don't, Janelle. I'm begging you not to, please. It could destroy everything. The life I've worked so hard to build."

"You should've thought about that before you started going into my daughter's room at night."

"I did think about it."

"Oh, you thought about it, and your brain gave you the go-ahead, is that it?"

"No. I mean, I wasn't thinking when I did it. That's the whole problem."

"You think okay on your job and you carry a fucking gun. You don't seem to have any difficulty making decisions out there, do you? I mean, you've never shot anybody because you were overwhelmed by the fucking moment, have you?"

"I suppose not."

"What in the world would compel you to do something like this in the first place?"

"I don't know."

"And then *keep* doing it?"

"I honestly don't know."

"Think about it for a minute! If you don't know, who the hell does?"

"I guess I wanted her to like me."

"What did you say?"

"I wanted her to like me."

"Oh, really. And this was a guaranteed way to do that?"

He just shakes his head.

"She never liked you, George, and I should've trusted her instincts from the start."

"I know that, but I kept hoping she would. It doesn't make any sense."

"And you really thought that by touching my daughter and forcing her to do things to you, that that would make her like you more? Am I getting this right, George?"

"Somewhat."

"Did you ever think about how she might feel because of what you were doing to her?"

"I thought she liked it."

I reach for the bouquet to throw at him, but decide it's not worth it. I grit my teeth and ball up my fist and back away from him. "You didn't say what I thought you just said. Did you?"

"She could've stopped me."

"How?"

"She could've said no."

"You expect me to stand here and believe that she didn't?"

"Look, Janelle. I don't want to argue about this. What I did was despicable and I want to get help. I don't like the side of me that did this."

I fold my arms, wishing they were bats. "What if they can't help you?"

"It doesn't matter. I know the magnitude of what I've done. It was wrong, and I can promise you that it will never happen again."

"And you expect me to believe you, just like that?"

"Yes."

"Let me ask you something, George. Did you do this to your own daughters, too?"

"Absolutely not."

"Oh, so my daughter was the prize, huh?"

"No, Janelle."

"How about any other little girls?"

"No. Look, I'm just as shocked by my behavior as you are."

"Really," I say. I'm not sure if I believe him or not. Thieves have usually been stealing a long time before they ever get caught. I will certainly find out.

"Janelle," he sighs, "do you really think I did this deliberately to hurt Shanice?"

"This isn't just about Shanice, George."

"Well, either of you?"

"You hurt us, all right. Big-time."

"But I didn't mean to. I swear it."

There is a long silence. I'm sick of talking to him. Sick of listening. He's not sorry. He's worried. More worried about what might happen to him than he is about what's going to happen to me and my daughter because of what he's done. He has changed our lives forever. No matter how much I wish it weren't true.

"And what about our promise to each other?" he's saying, as I move toward the stairwell for no reason other than to get away from him.

"What promise?"

"To get through the bad times together."

"This doesn't exactly fall under the 'bad-times' category, George."

"Then what about forgiveness?"

"Yes. Some things shouldn't be forgiven."

"Is that what you really believe, Janelle?"

"Some things are unforgivable."

"So—you mean all the Sundays in church when Reverend Mitchell preached about forgiving the intolerable, all that meant nothing to you?"

"Yes, it did mean something." I stop on the tenth or eleventh step and turn to look down at him.

"Then wouldn't you say this qualifies as some sort of test?"

"A test given by whom?"

"I don't want to say it, but I'll say it: God."

I was about to turn to keep walking until I heard the word "God." I don't play when it comes to Him. And as much as I hate to admit it, what George has said is true. Reverend Mitchell has given us so many examples of things people have done that hurt others so deeply, but he says that God gave us the capacity to forgive. Wants us to forgive. But I don't know how right now. I don't feel like forgiving him. I don't think forgiving him will make me feel any better. And what about Shanice? Is she supposed to forgive him, too?

"What about our baby?" he says.

I sit down on a step. The baby. There's a baby growing inside me. What in the world am I going to do with a baby? His baby? How will I feel having a constant reminder of him in my life? I couldn't take that out on an innocent child, could I? But what about protecting it? I haven't done such a good job with my daughter; how can I expect to keep this one from harm? And how would Shanice treat him, or her?

"Look, Janelle, I'm ashamed of myself for what I've done, but I'm glad you found out, because now an end can be put to it. It stops. I stop. And hopefully we can get on with our lives. I want our baby to be raised in *this* house, with both of his or her parents under one roof, under which there is a new sense of trust and love. Hell, we can get a bigger house. Fill it with even more love and trust than we ever imagined. I know it's something I'm going to have to earn again, but, baby, I'll work overtime to get it back. I promise you. I'm sorry. So very sorry. Can't we try to put this behind us, and think about our future?"

I try to stop the tears but I can't control them. I wish this was all just a bad dream, and when somebody snaps their fingers or turns the light on, it'll be over. That my daughter will be upstairs in her bedroom reading Goosebumps and I'll be reading a Janet Dailey novel and George will be rubbing his foot up and down my leg until he falls asleep. I have loved him hard, but right now I don't love any part of him. Can't. He used to make me feel protected and safe. How in the world can you ever get that back once you lose it?

George is crying, too. We both cry until I know for sure that our pain isn't the same. Coming from two very different places. I suppose he is sorry, but most criminals are after they get caught. I'm sorry for him. Sorry for Shanice. Sorry for me. But I'm not going to be a fool. Not take any more chances with my daughter's life. I look down at him and I simply say, "I want you out of here before this day is over. If you refuse, I'll call a few of your buddies in blue and you can explain it to them."

"Where am I supposed to go?"

"I don't know, George. But I hear they're looking for your kind in hell." I stand up and walk back down the stairs like I'm in a hurry. I bump into him to the point where he loses his balance. He does what he can to get his equilibrium back. But I ignore him, and head for the kitchen to straighten up, because he and everybody else knows that I like my house clean.

Hand
After
Hand

"You ready to call it a night, man?" Howie asks.

We been at the tables since I got off work. "What time is it?"

"Late. And I'm hungry. We ain't ate nothing in going on five hours. I need to eat something before I go home. Come on, Cecil. Let's cash in."

I look down at my chips. Hell, what's to cash? Chump change. I ain't got but two or three hundred. Howie in better shape than me, but some nights is like this. We pick up our chips and take 'em over to the change booth, where one of my least favorite clerks is working: Betty Sue, a redneck from Reno who shoulda stayed there. She got a high-and-mighty attitude to go with that thin brown hair that look like a rat's nest on top of her head. She act like it's downright painful when a black man cash in, and right now I'm a little pissed 'cause I ain't handling more than I am.

I don't say a word. Just watch her fingers flip through them bills like feathers. Howie get his take and we head on over to the restaurant. It ain't crowded, not this time of night. It's a Monday. No big conventions in town this week. Thank the Lord. Which mean maybe we stand a chance on making a few dollars around here tomorrow.

We sit in a booth, where we can still see the casino and folks walking back and forth picking which slot machine looks lucky, which dealer looks like he'll give you that winning hand after hand after hand. I would love to tell these knuckleheads that ain't no lucky machines or no such thang as a good dealer. The odds is stacked against the gambler. Casinos is in the business of making money. So—some days they let you win. But most days you lose. It's simple arithmetic. It shouldn't take all day to figure out which of them days you on. But, hell, I thought everybody knew that.

A redheaded waitress comes over to take our order: she's new.

"We'll both have the well-done steak and eggs with hash browns and white toast," Howie says.

She looks at me and I give her a look that says, "He said 'we,' didn't he?" She turns and walks away. Her orange uniform don't look so hot with her hair that color and her skin being so pale. I wouldn'ta took this job if I was her. There's hundreds of places just like this one in this town that got uniforms that would go a whole lot better with that copper-penny color. But I'm just a man, so what do I know?

"So how was it seeing your kids, Cecil?"

I take a sip of my water. "It's hard to say, Howie."

"What's that supposed to mean?"

"Well, I thank they mad at me."

"For not being over there with Viola?"

"That, and for being with somebody else."

"They just have to get used to it, then, don't they?"

"I guess."

Howie lights a cigarette and blows the smoke away from me. He know I'm allergic to it, but I'm so used to it now I don't know if it even bother me no more. He ain't got no wife or no steady woman in his life—just visitors, as he call 'em—and nobody but me for a friend. But he got a dog: a German shepherd he call Lassie, which I told him when he got him was a stupid name for the dog—considering—but Howie said he always loved that TV show and how much that dog could do, and he was naming his Lassie, he didn't care what I said. This Lassie's a mean son-of-a-bitch, too. The last thang he would even thank about doing is giving you his paw. This dog ain't never in a good mood, but I thank God he like me. Howie musta told him I'm his best friend.

"Did you tell 'em about Brenda?" he asks.

"I told my youngest, Janelle, but I betcha Viola had already heard something and probably told Paris and Lewis."

"You ain't committed no crime, Cecil."

"I know that, Howie."

"So what's the problem?" he asks, scratching the top of his bald head, which is so shiny it look like a varnished hardwood floor. Howie's eyes is the same color as his head: light brown, and his skin, which always smell like stale tobacco, probably used to be a golden color, but now he done gotten older and ain't kept hisself up like he shoulda and so his face and hands—in all fairness—ain't but two or three shades above me, and everybody know I'm darker than burnt fried chicken. Me and Howie done spent so much time outside in this hot desert sun we done both changed colors, although I can't see how I can get no darker.

"You just don't want your kids mad with you," I say.

"Mine been mad with me for a long time," he says, putting his cigarette out and motioning for the waitress. I know he wants a drink. He usually do it the other way around, but it's 'cause we on empty, he don't wanna be stupid. Howie got a weak stomach. We learned that years ago.

"That's different," I say.

"Mad is mad," Howie says.

"But it feel more like they don't like me, not that they just mad. I thank this got more to do with losing respect. At least that's what it sounded like I was hearing when we was talking on the phone. It don't feel good, Howie."

"Well, what you gon' do, run back home to Viola to please your kids?"

"Naw, can't do that."

"Well?"

The waitress brings our food, which look the sizzling-same as always, and Howie says, "Can I get a double Dewar's on ice, please? And a ginger ale for my friend here."

She smiles and winks and says she'll be right back. She remind me of that girl on *Gilligan's Island*. "You ever feel like sometimes thangs is happening so fast, and even though you the one doing it, you don't know how it happened?"

"Come again, Cecil?"

The waitress sets our drinks on the table. Howie takes a deep sip. "I guess what I'm trying to say here is, you know how sometimes, if you blink, a whole week can pass?"

"Sorta."

"Well, I been married to Viola for thirty-eight years, and now I'm with Brenda, and we fixing to have a baby."

"I been thinking about this baby business ever since you told me about it."

"Wait, let me finish my train of thought, would you, Howie?"

"All right, all right. I'm listening."

"Anyway, it seem like I just blinked and my whole life done changed right before my very eyes, except I feel more like a witness to it than the person 'in it.' Do that make sense?"

"Hell, yeah, it make a whole lotta sense. You done jumped into some new shit so fast you don't know how you got in it or how you gon' get out of it. Is that about right?"

"Sort of. But don't get me wrong. I like Brenda. A whole lot. I might even love her. It's just that I can't believe I ain't really with Viola no more."

"It ain't too late," he says.

"Sometimes it is too late."

"How you supposed to know that?" he asks.

"I don't know for certain. But I guess when it feel like you do on your last day at work before you go on vacation, only you wish you could stay on vacation."

"Well, can I ask you something, Cecil, and don't go getting all personally upset about it?"

"Okay."

"You sure that baby yours?"

"Well, yeah. I thank. I don't see why not. It should be. Why you ask me that?"

"She got pregnant awfully quick, don't you think?"

"She young. It happen fast when they young, Howie."

"Yeah, but be for real with me for a minute, now, Cecil. We done talked about this before, and you and me both know you been having trouble in that area for some time, and I just wanna know how you able to make a baby when you ain't been with the girl but a hot minute?"

"It's possible. But what you really getting at, Howie?"

"She had to been with different mens before you came on the scene, don't you think?"

"Of course. She attractive."

"That's a matter of opinion, Cecil. But you hear where I'm coming from?"

"Naw, I don't."

"You got a pension. You ain't got no responsibilities. You good at the tables. I'd say you was a good catch. I'd want you to be the father of my baby if I was young and homely with three kids in the projects and met myself a middle-aged old sum-bitch like yourself."

"First of all, Brenda ain't homely. I beg to differ with you, Howie. I'd stand her up against any of them orangutans you been known to spend time with, so shut up."

"To each his own," Howie says, chuckling. "Just something to ponder on."

I know he don't mean no harm. But I say, "Don't cause me to thank too much, now, Howie. I got enough on my mind. I'ma have to quit this job at Harrah's, 'cause I thank the IRS is fixin' to garnish my little piecey check. But back on the subject: I don't thank Brenda would lie to me about something like this."

"You ain't known her that long to say no shit like that, Cecil—now, come on."

"Well, she got a good heart, though."

"We ain't talking about nobody's heart right now."

"I know. But it could be my baby. I thank."

"How pregnant is she?"

"I don't exactly know."

"Well, watch the calendar, is all I gotta say about it. Don't be no old fool, now, Cecil, you hear me?"

"I hear you."

"What your old ass gon' do with a baby, anyway? That's what I wanna know."

"I don't know. What every man do with one: raise it and love it."

"You might be dead before you get a chance to do much raising, but you didn't hear it from me."

We both get a chuckle outta that one. I take a few sips of my ginger ale. It's good. They even put some lime in it.

"But tell me something, man," Howie asks, hunching over, like I'm about to tell him a secret or something. "What's it like getting it from a youngster?"

"To be honest, it all feel the same, Howie. Just a few different moves and a younger face."

"That's all?"

"From what I gather."

"Then you ain't doing it right."

"How can you sit there and tell me how I'm doing it?"

"Okay, wait a minute. Now, looka here. We all know that Viola's a big woman."

"That's putting it nicely."

"She ain't fat. She just husky," Howie mumbles.

"She fat," I say.

"Okay, you said it, I didn't. But Brenda don't look like she got a drop of fat on her. Don't that make some kinda difference?"

"Not really. Well, wait. I'm lying. I'll be honest. I like the cushion a body like Viola's provides. But in me and Brenda's case, I'm the one providing it, so it all average out."

"You feel like you really in love, Cecil?"

"You mean the way I loved Viola when I loved Viola?"

"Yeah."

"Naw, this love is different. It's smoother, easier. I ain't crazy this time."

"You think?"

"I know. But whatever kind it is feel pretty good. Better than the war I been in for the past few years at my house. I hope the old broad is feeling better, though."

"Check on her from time to time, man. Ain't nothing wrong with that, is it?"

"Naw. I don't guess."

We sit here for another ten minutes, scraping up all the yolk with the last of our toast. For five dollars, you can't get a better deal. When I get to the employee parking lot, I unlock my car and sit inside. I let the engine run for a few minutes. I need to call my kids. Just to touch base. To make sure they know I still love their mama and let 'em know that if there's any way we can ever get back together and be happy again we'll find it. It may not be today. May not be tomorrow. May not even be ever. But if it's meant to be, we'll find our way back there. In the meantime, I just want them to bear with me and try to understand that this is the first time in a long, long time that I can say that I'm what you might wanna call happy.

Throbbing

I ain't doing nothing but laying here watching *In the Heat of the Night*, 'cause I spent my last seven dollars on a forty, a fish fillet, a quarter-pounder with fries, a quick-pix lottery ticket, and a pack of Kools. It's been raining off and on all day, and since my car still ain't running and the bus service out here in Lancaster is pretty much nonexistent, it's too hard trying to go visit somebody. In my condition, I can't walk too far, plus, I don't even know where Luisa live. I remember her saying it wasn't far from me, but, shit, where's that? Besides, I owe her some money, so I really don't need to see her today. All the other women I know—damn, right now I can't think of a single solitary one of their names—live within walking distance, but I don't feel like being bothered with no female bullshit tonight, which is why I decided to stay in and watch some TV. At least till the rain lets up. And, besides, this is free.

Damn! I remember that Denise Nicholas chick from *Room 222*! She's still fine. I wonder what ever happened to that show? I take a sip from my bottle and just lay here without moving. I need a shower, but since I ain't going nowhere, I take my blue jeans and T-shirt off and throw 'em on the floor and get under the covers. After a few minutes, I realize I ain't the least bit interested in what's going on on the TV, but I don't feel like getting up to change the channel either. Times like this is when I wish I had a remote control. I saw a nineteen-inch one with a VCR in it for under three hundred at Circuit City. I wonder do they have layaway? Shit, I know I'm bored when I'm entertaining thoughts about how I can get a remote control—when that's as deep as I can get.

I'm glad that's all I'm thinking about, considering my current situation. But it ain't nothing I can do about none of it right now, which is why I ain't thinking about how pissed Mama and 'nem probably are at me for leaving the way I did, or the fact that they probably gon' put a warrant out for me in Vegas since I failed to appear, and if Woolery don't hurry up and pay me the three hundred he owe me I won't be able to pay my rent, get my car fixed, or send Donnetta at least a hundred dollars for my son. Shit, I forgot all about the child-support hearing coming up, and if I don't show up for that I'm in deep shit.

But I don't want to think about none of this right now, which is why I bend over and get my tube sock from under the mattress and politely put it on with my left hand, then use my right one to slide it up and down my penis until I see myself expanding, filling it up. The friction is getting it warm. Now warmer. I kick the covers off, 'cause it's starting to feel like somebody turned the furnace up all of a sudden. I need this: The heat. The friction. The juice. All of it. So I close my eyes and completely erase this nasty-ass apartment and everything in it.

"Yeah, baby."

I knew Halle Berry wanted to suck my dick the minute she laid eyes on me. But why wouldn't she? I got a pocketful of money, credit cards falling outta my wallet, and my Benz is parked out front. Shit, I smell good. And look even better than I smell. "Come on, Halle. Take it." And don't she take all of it?

"Oh, hell, yeah!" That's my girl. Halle, you working it, baby. Goddamn! She can perform miracles with those lips, I swear to God she can. I'm feeling smooth and hot, like a blister getting ready to pop, like the bristles of a hot soft brush is tickling me only it ain't funny but I'm grinning from ear to ear 'cause . . . Watch out, Halle! Toni Braxton said she can suck it better than you! Move over, girl, and let Toni do her thang. She told the whole truth and nothin' but truth!

I wanna look down, but I don't wanna open my eyes. I feel her stroking it like she's familiar with it, like she in love with it, like she been waiting to kiss it, touch it, hold it, and stroke it all her life. I whisper, "Take your time, baby." I'm starting to tingle. It's spreading through every single one of my veins, all the way out to the curve of my fingertips. Damn. My dick is throbbing. It wants to scream and tell the world how good it's feeling right now. Now I'm icy hot and some kinda electric current is shooting through my body and working its way down.

"That's it, Toni!"

I love the way she's singing to it.

"Work it, baby." It's moving to her beat. "Come on, Toni, hit any note you want to. Make it jump. That's it! Yeah yeah yeah, Toni, that's IT!"

I feel the sock getting wet and my body sinks into this raggedy-ass mattress, since I'm now back in the real world, but I can't open my eyes until I at least kiss Toni and Halle and lick their pretty nipples and thank 'em for being at my service tonight. They thank me. They wanna curl up here and spend the night, but I say, "Y'all both can't stay. It wouldn't be right." What a jam I done got myself into, but, hell, I can't choose, 'cause I love 'em both.

While they fighting over it, a knock on my front door makes 'em both disappear. I pull my sock off and toss it under the bed. I'll get it later. But I always say that. I wonder who the hell that is. As long as it ain't no more Clearing House Sweepstakes motherfuckers, or Luisa, I almost don't care.

"Hold on a minute!" I holler, as I put on a pair of clean sweats and walk out to the door. "It better be important. Who is it?"

"It's me, Jamil," a small, crackly voice says, "your son."

My son. Goddamn. I look like damn it to hell. Shit. My *son*. What is he doing here? I didn't even know he knew where I lived. Open the fucking door, Lewis. "Just a minute," I say, and run to put on a clean T-shirt.

"I can come back later," he says through the door.

"*No!* Don't go nowhere. Just give me one second! I'm coming!" I run and put on a light-blue T-shirt that ain't hardly got no wrinkles in it, grab my cigarettes and some matches, and limp back as quick as I can to the door. I open it. I'm shocked as hell when I see a miniature version of myself staring back at me. I can't believe this. "Hi," I say. "Come on in."

Jamil is wearing a black baseball cap pulled down awfully low, so I don't really see his eyes. His lips look like my lips, and so do his chin. He's grown. Must be about five eight or nine. And skinny. Can't weigh more than 140 pounds, if that. I don't remember ever being this skinny as a kid. I think he's thirteen. But I ain't sure. He was a runt the last time I saw him. A lot can change in a year.

"Sit down," I say. I'm nervous. I wanna hug him but I ain't sure if I should or not. I don't know if he wants a hug. He don't act like it. But, damn, this is my son. Here. In my apartment. He goes over and sits down on the couch, but he jumps back up, holding a bundle of crumpled-up plastic in his hand. Shit, I forgot about Bobbing Betty.

"What's this?" he asks, as her head drops into view.

"It's something stupid."

"Is this one of those inflatable girls?" He's blushing.

"No. Sometimes I use it going to work, when I'm running late and wanna drive in the carpool lane. I blow her up and sit her in the front seat."

He lets out a laugh, but I can tell he ain't buying this story. He slides Bobbing Betty to the other end of the couch and I walk over and sit on the chair across from him. When we look at each other, that's when I notice his left eye is black. And swole up. "What happened to your eye?"

"I got hit in it."

"Do it hurt?"

"It's throbbing."

"I'll get some ice for it. Who hit you?"

"My dad."

"Wait a minute. I'm your dad."

"I meant my stepdad."

"That white boy hit you in your eye hard enough to do this?"

"Yep."

"Why?"

"Because he found some weed in my backpack."

"You smoke marijuana?"

"Sometimes."

"That stuff ain't no good for you."

"Whatever."

"I thought you was into that ROTC junior-army stuff and everything." I get a cigarette out the pack and light it.

"I was. Those aren't any good for you."

"I know. Was?"

"I only did it because they made me."

"Who?"

"My parents."

When I hear the words "my parents" I know he ain't talking about me and his mama. Damn.

"What grade you in?"

"Eighth."

"And how old are you again?"

"Thirteen and a half."

"That's what I thought. But what exactly made him haul off and just punch you in the eye?"

"I sorta got smart with him, I guess."

"Where was your mama?"

"Standing right there, holding Heather, watching."

"What?"

"She never says or does anything. He runs the show around our house. She's like his puppet."

"Did you hit him?"

"After he hit me, of course I did."

"Really?" I'm trying not to let him see the smirk on my face, but right now I'm feeling proud that he's got enough balls to stand up for hisself. "What'd you hit him with?"

"My fist."

"No fooling," I say, but I'm thinking, Wow, that shoulda really put a hurting on him. "Did he hit you with his fist?"

"Yes he did. Quite a few times."

"Where is he now?"

"At home."

"And did they know you were coming here?"

"No. They don't know where I am."

"So have you, like, run away or something?"

"Exactly," he says.

"And where you running away to?"

"Right here. I wanna live with you."

"Damn," is all I can say, but what's really on my mind is how I'ma get out to their house to put my foot in this mother-fucker's ass. I swore if he ever laid a hand on my son I was gon' hurt him, and I meant it.

"Aren't you glad to see me?" he asks.

"Yeah. Of course I am. Just not under these kinda circumstances. I wasn't expecting you tonight."

"I can sleep on the couch. I don't mind."

"Wait a minute, Jamil. First of all. It's a little more complicated than you just coming over here to move in and sleeping on my couch. Your mama got custody of you. You're a minor. You can't just move in here with me 'cause you feel like it."

"Then why don't you get custody of me?"

"What's he do?"

"Todd?"

"Yeah, Todd."

"What do you mean?"

"You sure talk proper. Just like a little white boy."

He swerves his head around like Stevie Wonder. I guess he's

tired of hearing this. "But it's cool." I say it like I'm apologizing. "You sound smart."

And he do, and it wouldn't kill me to talk like I graduated from high school. Especially in front of him. I know better. And I know he can't be too impressed by the way I talk.

"Yeah, well . . . anyway, what do you mean about Todd?"

"What kind of work do—I mean—does he do?"

"He works for UPS but he had to have shoulder surgery, so he's been off work for a few months."

"What happened to him?"

"Well, because of all the lifting he does, the doctor said he tore about ninety percent of his rotator cuff. He was pretty messed up."

"Is that so?"

"Yep. He has to go to physical therapy twice a week, but the rest of the time, after Mom gets home from work, they're at church. They go three nights a week and twice on Sunday. I baby-sit Heather. The whole routine is driving me crazy. They even make me sing in the choir and I can't sing a lick."

I snort a little. "When's he going back to work?"

"In another month or so. But he said he'll have to be on limited duty for a while."

"But he was strong enough to punch you?"

"I guess so."

I grit my teeth. Try to regroup. Lighten up. "Can your mama cook yet?"

"Nope. Todd does almost all of the cooking and cleaning."

"No shit?"

"I kid you not."

"Does he do the laundry, too?"

"Only his and my mama's."

"Well, who washes yours?"

"I had to learn. I go to the Laundromat once a week. I have to buy my own soap powder and use my paper-route money for the washer and dryer."

"You're shitting me. Why they make you do this?"

"So I'll be responsible."

"That's bullshit."

"I agree."

"So—why you smoke weed?"

"I don't know. So I won't have to think so much."

"You still getting good grades?"

"Sorta. I was getting almost straight A's, but I got two B's and a C last grading period."

"It's the weed, Jamil."

"I don't smoke it that much. I was just stressing. Didn't really care what I got on my report card for a minute, but then I cranked it back up."

"So Todd hit you and your mama just watched?"

"She asked him to stop when she saw that he'd hurt me."

"He ever hit you before?"

"He threw something at me once."

"Really?"

"Yeah, but he missed."

"What'd he throw?"

"A bat."

"A bat, huh?"

"Yep. What's wrong with your hand?"

I try to ball it up into a fist but it won't go. "I got a little arthritis."

"But your fingers are really crooked."

"I know."

"Is that why you limp?"

"Afraid so."

"What can you do to get rid of it?"

"Nothing, really. Just take pills that make the swelling go down."

"Does it hurt?"

"Yes. It sure does, but I can deal with it. I've been dealing with it. Don't have no other choice but to deal with it."

"Do you have anything to eat?"

Fuck. I wasn't expecting no company. I'm almost scared to go over there and open the refrigerator. But I do, just to put on a front, like I'm surprised not to find nothing when I open it. "I just got back from Vegas and ain't had time to get to the grocery store. Your granny was in the hospital. She had a bad asthma attack. But she's doing pretty good now. I don't know what's around here to eat." When I open the refrigerator, it's sad. It is empty. Not so much as a stick of butter, a slice of bread, no kinda drinks whatsoever. I should be ashamed of myself. I know it. I feel it right now. I open the freezer. I got plenty of ice. I get a dish towel and wrap some cubes inside and ball it up.

"Well, I've got close to two hundred dollars. We can go get something."

"You got two hundred dollars on you right now?"

"Yeah."

"Where'd you get that kind of money?"

"I work—I told you, I deliver papers. But I'm not allowed to spend it. I lie about how much I make and hide some of it. This is my stash."

Just like his daddy for the world.

"Well, this is good that you have a job. It do teach you how to be responsible, I guess."

"I'm thirteen, Dad."

"Yeah, you told me."

"Is there a Tony Roma's anywhere around here?"

"A who?"

"Tony Roma's? It's a barbecue place."

"No, but we got a Arby's."

He frowns up his face. "How about McDonald's?"

All I'm thinking is, I already had McDonald's once today, and here's a opportunity to eat a real meal. I don't wanna pass this chance up, even though I have every intention of giving back whatever my son spends. I mean that. I hand him the ice and he puts it up to his eye and then I hear myself say, "You don't wanna eat that junk tonight, do you?"

"Well, what else good is within driving distance?"

"We got Marie Callender's. That's a nice, classy kinda place, and they got the best pot pies. How does that sound?"

"Good."

"But we have to walk. My car is out of commission right now. It's in the shop. Being fixed. Won't be ready for a few days, but could be tomorrow."

"I don't mind walking. What about you?"

"I can make it, but ain't it still raining?"

"It wasn't when I walked from the bus stop."

"How'd you get out here anyway? And who told you where I lived?"

"I took two Greyhound buses. It took four hours, but it was kind of cool. I've never been on a Greyhound bus before. Aunt Janelle gave me your address, because she said you didn't have a phone. Do you still play chess?"

I'm shocked that he remembers. It's nice that he do. That he got something good stored in his memory about me. "When I have a worthy opponent," I say.

"You've got one," he says, and heads for the door.

I hope he ain't too good, is what I'm thinking when I grab my jacket, but then I feel ashamed for even allowing this kinda thought to enter my mind. This ain't even about him. It's about me. I'm just tired of losing. Want to win for a change. Want him to see that I'm smarter than he is. I may not sound like it, but I am. I want him to gain a different level of respect for me when he sees how fast I move, how good I am at battle. I want him to watch his father think and act, and make sharp, intelligent decisions. I don't care if it's only on a board. Because victory can transcend. And victory is power. And if I had to lose to anybody, I just hope it ain't to my own son.

Credit

I didn't wanna be here when Al got home, so, right after work, I stopped by the liquor store and got my lottery ticket and then went to the mall to take back that stupid hat and that ridiculous diamond ring and got the money credited back to my credit cards. Then I went to Red Lobster and treated myself to a steak-and-lobster dinner and three Margaritas. They was weak. I still didn't feel like going home, so when I saw a movie theater I just parked, got a ticket to a movie I ain't never heard of, and went in and sat down to watch it, even though all I saw was the last twenty minutes, so I don't even know what it was about, but it was good enough to keep my mind occupied. I ain't said but two words to the kids these past few days. They know when something is wrong: I'm usually real quiet and then I explode. They been walking around on eggshells, just waiting. But I'ma fool 'em this time: I ain't blowing up. I'm keeping my cool.

When I get in the house the kids is eating the leftover oxtails I made last week, and I guess Tiffany called herself making some yams that ain't nobody eating but her. The kitchen is a mess, as usual, but I ain't saying nothing. I don't care if the fucking house collapse.

"Hi, Ma," Tiff says. "Don't worry. We're cleaning up as soon as we finish. Where you been?"

"Out," I say, and go sit in my chair. "Why y'all eating so late? It's eleven o'clock."

"We was waiting for you to get home."

"I'm touched," I say. "Leave that stuff and go on upstairs and get ready for bed. Right now."

They all scurry like mice, even Trevor, who ain't said a word to me except, "Ma, have you been in my room going through my personal belongings?" and I said, "No. Why? You hiding something?" and he said, "No, I'm not hiding anything, but some people want to keep things hidden because it's easier. But it's not." And on that note he closed his door in my face.

Al is watching the news. "Hi, baby," he says. "I was worried, wondering where you were. You work late?"

"No, I didn't work late. I had some errands to run."

"Is that right?" he says, not taking his eye off the TV. "They fixing to finally let them black Africans vote down there," he says.

"Down where?"

"In South Africa. They had this Mandela locked up for twenty-some-odd years for some stuff he tried to do, sorta like what Dr. King was trying to do here, and now he out, and people is turning out in droves to vote, and they didn't thank this many would come. Black people is something else," he says, chuckling.

"I'm happy for 'em," is all I can think to say.

"What's wrong, baby? Something happen at work today?"

"As a matter of fact, it did."

"Yeah," he says. He ain't listening. His eyes is glued to that TV, so I just say, "I quit my job today, 'cause I wanna be a full-time prostitute and make babies and then go find the daddies and make 'em pay up their asses in child support."

"Come again. What you talking about over there, girl?"

"I said, 'I want a divorce.' "

That shit gets his attention. He picks up the remote and turns the volume down and looks at me. "What?"

"You heard me, Al."

"Come on, Charlotte, not tonight."

"Why not tonight?" I say, and reach in my purse and get out that letter and throw it at him. He picks it up and starts reading it, and then let it drop in his lap. He don't say one fucking word, just sit there like all the bones in his body is leaving. His shoulders start drooping, and the next thing I know he slumped over like he about to fall.

"Sit up," I say like it's a order.

But Al don't sit up. His hand is cupped on his forehead to cover his eyes. "I was praying this day would never have to happen," he says. He's crying. Al is crying. But I don't really care.

"Well, it's happening," I say.

"I didn't wanna hurt you, Charlotte."

"Hurt *me?*"

"Yeah."

"I'm confused, Al. Some woman serves you papers for back child support and they take our income-tax checks and you sit here and expect me to believe that you didn't wanna fucking hurt me? Spare me, would you? You're too kind, Al. Who the hell is she?"

"You know who she is."

My heart feels like somebody's sticking darts in it. I know who she is? I'm scared to go over the women I know, and I ain't about to sit here and have no stroke trying to guess. "Who is it, Al?"

"Remember a long time ago when you found that note in my toolbox?"

"Her?"

"She went and had herself a baby on me, and 'cause me and you didn't break up, she told me as long as I sent her some money every month she wouldn't bother me."

"She had your baby?"

"Yeah, she did. A boy. His name is Raynathan. He nine going on ten. They live in South Carolina, which is where her people from."

"What's her name?"

"Alice. Charlotte, she didn't tell me about this till it was too late to do anything about it."

"You ever seen this boy?"

"Not in a few years. It was too hard. I never loved that woman, Charlotte, and she did this here hoping I would stay connected to her, and it worked."

"How good did it work, Al? Tell me that."

"Well, I been sending her regular money all these years, but you know what's been going on around here with the Laundromats and stuff, and we strapped some months, so I ain't been able to do what I been doing, and I guess she got mad."

"She got mad, huh?"

"Yep. She got mad."

"That's too bad."

"Why? I can fix this, Charlotte."

"You broke it, you should fix it, but you know what, Al?"

"What?"

"Don't waste your energy." I get up and head for the steps.

"Wait a minute, Charlotte!" he says, coming after me.

"No, you wait a minute, buster. I done gave you some of the best fucking years of my life, and you just keep on deceiving me and lying to me, and now I find out you got another baby— not just one, but two! I don't need to be married to no man I can't trust. And you? You can't be trusted, so all your little theatrics, save 'em for what's-her-name, Alice. Go tell Alice!"

"Charlotte, please don't do this. Just think about this for a minute. Let's sleep on it."

"No, you sleep on it, Al. Just make sure it ain't here. And if you here when I wake up, I'll go straight to the courthouse and get me a restraining order."

"For what? I ain't done nothing to you!"

"What did you say?"

"I mean, I ain't put my hands on you or nothing like that, Charlotte."

"Oh, but you have, Al. You have. You know what? You feel like a credit card I done had for a long time and now I'm over the limit, so I'm taking the scissors and cutting the mother-fucker up so I can't use it no more. I got enough credit, you know what I mean?"

"Naw I don't. Charlotte, baby, what about the kids?"

"The kids is gon' be fine. They grown any-damn-way."

"I don't want no divorce."

"No? I don't see why not. Then you can be free to fuck any-body anytime anywhere. That's probably what you been doing all these years in your big rig, huh, ain't it? Is that where you do it?"

"Stop it, Charlotte. I told you the truth. I ain't slept with an-other woman in ten years except you. I swear on my mama and daddy's grave that that's the truth."

"But you a liar, Al."

"Sometimes you gotta lie to protect folks' feelings."

"Look, I'm getting bored listening to you and I'm tired as hell and I wanna go to sleep." I walk up a few steps and then I hear him say . . .

"What you gon' do without me?"

I let my foot drop back down a step, and I turn to look at him, even though I ain't exactly sure how to answer this ques-tion or where to start. I just say, "A whole lot more."

"What's that supposed to mean, Charlotte?"

"You really wanna hear it, Al?"

"Oh, so is this something you been thinking about for a while?"

"Let me put it to you this way. I'm so tired of working at that post office I could scream. Let me give you a idea of what I do all day long. Today the computer broke down, so I had to fig-ure out how long everybody's frigging route was gon' take by hand, which meant I had to multiply the time it's supposed to take 'em to deliver the mail to each mailbox—which is eigh-teen seconds—by the number of houses on each of they routes.

Oh, I forgot to mention that four of 'em called in sick today, so I had to find backup carriers, and then one of the trucks broke down and I busted some of the carriers bullshitting when they was supposed to be sorting out they route, 'cause they'll do anything to get some overtime, and then we got labor disputes going on that they want me to read about in Lord only knows which damn contract, and then we get irate customers out front cussing and screaming 'cause their mail keeps going to the wrong address or they ain't getting it until six o'clock, and today I even had to drive to Hyde Park to some rich white bitch's house, 'cause her vicious-ass dog won't let the carrier open the mailbox 'cause he pepper-sprayed the dog a long time ago and now it won't even let him come close to the fucking box, so I had to go out and tell the woman to keep her dog in the house or she gon' have to come to the post office to get her goddamn mail, and the whole time the dog is licking my hand. I don't need to be doing this kinda shit. I got a brain, and I ain't using it! I'm a watchdog. That's what I am. A fucking guard dog. And you wanna know what I'm gon' do without you, Al? I'm taking my black ass back to school, that's what I'ma do."

"School?"

"That's what I said."

"Wait, you ain't quitting your job, I know."

"I am. I'm getting my 401(k) money."

"Don't be ridiculous, Charlotte. That's our retirement money."

"Our?"

"Yours, ours, it's the same thing."

"No, it ain't the same thing, Al. My name is on that 401(k), not 'Albert Toussaint,' got it?"

"All right, all right. You thinking about going to a real college?"

"I don't know. Maybe. All I know is I'm tired of getting up at four o'clock in the morning and at the end of the day don't feel like I've done nothing nobody even really gives a shit about. I wanna do something for me. Something that makes me feel good."

"I ain't never tried to stop you from doing that, Charlotte."

"I didn't say you did, did I?"

He takes a few steps toward the bottom step. "Don't come up here, Al. I mean it."

"What you wanna do to make yourself feel good, Charlotte? Tell me."

"I don't know right now. All I do know is, whatever it is, I wanna do it at home."

"Like what?"

"I just told you, I ain't sure! But I'll put it this way. I saw a commercial on television for this international correspondence school and I sent away for some information. I'ma look it over and see if I might wanna try something they got."

"Like what, Charlotte?"

"Why you keep asking me the same damn questions? Go! Leave!"

"All right, all right. But this is what I gotta say about this: I'm sorry. I didn't do this to hurt you. I thought I was protecting our marriage by doing it this way, but I was wrong. Sometimes, people make bad decisions, Charlotte, but that don't mean they bad, do it?"

"I don't know, Al, but I don't even know if I really know you no more. I don't know if you really the same man I married. And to be honest, right now I could care less. Good night," I say, and head up the stairs past the kids' rooms. I go in our room and lock the door behind me. I get in the bed with my clothes on and wrap myself inside the covers. I lay here listening, waiting, to see how long it's gon' take him to do what he's gon' do. I'm wondering if he gon' come up the steps and try to fight for me, or if he gon' be a coward and leave. When I hear his engine turn over and the garage door open and close, I guess I got my answer.

Cancer

The guy who built this house was stingy when it came to landscaping. The shrubs are downright dwarflike; the trees are sparse and nothing more than tall twigs. I can just about count how many flowers there are on one hand. The backyard slopes upward, and because the ground cover never quite took off, the sun and heat have turned the dark-brown bark to a grayish beige. He swore the evergreens would be at least twenty feet by now, but I'd be afraid to put Christmas lights on them. When we moved here two years ago, I promised myself I'd get around to sprucing it all up, and today is finally that day.

I'm basically killing time, waiting for two things to happen. After finally making the time to work on and finish what I thought was still a working draft of my proposal, I was shocked when the agent representing me for my cookbook told me that two or three publishers might be interested. She's supposed to let me know sometime today or tomorrow which one makes the best offer. I almost shit when she told me she wanted "six figures." But I'm not freaking out. I'll be happy with any amount that would help Mama get her condo and car and send her on her cruise. I want her life to improve. Want her to have some fun. Want her to stop worrying so much. Since submitting the proposal, I haven't managed to eke out enough time to write any of the text; haven't even started narrowing down the recipes. All I have is a concept: how to eat healthy and delicious gourmet-type meals in little or no time and for even less money than you'd think. The agent said they'd want to see a polished introduction within a few weeks. That I'd need to give them a better idea of the structure the book would take.

I'm also waiting for the landscaper to show up. He's black. This'll be a first for me, because 99 percent of all landscapers in California are Mexican. But one of my clients swears this guy isn't your everyday run-of-the-mill gardener: that he's really a "landscape architect." He actually does a design plan. She said he does amazing work, especially with ponds, those koi fish and all kinds of exotic plants. I like to spend my money "black" whenever I can, so this is kind of refreshing. He's already twenty minutes late, but I'm not going to hold that against him.

A pile of mail is sitting on the counter, and I start sorting it—making stacks. At least ten invitations from clients—I drop them in the trash. Two or three letters are for Dingus, from different universities. He's already gotten them from USC, UCLA, Stanford, and a bunch of other schools. He told me this would happen in his junior year. I never got a single letter from any college asking me to come for a visit. Jocks.

It's so quiet in here. So still. Birds are chirping outside, and I realize it's spring. The sun is bright. The kitchen looks like a photograph from a kitchen magazine. It's so perfect. Too perfect, really. I did it all by the book. Bought the best of everything. And here it all is: The Wolf range. The Miele dishwasher. The Gaggenau ovens. The Sub-Zero fridge. But who really gives a shit what I cook on, what I clean my dishes in, or how I chill my food? And did I just have to paint the room butter yellow?

I find myself sliding down the wall until I land on the floor. I wish something good would happen to me. I'm not talking about a cookbook contract. I mean something that would break up the monotony of working too hard. In fact, I should be in my office right now, planning a party or working on a week-to-week meal plan for summer. I'm always planning. Always about to. And it's almost always for somebody else. People I don't even want to know. What they don't know is that the joy of cooking is the cooking itself. It's starting to get to the point where even the presentation is becoming passé. Because, after they eat it, it's gone. No trace of joy is left.

My energy level is dropping. These are all negative thoughts, thoughts that won't help me do what I've got to do. I need a jump. I hook my foot around my purse strap and pull it over to me. My prescription bottle rolls out and I get one of my pills, swallow it dry, but then realize I'm sitting next to the sink, so I get up and cup my hands under the faucet and sip the water from my palms.

Without even realizing it, I lean over and look down into the silver drain. I can't see anything. It's too dark down there. I keep looking anyway. I hope that girl isn't pregnant. I know that's what's been bothering me, too, and I don't know why I'm trying to pretend like it's not. This isn't something I can control, and I'm going to have to confront Dingus about it. I really don't give a shit if he gets mad because I eavesdropped. I've spent the last sixteen years of my life, and his, raising him to be a responsible young man. Stressed time and time again the importance of getting a college education, especially for a black man. Instilled in him the importance of being honest, dependable, worthy. Strive to be the best even if he doesn't become the best. That'll be good enough. And how in the world is a baby supposed to fit into this picture? What if that girl decides to have it? Does this boy have any idea what it could do to his future? Please. Don't let this happen, God. My son may be stupid, but he's smart. He's worked too hard. I've worked too hard to come to this.

I don't even know which sister I dial until one answers. "Charlotte?"

"Yeah."

"It's me, Paris."

"What can I do for you?" she says, dryly.

You'd think I was a bill collector. "You don't have to sound so cold, Charlotte, my goodness."

"I don't sound cold, and if you called to give me another lecture, I ain't in the mood."

"I'm not calling to lecture you, so please don't hang up the phone."

"Well, what's going on?"

"I was just calling to see how you're doing."

"I'm doing just fine. Why wouldn't I be?"

Just the tone of her voice tells me she's lying. I don't know why it's becoming so hard for us to tell each other the truth, when we used to tell each other everything. "Relax, Charlotte. Why're you so defensive? You're the one who hung up on me the last time we talked, remember?"

"Look, Paris, I talked to Mama and she understood why I didn't come out there, okay?"

"Okay. That's not why I'm calling."

"Then what are you calling about?"

There's a click on the line. This could be my agent. "Can you hold on a second?"

"Yeah."

Before I press the receiver, I hear Miss Ordelle, the older lady who irons for me on Wednesdays, come in the side door. I see her bandana tied around her head. "Hi, baby," she says, almost to the floor.

"Hi, Miss Ordelle. How are you?"

"No worse for the wear," she says, and coughs ferociously. "But I'm here."

The phone clicks again.

"You gon' get that?" Charlotte asks.

I click it this time.

"Hello, Mrs. Price?"

My agent calls me "Paris," and anyway it's a man's voice, so then I think it's Dingus trying to pretend like he's Isaac Hayes or Barry White, but he's still at school. "Look. I'm on a long-distance call, and if you're trying to sell me something, the answer is I'm not interested, or I already have some, and, no, I don't want to change my long-distance company, and if you're not selling anything, who's calling and how'd you get this number?"

"This is Randall Jamison. I'm the landscaper. . . ."

"Oh, I'm sorry." Now I feel silly.

"No, I'm sorry for being late. I'm stuck in traffic. Apparently, a semi has flipped over on 280, and me along with about a hundred other cars are waiting to see when we can move. I just wanted you to know that."

"Well, thanks for calling, Randall. And don't worry, I've got enough to keep me busy until you get here."

Before I click back to Charlotte, I have to pause for a minute. What a nice voice. What a sexy voice. A landscaper. He's probably rough and ready and raggedy and ugly and dry and dirty, and I bet he stinks. Oh, who cares, as long as he can get the job done. I press the receiver. "Charlotte?"

"I'm still here."

"So—how are you, again?"

"I'm fine, Paris. Couldn't be better. How's Dingus?"

"He's fine. Except some little white girl might be pregnant by him."

"Yeah," she says, like she couldn't care less one way or the other.

"How about your kids? How are they?"

"They're all doing good. Real good."

"And Al?"

"Oh, he's fine. We're all fine."

"That's good. What are you doing for your birthday?"

"Nothing. I don't celebrate my birthday no more. It's just another day."

"Well, we're trying to decide what to do for Mama for hers, and we were wondering if . . ."

"Who is 'we'?"

"Me and Janelle," I lie. We haven't exactly discussed it again in any detail, but she'll go along with the program. She always does.

"I'm listening."

"Well, first I thought Mama wanted to spend a couple of weeks here. . . ."

"Don't she always?"

"No, she doesn't always, Charlotte. Would you let me finish, please?"

"I'm listening."

"Anyway, since Shanice is staying with her . . ."

"Since when did Shanice start living with Mama?"

"Since the end of March. You haven't talked to Janelle?"

"No. I ain't talked to nobody but a lawyer."

"A lawyer? For what?"

"I'm getting a divorce."

"Hold it a minute! You just said you and Al were fine."

"We are. This is the best thing that coulda happened to both of us. I shoulda done it a long time ago. Why is Shanice staying with Mama?"

"Because Janelle and George are having problems."

"And she gets rid of her daughter and not his ass?"

"Good point. He's supposedly gone."

"What happened between them two?"

"I don't know for sure. Janelle's not talking about it."

"Mama thinks he probably messed with Shanice, even though Shanice claimed he just hit her."

"Who told you that?" I ask.

"Mama. Why? Was it supposed to be a well-kept secret or something?"

"I don't know. I'm confused. This is just getting all fucked up. Everybody getting divorces. Splitting up. What's going on with you and Al, even though I'm not sure I want to hear this?"

"You ain't gotta hear it."

"Are you serious, Charlotte?"

"As cancer. He just got served some papers for back child support from some woman he slept with over ten years ago who just came outta no-damn-where and they done took our fucking income-tax return and everything."

"No shit. Who is this woman?"

"I don't know the bitch!"

"She had a baby by Al and he didn't know it?"

"Apparently, he did."

"I don't know what to say, Charlotte."

"You ain't gotta say nothing. It's a lotta things I been wanting to do with my life to get away from this post office, and, to be honest, Al ain't been doing nothing but keeping me down. We been in a rut, so this might just be a blessing in disguise. Anyway, what about Mama's birthday?"

I don't know what else to say about her divorce, so I'll let it pass for right now. It's not something you gloss over, but I'm not in any position to fix their problems, if in fact their problems are real. You never know with Charlotte. She can be so melodramatic. "Well, Mama told us to forget about doing anything for her on her birthday, but she was wondering if we could all chip in a little something so she could go on a cruise this summer with her friend Loretta."

"How much something?"

"I don't know yet. Probably no more than five hundred."

"That's a lotta money. For some of us."

"If you can, you can. If you can't, you can't. Don't worry about it, Charlotte."

"You'll take care of it if we can't come through, ain't that right, Paris?"

"I don't know. I've got a lot on my plate right now, too. Look, I just wanted you to know."

"All right. That's it?"

"I guess. But are you sure you're feeling okay, Charlotte?"

"Couldn't be better. Look, I gotta go, Paris."

"Okay, Charlotte, but call me if you need to talk."

"I will. And tell Dingus to make that girl get a abortion. He don't need no baby. He got a future ahead of him. Bye."

I'm in shock. She's getting a divorce? Charlotte loves Al, and he's been there for her and those kids since the beginning of time. Do you fault somebody for something they did a long time ago when it comes back to haunt them? It doesn't seem fair, but, then again, I'm not in her shoes.

I can't go into my office now. No way. I feel like I'm floating in a holding zone, waiting for this guy to show up and a call from New York. Why isn't she calling? Did the deal fall through? I dial my other sister, who answers on the first ring.

"How're you doing, Janelle?"

"I'm fine. And you?"

"Exhausted, if you want to know the truth."

"Me, too."

"You won't believe this."

"What?"

"Charlotte says she's divorcing Al because some woman from his past hit him up for child support."

"I can think of better reasons to divorce your husband than that. She's not divorcing him. Wait and see."

"I don't know. Have you talked to Shanice?"

"Yes, I have. She's fine. She and Mama are bonding."

"You miss her?"

"Of course I miss her."

"Well, when's she coming home?"

"I don't know right now."

"Why don't you know?"

"Because there's a lot of confusion around my house."

"Like what?"

"I don't feel like getting into it right now, Paris."

"Why not, Janelle? You never feel like talking about anything that really matters. Why is that?"

"That's not true. It's just that sometimes other people can't solve your problems."

"Did I say anything about solving your problems? No. But I'm your sister, bitch, and if something is wrong over there, I just wanted you to know you can talk to me."

"I know."

"Then why aren't you?"

"I am."

"No, you're not, Janelle. Something is going on with your daughter and your husband and you're not telling it."

"You're right. But, like I said, Paris, I have to work this out myself."

"But you're not very good at that."

"You don't know what I'm good at."

"I've only known you for thirty-five years, Janelle. We grew up in the same house. So—I think I do."

"Look, can we talk about something else? Like Mama's birthday, for instance?"

"She told me she just wants us to chip in so she can go on her cruise this summer."

"That sounds good."

The phone clicks. This has *got* to be New York. "Can you hold on a minute? I'll be right back. I promise."

"Okay."

"Hello?"

"Is this Paris?" somebody with a raspy voice is asking.

"Who is this?"

"This your Aunt Priscilla, baby. How you doing?"

"You mean Prison, Aunt Priscilla?" I ask, disappointed again.

"Well, yeah, since you put it that way."

This call means two things: she's out and she wants something. And it's always the same thing—cash—for the same thing—drugs. She's the oldest drug addict I know. I hope it doesn't run in the family. "Aunt Priscilla, is there a number I can call you back at? I'm on a long-distance call right now."

"Look, I just need a favor, is all. I just got out, you know, and I went to the doctor and he done told me I got cancer, and I wanna know if you can help me get the operation."

"What kind of operation?"

"The operation that's gon' get rid of the cancer."

This one takes the cake. "What kind of cancer do you have?"

"I think he said it's in my throat. A lump or something, and they need to get it out."

"Look, Aunt Priscilla, I'm really sorry to hear that you've got cancer, and I wish I could help you right now, but I'm broke. Don't you have insurance or Medicaid?"

"Broke? Everybody know you got money, baby. You ain't gotta lie to your Aunt Priscilla. When you do time you don't get no benefits," she says, and starts crying. "This ain't no way to come home: with nothing but a whole lotta something you don't need. You ain't even gon' try to help your auntie live a little longer?"

"How much is the operation?" I ask for the hell of it; I would love to come right on out and ask her how much does she need to get her through the day, but it's coming. I know it.

"I think it's only gon' be about a thousand, but if you could send me a hundred or two hundred today that would help take care of the doctor's visit and them X-rays they took."

"Are you staying with Aunt Suzie Mae?"

"No no no no no. You know Suzie Mae and me don't get along. I ain't got no permanent residence as yet."

"Hold on a minute, Aunt Priscilla." I click Janelle back on. "Girl, you won't believe this. It's Aunt Priscilla on the other line."

"Did she escape again?"

"No, she's out. This time it's cancer and she wants me to pay for her operation. I'll be right back." I click back.

"Aunt Priscilla?"

"I'm still here."

"I could Federal Express you a little something at Aunt Suzie's and you could go over and get it tomorrow."

"Is there any way you could Western Union like fifty or a hundred so I can have it today?"

"I can try, but I don't know, Aunt Priscilla, I've got a lot to do today. Have you talked to Charlotte? She's right there in Chicago."

"Suzie Mae just gave me her number, and I left her a message, but she ain't called me back yet. You know how she is."

"Look, I really have to go, Auntie. Just check back tomorrow."

"Wait! These days you can use a credit card and do it over the phone. You ain't gotta go nowhere!"

"Okay! I'll do it. But I've got to go right now, and I'm glad you're out. Again. Goodbye!" And I click the phone.

Janelle's still laughing.

"Don't ask. Anyway, what are you doing right now?"

"You mean right now?"

"Yeah."

"I'm out in the front yard counting all the red cars that go by. I'm up to seventeen. I guess I'm trying to decide if I want to have this baby or get an abortion."

I get a gigantic lump in my throat. "Oh, so . . ."

"So you were right. But I feel kind of weird, Paris. George is gone."

"For how long?"

"I hope forever. I just don't know what I'm doing right now. It's too much. I need to talk to somebody who doesn't know me. Just to explain how things have transpired."

"Please don't go to a psychic for this kind of shit, Janelle. Please."

"I'm too scared. I went to a Tarot reader and the first card she flipped over was too much, so I left."

"Out of pure curiosity, what was it?"

"The Hanged Man. Anyway, I just want my daughter to

come back home. To be honest, I don't know how I'm gonna take care of her, and I don't know if I should have this baby or not."

"You're not handicapped, Janelle. You can get a decent job. How far gone are you?"

"A little over two months."

"Whoa. That's cutting it close."

"I know."

Now here comes Miss Ordelle, standing in my doorway with one hand on her hip and holding a pair of jeans in the other. Something's wrong. I hired her just to iron, but she insists on washing anyway (when her stories go off she gets bored). We argued about it, but she won. I asked her not to wash my white clothes, because she uses too much bleach and she's stingy with the softener.

"Hold on a minute, Janelle. Yes, Miss Ordelle?"

"Excuse me, baby. But I don't know how this happened. See this red stuff, here? I think Dingus musta had something red in his pocket. But it done got on a whole lotta stuff, and I just want you to know—I didn't do it."

"It's okay. Don't worry about it, Miss Ordelle."

"You sho'? I mean, I can try to get it out, now," she says, "but this look permanent to me."

"If you can, fine."

"All right," she says, coughing hard as she heads back toward the laundry room. She smokes like a fiend. Outside the garage door. And it seems like once a month Miss Ordelle has an abscess and has to get another tooth pulled. She was homeless three years ago, even though she's got grown kids. I found her through an agency. She ironed as good as Mama taught me. But when she told me how much her take was of the fee they were charging, I offered her a few dollars more if she would come once a week on her own. That was two years ago. Since then, every week, when I ask her how she's doing, it's gone from bad to worse, so much so that she should've been dead about a year ago. "Sorry about that," I say.

"Was that Miss Ordelle?" Janelle asks.

"Of course it was. She loves interrupting me when I'm on the phone, you know that."

"Does she have on her bandana?"

"Yes, she does."

"How many teeth does she have left?"

"Never mind, I love that woman, so shut up. Look. I was just calling to reach out and make a sisterly gesture. Between you and Charlotte, I swear. Lord only knows what our wonderful brother's up to."

"Well, all I know is Jamil called over here a few days ago for his address."

"You're kidding me."

"No, I'm not. He wasn't very communicative, but I gave it to him. And that was it."

I hear the doorbell ring.

"Look, there's my front door and it's probably this landscaper I've been waiting for."

"I thought your yard was already landscaped."

"I wouldn't go that far. Anyway, this guy's just going to look at it, throw some of his ideas out, and then go work on some plans and give me an idea how much it'll cost to make it lush and pretty, although right now, to be honest, it seems really trite compared to what you guys are going through."

"Don't worry. Everything always works out. I didn't get a chance to ask—how're you doing?"

"I'm fine. I think I sold my cookbook, and I've been going bonkers waiting for my agent to call and let me know the deal."

"That would be so cool, Paris. This is right up your alley. It took you long enough."

"Yeah yeah yeah," I say, trying to peek around the corner, but can't quite do it without being spotted.

The doorbell rings again.

"Just a minute! Be right there!"

"Okay, so go, and I'll talk to you later."

"Well, try not to make any decisions right now, okay, Janelle?"

"I won't. Thanks, Paris."

I hang up and look at myself in the glass to see if I look like a housewife without a husband. I do. I'm a mess. I have on gray sweats and a pink sweatshirt that has coffee stains on it from this morning. I can't remember if I combed my hair or not. But who cares? This is the fucking gardener.

When I open the door it appears that the lump that had popped into my throat when I was talking to Janelle has come back. I can't open my mouth to utter a single solitary word. This is the first black landscaper I've ever met, and they send me one who looks like he should be on one of those sexy black-men calendars? And in my condition? A woman who hasn't so much as smelled a man this close in over a year, let alone touched one. I'll be damned. All I'm thinking is: At least I'd have something pleasing to look at for a month, or however long it takes to do this. If this works out.

"Hello, Mrs. Price, I'm Randall. I finally made it," he says, holding out his hand to shake mine. His nails are clean. His hands are full of thick veins, but they look like they get lotioned regularly, because his wedding band is dull.

I swallow. "Hello, Randall. I'm Paris. Glad you made it." I feel ugly and fat, and I should've combed my hair even if no one was coming over. That's the problem, no one hardly ever comes over except Dingus's friends. Why is that, Paris?

"I think there were a few fatalities, sorry to say. But I'm here. You have a beautiful home," he says, looking around.

I can't even believe myself. Getting all giddy over some stranger who's here to look at my yard. Get a grip, Paris. Please.

"You want to show me your yard?"

"Sure," I say, and point toward the French doors that lead

outside. "I'll be right out." I'm too hyper right now. I need to calm down. But the good news is that this hasn't happened to me in years. His being married doesn't concern me. In fact, I hope he's happily married. I'm just grateful to him for making me feel some level of excitement. I need to contain this feeling, trap it somehow. So—I pick up my purse and get out a pill and then decide to break another one in half. I take them both.

I walk out through the open doors and just stand there watching this man walk around my yard. He's up at the top of the slope, standing next to an evergreen that looks like it's got tuberculosis. He must be about six feet, maybe five eleven. Chocolate brown. Not more than thirty-four or -five at most. God knew exactly what he was doing when he made this one. His wife is one lucky woman.

When I step outside, he yells: "You want to tell me some of your ideas, and then I'll tell you some of mine?"

"Sure," I say, as I stand inside a puddle of sunshine. The heat feels good. For the next hour or so, I think I'll pretend that the only thing on my mind are flowers and ponds and koi and evergreens and shrubs. But tonight, when I close my eyes, I'm almost certain that this is the man who'll be lying in bed next to me. That's how it's been. That's pretty much how it is.

Puff on That

He beat me. But I didn't feel bad like I thought I would. As a matter of fact, it was sorta like playing myself, because my son is smart, maybe even smarter than me. But it's cool. They say each generation should be an improvement over the next, and he's living proof that it's true, which is why I guess I actually feel better about losing to him.

He's still sleep out there on the couch, and I've already been up and out this morning. I tracked down Woolery and got most of my money, enough to get the parts for my car, and even though it hurt me to pay it back all at once, I sent Miss Loretta the sixty I owed her and Luisa her forty. My buddy Silas spent all morning helping me get my car running, and now I'm just smoking a cigarette, waiting for Jamil to wake up so I can take him home. We were up till almost three o'clock, and I'm glad all I had in the house to drink was the rest of that forty, 'cause I just barely got a buzz. It was nice waking up with a clear head instead of the lead head I'm used to. I ain't got cotton mouth either, which means I could actually tongue-kiss somebody if somebody was here for me to tongue-kiss. I might have to try this more often.

A cup of instant coffee'll make these three Tylenols work faster. Early morning is tough, when I get out the bed and my feet and ankles hurt so bad I can't even think about putting no weight on 'em. This morning wasn't quite as bad, but by this afternoon, if I don't take something again, I could be mistaken for cripple. Sometimes I can't even move my fingers to hold my cigarette. Like right now, some of 'em are swollen and curving out toward my baby fingers. And in a little while, these knots in my wrists and elbows'll be on fire, daring me to try to straighten 'em all the way out. I don't want my son to see me in this much pain. I don't want him feeling sorry for me, because I don't want his pity.

"Hey, Jamil," I say kinda loud. "Wake up. Let's go get some breakfast, and then I'm taking you home. I want to talk to Todd."

His head pops up over the back of the couch. He slept in that baseball cap. "I don't like breakfast," he says.

"Well, I do. My stomach gets all messed up if I don't eat. Plus, breakfast is for champions, didn't you know that?"

He grins. The boy's got dimples. Me or his mama don't have 'em, that much I remember. Come to think of it, I don't know what it'll be like to see Donnetta after all this time. Right now, I ain't got no butterflies in my stomach except for the mere fact that she might bring up the child-support issue, but I got a court date for that and, plus, I'll show her my hands. Maybe then she'll see why I ain't been working.

While Jamil takes his shower, I smoke another cigarette and try to think of what I'ma say to Todd. I'ma be a man about this. I ain't going out there to make a fool outta myself or do nothing stupid, but I want him to know—from one man to another—that you don't put your hands on somebody else's child. That's it. I'll let him know that if he ever touches him again there'll be consequences. I ain't never hit Jamil. Even when he was bad, I just talked to him. Jamil was hardheaded, couldn't stand sitting in one spot for more than five minutes, so I'd make him sit for ten, then fifteen, then a half-hour. By the time Donnetta filed for divorce, he was up to two hours.

"I'm ready," he says. "You need to get some new towels, Dad. Yours smell like mildew."

"I know. All things in time. Let's go."

"How are we getting there?"

"My car's running."

"Cool," he says. "Where are we gonna eat?"

"Coco's or IHOP, which would you prefer?"

"I really don't care."

"IHOP is my favorite. My treat," I say.

"Cool."

If my back was turned, I'd swear this boy was white.

———

Jamil is busy changing radio stations when I get out to the car. He don't say a word about the smoke coming out of the muffler, or how old and raggedy this piece of shit is, and I don't say nothing either. I'm grateful to have transportation, even if it is twelve years old and hard to find parts for. This burgundy Riviera gets me around town when I take care of it. It's a gas guzzler, but I bought it off this Mexican for two hundred dollars, so I wasn't all that particular about what other colors it came in. And, plus, I ain't into cars that much. Not like when I was young. I just want something that can get me where I'm going. But, hell, if I ever hit the lottery, the first thing I'd do after paying all my bills is get myself a brand-new truck.

"You all right?" I ask.

"I'm fine. I guess. I hope there's not going to be a scene."

"Don't worry about that, Jamil. All I want to do is make sure this dude never puts his hands on you again. If he does, he's going to jail. And that's that."

There goes that grin again. We don't say too much for the next forty minutes, when we get to Simi Valley and pull up in front of their house. It's the same shade as cantaloupes, one of those cheap stucco things I was building before my arthritis got too bad. I don't know why they all have to be fruity colors, and all set back at the exact same spot as the next house. If you ever came home drunk, you probably wouldn't be able to tell your house from the neighbors'. But they're new. And people like new anything: shoes, cars, and especially houses. They like the smell of new. The look and feel of new. I can't much blame 'em. If I could afford it, I'd be living in one, too.

I wonder what possessed Donnetta to wanna live way out here? What a dumb-ass question, Lewis. She's got a white husband. Which means she probably thinks like everybody else: that the further away you get from black folks, the safer you'll be. But look what happened to Rodney King, which wasn't that far from here.

Jamil opens his side faster than I thought and is out the car and at the front door before I can even turn the engine off. By the time I limp up the sidewalk, Donnetta is standing in the doorway with one hand on her hip, squinting. She looks better than I remember. Her skin is still smooth and creamy, like it's been dipped in caramel. Her hair is sandy brown and wavy; now it's way past her shoulders. And for somebody who just recently had a baby, she looks good: thinner than I ever remember her being.

"What are you doing here?" she asks.

"I just came to talk to you and your husband. I didn't come out here to cause no trouble, so don't worry."

"Who's out there, honey?" I hear a man's voice that sounds almost like a woman's say, but he doesn't even come to the door.

"It's Lewis," she says, and I'm surprised when she backs away to let me in. "Please don't make me have to get another restraining order," she mumbles.

When I walk in, I realize some things don't change. The house may be new but the stuff in here is old and out of style, with the exception of that big-screen TV. She's got that same J. C. Penney's couch we bought right after we got married and the La-Z-Boy, too. The tables weren't even real wood, but I didn't care back then, it was all we could afford. I see what must be four years of trophies and pictures of Jamil in his soccer and Little League uniforms on three glass shelves. It smells like Glade air freshener in here, but that's about it.

"How're you doing, man?" I hear that voice say, and when I turn, here goes Todd, the tin man. No wonder he punches kids. That's probably all he could get away with hitting. He ain't even close to handsome, and he's downright lanky to be about my height, he can't weigh more than 140, 150 tops. And his head looks too small for his body. He's clean-shaven and got beady little eyes. When he reaches out to shake my hand, I just look at him.

"I'm not staying long," I say.

"What brings you out here?" Donnetta says. "And where'd you run into Jamil?"

"I didn't run into him. He came over to my house yesterday."

"He probably told you a bunch of lies, then," Todd says.

"I don't know how many lies he told, but I've got some questions I want answers to."

"Like what?"

"Like why would you hit a thirteen-year-old kid in the eye with your fist?"

Todd starts walking around the dining room like he's trying to think of a good answer. Jamil, who ran straight upstairs when we got here, is now standing at the top of the steps looking down at us, like this is some kind of show he's about to watch.

"Look, Todd. This is the deal. I do not appreciate you putting your hands on my son and I do not think it's appropriate for you to be punching on a kid like he's a grown man."

"Hold on a minute, buddy. First of all, did he tell you what he did?"

"I ain't your buddy, Todd. Let's get that straight right here and now."

"Did he tell you what he did?"

"What did he do that was so bad besides smoke a little marijuana?"

"I don't believe my ears. Are you a God-fearing man or not?"

"What's God got to do with this?"

"There is no way I'm going to allow a thirteen-year-old child living under my roof to indulge in any kind of drugs. Not in this house."

"But he's not your son!"

"Well, I'm the one who's been taking care of him for the last four years."

"Oh, is that right?"

"Lewis, please," Donnetta says, getting up from the dining-room table where she been sitting with her hands folded. "This is getting a little out of hand and I don't feel comfortable. Let's just deal with this over the phone."

"Why don't you be quiet, Donnetta," Todd says.

"Yeah, shut up, Donnetta."

"Don't tell my wife to shut up."

"She used to be my wife and I can tell her to shut up if I feel like it. If you can hit my son in the face with your fist, I can tell her to shut the fuck up ten thousand times if I feel like it."

"Not in this house, you can't."

"Look, I just want you to know that if you've got a problem with anything Jamil does, before you raise your hand to hit him again, you better think twice, because I'll be on your ass like white on rice."

"Are you threatening me?"

"What does it sound like, motherfucker?"

"If he disobeys me, if he disrespects me, I will discipline him the way I see fit and considering the fact that we can count on one hand how much you've contributed to his well-being in the past four years, I don't think you have much say-so here. Now would you kindly leave this house?"

Before I even know what I'm doing I haul off and sucker-punch this blond motherfucker so hard he falls past the dining-room table and into the kitchen, and I hear Jamil yelling: "Kick his ass, Dad!" and I'm assuming he means me, and then I hear Donnetta scream, "I'm calling the police!" and when I look up

Todd is coming at me with a sponge mop and I snatch it out of his hand like I ain't got arthritis and start whopping him all over his body with it until the wooden part cracks in two and my hand is bleeding and everybody's screaming and yelling and all I can think is that I bet he won't hit my goddamn son no more.

When the police get here, they handcuff me, put me in the back of their car, and take me to jail. I don't really give a fuck. I made my point. Donnetta ran and got her little half-white baby she kept hidden from me the whole time and just stood there with it in her arms, shaking her head. Todd was still on the floor, acting like he was half dead. I didn't hurt that mother-fucker, not with that skinny-ass handle, but he still pretended like he couldn't get up when the cops pushed me out the door-way.

The police said my bail is probably going to be in the neighborhood of $50,000. Damn. I can't call nobody and ask for any five grand to get me out. Just what I need: another fuck-ing court date. Paris is already pissed at me for what happened in Las Vegas, so I can't even think about calling her. And Janelle's money ain't hers, so I can forget about her trying to explain to George why she would need this kinda cash. And then there's Charlotte, who I know would probably cuss me out when she heard the word "jail" and then hang up in my face. So fuck it. I'll just have to wait it out. Why'd this have to be a Saturday? Which means I won't even get arraigned until Wednesday.

One officer tells me that I'm being charged with assault and battery, and disturbing the fucking peace. That Todd is defi-nitely pressing charges. I have never been convicted of a vio-lent crime, and I ain't exactly sure what this means, but when we get to the jail, I ask if I can smoke a cigarette before I go in and how much time am I looking at? They both kinda chuckle, and then one of 'em says that I won't be walking on no streets in street shoes for at least the next twelve months, and for me to puff on that.

Lucky Strikes

"Granny, are we gonna make the pie for your birthday or not?" Shanice is asking me.

"I done told you at least a hundred times, girl: I don't roll nobody's crust or cut up no kinda apples." I love this child to death, but she is getting on my last nerve. Can we make this? Can we go here, can we do that? She think I'm young, and I had to remind her that as of today I'm a certified senior citizen, so cut me some damn slack. I'm exaggerating. Some. I guess I'm just used to complaining and glad I got somebody here to listen. Right now, I'm laying across my bed, halfway watching *Oprah* and reading my birthday cards. I just took a shower and gave myself a breathing treatment, and now I'm trying to sneak in a little hour or two nap before we leave for the bowling alley. It's been one helluva day.

"I told you you should've just let me make you a cake," Shanice says from the living room.

"First of all, you don't *tell* me what to do, missy, and, besides, it's *my* birthday, and I don't like cake. They always too sweet, too thick, and too dry, and especially with these Kmart teeth I got in my mouth right now. I like pies and cobblers, and a bread or rice pudding every now and then."

"Then can we get a frozen one?"

"You know how stingy them white folks is with the apples?"

"Not Mrs. Smith's," she says.

She just won't quit, will she? "Hers is the worst. But I'll tell you what. We'll get one on the way to the bowling alley and leave it in the car to thaw out and buy three or four apples, which you can cut up, and when we get back home the crust should be soft enough to cut open, and then we can add some cinnamon and brown sugar and lemon juice and vanilla and a few dabs of butter to spruce it up and make it taste like we made it from scratch."

"By the time you do all that, Granny, couldn't we have just made it from scratch?"

"Why don't you go sit your little narrow behind down somewhere and find something to do to keep you occupied? No. On second thought, go get Granny's bowling ball and put it in the backseat of my new car, would you?" When I hear myself say this I can feel my cheekbones tingling. I love the sound of that: "my new car." Paris is too much sometimes, I swear. When you got money you can buy damn near anything you want to without even leaving your house. All you need is a phone, a credit card, and Federal Express.

Last night, right before *Arsenio Hall* was coming on, my sister Priscilla called me collect to wish me a happy birthday and had the nerve to sound happy because she had just run into Precious, her damn daughter, in the same prison she was in. I guess I was supposed to jump for joy, but I didn't. Precious is thirty-five. I didn't even ask what she was in there for, 'cause their whole situation is just ridiculous. First Boogar and Squirrel, and now her only daughter. They all got caught up in some shit I don't understand. I told Priscilla I was falling asleep when she called, and after I told her I couldn't send her no more than twenty or thirty dollars, I said goodbye. I was still shaking my head when the phone rang again. It was Paris, calling to wish me a early happy birthday 'cause she said tomorrow she had to go with some gardener to pick out some trees and plants and rocks and slate and some kinda shy fish and she didn't know what time she'd be back and she wanted to make sure she caught me at home. I told her she caught me at home all right, that I was half sleep, so hurry up and say what she gotta say so I could go back. She told me to wake my fat butt up if I wanted to hear her good news. I made myself sit up and told her I was awake now, now hurry up and get to the damn point. And that's when she said she sold her cookbook for a good amount of money and that I could not only go down to that dealership after ten-thirty this morning and pick up my brand-new navy-blue Mitsubishi Galant, but to drive that sucker to the best dentist in town and make an appointment to get fitted for some brand-new dentures, and then she said turn every corner I feel like it until I see a condo I might want to live in and park this sucker in the shade and go talk to a sales agent about buying. At first she didn't even give me no price range, but then she did say to make sure the price had a "one" in front of it, and for me not to go crazy. Hell, here in the Valley, for one hundred thousand even a damn fool can live good. And since I'm nosy as hell anyway, I just had to know how much she got for a cookbook she ain't even wrote yet, and especially since she the one sound like she going a little spending crazy, but she just said, "Enough nuff," so I let it go at that.

Me and Shanice was way too excited when we drove that baby off the lot to go looking for some new teeth or at any kinda condos. We went straight to Red Lobster to celebrate, and who in the world did we run into? Cecil and his new family—looking like the black Flintstones—but I didn't even "trip"—as Dingus would say. Cecil was just about to put one of them little shrimps in his mouth when he saw us, and I just nodded a hello to him and then to that mushroom-looking wench he was sitting next to, who look young enough to be his grand-daughter, and who need to make up her mind which hairstyle she really interested in and settle on one instead of the three or four I saw. Look like finger waves was pressing against the left side of her head. The top was part ancient Jheri Curl and part reddish-blond braids that hung down over some of the waves. Hell, maybe they was supposed to be a waterfall, I don't know.

But the right side was cornrows that had been wove with purple yarn all through 'em. What would possess her to do this to herself? And this was only the front view.

Then there was three halfway-cute little kids who looked like they could use some Dixie Peach around their nappy edges, them gray elbows and knees, and a hot bath wouldn't hurt, since it look like Cecil musta took 'em to his favorite store in the whole world—Target—for them brand-new outfits they was wearing, but he shoulda kept on walking till he hit the shoe department. I just smiled and pushed Shanice past the whole group and led her to a table way back in the corner, where we couldn't see none of 'em.

But what did Cecil do? Come back to our table and just stood there, and said, "Happy birthday, Viola."

"Well, how nice of you to come to my party, Cecil. Thank you," I said, and picked up my menu and started reading it. When the waitress came, I ordered me a Margarita and Shanice a Shirley Temple. Cecil just kept standing there like a damn fool. "Go," I said. "Go on back over there with your new family."

"You gon' be home later?"

"No, I will not be home later. It's my birthday. I'm celebrating it."

"I wanted to drop something off for you."

"I got a date."

"You got a what?"

"A date. Just like you on a date. I'ma be on one, too, tonight."

"With who . . ." Shanice was about to ask until I kicked her under the table. "Oh, him, yeah, I forgot about him."

"I just wanted to give you a little something, Viola. It ain't got to be tonight."

"Then don't let it be tonight, Cecil. Look like you got enough to keep you busy. Now go. Go on."

"All right," he says, and turns and walks away like his bunions hurt. Good enough for his old ass. Sometime I wish I had a giant vacuum cleaner so I could suck up all the stupid men in the world and put 'em in a big hole and bury 'em in hot mud and not let not a one of 'em out until they realize that the women they married—the ones that stuck by their sorry asses all them years—is the ones that truly loved 'em, and even though these new and improved models may give 'em a quick thrill, it won't last longer than the time it takes to get 'em off a few times. What do he think a young girl with a houseful a kids could want with his ancient behind? The idea that Cecil and the rest of 'em actually think these girls might like (and we don't even wanna use the word "love," but let's say "love") 'em, you know they must be "tripping"—as Dingus would say. All these old farts really got to offer 'em is some hard plastic and hot cash. But I didn't spend thirty-eight years of my life to fatten no frog up for no snake. And just watch: when he ready to come crawling back home, my back gon' be turned or I ain't gon' be nowhere around. They always a day late and a dollar short, but that ain't my fault, and it sure ain't gon' be my problem.

"Granny, I don't see your bowling ball anywhere . . . ?"

"Then look for it! How many different places could it be in this mansion?"

"I gotta do everything around here, don't I, Granny?"

"What you say, baby?"

"I said: do I have to do everything around here?" Now she standing in the doorway, shrugging them little bony-pony shoulders, but she just messing with me. She doing good. Smiling. Laughing out loud. And I ain't smelled no liquor on her breath. As much as I wanted to get rid of all of it, I couldn't bring myself to do it. That stuff cost too much money, and, plus, every now and then I need a little som'n—som'n to pick me up. I marked the bottles and don't think she found out where I keep my stash, 'cause it seem like I'm the only one who been crossing out the lines and making new ones.

I think she might be healing. I don't know. I hug her every day. Try to make her feel special, but she is special. And she fast. She might could be the next Flo Jo. But deep down, I don't really care how fast she is, as long as she ain't gotta run to get out of harm's way. And that's why she here with me. I want her to know what being safe feels like.

Some nights she sleep in here with me and we read together. Her mama used to send me all her old romance novels, but I got tired of reading shit that don't never happen, so I started going to the Native Son bookstore, down on "D" Street, and that nice black man in there gives me a senior-citizen discount on paperbacks.

In her own way, I think Shanice think she protecting me some kinda way. I like the fact that she care. It's a good feeling being around folks who care about you. I done also got her to stop pulling out her hair so much. I just told her it didn't make no sense hurting herself when other people done already done a good job of it, but don't think for a minute that they done got away with it. God don't work that way. I told her to let happiness be her payback. Let feeling good be her revenge.

I throw a piece of peppermint candy at her and wink. "You ain't paying no rent around here, so, yeah, you might as well think of yourself as my young slave."

"Granny!"

"Did you say you talked to your mama?"

"Yes I did."

"You didn't tell her I kept you out of school today to go with me to get my car, did you?"

"No way."

"And what she talking about?"

"She called to wish you happy birthday, but that's when you were taking Miss Loretta for a ride in your new car, and Mama said she was having some kind of female problem and had to stay in bed for a couple of days."

"What kind of female problem?"

"I don't know, Granny."

"Dial the number and get her on the phone for me, would you, baby?"

But soon as I get the words outta my mouth, the phone rings. "Shanice, would you get that for your granny, please? Never mind. I'll get it myself." I grab the receiver and say, "Yep."

"Happy birthday, Ma."

"Charlotte?"

"Yep."

"Why, thank you. And happy birthday to you. Did you get my card?"

"Yes, I did. Yesterday. It was very nice. Thanks. Anyway, Mama, I been running around since early this morning and I been meaning to call you all day and just now getting around to it. You know your card is in the mail. You should be getting it by tomorrow or the day after at the latest."

"No biggie. What you doing to celebrate?"

"Nothing."

"What you mean, nothing?"

"Just what I said. I don't feel like celebrating."

"You mean to tell me Al didn't do nothing for you for your birthday?"

"Al is gone."

"Gone where?"

"I don't know. I filed for a divorce, but I don't wanna get all into that right now. It's your birthday. The kids wanna say something, hold on."

A divorce? She kill me just dropping bombs on you like this, and you just supposed to accept it like it ain't no big deal.

"Happy birthday, Granny!" I hear all three of 'em scream at the same time. "We got you something pretty!"

"Why, thank you," I say.

Then Charlotte gets back on the phone. "So what *you* doing to celebrate?"

"Wait a damn minute, Charlotte. You just said you getting a divorce. . . ."

"Mama, can we talk about this another day, please?"

"Okay," I say—since she don't feel like talking about it, then to hell with it. "Well, then, have you talked to Paris lately?"

"Not in the past few days, why?"

"You know she sold her cookbook, don't you?"

"No, I didn't know she was writing a cookbook."

"Yes you did. She told all of us last Thanksgiving that she'd been putting it together for years. Anyway, she got a whole bunch of money for it, and she bought me a new car!"

"What kinda car?"

"A Mitsubishi Galant. Navy blue."

"That's nice," she says like she don't really mean it.

"Wait. I ain't finished."

"You mean there's more?"

"Oh, yeah, baby. I'm getting some new dentures—the best money can buy—and tomorrow I'm going to start looking at some brand-new condominiums!"

"Paris is buying you a condo?"

"Yes indeedy."

"What else did you get for your birthday?"

"Shanice made me a cup in her art class, and Dingus sent me a pair of gold hoop earrings."

"Real gold?"

"I don't think so, but what difference do it make? It's the thought that count. Anyway, my good friend Loretta—the one I might be going on a cruise with—she crocheted me a pretty gold, purple, and hunter-green throw to go over my old couch."

"Ain't she white?"

"Yeah, so?"

"I just asked."

"And that's about it."

"Janelle and Lewis didn't get you nothing?"

"Janelle gives me the same thing every year. A gift certificate to Nordstrom's."

"What kinda store is Nordstrom's?"

"A very high-class department store. It ain't quite Neiman Marcus, but close enough for my taste. Anyway, I ain't heard from Lewis, which means he probably in jail, 'cause he don't forget my birthday."

"Well, you did it again, Mama."

"Did what?"

"Threw dirt in my face."

"What the hell are you talking about, Charlotte?"

"You just had to brag about what everybody else did for your birthday except for me and my kids. Can't you see it?"

"You asked me what I got, so I told you!"

"Yeah, but look at *how* you had to tell me!"

"What you want me to do, whisper it? Tell you like I'm disappointed 'cause my other daughters think enough of me to do something for me on my birthday and you don't? I still ain't figured that one out. Is it something I done to you that's making you treat me like a stepmother, or are you just plain nasty?"

"No, I am not, and you should think about a lotta things you've done to hurt me that you don't seem to ever fucking remember!"

"You better come down off that high horse you on and watch the way you talking to me. You always coming up with a reason to bring the problems back to Charlotte, don't you? Don't make no difference what's going on, it always comes down to poor Charlotte. You always the innocent little victim. Well, I ain't never done nothing deliberately to cause you harm, and I swear on my mama's grave that's true."

"Yeah yeah yeah."

"I can't help it if you and my damn grandkids didn't send me nothing for my birthday."

"They just told you they got you something!"

"Then where the hell is it? My presents to them always get there on time. And you? You always so busy—too busy to . . ."

"Look, I don't need you to try to make me feel guilty."

"You don't sound like you feeling no kinda guilt, so who you fooling?"

"You right, Mama! I *don't* feel guilty. And from now on, I *ain't* gon' feel guilty about a damn thing I do or don't do! I'm *sick* to death doing what everybody thinks I should be doing. *Sick* of living my life to please everybody but me. So, yeah, I'm tired of feeling guilty 'cause my own mama likes to make one daughter feel bad by throwing dirt in her face about what her other kids is doing!"

"That is not what I'm doing, Charlotte, and you know it."

"Oh, yeah! That's what it feel like to me. So you enjoy your birthday in your new car and make sure you wear your new earrings and drink something hot in your new cup and rest your head on your blue-and-orange throw, and when you move in your new condo, don't bother picking up the phone to call me till you can learn how to talk to somebody, because it's gon' be a cold day in hell before I call you back!" Click.

Here we go again. And on my birthday! This little wench done hung up the phone in my face one too many times. Al musta done something really low, 'cause she's tripping hard.

"Dag," Shanice says. "She tripping real hard."

"You still on this phone, girl?"

"Yep. This is better than the soaps, Granny. What's up with Aunt Charlotte? She was totally out of line."

"Do this. Don't mention her name in this house until I tell you to, okay?"

"Okay."

"Now get your mama on the phone and be quick about it."

"Okay." I hear her dialing the number from in here, but when I pick up the phone, it's Suzie Mae. How'd this happen?

"Vy? You there?"

"Yeah, Suzie, I'm here."

"I just was calling to say happy birthday. At first I couldn't remember whose birthday it was, and then it hit me. It's yours and Charlotte's. Both on tax day."

"Thanks for calling, Suzie, but can I call you back later?"

"Sho'. I wasn't planning on talking but a minute no way. Rates is sky-high this time a day. You feeling all right?"

"Feeling fine."

"You got your papers in order?"

"What papers?"

"You know, in case you die or something."

"Ain't nobody doing no dying around here no time soon, Suzie Mae."

"You never know. Better to be safe than sorry."

I don't know how she got to be my sister, I swear I don't. "Anyway, my papers is in order."

"You don't want the kids fighting over all your personal belongings, now, do you?"

"Not like yours will, huh, Suzie?"

"I ain't got no kids."

"You also ain't got no personal belongings."

"I heard Cecil's gone."

"So you do watch the six o'clock news, huh?"

"It's about time," she says. "He wasn't worth all them years, but you didn't hear it from me."

"Bye, Suzie."

"Bye, Vy. I'll call you again on Sunday, when the rates is low. Wait a minute! You heard from our sister?"

"Don't mention that dizzy bitch's name to me right now, okay? I'm sick of stupid women, and I don't know who's on the top of my list right now."

"Long as it ain't me. Bye."

I chuckle, and then dial Janelle's number myself.

"Happy birthday, Mama." She sound groggy and tired.

"What's wrong with you, Janelle?"

"I'm just having cramps."

"Since when did you start having cramps?"

"I get them from time to time, depending on the season."

"And what season is this?"

"Spring, Mama. It's spring. Where's Shanice?"

"She's in the kitchen. We going bowling in a little while, if I can ever get my nap in."

"I want her to come home."

"That's nice, but she ain't ready to come home yet."

"But I need her to."

"Look, Janelle. You done already put the girl through a whole lot of unnecessary bullshit. Now, she ain't been here but a few weeks and she doing good in school, she on the track team, and we done signed her up for a week at sleepover camp with some girls she met at Victory Baptist that she hit it off with, and it just so happen it's the same week as my cruise. Now. School'll be out the first week of June, and I ain't taking her out. You just gon' have to wait till we both get back. How that sound?"

"Okay okay. I'll be job hunting, anyway."

"What else is new?"

"Ma, not today. So—I guess you've heard about Lewis."

"What about him?"

"Paris didn't call you this morning?"

"She called last night."

"And she didn't say anything about him?"

"Get to the damn point, would you, girl?"

"He's in jail. But this time he's going to be in there for a while. Maybe even as much as a year. It depends. His case might end up going to trial."

"What? For what?"

"He struck Donnetta's husband with a sponge mop."

"What you mean, struck?"

"He hit him with the wooden handle of a mop."

"I know you lying."

"I wish I was."

"I don't even wanna know the details. This day been chock-full of some of everything, I know that much. He done hit . . . I swear to God, I don't know where that boy was when they was passing out common sense."

"I might go see him next week."

"You knock yourself right on out. Where's George?"

"He's not living here anymore. I told you that."

"We'll see," I say. "But let me say this: if he stay gone, I'll give you a whole lotta credit."

"I'm trying, Ma. I'm trying. Kiss Shanice for me. I took a pill that's made me sleepy and I need to close my eyes."

"Then don't let me stop you. Talk to you later. And thanks for my birthday present. As soon as I lose ten or fifteen pounds, I'm going straight to the Savvy Department. Thank you, baby." I make a kissing sound into the phone and then hang up. "Shanice!" I yell. "Unplug that phone from the wall, would you? I don't wanna talk to another soul."

"Okay, Granny. But what about the door? I think Grandpa Cecil just pulled up."

"Shit! It's my birthday and I wanna take a nap!" I say, and crawl over the edge of the bed and go straight to the front door and open it. "What can I do for you, Cecil?" He still wearing that Sammy Davis shirt and them James Brown pants. Some things just don't change.

"I told you I wanted to bring you a little something for your birthday."

"What is it?" I ask, talking to him through the screen door. I ain't opening it until I feel like it, and he ain't coming in here, I don't care what he got for me.

"Whose car is that in the driveway?"

"My friend's."

"What friend is that?"

"That would be none of your business, Cecil. Now, what you got? 'Cause I'm supposed to be getting dressed."

"Where you going?"

I take a deep breath. And then, just to satisfy his curiosity, I say: "We going bowling."

"Yeah," he says. "Do I know this fella?"

"I doubt it. I just met him myself, how you gon' know him, too?"

"Vegas ain't that big," he says.

"Look, Cecil, you gon' give me the present today or tomorrow? 'Cause I ain't got all day," I say, cracking the screen door open wide enough for him to hand me something through it.

"Here," he says, and hands me a plastic bag that looks like it's from Philmon's Hair Emporium, where I used to get my hair done till I decided to do it myself. But Philmon's is a bookstore, too. So, when I open up the bag, it's a book.

"Thank you, Cecil. It was very thoughtful of you."

"You're welcome. I guess we probably might need to be talking real soon about what we gon' do about this house."

"You can do anything you wanna do with it."

"What you mean by that, Vy?"

"It means that I'm moving soon."

"You moving with that man in there?"

"Lord, no. I wouldn't live with another man at my age if you paid me. You cured me of that, Cecil. No, I'm doing one better than that. Paris is buying me my very own condominium."

He actually gets a smile on his face. "Yeah," he says, rubbing what might be new growth 'cause I see little gray prickly stubbles coming outta his face. "That's our girl."

"She certainly is."

"We did something right, didn't we, Vy?"

"I guess so. But, like I said, Cecil, I gotta go. And thanks again."

"You're welcome. Can I give you a little sugar? Not on your mouth. On your cheek."

"That ain't really necessary, Cecil."

"I know. But I need to, Vy."

"Oh, all right," I say, and turn my face so my right cheek fits into the space I left open in the screen. His lips is dry, hard, and crusty, like he ain't been kissing nothing. I almost feel sorry for him, but, then again, I don't.

"Happy birthday," he says, and turns and walks down the sidewalk and get in his red Lincoln, which, to my surprise, starts right up.

When I turn to look at Shanice, her mouth is covered with both hands, I guess from laughing so hard. She's easing out from beside the refrigerator, where I see she been hiding. "You're good, Granny."

"Sometimes you gotta lie. I just don't make it no habit. Now, let me go on and get ready and let's get the hell outta here. To hell with taking a nap!"

I go on back in my bedroom and I'm pulling my yellow bowling T-shirt over my head that's got "Lucky Strikes" in big red letters on the back when the phone rings.

"Shanice, I thought I told you to unplug the phone!"

"I did, Granny, but you didn't unplug yours!"

"Shit," I say, and answer it. It's Essex. "When you gon' get here, gal? We waiting on you!"

"I'm coming, I'm coming! Give me fifteen or twenty minutes, Essex."

"Okay, but hurry up." Essex been bugging me to get back down to the lanes ever since I got home from the hospital. I'm one of the few on our team that bowl 170, so they need me. They need me bad. LuEsther average 155 to 170, but she fluctuate from one week to the next, depending on how many hot flashes she having. Essex been bowling in the 180s for years. Me and him on a doubles team, but since I been out, he been forced to roll with Mr. Kentucky, who got a odor but don't nobody have the nerve to tell him. We just get out his path when he roll, 'cause he can bowl his ass off.

On the way, we stop by the grocery store and Shanice runs in and gets the pie, some apples, and some vanilla ice cream. When we get inside the Showboat, we walk down to the lanes, and when I look to the left, I don't see no familiar faces, so then I look to the right, and I still don't see nobody I know from our team in our usual lanes. I know I got this right. This is our "house." I start walking over to the bar area to ask Zenobia if she would put this ice cream in the freezer and where the hell everybody done disappeared to, and she just grins at me like a damn fool—showing off them two gold teeth that long ago stopped shining—and that's when, from behind me, I hear a whole bunch of Negroes yelling at the top of their lungs: "SURPRISE! HAPPY TWENTY-FIRST BIRTHDAY, VIOLA! AND WELCOME HOME, HUZZY!"

I'm scared to turn around, 'cause I might have a heart attack, but that's a chance I'm gon' have to take. When I do, Essex and the whole crew is holding a giant sheet cake with my name written in pink letters right across the middle and big yellow-and-mint-green roses up in two corners that I know they got from Costco. I forgot to tell Shanice that I do like Costco's cakes, 'cause they don't stick to the roof of my mouth like the other ones do, but I figure, if I let her roll my ball a few times, I can sneak and eat a little piece and maybe she won't even notice.

Burnt Toast

I don't know why I'm not scared. I should be, in this neighborhood: South Central. Jimmy was killed out here in a drive-by shooting. That was in 1985, when the term wasn't part of our vocabulary yet. It doesn't seem like it was nine years ago. In fact, if I were to drive down two or three blocks and turn a few corners, I could be right in front of the house where it happened. But I don't want to see that porch or the steps leading to it. I don't want to see the red grass or the burgundy sidewalk; the broken glass shattered and scattered like a map of the world ripped apart until every country landed in the wrong place. I don't want to remember the screams that sounded like sirens and the sirens that sounded like screams. Or the crowd, too many people—even little kids—rushing to form a thick circle so they could experience the thrill of seeing another dead body being carried off to the morgue: another casualty in their own neighborhood caused by someone from their own neighborhood.

Jimmy never hurt anybody. Even after he got his degree and became a high-school coach, he still spent his summers out here, volunteering, helping to train young track hopefuls for the Junior Olympics. His heart was big, and I'm glad I was lucky enough to feel it. He was the best thing that ever happened to me. I'm sure if he were still here Shanice and I would be happy. He wouldn't have let anything happen to her or me. He was a protector, and the sad thing is, no one in his neighborhood even cared. I think it was Malcolm X who said that when we kill each other senselessly it's genocide, and the white man is smiling, watching us do a job he doesn't have to anymore. I'm sure this is why they never found out who killed my husband. They just never looked that hard.

I pass Normandie Avenue and Western and Crenshaw Boulevard and realize how Rodney King made these streets famous. They still don't look too inviting.

I searched high and low for Arlene's number—she's George's ex-wife—and I found it in one of the very same Christmas cards she'd sent him four years in a row. On a separate piece of paper she always asked that he call her before the holidays and make sure he didn't forget to send her some money like he promised or she was going to have to get ugly. Each time George simply said, "Bitch," and tossed them into the trash. I kept the first one and put it away. This morning I tried calling the number she'd written inside, but it belonged to someone else. I knew she was still in the same place—rent-free—because George owns the duplex. I guess this was a form of alimony, since, from what I gather, Arlene has never worked.

This place looks like it's one of the few houses on the whole block that have been maintained. It's old, but the paint is fresh. It's either a pale yellow, or almond, I'm not sure. There are several round flowerbeds surrounded by little mesh fences on the patch of grass that's posing as the lawn, which I can tell has recently been cut. Some kids are rollerblading at the end of the block, up what appears to be a jump that they made out of plywood planks. Two elderly black men are sitting on the sidewalk in kitchen chairs with their legs crossed, drinking Pepsis.

I park in front of a rusting blue Escort and walk up to the door and knock. I don't exactly know what I'm going to say to her if she's here. What if she slams the door in my face? What if she could care less that I've come? What if she doesn't care what has happened to my daughter?

"Yeah, who is it?" a husky voice says through the door.

"Is Arlene Porter at home?"

"Who's looking for her?"

"Janelle Porter."

"Say what?" And I'm surprised when a handsome woman who must be about fifty-three or -four opens the door. "What you doing way over here?" she asks. "Is George dead?"

"No, I'm afraid not."

"Then what can I do you for?" she asks, not moving. I can see over her shoulder that her little place is clean and neat. That she has taken great care of what she does have. She seems to have taken good care of herself, too. Even though her roots are gray, I can tell her hair has recently been permed because of the way it's lying flat against her head. Her skin is flawless—and such a beautiful shade of brown—with not a wrinkle in sight. She could be from one of those Caribbean islands or something. And her eyes. They look green or gray, but I can't really tell. What in the world did she see in George?

"I wondered if I could talk to you about something? It won't take long."

"You mean you wanna come in?"

"If you don't mind."

"I don't mind, but I was just about to walk out the door."

"Oh, I'm sorry if this is a bad time."

"Well, all I got is about a minute, 'cause I gotta get to Ross to pick up something I got on hold before they close, which is about fifteen minutes from now, so come on in but make it quick."

Once inside, she motions for me to sit down on the couch, which I do. Her taste is very seventies, but it's understandable. I see pictures of her daughters as they were growing up, all over the living room in old frames. Only one favors George. In what looks like high-school photos, it's easy to see that they grew up to become attractive girls. I don't know who's who, but one is playing basketball, and looks like she's dunking it. There's a

Polaroid of one of them holding a baby. She looks to be about eighteen. Don't know which one it is or how long ago it was.

"How are your daughters doing?" I ask.

"They fine, why?" Like I've asked her about something I shouldn't have.

"I was just curious."

"You didn't drive all the way out here just 'cause you curious," she says, and reaches for and lights a cigarette from her purse. She takes a deep drag, and when she looks at me, her eyes tell me that she knows exactly why I'm here.

"How old are they now?"

"JaDonna's twenty-six and Yolanda's almost twenty-four. Why?"

"Do they live here in L.A., still?"

"Yeah. JaDonna stays here with me, and Yolanda's living somewhere around here in South Central. But I ain't seen her in going on two years."

"Why not?"

" 'Cause we don't speak."

"Why not?"

" 'Cause we ain't got nothing to talk about."

"Is JaDonna here right now?"

"Yeah, she back there in the bed."

"Is she sick?"

"I guess you could say that, but not really. She have her good days and she have her bad days."

"What's wrong with her?"

"She on medication."

"Medication for what?"

"Depression. They say she's manic-depressive. I don't know. Sometime I think she just lazy, but I can't throw her out on the street, you know. She's been through a lot and, plus, being my firstborn and all."

"Yes, I know."

"How you know? You on medication, too?"

"No."

"So, whatever it was you wanted to talk to me about, I think JaDonna can probably fill you in, 'cause she love to run her mouth and she'll give you a earful. She know everything that's gone on in this house, and, besides, the clock is ticking and I gotta get where I'm going."

"Mama, who's that out there?" a voice from down the short hallway asks.

"It's your daddy's fourth wife, Janelle!"

"Third," I say.

"Fourth," Arlene says, correcting me, and kind of chuckles. "I was second."

I feel a hole forming in my throat. Fourth? I take tiny sips of air in order to breathe. That's lie number one.

"Go on back there, it's the first door on the left. Ain't but two. You can't miss it. I won't be but twenty or thirty minutes, tops, but if you ain't here when I get back, I'll understand. Believe me."

"Okay, then."

I want to correct her English so badly I almost can't stand it. I can't believe George tolerated her speaking like this.

"Tell me something, Janelle: is there a wife number five on the horizon?"

"I don't know."

"He's getting too old for all this. I'm surprised you lasted this long. Where's my keys? JaDonna, you seen my keys?"

"Why are you so surprised, Arlene?"

"No, Mama! Try the top of the 'frigerator!"

Arlene puts her cigarette out and walks over to the tiny kitchen area, and, sure enough, her keys are up there. "Because he don't know how to treat a woman. First he spoil you to death by taking care of you, then he gets you to love his last year's drawers, and you trust him, grow to depend on him for everything, and then you find out he been cheating on you the whole time. Didn't you know that?"

"I'm finding out the hard way."

"It took me sixteen years to see the light, but it look like you and LaVerne done seen it, too."

"LaVerne?"

"Yeah, she was number three. She shot his ass, but I guess that didn't stop him."

"Shot him? George said that wound was from a robbery gone bad."

"That's true, in a manner of speaking."

"Do you know where she is?"

"I heard she took her daughters and moved back to Dallas, but I don't know for sure. Ask George."

"I can't."

"Look, it don't make me no difference one way or another. I got me somebody. And he's decent. Anyway, I done said more than I planned to. I gots to go. After you finish talking to JaDonna, if it's anything else you wanna talk about, fine, maybe I'll see you when I get back. Otherwise, slam the door hard behind you till you hear it click."

And she was gone.

I stand here for a minute, not quite sure what to do now. I really am afraid to go back into JaDonna's room, and find myself taking baby steps in that direction. When I turn into her doorway, a woman who looks like she's in her forties is lying on her side eating Cheez Doodles and watching TV. She must weigh at least three hundred pounds. She couldn't possibly be one of the girls in the pictures, but of course I know she is.

"Hey, Janelle. What lies Mama done told you about us?"

"What do you mean?"

"She lies big-time."

I'm still standing in the doorway. There's nowhere to sit, really. This room is small. Stuffy. The one window in here is partially covered with a black towel, apparently to keep the light from shining on the TV screen. "Would you mind if I sit here on the floor?"

"Knock yourself out. What brings you all the way over here to the Black Beverly Hills?"

"Well . . ."

"Wait, let me guess. Mr. Fuck Fuck Fuck done fucked your little girl, too. Now, tell me I'm wrong?"

I cannot believe my ears. I didn't expect anything close to this to come out of this young woman's mouth. But all I can say is, "You're not wrong."

She claps her hands together hard. "He just won't quit, will he?"

"So—you're saying that he did this to you and your sister, too?"

"Oh, hell, yeah."

"When?"

"When we was kids *and* when we was teenagers."

"Why didn't your mother stop him?"

She cuts her eyes at me like a knife. "Stop him how?"

"Didn't you tell her?"

"How long did it take your daughter to tell you?"

"Actually, she didn't. I found out the hard way."

"See there. He blackmails you, making it so hard for you to say anything that when you finally just get tired and say 'fuck it' and drum up enough nerve to tell, you realize you got a mama who's so goddamn stupid and so in love with the mother-fucker that she swear up and down you making the shit up just 'cause she don't wanna believe it, even when you finally turn fourteen and get pregnant by your goddamn stepfather and you say, 'Now do you believe me?' and she just accuse you of being a little ho' and make you get a abortion and all you know is this ain't the way you fantasized losing your virginity and you never dreamed in a million years that the first time in your life you'd get pregnant it would be by your fucking stepfather, and since he ruined everything that was meant to be precious, after that you get pregnant again but this time you don't know and you don't care who the daddy is 'cause you been giving it to anybody who want some and that's only because you said, 'Fuck it, fuck everything,' and the next thing you know you ain't got nothing in you that wanna get up and do shit so you just let your mama take care of you and your baby since it's her fucking fault you got like this and you just kick it and take it easy and watch TV and eat as much as you want to and let the days pass by and wait till things get better but you know that that ain't never gon' happen, so here I am. Chillin'."

I don't say a solitary word.

"Say something."

"I don't know what to say."

"I know. This some of that *Sally Jesse* shit, ain't it?"

"George isn't your father?"

"Oh, hell, no. You didn't know that?"

"No, I didn't." For a few seconds, I'm at a total loss for words here. "How old were you then?"

She closes her eyes and opens them real fast. "Five or six, I guess, 'cause she married Mr. Fuck Fuck Fuck when I was seven. He used to live downstairs in our building. He was married to wife number one, and then Mama took him from that woman."

"Really."

"She said her pussy was that good."

I grit my teeth at her bluntness.

"But turns out it wasn't as good as mine and 'Londa's."

"So—you mean your mother knew George was doing this to you guys all along and didn't do anything about it?"

"She didn't want to believe us. She believed him."

"You mean nobody reported it?"

"Report it to who? If your own mama don't believe you, who else gon' fucking believe you?"

"Didn't you tell somebody else? Relatives?"

"She told 'em 'Londa wasn't right in the head. Which wasn't no lie at the time."

"But what about you?"

"I gave up a long time ago. I didn't get out the bed for six months, till they put me on this medication. But, hey, ain't nothing wrong with 'Londa's head except she just hates Mama big-time, and that hate done turned in on her."

"And you don't?"

"I feel sorry for her, really."

"Why?"

"For being so pitiful and stupid. I think something is wrong with her, to tell you the truth. The man she got now—Charlie-Z is his name—she took him from a woman who supposed to have been her friend. They lived right across the street. They been knowing each other since high school. But Mama say she ain't done nothing wrong. She said she can't help it if Sheila's man got tired of her. But Mama like taking things that belong to somebody else. It took me a long time to see that this how she got all her men. It's like a game she play to see if she can win. But what do she really win? These ain't *real* men. They pretend to be good, but inside they smelly rotten. I don't know why she can't see it. She the main reason I don't care if I never love nobody, 'cause, if love can do to me what it's done to her, I don't want none."

"What about Yolanda?"

"What about her?"

"Where is she? And how is she?"

"She's around. She do a little crack. Let me stop lying. She do a lotta crack. But I think she might be in rehab now. She in and out. She keep trying to get it together, but it's hard for her. She ain't spoke to Mama in going on four years."

"Why not?"

"'Cause she said she ain't gon' never say another word to her until she apologize for not admitting that she knew George did what he did to us."

"Why won't she do that?"

"'Cause she still swear up and down he didn't."

"But you all know that she knew."

"Oh, hell, yeah. She knew."

"Don't you hate him?"

"More than burnt toast."

I nod my head up and down in agreement.

"How old is your daughter now?" she asks.

"Almost thirteen."

"She's gon' be fucked up, I can tell you that right now. Ain't no getting around it."

"Oh, I wouldn't be so sure about that. But I'll tell you something, JaDonna," I say, rising to my feet, "I'm going to do everything I can to make sure she doesn't get fucked up, and I'm going to start by stopping George from doing this to someone else."

"You do that," she says, picking up the remote and flicking the channels.

"Can I ask you something else?"

"Don't stop now."

"When you got older, did you ever confront him?"

"No."

"Why not?"

" 'Cause he's a good pretender, too."

"Why didn't you or your sister just report him?"

"To who?"

"The police."

"He was the police!"

"I know that, but that doesn't mean he couldn't go to jail."

"You really believe that shit?"

"Oh, you just watch and see," I say.

She looks at me like she believes me. "Mama said me and my sister woulda ended up in foster care if somebody hadda believed us. And we wanted to stay together."

"Look, do me a favor, JaDonna. Tell your mother I said thanks for her time, and you try to take good care of yourself."

"I will," she says. "Mama wasn't *even* going to no Ross store."

"No?" I say as convincingly as I can.

"Hell, no. She ain't got nothing on hold nowhere. She bee-lined it outta here 'cause she was scared a what you really came here for. I mean, it ain't like you drop by to kick it with us all the time, now, do you?"

"No I don't."

"Look, before you go, would you mind grabbing me a beer out the 'frigerator and then make sure you pull that front door tight, or else it won't lock, and Lord knows I do not feel like getting up to do it."

"No problem," I say, and head out toward the kitchen to get her beer. Before I get back, I wipe the smirk off my face. It was no accident that Arlene sent us those Christmas cards. And Arlene knew JaDonna would tell me the truth. Because she couldn't. She's probably been waiting a long time for her daughter to tell her story to the right person. For a moment, I'm tempted to hang around just to wait for her. To let her know that I appreciate what she's done. That I understand how hard it's been for her all these years. But I know she won't come back until my car is gone.

When I get back to the room, JaDonna has actually sat up. She has on a light-blue sweatsuit. I feel so sorry for her. She looks like a giant baby. And that's when it occurs to me that I haven't seen any sign of her child. "Where's your daughter?" I ask.

"In foster care," she says. "Where else?"

I turn to leave, and when I get outside the front door, I pull it so tight that I actually scrape the knuckles on my hand against the doorframe. I look up and down the street. A new set of children are racing. If Jimmy were here, he'd walk right over and ask if they'd like to try running on a real track. On a team. He would tell them that they look fast enough to win medals. Even if they weren't he'd make them believe they could. I wish he were here to help me believe that all of this is going to work out.

At eight-thirty on Monday morning, I pick up the phone and dial the number of the Child Protective Service Agency and tell them that I'd like to report a case of sexual abuse. For the next hour or so I answer all of their questions and explain what has happened. They tell me how they'll cross-reference the information I gave them and file a report with the police. They ask if George is still in the house, and I tell them no. They ask if my daughter is, and I tell them she's in Las Vegas with her grandmother. They're pleased to hear this. I tell them I don't know where George is living but I know where he works. They aren't moved when I say he's a police officer. They will arrest him at his job. He'll be charged and held, pending further investigation. They say he'll probably post bail and be released until enough evidence has been gathered to build a case against him. And the only way to do this is if Shanice agrees to undergo a physical exam and consents to being interviewed on videotape by a child advocate. I know she won't do this. The social worker says a lot of kids don't want to go through this, for obvious reasons. I take a series of deep breaths before blurting out the words, "I want him stopped," and then I sit there for the next hour or so trying to figure out the best way to finally tell my family the truth.

Refills

"Hello, this is Paris Price calling to see if my prescription is ready."

"Is that a new prescription or a refill?"

"It's a refill. I called it in yesterday," I say as I swivel back and forth on my kitchen stool.

"Can you hold a second while I check?"

"Yes, I can." I look over at the clock. It's almost three-thirty. Here I go again. Waiting. He's late again. Something told me I should never have started to work with this Randall. I mean, I tried to show the brother some respect, gave him the benefit of the doubt, because I'm not one of those people who believe that black folks are poor at handling our business—hell, I can use myself as a good example—but it's guys like this who give the rest of us a bad name. He has called and canceled the last three appointments and all he had to say was it was an emergency and he was sorry, could he reschedule. Reschedule? My backyard looks like a battlefield. And this of course is after I've already paid him a third of his megafee because he had me drooling over the plans, fantasizing about how lush and beautiful it was going to be when he finished. Hah!

He was supposed to be here between one-thirty and two. This time, I didn't even get a phone call. I guess when he met me he saw "fool" written all across my forehead. He's probably partying his ass off with my money. But he *will* finish my yard. He *will* fill and refill those damn trenches with all that expensive dirt and shit he insisted I buy. If he doesn't, I'll take him to court so fast it'll make his head swim.

"I'm sorry, but the doctor hasn't called to okay your prescription yet."

"What? Why not?"

"I don't know why. You should call your doctor. Sometimes they forget."

I hang up. "It's my dentist!" I say into the phone as I speed-dial his number. "Hello, Sylvia, this is Paris Price. I was hoping to get a refill on my prescription, but the pharmacist said that Dr. Bronstein hasn't called it in. Is there a problem?"

"Hold on and let me put Doctor on."

More waiting. I'm waiting for Dingus to walk through that door, because last night I decided to ask him if this girl is pregnant by him or not. I'm tired of walking around here like everything is just hunky-dory. I'm also waiting for a client to fax me directions to her home, which is at least an hour's drive from here, all the way in Hillsborough, somewhere up in the hills, off a windy road. She's the CEO of one of the top advertising agencies in San Francisco. And throwing quite the shindig for Lord only knows who. What I am sure of is, she's willing to spend the hundred thousand plus that I quoted her. I just need to see the place in person.

"Paris, this is Dr. Bronstein. I didn't refill your prescription because I'm wondering why you're still experiencing discomfort with your gums after all this time. If you are, then you need to come in and see me right away and let me take a look to see what's going on."

Without even thinking, I hear myself lie: "It's not my gums, Dr. Bronstein, I think it's my tooth, the one in the bridge that we talked about before."

"Oh, yes. It's starting to give you trouble, huh? Is there any way you could come in to see me today?"

"I can tomorrow, but not today."

"Okay, then. Hold on and I'll put Sylvia back on to set it up, and I'll see you sometime tomorrow."

"Wait! But what about today?"

"Are you in that much pain?"

"Yes, I am."

"Have you tried Tylenol or Advil?"

"They don't work."

"I'll call in six Vicodin. That should get you through until tomorrow, and we'll see if we can't get you fixed up. Take care, Paris. Here's Sylvia."

After scheduling the appointment, I know full well I'm not going to see him tomorrow, because there's nothing wrong with my tooth. The kind of pain I'm feeling doesn't ache or throb. In fact, I think I'm finally starting to catch on that it's not pain at all. I *want* to be distracted. I want not to care what happens one way or another. I want things not to bother me. I would like to be more nonchalant, less emotionally charged up. The problem is, a lot of things bother me that I wish didn't. Things I can't control. When I take one or two pain pills, it helps me pull back, hand the reins over to the gods in charge.

Fortunately and unfortunately, I happen to care whether or not my son is going to be a father at seventeen. I care whether or not my mother is going to be happy living in her new condo, alone, without Daddy there to irk her, but with her new teeth, driving her new car. I know that's not going to be enough. Even though I'm pissed at Daddy for what he's done and how he left, I'm worried about him, too. I'm worried that this young chick is using him, and what'll happen when she's through with him. I don't want to see him hurt either. Don't want to see him kicked to the curb. He doesn't deserve that. Not at his age. He's worked too hard for too long. All of us know that Mama shut him out a long time ago. We all saw it. But what can you do to fix your parents' lives when yours isn't perfect?

I'm lonely. I admit it. But it's not something you want to go around broadcasting—don't want to share it with the world—

especially your family-world. It's embarrassing, really, to be lonely. It makes you feel inadequate in some way. Like you don't measure up in this area of your life. It doesn't even seem to matter that I'm successful, because I feel like a failure as a woman, and I hate feeling like this. I know it doesn't make any sense, and I've tried to trick myself into believing that it's okay to be lonely, that it's not the end of the world, that I'll survive, but it still makes me feel like I'm lacking in something. Missing out on what other people have. In some ways, it even seems like a form of punishment, except I can't figure out what crimes I've committed.

This is just one more reason on the list I can think of as to why I've been taking so many of these stupid pills. They're no panacea, I know that, but they have helped me not think about how long it's been since I've been kissed and held. They help me forget all about passion. I honestly wish that my son's love was enough to sustain me. Wish my work was enough, but obviously they're not. And until I can come up with better, smarter solutions, this is just a temporary thing.

"Hi, Ma," Dingus says, coming through the door with the mail. He bends over and kisses me on the cheek and drops the pile on the kitchen island, then lets his backpack crash to the floor. He goes through each envelope, magazine, and catalogue and pulls out what apparently are eight or nine more letters from colleges. I think he's up to about eighty of them now. He keeps them in shoe boxes under his bed.

"Hi," I say, not budging from the stool I'm still swiveling on.

As usual, he opens the refrigerator to see what he doesn't want, closes it, then changes his mind and grabs the gallon carton of orange juice and goes into the pantry to find a bag of cookies or chips—it doesn't matter—and comes out and heads toward the hallway. But before he reaches the doorway, I say, "Hold it!"

He stops dead in his tracks. "Yes, Mother Hubbard," he says, turning to face me.

"Would you look and see if there's a fax in there?"

He disappears and immediately returns, holding it between his teeth. "It looks like directions," he says.

"Thanks. Now sit," I say, taking the paper from his mouth.

"But I've got tons of homework and I need to clean my room."

"I said sit. Your room was dirty yesterday. It can wait. And homework isn't that important."

"What?"

I knew this would get his attention. "I want to know what's going on with you and Meagan."

"Nothing. Absolutely nothing."

"I overheard something on the phone a while ago that didn't sound like it was about nothing."

"Oh, you mean about her maybe being pregnant?"

"That would be it."

"She made it up."

"What do you mean, 'made it up'?"

"She was faking. Scheming. Trying to run a game on me."

This is a relief, but something's still not right about this whole thing. I have a sour taste in my mouth. "Okay, so, Mr. Sex Machine, she 'faked it' this time, but what about the next time you decide to get on top of her without a goddamn condom? What if it's when you're about to head off to Stanford or UCLA or US-fucking-C! Do you think she'll fake it then?"

"Ma, settle down. It's okay. I'm not seeing her at all anymore. Bet."

"Bet, my ass. Don't be so stupid, Dingus. Girls do this shit every day of the week. Back in the seventies and eighties . . ." And then he gets that "here-we-go-again" look on his face, but I really don't care. "Look, this is the little game pretty girls played who didn't have a future of their own mapped out. They'd get these jocks who were headed for the NBA or the NFL or the major leagues all strung out and so grateful to have them as trophies that they'd marry them, and these girls would be set up for life. The point I'm trying to make here Dingus is this: love who you want to and I don't care what color she is really, but know that the ones who don't have at least a two-point-seven grade point average—and aren't thrilled about the idea of going to college—are the girls who usually have an agenda. They want to marry up and they want to marry well. But when and if they ever divorce you, it's pretty much bankruptcy for you. So you won't have too much left to offer the next wife and new batch of kids. It'll be a struggle, even though you might be making millions. Get the picture?"

"I get it, Ma! Dag. I get it! Why don't you take a chill pill?"

"I have taken a chill pill," I say, not meaning to.

"Can I say something here to defend myself?" he asks, walking over and patting me on the head.

"I'm listening," I say, trying to duck away from his hand.

He gets a big grin on his face. I wish his daddy could see him now. "Okay. I'm not being as irresponsible as you think, Ma. I did use protection, and I was told that there had been an accident but now I know exactly what time it is, so no worries. She thinks she's clever, but do not fear, Mother Dear, I will not be throwing away my future over some girl, regardless of what color she is. *Comprende?*"

"*Comprende,*" I say, feeling relieved as hell. "What ever happened to Jade? If you don't mind my asking."

"We're cool."

"What does that mean, Dingus?"

"It means I like her, Ma."

"Why doesn't she ever come visit?"

"Why should she, when I see her at school?"

"I mean to watch a movie, or for dinner, or something. Do you ever take her anywhere? I mean, do you guys ever go on a date?"

"We go to the movies once in a while."

"Take the girl on a date, Dingus. Spend some of your allowance on her."

"Okay! But can we please quit now?" he yells.

"Okay!" I yell back.

"She's my date for junior prom."

"Hallelujah."

"Anything else while I'm standing here?"

"Actually, there is. I have to run out to see a client in Hillsborough so you can order a pizza or something. But— remember when I canceled my London trip when Granny got sick?"

"Yep."

"It was rescheduled, and I'm going over sometime in early June."

"I wish I could go with you."

"Why can't you?"

"Ma. Spring training leads to summer training, plus I'll have a job, remember?"

"Yeah yeah yeah. I'm trying."

"Any parting words?"

"Yes. Get out of my face and make sure that room is clean by the time I get back. Or else."

"Yeah yeah yeah. I'm shaking all over," he says in the good-spirited way I love.

———————

It's four-thirty. Rush hour. What the hell am I doing on the 680 Freeway at this time of day? Oh hell! I'm stuck trailing behind some hippie driving a lime-green Volkswagen bug with that Westphalia thing on top, which I have never figured out what the hell it's for anyway, and of course they're driving below the speed limit and I can't change lanes. Other drivers are just whizzing by us, like the two of us are in some kind of tailgating party. How stupid could I be to have scheduled this meeting at this hour on a weekday? I feel myself grinding my teeth, and I hate it when I do this. I reach down for my purse, but when I look inside that orange plastic bottle, only two pills are rattling in the bottom of it. Shit. I'm somewhat surprised when I feel myself panic over this but then I immediately feel a sense of relief knowing that I have six more waiting for me at the pharmacy. But wait a minute: only six? Those'll get me through one whole day, but what about the next day? The pharmacy closes at nine, but, hell, I'm a long way from home and I don't know if I can wrap this up in two hours or not. I'm going to have to. Simple as that. Or—I could call and ask Dingus to pick it up for me, but I don't know if he has any money or not. Shit. Why didn't I think of this before?

I pick up the car phone and speed-dial my regular doctor. He's so nice. He reminds me of Dr. Welby. The receptionist answers. "Yes, hi, Lisa, this is Paris Price calling, and I was wondering if I could speak to Dr. Lerner."

"He's with a patient right now. Is it an emergency, or something that can wait a few minutes?"

"Sure, I can wait. Should I call him back?"

"Why don't you do that. Ten minutes would be good."

"Okay," I say and hang up.

I look at the clock. It's 4:45. His office closes at five. Traffic is picking up, moving a little better at least. I'm almost on the 580, but still have to go over the Dumbarton Bridge and then drive another twenty minutes or more. Shit.

I dial my answering machine to listen to my messages, because I was trying to finish up the final proposal for this meeting and didn't answer the phone all day. "Hello, Paris, this is Frances Moore, and I do so apologize for any inconvenience this may cause you, but I've had a death in the family and have had to fly to Boston, so I won't be able to personally meet you today, but you can feel free to come out and look at the house. Sophia, the housekeeper, will let you in, and you can take your time and look around for as long as you like. I should be back in four or five days and I'll look forward to hearing your thoughts. Goodbye."

I'm sorry to hear that she has a death in the family, and I sure feel like turning this car around and going home. But of course I'm almost here now, and it would be stupid, because I'll just have to come back anyway. Actually, this is great, because now I won't have to talk to her. I can just cruise through the house to get an idea how we can use the space and I'm out of there.

Message two: "Paris, you there? This is Mom calling. Pick up. She ain't there. Okay, then. Anyway, I just wanted you to know a few things. First of all, my teeth look good but they hurt like hell and the dentist said it was gon' take a few weeks to get 'em adjusted just right, but I look like a million dollars when I smile now. And since it's been so hard for me to chew, I done lost nine whole pounds. If I'da known I could lose weight this way, I'da got me some new teeth a long time ago. Anyway, baby, I get to move in my new place next week. They repainting the whole place even though it don't really need it, and I picked out a different color carpet I like and I need to know if you can do me a big favor and I promise not to ask you for nothing for a long long time, I promise. Can you let me borrow or either just send me two thousand dollars so I can put this dining-room set in layaway at Thomasville that would look so good in my new place, and to pay for the difference in the upgrade for the carpet? If it's asking too much, I will understand. You done done enough for me, but I'm just excited. Love you. Call me as soon as you get this message. And tell my grandson to call me!"

Mama Mama Mama. She loves her some Thomasville, I swear. Nine pounds? She also loves to exaggerate. I'll have to see this to believe it. I should ask her to take a picture, and I bet she comes up with some kind of excuse. She's too much. But I love her to death. She's having the time of her life right now. Living in a fantasy world, which she and all of us deserve to experience at least once in our lives. So—yes, Mama, you can put your dining-room furniture in layaway and get your upgraded carpet and move into your almost-but-not-quite-new condominium.

Message three: "Paris, this is your sister, Janelle. Hope you're doing okay. I'm better. Want to talk to you, about George. Among other things. But. I've had him arrested. I know you're not surprised, but call me when you get this message. Oh, and by the way, our brother's in jail again. He goes to court next week for sentencing. He's probably going to get the electric chair. I'm just kidding, and I know I shouldn't be. But, anyway, he shouldn't get more than a year. I'm surprised he hasn't called you. Have you talked to Charlotte lately? She's going through some serious changes. But then again, aren't we all? Call me. Hi to Dingus."

Wow. Damn. As the World Fucking Turns, again and again and again. I dial Dr. Lerner again, and when the receptionist answers and I tell her it's me, she puts him right on. "Hello, Paris. What can I do for you?"

"Well, Dr. Lerner, a few days ago I was jogging and I pulled a hamstring and fell on the pavement and I went to the Emergency Room and they checked me out and I was fine but they gave me some medication for the pain and they told me to follow up with my regular doctor, and I'm calling to see if you can give me a refill on the medication because I'm out of it and it's still hurting something fierce."

"Oh, gee. When did this happen?"

"Four days ago."

"Was it on the Iron Horse trail, by chance? I've taken a few bad falls along there myself."

"As a matter of fact, it was."

"Gotta be careful. So—you saw someone in the ER over here at the Regional Medical Center, did you?"

"Yes I did, but I can't remember who I saw."

"It's okay. I know all those guys anyway. But what kind of pain medication did they prescribe for you?"

"I think it's called Vicodin, and it has an 'E.S.' after it."

"Un-huh. You must've taken a pretty hard fall. You have bruising, do you?"

"Sure do."

"I'll call in twenty for you. Would that hold you until I can get a look at you in a few days?"

"I'd like to think so, but, unfortunately, tomorrow I'm going out of town for a week, so maybe we should make it for thirty, just in case?"

"No problem. How about we just make it for forty, and this way you won't have to worry about having any discomfort?"

"Thanks, Dr. Lerner."

"What pharmacy should we call?"

"Walgreens in Danville."

"We'll call it right in. Are you icing it?"

"I am."

"That's good. And keep your foot propped up as high as you can, to keep that blood circulating."

"I'll do that. Thanks, Dr. Lerner, and I'll call you as soon as I get back."

"Have a good trip," he says.

As soon as I hang up I feel both relief and shame. Why am I doing this? Lying to my nice doctor to get some pills I don't need? I mean, how long have I been doing this? Think about it, Paris. It's not until now that I realize I've long since driven over the bridge and am actually approaching my exit. As I start to change lanes, someone is honking at me, and when I turn to look, it's some guy in a truck holding up a giant rubber hand that's giving me the finger. I guess I must've cut him off, but I just give him the finger right back. When I get off the freeway, I pull the car over and stop and drop my head back against the headrest and close my eyes.

But I can't think. Of anything. And almost as if by rote, I reach inside my purse and dump out my last two pills and open my water bottle and swallow them. I drop my head against the cushion, but this time it seems as if knowing I've paved a way for my immediate comfort, I can perhaps begin to think about when my so-called long-term discomfort first started.

Last year. Right after I had my breasts lifted and they prescribed Vicodin and I realized that I liked the way it made me feel. That I could think about one thing at a time when I took one. Even then I wasn't in that much pain, nothing a couple of Advil couldn't have remedied, but I remember getting the refill when I didn't need it, and later calling that doctor back and asking for yet another one, and he gave it to me. I did that four times in four weeks. It was right after that, that I had the first of a series of gum surgeries and once again I felt lucky when I was prescribed the same medication.

Back then, I took one every four hours, just like I was supposed to, but now I do believe that I'm up to six and sometimes eight of these things a day. How and when did this happen? I'm nobody's drug addict, am I? Is this what they mean by getting dependent? No way. No fucking way. I just won't take any more. Period. I can get through a day without a pill. It's not like they cure anything. They haven't fixed anything. Haven't changed anything. Problem solved. I'll just stop taking them and grow up and face the fucking music. I mean, what am I complaining about anyway? I live a good life. I've got lots of money. A nice big home. A good kid. I'm alive. And I'm no drug addict. No fucking way.

However, I am truly shocked, ashamed, and embarrassed when I realize that I'm weaker than I thought, because, after the housekeeper gives me a tour, and upon reaching the master bedroom, when the doorbell rings and Sophia excuses herself to go downstairs to answer it, I find myself rushing into the master bathroom and opening one of two medicine cabinets that look like shelves in a pharmacy, and I pass right over the Percodan, the Percocet, the Darvocet, as well as the antibiotics, Prozac, and Xanax, until I spot two giant bottles of Vicodin. I quickly open one and dump a pile into my palm and then drop them into my jacket pocket. I do the same thing with the other bottle and then close the medicine cabinet and walk out into the hallway. When Sophia comes back and asks if there's anything I need, all I can think to say is that a glass of water would be nice.

Sinners

Me and Brenda went to church two weeks ago and she got saved. I was scared to death when she jumped up and threw both her arms over her head and balled up her fists and started boxing the air, and then she musta been doing that call-and-response business, 'cause she yelled back to the choir, "Yes, He is worthy!" I guess that song is what did it, 'cause, right before that, Reverend Xavier Jones had preached a hefty sermon about redemption and how good God is for forgiving us for our sins, and sweat was dropping down Brenda's temples and tears was rolling from her eyes, but she didn't move that much. The reverend broke it down so good that Brenda, and it seem like everybody else in there, started whooping and hollering, fanning fans, and moaning "Amen"s and "Hallelujah"s and "Thank you, Jesus"s, "He who died for our sins," and what have you. Everybody probably except me. It take a lot to get me excited. I was moved, just not to the point of yelling, speaking in tongues, or jumping up and down. And before the reverend could finish calling folks up to join his congregation, when the choir started humming and singing in the background, Brenda was already up there, dropping to her knees. I could hear her crying and she was shaking her head back and forth so fast one a her hoop earrings flew off but she didn't even notice. "I'm sorry, I'm so sorry," she was saying. I wanted to tell her she ain't got nothing to be sorry about, but I couldn't go up there, 'cause I wasn't feeling the Holy Spirit on this particular Sunday the way Brenda was, and if I was to go up there with her, I'da been faking it. And that ain't a good thing to do in the House of the Lord. Some older woman wearing all pink wrapped her arm around Brenda and rocked her till she calmed down. Good thing the kids was in the next building in Little People's Church, 'cause they wouldn'ta been able to handle watching their mama in such a state. It was hard for me, too. But when Brenda came back to her seat, she looked different. Like she just took a shower or something. All I know is when she took my hand and squeezed it, I felt closer to her at that one moment than I ever remember feeling with Viola.

Afterwards, when we in the car, I come right on out and ask her: "You all right, Brenda?"

"I'm fine. Never felt better."

"Well, what just happened in there?"

"I ain't sure, Cecil. But all I know is I felt the power of God move in me. I been feeling bad for not being a good mother, for dranking like a fish all these years, and here I am pregnant again and all I been doing is cutting back some, and it's shameful. I know I can do better than what I been doing for myself and my kids. I ain't dumb. We shouldn't be living in no projects, 'cause I got good sense."

"I know that, Brenda. It's one of the thangs that attracted me to you. Did God tell you anythang in particular? Like what to do next, anythang of that nature?"

"No. I just feel cleansed. And I ain't finished. I need to purge myself. I need to look into the light instead of the darkness. That's what I been doing all these years, living in darkness."

"Who told you that?"

"Nobody. I grew up in the church. I left when I started doing a whole bunch a unnecessary things to myself. But Cecil," she say, looking over at me like she pleading, "I feel like God done gave me another chance to make my life right with you. You a blessing. I know you older and all, but it don't matter to me. I wanna spend the best years of my life, and the best years of the ones you got left, with you."

"You can put money on that."

"Will you join with me?"

"You mean church? If I have to, I will, but I don't like going to church every Sunday, Brenda."

"I didn't ask you to go every Sunday, now, did I?"

"No, you didn't. But, Brenda, please don't turn into one of them Holy Rollers and try to save me and everybody else just 'cause you been saved. Please promise me you won't do that?"

"I promise, Cecil. I just feel like it's time to clean up my life. I think that's why I came to church today. Something led me here."

"I'm happy for you, Brenda. I'm just glad you can't sang."

"Why is that?"

" 'Cause I ain't gotta worry about you joining the choir."

"Is that right?" she say, and then she just let out a hoot and hit me with her purse and started singing "Amazing Grace" real loud, like them people who get pulled off the stage with the rod on Amateur Night at the Apollo.

We done seen two miracles around this house: Brenda ain't had a drop to drank since she found God, and I done lost eight pounds since I started walking evenings a little over a month and a half ago. I sure like her sober, and she say she certainly like what's left of me.

Right now, we sitting out here at Lorenzie Park watching the kids feed the ducks. She mad with me. Ain't said a word in the last ten minutes. She just put Sunshine on her left hip and started throwing breadcrumbs out in the water, too. Miss Q keep trying to count the ducks, but they keep flying away, and she get mad 'cause she have to start all over. For five, she don't count too fast, but I been trying to help her, using toothpicks. I bought my fishing pole out here just so Hakeem could hold it in his hand to see what fishing feel like, but he keep wanting to

run in the water to catch hisself a duck. I wanted to take 'em to
McDonald's and then over there to the Sammy Davis Theatre
to see a little kids' movie, but I don't know now. Depends on
what Brenda feel like doing.

She getting big. Her stomach is starting to poke out. I thank
it's cute. Been a long time since I been around a woman with a
baby inside her. I been thanking about what Howie asked me,
and I come to the conclusion that I don't care if this baby is
mine or not. I'ma pretend like it is, and that's what's gon' make
it mine. I been wanting to ask Brenda off and on ever since
Howie brought it up, but I just can't brang myself to do it.

I love her. And these kids is growing on me. I'm even learning how to braid hair. Brenda showed me, 'cause Sunshine's
hair sticks out all over the place and she look too wild to be
such a little-bitty thang. I musta bought at least twenty books
for these kids. They was so excited, it was like they ain't never
had they own books before. I told Brenda that reading is important. Especially for black kids. I would write and talk a
whole lot better if I'da learned how to appreciate reading when
I was younger. I been reading to 'em before they go to bed, at
least on my nights off, and Brenda started doing it when I ain't
there. She say she love that *Goodnight Moon* more than the
baby, and *If the People Could Fly* makes her happy. She said
she never knew reading could be so much fun. That words
could make you feel so good. This is one more reason why I
like Brenda: she say what's on her mind. Uh-oh, here she come
now. Sunshine done fell asleep on her shoulder.

"Can you take her for me, please, Cecil?"

"Sure can."

And then she stands there with her hands on her hips. "You
want me to make you some gumbo tonight?"

Hot damn. Don't she know how to get what she want from
a man. "Yeah, if it ain't too much trouble."

"You know how much trouble it is, but if I didn't wanna do it,
I wouldn'ta mentioned it, now, would I?"

"Thank you, Brenda."

"You're welcome. You ready to go home?"

"I wanted to take the kids to McDonald's and a movie."

"I'm tired, Cecil. Let's go to the drive-up window so we can go on home. They can watch a video, they don't care."

"Okay, then."

"So—you thinking about what I asked you?"

"Yeah, I'm thanking about it."

"And what you thinking?"

"I'm thanking that maybe you right. That we living in sin in front of these kids and we need to do it the right way."

"So when you gon' go down there and file?"

"Monday morning."

"You sure you wanna do this, Cecil?"

"I can't go back to Viola, Brenda. Not now."

"Why not now?"

"With the baby coming and everything."

"What if I told you I ain't sure if this baby is yours, Cecil?"

"You got reason to doubt?"

"Maybe. But maybe not. I don't know. I'm trying to be honest about it."

"I don't truthfully care one way or another, Brenda. I like being around you and these kids."

"And I love being with you, Cecil. I love how you treat my kids. I love how you treat me. That's why I'ma make you some gumbo tonight, but you gotta go to the store to get the stuff."

"I don't mind."

"When you think we gon' be able to move?"

"Soon. Viola's moving out the house next week. I went down there to talk to them IRS folks, and turns out I can put the house up for sale and pay what I owe from the proceeds. I should have enough change left over for us to find a decent place."

"What's wrong with that house?"

"We can't live there."

"Why not?"

"I can't bring you into that house, Brenda; now, thank about that."

"I wouldn't care. It ain't like we'd be sleeping in the same bed."

"No. And that's all I gotta say about the matter."

"Okay. But when we gon' start looking?"

"When we get a offer on the house."

"We?"

"Well, that would be me and Viola. Whatever I get, I gotta split it with her."

"Hakeem! Miss Q! Come on! Let's go. We going to Mc-Donald's!"

And here they come.

I can tell she mad again, but it's too bad. Wait till she hear this: "Speaking of Viola, I gotta stop by there to get my stuff out the carport."

"Today?"

"It won't take but ten or fifteen minutes at the most."

"You sure you know what you doing, Cecil? I mean, I ain't one to pressure nobody. I done took care of my kids by myself all this time, I don't want you to feel obligated to me."

"Brenda, stop."

"You right, Cecil. I'm sorry. Glory be to Jesus. I know I'm blessed, and here I go being ungrateful. I ain't got no hard feelings toward Viola. None. She been your wife longer than I been born, so I understand you kinda tied to her. Just don't change your mind about us, Cecil. Please."

We almost at my car in the parking lot. "I was thanking that if and when the house sell, I might should trade this old thang in and get us a van. Something the kids can be comfortable in. What you thank about that, Brenda?"

"I like it. I like that idea a lot."

After we put the kids in they car seats, I bend over and give her a kiss on her lips. Brenda is a good kisser. A very good kisser. She just don't know how blessed I feel, and I ain't even close to being saved.

————————

Is that fella back again? This is getting a little ridiculous. I mean he spending a awful lotta time over here with a woman who ain't even divorced yet. He don't feel no kinda shame, do he? I should ask him. But naw. I can't talk about sinning. What I thank I been doing for the past five months? I still wonder what him and Viola been doing in there. I had a hard enough time trying to get her in the same bed with me, let alone getting her to do anythang else. I wanna see this fella. See what he sporting that I ain't got.

When I get up to the front door, before I get a chance to even knock, Viola opens it, and I have to rub my eyes, 'cause I know I'm seeing thangs. This look like the woman I was married to ten or fifteen years ago. This can't be the fifty-five-year-old Viola. Not looking like this.

"You can't speak?" Now I know it's the Viola I left five months ago, but she still look good enough to kiss right now. If only she could change the tone of her voice so she don't sound so evil.

"How you doing, Vy? You sho' looking good, girl. Don't tell me you done went and had some of that plastic surgery?"

"Hell no, I ain't had no damn plastic surgery. What about you, Cecil? You looking like you done had some liposuction. Where's your stomach?"

I look down. Some of it *is* gone. I suck it in a little more and stand up extra tall. "I been exercising."

"What took you so long to start?"

"Look, Viola. You got company?"

"No, I don't."

"Well, last time I was here you said that car belonged to a male friend. Did he give it to you?"

She break out into a big smile, and hot damn if her teeth

ain't pretty and white. What she been doing over here? "Viola?"

"What?"

"What happened to your other teeth?"

"Paris got me some new ones."

"Them don't even look like dentures."

"That's 'cause they ain't cheap like the other ones was."

"You look like you done lost quite a bit a weight, too."

"I have. And still losing. I got ten or fifteen more to go."

"Me, too," I say. "Is your friend in there?"

"No. And that's my car, Cecil. Paris bought it for me."

"So do this mean you ain't got no friend?"

"Did I say that?"

"No, you didn't."

"Then don't let it concern you."

"I just came over to get my stuff."

"It's out there."

"You gon' need any help moving?"

"I don't know yet. A lot of this junk ain't going to my new place."

"What you mean by junk?"

"That bedroom set, for starters."

"Ain't nothing wrong with that bedroom set, Viola."

"Then you can have it."

"No, I can't sleep on that."

"Then shut up, Cecil."

"You looking good, Vy. Healthy. I'm glad."

"Thank you, Cecil. Now. I wish I could stand here and talk to you, but our granddaughter got a track meet and I been watching all that O. J. Simpson mess on TV and I'm almost late."

"He kilt them people as sure as I'm standing here. Shanice still here?"

"You don't know that, Cecil. She ain't going back home till next month."

"We'll soon see, won't we? How the kids doing these days?"

"Damn it, Cecil. I just told you I gotta go. I'd be standing out here all night if I was to tell you what they all doing, but let me say this. Janelle done finally put George out, and he might be going to jail."

"Say what?"

"You heard me. Charlotte ain't speaking to me, and I suggest you try calling her, 'cause I'm through with her ass. I mean it. Your son is in jail again. I think they said he might get up to a year for beating up Donnetta's husband with a sponge mop handle."

"Say what?"

"And Paris still over there in California trying to be Superwoman, popping pills like them women did in *Valley of the Dolls* to keep that fast pace up, but she don't thank nobody know it."

"Say what?"

"If you say 'say what' one more time, I'ma slap you into next week. Now, get outta my way, 'cause we ain't got no more kids to discuss. And don't touch my lawnmower or take nothing that don't belong to you. Goodbye."

I just stand there and watch her lock the front door that I had the keys to for twenty-some-odd years. But my keys don't fit this door no more. I walk over to the carport and turn around and watch Viola get in her new car. She don't just look younger, she look happy. I ain't seen her look like this in years. I wonder, as she wave to me backing out the driveway, if it's because I'm here, or because I'm gone.

A New
Life

"I still can't believe Jackie Onassis is dead; can you, Loretta?"

"I can't believe I'm not dead," Loretta says, laughing.

"She was too damn young to die. And as pretty as she wanted to be. You remember when President Kennedy was shot?"

"Of course I do, Vy. Everybody remembers that day. Okay, let's not talk about dead people right now. We're alive and kicking right here in your brand-new condo, and it's beautiful! Just beautiful, Vy!"

"It is, ain't it?" I say, looking around. It certainly is. And far enough from my old house that I get to go to a different grocery store, bank, and post office. "Thank you, Loretta. I told you you would love it." It took all the patience I had to hold off showing her till now, but I wanted to wait till after they put in the new carpet and painted it, so she could get the total effect. But with Memorial Day and everything, they couldn't do nothing till this week, and they took their sweet-ass time. They just finished two days ago, and we go on our cruise a week from today—on the sixteenth, and I got a million and one things to do between now and then.

Since I can't move in for another few days, I wanted to bring something over here so it feel like I'm gon' live here, so me and Loretta stopped by Target and picked up two $7.99 houseplants. She also helped me bring over my good towels and sheets and glasses that I keep hid. I'm trying to decide if I wanna put one of the plants in the kitchen window and the other one in my master bathroom. I don't know. Hot damn! If I don't like the sound of that: master bathroom. But if there ain't no master, can I call it a mistress bathroom? Naw, 'cause I ain't nobody's mistress neither. Hell, it's *my* big bathroom. That's good enough. I got two sinks! So I can take my pick which one I wanna brush my teeth or wash my face in. They look just like marble even though they ain't, but, hell, I don't care. I still can't believe it. "Don't you just love this dark teal I picked out for the carpet, Loretta?" I say, and then I sneeze.

"Bless you. I do, Vy. You've got such good taste."

"So do you, Loretta. What you talking about? I just don't like ruffles as much as you do, that's all. Come on around this corner and see how big my bedroom is."

"I'm coming," she says. "Boy oh boy, these ceilings are so high. And you've even got a little backyard out there. This is just perfect. I wish I had a daughter like you."

"I feel blessed to have all my kids, even when they make me mad," I say. "I can't wait to put my new bedroom set in here, and I'm still gon' have plenty of room. When I start taking that class to get my day-care license, and if I get a job that won't mess up my Social Security checks, I might buy one of them loveseats or a chaise lounge, like Marlene Dietrich used to lay on, remember those?"

"Of course I do. You're still thinking about working at a day care, Vy?"

"I don't know, Loretta. I can't hardly add two and two no more, I don't know what kinda class I'ma take, but I'ma learn how to do something. That much I do know." I sneeze again.

"Bless you."

"Thanks. Okay, Loretta, get the camera and hurry up and take my picture. I gotta get outta here, 'cause this paint is starting to get to me, I ain't lying."

"It could also be the new carpet, you know. I read somewhere that people with asthma shouldn't be around new carpet, because something they treat it with can trigger an attack." She reaches in her big purse and gets out the Polaroid. "Lean against that wall there. It'll look more professional with a white background."

And I do. I smile, showing off my new teeth, and turn a little to the side, showing off my new body. I'm wearing those leggings all the young girls wear and a black cotton T-shirt.

"Say 'pizza'!"

"Pizza. I know that, Loretta. That's why I ain't moving in till next week. So let's go. Plus, I gotta stop and get some gas, and pick up my prednisone and theophylline prescriptions, 'cause I'm all outta both of 'em, and then get Shanice. She only got a half-day of school today. Will you take another one, just in case?"

"Okay, Vy," she says, "say 'pizza' again!"

"I wanna say 'cheese'!" And the flash goes off.

"The first one came out really nice. You look so much younger," Loretta says, and starts putting her shoes back on. I made her take 'em off when she came in here. I took mine off, too. But when I move in, I ain't making nobody take off they shoes, except if they look too dirty. "Is Cecil helping you move?"

"I wouldn't ask Cecil to help me move if he paid me. I'm starting a new life, Loretta, and he ain't nowhere in it. Simple as that."

"Well, I just wondered, Vy."

"I know, Lo. I didn't mean to get testy about it."

And then she looks like she just saw something that excited her, but she couldn't have, 'cause we just walking over to my garage. I love it when I press my Genie and that door starts going up and I see my new car sitting inside it. Now I know what living good feels like. My teeth ain't even hardly hurting me no more, and I done lost nineteen pounds. It don't get no better than this. Lord knows it don't.

"Vy, guess what?"

"What?"

"I'm already packed," Loretta says, blushing like a little girl—wrinkles and all.

"I'm right behind you," I say.

"You mean you started already, too?"

"Finished. When would I have time to pack when I move? And how in the world would I be able to find anything? You know how much junk I got?"

"Yes, I do."

"Shut up, Loretta. See you later."

She starts laughing, waves to me, walks over to her white Cadillac, and gets in. Loretta know she don't need that big old car, but her husband left it to her, and she said she'll drive it till whoever dies first.

It's hot as hell out here. I know that much. But I don't care. I got air conditioning in my car. And I got air conditioning in my new condominium. Hot damn! I pull straight into a handicapped space when I get to the pharmacy and put my card on the dashboard so the police can see it while I run in and get my medicine. I love having this handicapped sign, 'cause you always get a parking space. When I pull into the gas station, I forgot I just used most of my cash, and I ain't cashed my check yet, so I hurry up and put five dollars of unleaded in, 'cause I can't tolerate the smell of this gas and it's hard holding my breath when I'm filling up, but sometimes when I plug my nose up people look at me like I'm crazy. I'ma just have to look crazy again today.

Shanice is standing at the curb outside Hyde Park Junior High School talking to some boy with little braids in his hair. He sure is cute. No wonder she like it here. This is one of them Magnet schools they made so that all kids could get a good education and not just white ones. I feel like honking this horn, but I don't wanna embarrass her. She swings her head around, and when she sees me, she tells this boy something and runs over to the car.

"Hi, Granny," she says, and gives me a kiss on my cheek.

"Hi, baby. Who was that boy?"

"Gerard. He's in my science class. We've been doing our final project together on the senses."

"And which ones would you be dealing with?"

"Taste and smell."

"I betcha."

"Granny! Stop it. Wait a minute. Where are we going?"

"We splurging. We going to the Mirage to eat lunch at their buffet, and then we going home and start packing. Get Granny one pill outta each bottle and then hand me that Pepsi rolling under your foot, would you? And get my spray outta my purse while you at it, please? Between that paint and them gas fumes, I swear."

"Granny?" She hands me my pills, opens that warm soda, and gives me my inhaler.

"Yeah," I say, after swallowing them and taking a puff, but I start coughing, 'cause my chest been feeling tight and this is what happens when it starts opening up. I take another puff, just to make sure.

"You all right, Granny?"

"Yep. I'm okay now, baby. Here, you can put it back."

She drops the inhaler in my purse. "Would you be mad at me if I told you I don't wanna go home when I get back from camp?"

"No, I wouldn't be mad. But why don't you wanna go home? George done been arrested. And your mama's there all by herself."

"That's true, but Mama said they can't keep him in jail unless I let them examine me and do that stupid interview, which I am not doing. Period."

"Why not? If that's what it's gon' take to put that son-of-a-bitch where he belong—in San Quentin somewhere—why won't you?"

" 'Cause I can't. I just can't. I want to forget about this whole thing, and every time I look around here comes another reminder."

"Maybe you just need a little more time to think about it. Those social-service people I been talking to seem real nice. They trying to protect you, Shanice. They got your best interest at heart, you know."

"I've heard. But I'm not interested. As you always say, Granny, 'they're a day late and a dollar short.' "

"But it ain't they fault."

"I can't go back to that house. And I'm not setting one foot in there ever again in life. So, if Mama wants me to come home, then she's gonna have to find us another place to live."

"Then you need to take that up with her."

"I will."

And we don't say another word about it. I stop by the bank and cash my Social Security check and then drive till we pull into the Mirage, and I let 'em valet-park my car, and we go in and eat steak and crab and lobster, and we licking our fingers when I see some horses on a big screen in another room running around a track. Now, I know the Kentucky Derby was damn near a month ago and I know I ain't got no business doing this, but for some reason I feel lucky, so, without even realizing what the hell I'm doing, I grab Shanice by the arm and the next thing I know we standing in this big old curved room with giant screens all around us and all kinds of races is going on.

"Granny, what are we doing in here?"

"I wanna bet on a horse."

"Which one?"

"Hell, I don't know," I say, looking up. "Let me go ask somebody."

And that's exactly what I do. I walk over to some old black

fella who look friendly with a wrinkled-up newspaper in front of him that turns out to be a racing form. "Excuse me, honey, but what racetrack is this?" I say, pointing to that screen.

"That's Hollywood Park."

"What would I do if I wanted to bet on a horse?"

"Which one?"

"I don't know."

"Well, you need to know which one. Or how many. And if you wanna bet on one to win, place, or show."

"I know that means first, second, and third place."

"That's right."

"Which horse you betting on?"

"These two right here," he says, and shows me the ones he's circled: "Moneychaser" and "Imflyin."

"Thank you," I say.

"Good luck," he says. "And if you're gonna bet on this race, you've got three minutes to do it."

"Shit," I say to Shanice. "I mean, shoot. Sorry, baby. Reach in Granny's purse and hand me my wallet."

She do, and I run over to the window where you place your bets, and when they ask me which horse, I hear myself say, "I wanna put five dollars on all of 'em to win, place, or show."

The man just looks at me like I'm crazy. "That's fifteen dollars each."

"It is? I mean, I knew that." But hell if I did. This just sucked up almost all my little check, but for some reason I don't even understand myself right now, I don't really give a damn. Maybe this is how Cecil been feeling all these years.

"That *was* for all of them?"

"That's right."

"Whatever you say," he says, and hands me my tickets.

I hold 'em in my hand real tight and order me and Shanice a Shirley Temple, and when that race starts my heart is pounding so fast, and I hear people screaming and hollering, getting louder and louder as the horses get closer to the finish line, and then a whole bunch of moaning and groaning when the race is over. All except me. My horses won. I sit and wait and then don't know what the hell I'm looking at when all them numbers start scrambling up and down like they do at a train station, so I walk back over to that same man and ask him how much did I win? He just look at my tickets and start laughing and shaking his head at the same time. "Beginner's luck," he says.

"How much?" I ask.

"Wait a minute," he says. "Watch that screen over there. It'll tell us in a minute. But you won some money today, sweetness, that you did."

I just stand there holding Shanice's hand real tight, and then, when I see the numbers finally stop, I look back at the man and ask him again: "How much did I win?"

"Well," he says, going through my slips, "somewhere in the neighborhood of about eight or nine hundred dollars."

"I know you lying," I say.

"Go on over to the cashier, and they'll tell you," he says, "and congratulations. You wanna be my bookie?"

I just laugh and take my tickets over there, and, sure enough, they count out $898 and they put it all in my hand and I can't hardly control myself all the way outside. When that valet boy brings me my car I give him a five-dollar tip, and when we get in I give Shanice a brand-new crisp one-hundred-dollar bill. We laugh all the way home.

When we pull in the driveway, some white man in a beige suit is getting out a white Saturn in front of my house, but I ain't got a clue who he is. "Can I help you?" I say.

"Are you Viola Price?" he asks.

"Yes I am, why?"

"I have something for you," he says, and walks over and hands me a envelope.

"What's this?"

"I'm not sure. But could you sign here for me, please."

"Okay," I say, and sign on the line next to my name.

"Did I win something?"

"Could be a trip or something," he says, and gets back in his car and drives off.

It's kinda obvious that this ain't no trip or no Clearing House Sweepstakes kinda win. After I get in the house, I sit on the couch and even without my glasses I can see this envelope is from Family Court. I open it. It's divorce papers from Cecil. "Shanice! Get Granny's spray, would you?"

"Where's your purse?" she asks.

Shit. "I left it in the car. But it should be one by my bed. Hurry up."

My chest is getting tight again. Shit. I ain't in the mood for this right now. Cecil want a divorce, huh? Well, good-goddamn-riddance. You just beat me to the punch, buster. Save me a whole lotta money. You can have a divorce all right.

"Here, Granny."

After two puffs, I feel better.

"Are you all right?"

"Yeah. Look in the second kitchen drawer on the left and get your granny a pen and then go in my bedroom and pull out that night-table drawer and get me some envelopes, the writing tablet with the birds on the front, and one twenty-nine-cent stamp. And see if we got any messages on the machine while you in there. Paris been in London for damn near a week and I ain't heard a word from that huzzy. I asked her to buy me one of them Princess Di hats. She could call some-damn-body."

"Okay, Granny. You sure you're all right?"

"Yeah, I'm just wheezing. Too much excitement. Fresh paint and gas kinda gets to me. I just need to sit here and relax, do a breathing treatment, and I'll be fine. Damnit! I missed my stories today! Would you turn on *Oprah* for me? Wait a minute. On second thought, I don't feel like listening to her ass today. Put it on BET."

"Okay, Granny."

"And could you run and get the mail?"

"Okay, Granny."

I hear Paris's voice: "Hi, Mama. Hi, Shanice. I'm having an amazing time over here. And don't worry. I got your hat. Shanice, I got you something cute, too. Hope everybody's doing fine. I'll be home in a couple of days. It's been a very fruitful trip. All around. Call Dingus at his friend Jason's house if you feel like it, Mama. I left you that number, remember? Anyway, I love you. Call you when I get home."

When Shanice comes out with what I asked her to get, I pick up them papers and sign 'em so fast it makes me laugh out loud.

"What's so funny, Granny?" Shanice asks, after coming in with the mail and slamming that screen door.

"What's 'a fruitful trip' mean, and how many times have I asked you not to slam that door?"

"Sorry, Granny. It means productive, good, something happened that you wanted to happen."

"Where you learn such a big word and you ain't but in the eighth grade?"

"It's not a big word, Granny."

"And sorry my behind. Slam that door one more time and I'ma make you go get a switch off one of them trees out there I ain't got. Any good news?"

She's laughing now. "This big envelope's from Dingus."

"Open it, would you? And hurry up, hurry up!"

"What's the rush, Granny?"

"I wanna see! I just wanna see! He promised to send me a picture of him at his junior prom and some of them college letters he been getting. I just wanna see some for myself 'cause I ain't never seen no letter from no college asking nobody to come to their school. I'm so proud of that boy I don't know what to do."

"What about my mom and Auntie Paris?"

"I don't mean them kinda letters. These colleges is begging Dingus to come. Hurry up, Shanice!"

After taking her sweet time and finally getting the envelope open, she holds up what I know from the back is a picture. "She's cute," is all Shanice says, and then hands it to me. "Dingus might look a whole lot better when he gets all that metal out of his mouth, and he may not know it, but Clearasil and Oxy Pads could help his cause. Nice tux, though."

"Be quiet, girl." I turn that picture over and see my handsome grandson, who don't look like he got no pimples on his face, standing with his arm around this pretty little chocolate cupcake of a girl, and it's written all over her that she come from good stock. Paris said her daddy's a preacher, so that mean she been raised right and probably ain't fast like a lot of 'em is these days. "He sho' know how to pick 'em, is all I gotta say," and then I start flipping through what looks like eight or nine different letters Shanice just handed me. "Would you get Granny's glasses for her, baby? Please?"

"I don't know what you'd do without me, Granny. Don't you want me to stay and be your private maid?"

I'm nodding my head yes, chuckling, and getting teary-eyed at the same time when I start reading the names of the schools written in big colorful letters across the top of each piece of paper that I don't need no glasses to read: Stanford University and the University of Southern California and Michigan State University and Ohio State University and the University of California at Berkeley and the University of Miami, and I stop right there, 'cause it's enough. My grandson is going to college all right. And he got choices. And they asking him do he wanna come to their school. Times have sure changed, thank you, Jesus.

"Shanice, what exactly do a three-point-eighty-seven GPA mean?"

"It means he's getting almost straight A's, Granny."

"Un-huh," I mumble, and read every word of each one of them letters even though they all said the same thing. He's a great quarterback. He's had a great junior year. His grade point average is impressive, and they hope he considers playing and getting his degree at their school, and then they list all the reasons why he'd like it there. I let the letters fall in my lap, and Shanice comes over with a Kleenex and wipe my eyes.

"I hope I can make you proud one day, too, Granny," and she gives me a big hug and squeezes me so tight that I accidentally pull off her little curly hairpiece, which, to my surprise, she just throws on the cocktail table.

"You know what, baby? I'm already proud of you. I'm proud of how well you've handled all this terrible stuff that's happened to you, and I pray on my knees every single night that you grow up and become a strong, healthy woman. I pray that, if you can't forget this, which you probably won't, that you bury it somewhere so deep you can't find it. So deep that it won't never have to haunt you. Watching you smile makes me happy. I won't lie, now that I know what a GPA means, yours was a three-point-oh if I'm not mistaken, so you might wanna work on getting it up a little higher next year—which will be your first year in high school, am I right?"

"You're right, Granny."

"And don't worry: I'll be there to watch you run that hundred and two hundred and them relays faster than Flo Jo. How's that sound?"

"It sounds good, Granny. It sounds real good."

"Okay," I say as I open up my tablet and start writing.

"What are you writing, Granny?"

"None-ya."

"None-ya?"

"None-ya business. But when I finish writing whatever it is I'm writing, I'ma want you to take it over to Miss Loretta's for me, okay?"

She nods her head yes, and I start.

———

I been tossing and turning all night, 'cause my chest been getting tighter since this afternoon. I took my pills, gave myself a breathing treatment. Hell, what more can I do? I ain't feeling too swift, I know that much. I been here too many times before. But I'ma just lay here a little longer and see what happen, plus, I don't wanna scare Shanice if I have to call 911. Sometime this mess pass. What time is it? I look over at the clock and it say 1:40. Shit. I start coughing again and put my hands over my mouth, 'cause this girl laying right up under me, but I can't stop. Shit. I been wheezing all day. I knew I shouldn'ta stayed in there with that paint or that carpet for as long as I did. Shit. What difference do it make? I'm hungry. Maybe if I eat something I'll feel better.

I ease out the bed and go on out to the kitchen and open up the refrigerator. It's some leftover spaghetti and meatballs in here, and that sauce was good. It ain't been in here but three or four days. It should taste even better now. I put some in a bowl and microwave it and sit at this raggedy table that I can't wait to get rid of once I get my new set outta layaway. I'ma put some of my horse-winning money on it to lower my balance.

After I finish, I put the plate in the sink and get a can of ginger ale and take it back to the bedroom. Shanice done turned her back away from me, thank the Lord. I take a few swigs and lay on back down. My chest is still tight, and I ain't feeling no better. Shit. I ain't in the mood for this. Not tonight. I reach over and take a puff off my inhaler and lay on back down. And wait. It ain't helping. I know I should call 911, but if I lay here for a few more minutes, maybe it might let up. Sometimes it do. You just never know. I feel like turning on the TV, but that might wake Shanice up, and I don't wanna do that when she gotta get up and go to school. Wait a minute. No she don't. Tomorrow is Saturday. Maybe if I turn it down real low she won't hear it. I pick up the remote control and some old movie is on, something I almost remember but I can't put my finger on right now. I need something to take my mind off my chest. It ain't working. Shit. My throat is closing up and I can't hardly get no air. Shit. I push Shanice as hard as I can and say as loud as I can, "Call 911."

But it came out like a whisper. She rolls over, wipes the sleep outta her eyes, and when she see me looking like I'm gasping for air, she screams, "Granny!"

I grab her arm so hard I know it must hurt but it's the only way I can say, "Call," again, and this time she jumps over me and dial 911 and I hear her yelling: "My granny is having an asthma attack. Please send an ambulance right now to 4807 Bledsoe Avenue! It's a light-blue house! Hurry up, please!"

Seem like I feel a little relief. "It's okay, Shanice," I say, fanning myself with my hand. "I just need to sit up and try to be still. They'll be here in a minute and it'll be all right. It's gon' be all right." I sit all the way up and fall forward, 'cause it's the only way it helps you feel like you can breathe easier. Sweat is starting to run down my face and my nightgown is getting sticky. I wish I could take it off.

"Granny, you want me to get your machine under the bed? Want me to get it out for you?"

I cough so hard that all this mucus comes up and when I try to sit up it feels like my neck and chest and ribs is being pulled like rubber bands. I don't wanna scare my granddaughter, but my chest is hurting again. Now my nostrils is flaring out, 'cause when I try to inhale ain't hardly no air coming in. I open my mouth and try to take little sips, 'cause it's all I can do. But now it feels like somebody got a straw down my throat blowing a tiny tunnel of air. This ain't enough. I'm trying not to move, trying not to cry, but now I'm scared. Please hurry up and get here. Please, God, let 'em hurry up and get here. Be still, Viola. Keep your big ass still. One. Two. Three. Buckle my shoe. Four. Five. Six. Shut the door. Seven. Eight. Nine. Pick up sticks.

I hear the sirens coming up the block and I close my eyes and wait to hear that loud knock on the front door and I say thank you Jesus to myself. Poor Shanice, she been standing in that doorway watching me and watching the front door, then she disappears and I hear her open it.

"Where's your grandmother, honey?"

"In there!" Poor thang. She don't need to be here. She don't need to see me like this. Somebody get her outta here. Please. Two paramedics come through the door and I hear the sound of the gurney popping open and then one comes over to me with his bag and look at me sitting here with my head down in my lap, rocking. "How you doing, ma'am?" this one say grabbing that thing out his bag and clipping it to the end of my finger.

I nod my head up and down and say, "I'm fine."

"That's good. Don't worry, we're gonna get you fixed right up here."

I try to grab onto the sheets and at the same time he tries to open my gown up and I grab his hand and he press that cold thing against my chest and say, "Try to calm down for a second, ma'am. I need you to take a deep breath for me."

But I can't.

"Come on. Let's try once more."

I try again, but don't know if I do it or not.

"I've got wheezing in all fields!" he says.

I hear the other guy say, "Her respiratory rate is over 33. Can you try to relax, ma'am? We need you to slow your breathing down."

If I could I would, don't he know that? But I can't. Just hurry up and give me something! Look at my eyes, goddamn it!

"I'm gonna put you on some oxygen now and this should help you breathe easier," he says. The next thing I know that mask is covering my nose and mouth and for a minute I feel relieved.

"Her number's still low. Get the albuterol," one says, and then I hear Loretta's voice.

"Vy, it's gonna be okay, sweetie. Don't you worry about anything."

I open my eyes as wide as I can, 'cause it seem like maybe

some air might get behind 'em and slide all the way down to my lungs, but it don't work, and when I look at Loretta she know exactly what I'm saying, 'cause she say, "Don't worry. I won't forget. Now, shush, and relax. Do what they tell you to do, Vy. Come on, sweetie."

"Granny!" Shanice is crying and I can't take her seeing me like this.

"Shanice, sweetheart, come on out here and let these nice men help your granny, dear. Come on." Loretta puts her arms around my granddaughter and now my eyes just say thank you and she put her finger over her mouth to tell me to shush-up again, her favorite thing when she think I'm running my mouth too much, and I shake my head real fast to tell her that's what I'm about to do. Is shut up. And be quiet. But thank you for taking my granddaughter outta here. Thank you for being such a good friend, Loretta. I hope she saw all that in my eyes.

Now something is going down my throat and I know this is that other stuff they try when the first one don't work. "Her blood pressure's hypertensive: 170 over 104; and the pulse is tachycardic: 160. And we have ectopy on the heart monitor. Let's watch her for a second. If no change, let's do another albuterol. How you doing, ma'am?"

All I can do is shake my head back and forth, and I think I got this whole sheet balled up in my hand. It's too hot in here. Can't somebody open a damn window?

"Ma'am, I'm gonna give you a shot in the arm. But I need you to sit still. And then we're gonna give you an IV and put you on the gurney and we're gonna take you to the hospital, all right? Try to relax and we'll have you there in a few minutes."

I wish he would stop saying that! How in the hell can I relax when I can't breathe? I feel 'em sticking me with more than one needle but for some reason it don't hurt. Now I feel like I'm about to gag, and, sure enough, here come that spaghetti.

"Oh, no, she's vomiting!"

My head is thick and hot and now I know I won't get no

more air. Even when I feel that other tube coming down my throat I know this ain't gon' work either. When they pick me up and put me on that gurney and strap me in and prop my head up, something cold slides between my legs. It's usually colder than this. My hands is puffing up. My arms is, too. I'm swelling.

One fella picks up a little telephone and says, "Base, this is Rescue 4. I'm in route to your facility, Code 3. My ETA is two minutes. Have a patient with a severe asthma attack. Does not appear to be getting better with the treatment given." And then he hangs up and looks down at me. "Hang in there, ma'am, you're gonna be just fine."

I know he lying. But it's okay. It really is okay. Ain't no use fighting it no more. As much as I wanna stay and move into my new condo and go on my cruise with Loretta, this feel so much easier to do. It don't take no energy. It don't take no strength. Why'm I feeling so much better all of a sudden? It feel like I don't even need to breathe. Lord, this is nice. This is so nice.

"She's unconscious. Her heart rate's dropping and she's turning blue."

I ain't unconscious. And I ain't turning blue either. What island is that over there, Loretta? Is that Jamaica or St. Thomas? Where the hell we at today, girl? Yeah, I'll play a little bridge, but only after we do some putting. Wait a minute. We home already? Cecil? You in there, baby? I know. I know. I do, I still do. You should know that. But I want you to be happy, especially after all this time. Right now, I'm happy. I don't think I ever been this happy before. I feel good. Just like I did right before I went into labor with Paris. My head is crystal-clear. I feel like I could fly and float and turn a few flips if I wanted to. Right this minute. I could. I know I could. I feel warm and cool at the same time. Soft. Moist and lush. Like Chicago on a hot afternoon right after a good thunderstorm. Whew. What kind'a medicine they done gave me? Lord, give me some more. Give me as much as you want me to have, 'cause right now, right this very second, it feel like I got everything I need. I don't know why it took me so long to get here. Why I been resisting all these years. When I coulda had this smoothness. This calm. This ease. I can't hardly describe it. I never woulda believed it would feel like this. And it's okay. I *like* this. I ain't worried about nothing right now. Except my kids. Lord, what they gon' do? Please don't let 'em take this too hard. Please don't let 'em fall apart. Please let 'em remember everything I taught 'em. Let 'em find their places—the place that was carved just for them since they was born. Don't let 'em hurt too much. And especially each other. Let 'em know that the one thing they'll always have is each other. And please let 'em find out what happiness feel like. Let 'em have every drop of my courage, my guts, my strength, 'cause I ain't gon' need none of it no more. Give what I had left to all four of 'em. Help 'em to remember how to backstroke and breaststroke instead of just treading water. And please, whatever y'all do, don't drown and don't let nothing or nobody make you sink to the bottom. Y'all supposed to rise to the top, 'cause that's how I raised you. That's how I raised all four of you. To be good. And then, be even better than that. To yourself. To each other. And to everybody that mean something to you. Don't forget that I loved y'all with every breath in my body, and if I had it to do all over again— all over again—know that each one of y'all could have this last breath, too.

Why Am I
Wearing My
Mama's Shoes?

I should be ashamed of myself. The phrase "shop till you drop" does not apply to me because I'm still standing. But, then again, this hotel room is small, and not by any stretch of the imagination even close to the standard suite size I'm used to staying in, in the States. But, if this were, say, a typical woman's side of a California walk-in closet (which is pretty much what it feels like), it would probably be close to full. It's wall-to-wall hatboxes, garment and shopping bags, so many that I actually have to brush my way through a sea of tissue paper just to get to the bathroom.

How am I going to get all this shit home? I have to save the pretty bags for Mama, because she collects them. She brags (and, from what I gather, sometimes even lies) to her bowling buddies that she's shopped in these stores, but mostly she carries them like an extra purse to draw attention, because not only do they come in such an amazing assortment of colors, but the embossed name screams out that it's not from any store in Vegas.

I kick one of the hatboxes so that the top flips off. When I see orange, I actually giggle. I can't even remember buying an orange hat, but I don't care right now because I've had so much fun these past five days I can hardly stand it. Everyone's been so gracious and hospitable. They're all ethnically diverse chefs and restaurateurs, and they certainly know how to cook—in every sense of the word. I've eaten East, West, and South

African food; East Indian dishes like I've never tasted any-where; the spiciest, tangiest, most sensuous Jamaican fare ever, and some of the meals were prepared in private homes! I even got a chance to taste authentic Vietnamese food, although over here they call it "Eurasian"—which makes no sense to me, but it was better than any Pan-Pacific food I'd ever had.

Last night, Bernard, a Grenadian chef, took me to some nightclub where half-dressed men and women danced in cages that hung from the ceiling. The music was thumping and I wore this "slutty" hot-pink dress I bought on Sloane Street with a pair of FM pumps that I know Charlotte would just die for. I danced so hard and long that I finally had to take them off. That was at four o'clock this morning. It felt good dancing like a madwoman. I felt like I was twenty-five again. I need to get out more often. It didn't take me all night to realize that. And I vowed to do just that when I get home. Once a month: go danc-ing. Even if I have to go by myself!

As I sit here in this yellow, white, and blue floral room, it feels like I'm waking up from a dream. I've spent a ton of money, done some real damage, but I enjoyed every minute of it. At home, I never splurge. Always trying to do what makes sense. For some reason I don't understand, I didn't feel like holding back.

I'm also feeling very sexy here, like I should've brought something satin or lacy to sleep in, but of course I didn't. What would be the point? As I kick off these slingbacks, I look around and realize I probably need to buy two more suitcases.

I got something for everybody. Mama's hat came from Har-rods and she's going to love that green bag! I got Daddy some hand-rolled cigars from Covent Garden. Shanice: an outfit from some teenybopper boutique. Right this minute, I can't re-member exactly what I bought Charlotte, Lewis, and Janelle. Dingus gets underwear from Marks & Spencer, and a weird pair of jeans. I wonder what he's doing? Probably with Jason.

I pick up the phone and call home to see if I have any personal messages, since I haven't checked in four whole days. I'm not even going to bother calling my business line, because I don't want to know. Only three messages! At first I feel relieved, and then, immediately, unpopular. Where are my stupid pills? I drag the phone over to the table next to the sofa, open the drawer, move the Bible, and push my hand back until I feel the bottle. The name on the prescription is Dingus's. Right before I was leaving to come here, I had exhausted all my "sources" for refills, but I remembered that during spring training Dingus had torn a ligament in his Achilles tendon and then, two weeks later, strained his hip flexor, so his doctor wrote two different prescriptions: an anti-inflammatory for swelling and Vicodin for pain. I took the Vicodin, because Dingus said he didn't like the way it made him feel. I wish I had that problem. There was one refill on it, and after that I called the doctor and told him that Dingus had had a little setback, that he'd been taking the one medication called Vicodin, and since it seemed to be alleviating his pain, would he mind giving him another refill. And here they are. I take one. I'm afraid if I take two I'll run out while I'm here and then I'll be up shit's creek.

The first message is a hang-up. And then I hear the sexy voice of the infamous landscaper who disappeared off the face of the earth. This better be good. "Hello, Paris. This is Randall Jamison calling. I know you're probably angry as I don't know what at me and you have every right to be. But, please, hear me out. First, I want to apologize and let you know that this is *not* how I normally do business. I mean, because you entrusted me with such a large project, I think I owe it to you to be honest and just tell you what's been going on in my life. I've been going through a nasty divorce and custody battle with my wife, who happens to have a huge substance-abuse problem. And to top it off, I just found out that she's been robbing the business blind behind my back. I've been so stressed out that it's taken all my time and energy to get everything straightened out and under control again."

Beep.

"It's Randall again. Your machine cut me off. Anyway, Paris, I truly apologize for any inconvenience I've caused you, and I will make it up to you. I promise to finish your yard in the next two months, and I'm willing to do the koi pond at cost. So, if you haven't fired me already, I'll actually be refunding some of your money, and real soon. I have a daughter. She's ten, and I hope I end up being her new mother and father, if the courts recognize the situation she's in. Anyway, I've rattled on and on, and it's only because I don't want you to kick me to the curb on a professional level. I can't wait for you to see how beautiful your yard's going to be. I won't disappoint you, I promise. So—I hope to hear from you real soon. But, please, don't be another person calling to cuss me out. Could you just pretend to be my friend and leave me a nice message? Take care, Paris. Bye."

Holy shit. I press the three button and listen to the entire message again. Wow. A divorce? Whew. And his wife's a substance abuser? Damn. I sit down on the couch and then jump up and open the drapes and look out at Hyde Park. It's raining again. But I don't care. We must've spent at least ten or twelve hours going to different nurseries looking for plants and trees, and I admit that I looked forward to each time. We talked about everything from why we do what we do to what we love about living in the Bay Area. We even debated about why it's not too late for either of us to have another child. He was rather convincing. In a warm, sincere way. I wonder what kind of substance she's been abusing? Or was it more than one? Oh, what difference does it make? And just how long have I been taking Vicodin? Shit. Almost a year.

Something told me Randall wasn't a flake. Maybe I could stand to trust my instincts more. Even still, I decide to call him when I get back to California, which is only two days from now. It's going to take all the strength I have to wait. I get under the covers, afraid to close my eyes because, if I do, Randall's going to be under this floral comforter waiting for me, and right now I'm not in the mood for pretending. Not when there may be a possibility that I—the Petrified Woman—might actually have a real opportunity to perhaps do more than smell a man up close.

I wake up starving. I look over at the clock and can't believe it's quarter to ten. For some stupid reason, before brushing my teeth and washing my face like a normal person, I find myself opening the Harrods hatbox. Mama's going to die when she sees this one! I put it on and look at myself in the mirror. This is a tough hat, anyway you look at it: it's black velvet and looks like a tamer version of a Dr. Seuss hat. It's not working for me. Not with this tired hairstyle. This wet and wavy look has played out, and I'm due for a new one so bad I can smell it.

I open a shoe box and try on a pair of hot-pink, mint-green, and lavender sandals. Mama and Charlotte both would have a stroke if they saw these babies! All three of us have shoe fetishes and even wear the same size. How'd that happen, I wonder?

I'm still starving. That much I do know. I'm just about to dial Room Service when the phone rings, scaring the hell out of me. Who in the world would be calling me here? It can only be one of three people, and it's 3 A.M. back there. "Hello," I say, cautiously, hoping it's a wrong number or someone with a British accent.

"Is that you, Paris?"

Whoever it is, is not British. "Yes, who's this?" I ask. It sounds like I've heard this voice before, but I can't quite place it right now.

"It's your mom's friend Loretta, dear."

My heart drops.

"Miss Loretta? What's wrong, did something happen to Mama? Please don't tell me something's happened to her?"

"She's at the hospital, dear. She's all right. I was here with

Shanice when the paramedics took her about a half-hour ago, but we couldn't find a number anywhere for Cecil, and then Shanice told me where your number was, and the next thing I know I hear her starting up Viola's car, and when I look out the window she's following behind the ambulance. I didn't know what to do, so I called you first, and I'm going to go on down to the hospital to get her and then call her mother."

I think I'm hearing things, but I know I'm listening to Miss Loretta's voice right here at the Dorchester Hotel in London, England, where it is raining outside. Just to be on the safe side, I ask: "What did you just say?"

"It's all right, dear. I'm sorry to call you at this hour. What time is it there?"

"I don't know. What hospital is Mama in, Miss Loretta?"

"Sunrise," she says, and then gives me the number.

"I'll call you back. Thanks, Miss Loretta."

I don't wait for her to say goodbye, because my heart is beating so fast I can hear it. I dial the hospital but it doesn't go through. I try again. No good. Why is it taking so fucking long to get an outside line? I finally get one and as soon as someone answers, I just say: "Emergency Room, please."

They transfer me, and then a nurse comes on. "I'm calling about my mother, Viola Price. Is she all right?"

"Hold on a minute, ma'am, and I'll put the doctor on."

I bite my bottom lip while I wait for what seems like an eternity, and then I hear a man's voice. "This is Dr. Glover."

"Yes, this is Paris Price. I'm Viola Price's daughter. Is my mama there?"

"Yes she is."

"Is she going to be okay?"

"Yes, your mother's going to be okay. But, unfortunately, she's not going to be okay in this world."

"What do you mean by that?"

"Well, she's passed on."

What did he just say? I know he didn't just say what I

thought he said. Did he just say "she's passed on"? Did he? No. Yes, he did. He just said that my *mama* has passed on. Passed on to where? To what? Why? Wait a fucking minute, here. I take a deep breath, but it feels like helium has somehow gotten into my head and it's spinning a million miles a second, so I blow air balls out in spurts and try to control myself, because I know I'm hearing things, I know that this man pretending to be a doctor on the phone did not say what I thought he just said. "What did you just say?"

"I'm sorry, Miss Price. But in my fourteen years as a doctor, I've never had to do this over the phone. I'm so very sorry."

"So you're telling me that my mama has died?"

"Yes, she has."

I sit here for what feels like forever, and then what the doctor has said registers in my brain, but then I want to know something else. "Did she suffer long?"

"No, she didn't. It happened very quickly. I can assure you of that."

How long is very quickly? And how does he know she didn't suffer? My stomach starts heaving in and out and won't stop. It feels the same way it did when I was sixteen and I'd pitched a fast ball to Esther Washington and she hit it anyway, a line drive right to my navel at about forty miles an hour, and knocked the wind out of me. Just like now. I press both hands against my belly to stop it from jerking, but it doesn't help, because now I'm crying so hard I can hardly breathe. What happened to the air in here? And my shoulders hurt. Now they're burning. And my chest feels like somebody just stuck me with an ice pick. Stop this! She can't be dead. My mama's not dead. She can't be. I just bought her a new hat and a new pair of shoes and she has to wear them. She has to. She asked for the hat, but the shoes are a surprise. I want to surprise her. I love surprising her. My mama cannot possibly be dead. She's only fifty-five fucking years old! She has asthma. She's had lots of asthma attacks and survived them all. Other people's mothers die when they're old. My mother is not old, so this has got to be some kind of mistake.

I think I may have let out a long howl, I don't know. I do know that now my stomach is shivering and my hands have no feeling whatsoever, which is why I suppose the phone falls to the floor and stays there until I'm able to stop screaming and crying. When I do, I look around this room. What an ugly room it is. Too many flowers. Everything's so fucking bright. And why did I spend so much money on all this bullshit I don't need? That nobody needs. I mean, who really gives a shit what color my sandals are or how many hats I wear? Who gives a fuck if I wear a Vivienne Westwood scarf or a dress from Voyage or a slick silver coat from Harvey Nichols, or that I bought black caviar and quail from Harrods? Who really gives a flying fuck?

I look down at the phone and pick it up in what feels like slow motion. I'm surprised the doctor's still on the line. I grab my prescription bottle and pop two pills and swallow them dry before I press the phone against my ear. I can't tell if it's cool or warm.

"Your mother's friend Loretta Susskind is on her way here to pick up your niece to take her home with her. I understand you have other siblings?"

"Siblings?" I reach for the glass of water I had last night and swallow some. It's warm. This much I do know.

"Yes. I'm positive Mrs. Susskind's calling the little girl's mother, but will you be able to call the others?"

"Me? Did I tell you I'm in London?"

"No. My gosh. Look, I can call them if you're not up to it."

Before I can even think about how I'm going to do it, I simply say, "I'll call them."

"Okay, then. And, Miss Price, you might want to start making arrangements."

"Arrangements? Arrangements for what?"

"Funeral services. If that was your mother's wish."

Arrangements? Funeral services? Wish? Funeral services for who? Who died? I mean, nobody's dead here. Is this the Make a Wish Foundation call? Is that what this is about? Because, if not, this has got to be some kind of huge, I mean humongous mistake. I know it is, because somebody has just called here and played a dirty rotten trick on me and told me that my mama has died.

The next thing I know, I hear myself say, "Goodbye," and I hang up. Did I say thank you? I don't know. And what exactly would I thank him for? I bite my tongue to see if I can feel it, and it hurts. I look down at the phone again. Didn't I just have it up to my ear? And didn't Miss Loretta call and tell me to call the hospital? Did I actually do that? Did I really talk to a Dr. Glover and he said that my mother has passed on? That my mother is dead?

I think he did. Didn't he? I sit on the edge of the bed and lick my lips until the salty taste of blood and tears is gone. I look over at the clock. It's ten after eleven. I look down at my feet. Why am I wearing my mama's shoes? I take them off and begin to put them back in the box. She's going to love these babies. I just know it. I know what she likes. I know her taste in things. But as soon as I lift the lid to the box, I look at my hands and realize that I'm still holding the phone. I blink five or six times to make sure I'm still in this hotel room, and then I pinch my arm to make sure I'm still alive. I am. And I'm surprised.

I take the phone with me over to the window and look out at that park. The grass is glistening green. The leaves on the trees are, too. I'm so cold I'm trembling. But all I can do is stand here and watch drops of clear water roll down this window until I'm blind. Until I'm frozen. When I do move, I collapse against the wall, grab the drape, and wrap it around me until I begin to feel warm. I hold it like this until it feels like I'm in my mama's arms again. I squeeze so hard that, when the drape comes off the rod and drops to the floor, I do, too. Once I get here, I look around this room again. I stare until all the flowers on these walls, these chairs, and the sofa begin to wilt and die and I cry dry tears because I feel vacant inside, like a thief has stolen something from me that no one can ever replace, like the best part of me has just evaporated.

Sorry

"**Ma, what's all** this stuff about?" Tiffany's sitting at the kitchen table, where I got all the information I sent away for from the International Correspondence Schools spread out.

"It's career information."

"What kinda career? Look like a whole lotta different ones here. They look like stamps!" And she starts laughing. But ain't nothing funny about it to me.

"Just don't mess it up. Where's Trevor? I wanna know where he put my lottery ticket. The drawing'll be on in fifteen minutes."

"Which one of these do you like, Ma? You gotta have some idea."

"I'm thinking about catering or learning how to be a gourmet chef. I don't know."

"You mean like what Auntie Paris do in California?"

"No! I would do my business different. I definitely wouldn't do it like her. Monique! Please close that door while you practicing that flute tonight, 'cause I got a headache and can't even hear myself think."

"Why not? She make a lotta money."

I hear the upstairs door slam. "Because I got ideas of my own."

"Like what?"

"Why don't you stop bugging me, Tiffany?"

"Ma, I just asked you a simple question. Dag."

She's right. But, hell, I ain't got no answers right now. Kids is so nosy. Ask too many questions at the wrong time. But. What I ain't told none of 'em is, I bought a book on mail-order businesses and read it cover to cover and I'm having a consultation with this lady tomorrow who'll listen to my ideas and sign a piece of paper to make sure she don't steal none of 'em and she'll tell me if she think any of 'em can work. But one of my ideas is in her book, so how could I go wrong? "Okay, let me ask you a question, Miss Grown-Ass?"

"Ma, please don't call me that."

"Okay. You right. Sorry. What do you think you wanna be when you grow up?"

"I don't know."

"Think about it for one whole minute."

"Dag, Ma. How'm I supposed to know? I'm only thirteen."

"So what? You write that poetry all the time."

"Yeah, but it ain't that good."

"It is good."

"Yeah, but you can't get no job being no poet, Ma."

"Maya Angelou seem to be doing all right."

"That's true."

"Then look into it. Read some books about poetry or something. That's the only way you gon' find out."

"Okay, Ma!"

She still flipping through the career stamps, but now I can tell she ain't really looking at 'em. She got exactly ten seconds to get her behind over there in that kitchen. One. Two. Thr—

"Ma, we miss Daddy and want him to come home."

Shit. "I know y'all do, but sometimes married people have problems that kids don't understand."

"We do understand, and we think it's stupid that you put Daddy out and wanna divorce him for something he did centuries ago. It's kinda like crying over spilt milk."

"Who the hell is we?"

"Me, Trevor, and Monique."

"Is that so?"

"Yep. Ma, you don't know how many kids at school's parents is divorced. And I been so happy all these years that I could say my parents ain't even thinking about getting no divorce, and that I got a very cool dad. I mean, come on, Ma, Daddy does everything around here, and he takes us places, and not every father will wash and braid his daughters' hair."

"Girl, that was so long ago."

"Me and Monique ain't forgot it. And even Aunt Suzie Mae think you way off base."

"Is that so?" I say, even though what I really feel like saying is, "FUCK ALL Y'ALL," at the top of my lungs, but I know that would be wrong. I bought this book a couple of weeks ago about feeling good, and one part of it was about controlling your anger, and it said people need to learn how not to say the first thing that comes into their mind, 'cause sometimes it can be more hurtful than you think. This is some hard shit to do. The book even said you can control your thinking, which is news to me, but according to this stupid test I took, a lot of my thoughts is negative, which means sometimes I may not be seeing things the way they really are. I don't quite buy that. But some of it do make sense. And some of it don't. Do I always think I'm right? Yeah, 'cause most of the time I am. I don't say nothing if I can't back it up. I had to stop reading that book, 'cause it was getting on my nerves, just like Tiffany is now. But it did get me to thinking that maybe I might need more than a book. Maybe I might need a real person to talk to.

"Hi, Ma," Trevor says, coming into the family room and handing me my ticket. "Here you go. And as we always say: Lotto Love!"

"Would you get me a drink, please?"

"Certainly. What might I make for you this evening?"

"I don't care. Just as long as it bite."

"Okay, Ma, what was it you was saying about Daddy?"

"Nothing. Y'all just gon' have to wait and see what happen. Just like me."

"Wait and see?" Trevor says.

"That's what I said."

"Where's Daddy staying anyway?"

"With one of his buddies." I turn the TV to Channel 9. I been doing this every Monday, Wednesday, and Friday for I don't know how many years. One day I'ma win. I just know it. And when I do, me and Mama been had a deal going for so long that whoever hit first split it. I'd be so happy to have a little bit of money to share with her. It wouldn't even matter if we ain't speaking. A deal is a deal. Plus, it would be one thing I could give her on my own.

"Which buddy?" he asks.

"Why y'all so worried about your daddy? I'm the one that got the raw end of the deal here."

"No, you didn't," Trevor says. "From what I gather, you're charging him for a crime he committed a long time ago. Haven't you heard of the statute of limitations?"

"The what?"

"Even I know that," Tiffany says. "It means after so much time passes you can't be found guilty of the crime. And this was way over ten years ago, wasn't it?"

"Look, after me and your daddy talk next time, I'll let everybody know what the verdict is, but until then could we skip the subject, please?" My jawbone is jumping, I'm getting so mad. I hate being put on the spot like this. I don't know why they taking his side, especially when they don't know the whole story.

"Okay, then, Ma?" Tiffany says, finally running some dishwater. "How come you ain't said nothing about my report card?"

"Where is it?"

"Right next to you, by that *Ebony*."

I pick it up and lift up the top part. I can't believe my eyes. Is them B's I'm seeing? And an A? "Tiff! Baby! When did you get so smart? I mean, I'm so proud of you! How'd you do this?"

"I listened harder," she says, smiling. "My tutor said that whenever I didn't understand something, instead of pretending like I did, to raise my hand and ask the teacher to explain it till I did. And guess what, Ma?"

"What?"

"A whole lotta kids in my classes was glad I asked, 'cause they didn't get a lot of that stuff either."

I give my daughter the thumbs-up. "Right on, Tiffany. I told you not to be scared to speak up, didn't I? I'm going down to Kinko's first thing in the morning and make a copy of this and mail it to your granny." She nods her head up and down like she hearing music all of a sudden. I know she smart. She just been acting stupid. I hope this is the beginning of a trend. If it is, this make two down and one to go. Monique tries harder than anybody I know, and maybe one day it'll pay off for her, too, especially when she grow up and don't need no medicine to think. But, come to think of it, seem like her grades was better before they put her on this mess. She slowed down like them doctors said she would, but, shit, maybe too much. She don't like taking it, that's for damn sure. And maybe I might take her off this stuff and see how she do. White folks got us believing everything they tell us just because it might be true about them, but it ain't necessarily true about us.

"Okay, Ma, I thought you was fixing to ask me a question a while back."

"I already did. About college. And do me a favor? Work on your English, would you? You sound downright uncouth half the time. If you can write the shit right, try speaking it right."

"Okay. I thought we was, were, talking about food or something."

"Oh, yeah, what do I cook best?"

"Pies," Trevor says, handing me a glass of something light yellow. Probably Squirt and Tanqueray.

"Yeah, all your pies are the bomb, Ma, but you make good

cakes, too. And some of them cookies be jamming. Why, you think you might wanna cook this kinda stuff?"

"I don't know. Maybe. We'll see."

"But what would people eat to go with it?"

"You can specialize," I say.

"I know that," Trevor says. "That's what Felix and I plan to do."

"Felix is a fag," Monique says, standing in the doorway in her pajamas. She's laughing, and then Tiffany starts in, too.

"So what, so am I," Trevor says, and I almost choke on my drink.

"We been knew that," Tiffany says. "Everybody know it, so what's the big deal?"

I don't say a word. As a matter of fact, I pretend like I didn't even hear him say it. I just stare at the TV and drink my drink until it's gone.

"No comment from you, Ma?" he says, looking up at me.

I swallow hard. I'm trying to figure out the right thing to say, but I don't know what that is. My daughters don't seem to be having no problems with this news, which apparently ain't news to them. Shit, he's their only brother and he act like a damn girl.

"It's okay, Ma," he says.

"No, wait a minute. All I can say right now is this. First of all, I thought the correct word was 'homosexual.' "

He looks shocked. So do Tiffany and Monique. I almost feel a grin coming across my face, but I don't wanna push it.

"That's the technical term," he says.

"Well, whatever you think you are, or whatever you wanna be, is up to you. I can't stop you from doing or being whatever is in you, just as long as you ain't going through these antics to get attention."

"Why would I wanna do that?" he asks.

"I don't know. But pour me another drink, would you,

Trevor? Y'all getting on my nerves. And, Tiffany, there's a stain on the back of your shorts."

She twists her neck around and looks down at her behind, but she can't see it like that. "Never mind, Trevor. I'll get it myself." I take my empty glass over to our little bar. "Tiffany, let me ask you a question, since we all in a confessing mood. When was you gon' tell me you got your period?"

"Ma, you should get over here," Trevor's saying.

"Wait a minute! I asked you a question, missy."

"I did tell you, Ma."

"No, you didn't."

"Ma, I'm serious!" Trevor screams.

"Goddamn it, I said just a minute!"

"Yes, I did. Three months ago."

"Then how come I don't remember it?"

" 'Cause you had been drinking a little bit that night, I guess."

"Ma, you've got all five of the Little Lotto numbers!"

"I don't drink that . . . What did you say, boy?"

"You got all five of the numbers! I kid you not! You hit the jackpot! It's like two hundred fucking thousand dollars, Ma!"

"No shit," Tiffany says.

"Damn," Monique says. "It's about fucking time."

I thought I heard 'em all cuss. I know I just heard 'em all cuss, but I can't believe this shit either until I walk over and grab that ticket outta Trevor's hands and compare it to the numbers on the screen. He's abso-fucking-lutely right! While everybody's jumping up and down I flop down on the couch. "Y'all, relax, and let's not get too excited till I find out how many people I might have to split it with."

"Oh, yeah. We forgot about that," Trevor says.

"Well, we'll just cross our fingers," Tiff says.

"Maybe we should pray harder tonight," Monique says.

"Now, that's a good idea," I say, and rest my head on the back of the couch and close my eyes. I wanna call Mama so bad, but I better wait till the morning. I don't wanna get her hopes up too high. Right now all I wanna do is thank God for answering my prayers. I promise to be a better person, a better mother, a better wife, a better sister—a better everything. 'Cause this is a sign. I guess the kids musta heard me say, "Thank you, God, for blessing me and everybody in this house," because, the next thing I know, I hear Trevor say, "Oh Lord, Mama's getting religion on us."

I'm the first one up. After the kids leave for school, I do everything I can possibly think of around here to make that clock move a little faster. Just get to nine o'clock, please. When it finally gets here, and I call, it turns out that only two of us picked these numbers. But what the hell: I'm still $104,000 richer! All I gotta do now is be patient, because it takes four weeks to get the money. I can wait.

I dial Mama's number, but she ain't home. I get her answering machine. "Mama! Mama! Hi! This is Charlotte! I know you still mad at me and everything, but forget about that. Guess what? I got a present for you! Fifty thousand dollars! You heard me! Guess who hit Little Lotto for a hundred thousand bucks? Me! Yeah, me! Call me as soon as you get this message, and don't worry, I won't hang up in your face. I promise. They got any room left on that cruise you going on? I ain't never been nowhere. I might wanna go. And when you moving? I wanna buy you something for your new condo. I do. I love you, Mama, and I'm sorry for being so nasty and hanging up in your face all them times. I swear I am. I'm sorry. Truly sorry. I love you again. I been waiting a long time to do something nice for you, and I'll finally get a chance to do it. So call me as soon as you get this message! Byeeeeee. Oh, I'm quitting the post office and selling the Laundromats, and I'm probably gon' start my own mail-order business where I sell nothing but desserts. I'll tell you all about it when I talk to you, but, no, I won't, 'cause . . ."

Beep.

The machine cut me off. I'm tempted to call back, but I'm too excited. I ain't got no choice but to call in sick, and when I do I plug my nose and cough a little bit to make it sound good, and then I spend the rest of the day daydreaming and doing nothing. I could get used to this.

———————

For some reason, when the alarm go off like it do every morning at four-thirty, I can't hardly move. I went to bed too early, is what probably made me tired. My body ain't used to relaxing. That's it. Get up, Charlotte. Get your rich ass up! Which I do. I can't wait to get to work to tell Belinda. She about the only one there I can tell. But I ain't quitting today, that's for damn sure.

I press the alarm off and get in the shower, but as soon as I do I swear I hear the phone ringing. Now, who in the hell would be calling me this time of morning? I know it ain't Al, 'cause he ain't had too much to say to me since I put him out. But you never know. I grab a towel and wrap it around me. This better be important, that's all I gotta say. I hurry up and pick up the portable right next to the bed. "Hello," I say, and my voice cracks, 'cause I ain't talked since last night.

"Charlotte?" somebody's asking whose voice sound worse than mine.

"Who is this?"

"It's Paris."

"Paris? What you doing calling me so early in the morning? And what's wrong, you sick or something?"

"No, I'm not sick. I'm in London."

"What you doing over there? And what's the time difference?"

"It's not important right now, Charlotte."

"What you mean? What's going on, Paris? Talk to me."

"Something's happened to Mama."

"What you mean 'something'?"

"The worse thing that could possibly happen to her," she

says. I hope that ain't crying I hear, and I hope she ain't saying what I think she saying.

"Wait a minute, Paris," I say real slow. I wanna make sure I'm getting this right. I wanna make sure I'm hearing what's coming outta her mouth through this phone, in my ear. "Okay. Now, what has happened to our mama?"

And then all I hear is her crying and making sounds like she trying to talk but she can't, and then I know. I start crying, too, and don't stop till the kids come in the room and hold me and rock me and put me under the covers, where I stay for the next two days, until Al comes over and helps me get up, and Aunt Suzie Mae comes over and tells me that she ain't going to Mama's funeral 'cause she don't care what nobody say: her sister ain't dead. I wanna tell her she crazy as hell and to get her crazy ass out my house, but Al do it for me.

My mama is dead. And I won't ever be able to talk to her again. I won't ever get to make her proud. I won't ever get a chance to tell her how sorry I am for all the times I said things I had no business saying to her. But I'm sorry, Mama. I'm sorry for cussing at you and raising my voice. Sorry I accused you of playing favorites when I know you didn't do it on purpose. I'm sorry for competing with the other kids for all your attention. Sorry for hating Paris all these years when she ain't done nothing to me but try to be my big sister. And I'm real sorry for not going to college like you wanted me to. For not listening when you told me not to be in such a hurry to grow up. Look at what's happened 'cause I didn't listen to you. Eighteen years at the post office and a husband who cheats. I love my kids, but this ain't what you dreamed for me, is it, Mama? It ain't what I dreamed for me either. I know that now. I'm so sorry. But what I'm even more sorry about is that I won't get another chance to tell you just how sorry I am. I hope you listening. I pray you can hear me. Can you? Can you hear me, Mama?

Dreaming in
Black and White

"¡Espera momento!"

All I do is grit my teeth.

"Okay. *Aqui estoy. Hola.*"

"Collect, from Lewis," I say.

"*Sí.* I mean, yes. I will."

"Hi, Luisa. This is Lewis."

"I know that, Lewis. You must be in jail, too, hey?"

"Too? Who else you know is in here?"

"Just my little brother, my cousin, and two of my uncles. That's only the boys. W'az up with you, Papì?"

I turn toward this cold brick wall so none of these dudes waiting behind me can hear what I say. "Look, Luisa. I only have about ten minutes, okay, and I need you to do a few things for me if you can. I know I haven't called you in a while, but I've been in Vegas since my mama got sick, remember?"

"Yes, I remember. Is she better?"

"Much better. Thanks for asking."

"*Es* good. *Su mama es* a *muy importante* part of you. Glad to hear she's doing well. Maybe I'll meet her one day, Papì, hey?"

"We'll see. Say, you got the forty dollars I mailed you in that Easter card, didn't you?"

"*Sí.* I couldn't believe you didn't forget. So why are you in there, Papì?"

"It ain't important. It was just a misdemeanor."

"Honestly?"

"I don't have to lie about it."

"True. So you already went to trial and everything?"

"Yeah."

"You should've called. I would've come. I love going to trials."

"You and every old lady in the Valley with silver hair who ain't got nothing better to do than sit in on hearings of people they don't know."

"I know. But you learn so much, Papì."

"Like what?"

"You see what's important to people. What they steal. Who they rob. Who they kill. You see that they don't value human life except when their own is on the line. Then it's get out the violins, hey, Papì?"

"Everybody in jail ain't necessarily a criminal."

"You're right. But when you do something wrong and you get caught, you should be punished. God is fair."

"Yeah, well, that's a matter of opinion."

"You're not saying nothing against God, are you, Lewis?"

"No—hell, no. I believe in God as much as you. All I'm saying is that it just makes you feel like a spectacle, or free entertainment, with strangers sitting in the courtroom learning stuff about you they don't need to know. But, anyway, that's not why I . . ."

"How long you in there for?"

"They only gave me ninety days, but I thought I might be in here for a year, so I got lucky. I gotta go to anger management once a week for three months, and AA once a week for six months. But with work-time/good-time, I could be out in a few weeks."

"I know from work-time/good-time so much I'm sick of work-time/good-time. So why you took so long to call me?"

"I haven't exactly been in the mood for chitchatting, Luisa.

I ain't even talked to my sisters. Look, my time is almost up. Hold on a minute."

I turn to the dude behind me and say, "One Top Ramen for five more minutes?"

He nods his head. "Shrimp, chicken, or beef?"

"What kind you like?"

"Shrimp," he says.

"Then I've got shrimp."

He goes over and sits down and starts watching TV.

"Luisa?"

"I'm still here."

"Can you go over to my apartment and check on my car to make sure it's all right?"

"*Sì.* You mean, see if it's still there?"

"Yeah. Do you remember meeting Woolery, the guy I work for sometime?"

"The one with that nose?"

"Yeah, him. You remember where the place was?"

"*Sì.*"

"Well, he owes me some money. And I need you to go get it and pay my rent so I don't get evicted. Right outside my doorstep, on the left-hand side, is a piece of crumpled-up rawhide under a bush that looks like trash but my key is inside it. Use it, and check to see if everything in my apartment is okay. I've got some important documents in there I don't want nobody to steal."

"Like what, Papì?"

"Formulas and ideas."

She starts laughing. "You're not just a criminal but a scientist, too?"

"Fuck you, Luisa."

"Can't you take a joke, Lewis?"

"Yeah, but I ain't in no joking mood. Anyway, can you do this for me or not, Luisa?"

"*Sì*, Papì. But not today. Tomorrow. I gotta take my kids to the doctor today."

"Thanks, okay? I mean it. And I'll take care of you when I get out, don't worry. I really appreciate this."

"You're a good guy, Lewis. But stay out of jail. I'm getting tired of these collect calls. Can you call back tomorrow night after *Jeopardy!*?"

"What time does *Jeopardy!* come on, Luisa?"

"Do you have cable in there?"

"I'll call somewhere around eight, all right?"

"*Muy bien.* And I'll give you the scoop. Like that? The scoop?"

"I gotta go, Luisa. Thanks. And say hi to your son for me."

"Remember there's three!" I hear her say, but I'm already hanging up, even though I pick the handset right back up and wave it to the dude who's been waiting for me. When he gets up, I go get his Top Ramen from the vending machine and give it to him. I go sit back down and pick up a *GQ* magazine, then toss it back on a pile and pick up *Life*. I flip to a picture of some gold hills that look just like a desert, and then to a whole page of fog, and then comes an emerald-blue sea with a boat sitting out in the middle of it, just sitting there, doing nothing but floating. I betcha that would be nice. To be out in the middle of some water in a boat, rocking back and forth to the rhythm of nothing but waves. I bet I could sleep like a baby and dream in color instead of black and white, like I've been doing in here.

I look around our unit at all these black and brown men. Only about thirty of the 170 dudes are white. But all of us are in here for doing stupid shit like stealing and driving drunk and getting caught with a little dope but not enough to be considered a felony. And then there's people like me that they don't consider violent enough to put in a maximum-security pod with murderers and people who shot somebody and shit, but we're still guilty of domestic violence, so they put us here in minimum security. One deputy even calls some of these dudes "felony stupid"—things they shoulda taken care of or they wouldn't be here: driving without a license, warrants for unpaid parking and speeding tickets, and failure to appear in court. I just keep my mouth shut, 'cause all my numbers ain't up yet.

Everybody's watching the NBA playoffs. I don't even know who's in it. And don't care. I'm trying to strengthen my mind while I'm here and figure out what to do when I get out. I can't keep doing what I've been doing, that much I do know, 'cause I ain't getting nowhere fast. Except here: and this ain't exactly a hotel. It could be worse, that much I can say. A lot of people would be shocked if they were to come in here, if they've never been inside a jail. Everybody thinks it's these little cells with bars on 'em. But not here. Not in this day and age. We're in dorms. And instead of bars, it's Plexiglas that faces out here where I'm sitting. We've got two TVs and they're mounted up on the wall in metal boxes. But, hell, everything in here is metal and mounted to something: our bunk beds are molded into the wall; the sinks and toilets are stainless steel; the tables and stools we eat at are metal and drilled into the floor. At least the walls are off-white, so it ain't as depressing as it could be. Volunteers come in here twice a week with a cart full of books, and then a few of these dudes that're in here for a year or more get magazine subscriptions to *Playboy* and *Penthouse*, but they won't let *Hustler* in here, 'cause they say it's too freaky, but, for a pack of cigarettes and a Top Ramen, sometimes a dude might let you "rent" a few pages of something for a half-hour.

It ain't home and I'm not trying to make no new friends in here, but I'm friendly. I've just been making a list of all the things I'm going to try to do, once I'm free. I hope nobody don't find it and take it.

"Here you go, Lewis. You said you wanted to read some of these when I finished, right, man?"

This dude named Hector, who happens to be black and Puerto Rican but looks plain black to me, is handing me two entrepreneur magazines that tell you how to develop a business plan and what to do with your ideas. He's in here for two thousand dollars' worth of parking tickets. "Thanks, Hector. I'll give 'em back in a couple of days."

"Keep 'em, man," he says. "Once you know it, you know it."

The nurse yells out that it's time for medication and everybody who's got a prescription or takes any other kinda pills goes over and she gives 'em to us. I get my three Tylenol, drop my magazines off in my dorm, and take a quick shower. When I get back, I read one of the magazines cover to cover till the TVs and radios shut off and the lights go black. I weave my fingers together like I'm about to pray, and I'm thinking about what I would pray for if I was about to pray, but then I just close my eyes and lay here and pretend like I'm twelve years old and this is sleepaway camp and I pray I don't get eaten up by mosquitoes when we go fishing in the morning. Or maybe I'll try canoeing out in the middle of that lake.

"Price, wake up. Wake up."

When I turn around I see the deputy standing in front of my bunk. "Yeah?" I say.

"You need to get up."

"Why? What's going on? What time is it?" I ask.

"It's about four-thirty. You have a sister named Paris, is that correct?"

"Yeah," I say.

"Well, she called from London and said there's a family emergency, and we're not sure what that emergency is, but she's going to be calling you back in exactly thirteen minutes from now. You need to get dressed so I can take you out to one of the interview rooms, where the switchboard will ring the phone when she calls. You can just pick it up and talk to her from in there. Is that all right?"

"Yeah, I guess. She didn't say what kind of emergency it was?"

"No, she didn't. She'll tell you herself. Now, maybe you wanna hurry up and get dressed."

"All right." I slip on a pair of sweats and a T-shirt and follow him out through the pod down a hallway to the visitors' center, where they put me in Interview Room B.

I'm just sitting here, not knowing what the hell is going on, and I'm scared to even think what it could be, so I just try to make my mind go absolutely blank and keep it like that. I even close my eyes, so I don't see nothing but gray space and I don't care if the deputy sees me doing this or not. When that phone rings, I don't jump. I answer it on the second ring. "Hello."

"Lewis?"

"Yeah, Paris. What's going on? What kind of emergency is it?"

She's crying. Goddamn it, she's crying. This can only mean one thing. It's Mama. It's our mama. Something's happened to our mama. Tears are starting to form, and that gray is turning red. I open my eyes. "Is Mama dead, Paris?"

And she says, "Yes, Lewis. She had an asthma attack a couple of hours ago and I'm here in London and Miss Loretta just called and told me that Mama was on her way to the hospital but, Lewis, she didn't make it. Mama didn't make it!"

I wish they would open this door. This Plexiglas is getting all fogged up and it's feeling like a furnace in here. Can't they crack a window or something? I forgot, ain't no windows in here. The phone is burning my ear and I wanna drop it on the table and run back to my dorm, but I hear my sister's voice again.

"Lewis? You still there?" I wish she wouldnt'a called me. Not in here. Not like this. I wanna call Mama and tell her that there's some things I still needed to do before she died, so could she wait at least another year so I can prove to her that I'm not going to spend the rest of my life as a drunk? Can't she postpone dying a little longer so I can show her how smart I really am? 'Cause I'm ready to prove it. I feel strong enough now. Is there any possible way she could wait and do this another time? Because this is not a good time for her to die. I mean, fuck, I'm in jail! How the hell am I supposed to get outta here to help her? And where's my wife when I need her? Where the hell is she? Married to somebody else. Remember? That's right. I'm divorced. But I need a wife. And I wish I had one right now.

"Lewis!" Paris screams.

And then I realize I'm not the only one who just lost Mama. All of us have. All four of us.

"Yeah, I'm here, Paris."

"Lewis, I don't know what . . ."

"Are you okay, Paris? You're all the way over there by yourself?"

"Yeah. But I'm leaving in a couple of hours. Don't ask me how."

"What are we supposed to do without her?" I hear myself ask.

"I don't know," she says. "I don't know."

And then we just sit there for I don't know how long and don't say anything until, finally, the deputy comes over and knocks on the Plexiglas and asks if there's anything he can do and I just tell him no, but thanks, and he asks me if I want him to get the chaplain and I say no, but thanks, and then Paris asks me can I get outta here in time to go to Mama's funeral and I just tell her I don't know, 'cause I've never been in jail when my mama died before, and it's something I have to look into.

Two of Wands, or Hanged Man, Reversed

Apparently, everybody in my family has just been waiting to see what I was going to do about George. Mama's certainly relieved, and the one thing I'm grateful for is that she didn't throw it back in my face when I told her I'd had him arrested. She just said she was glad I finally stood up for my daughter. I've already been interrogated. The police came to our home. They wanted to know why hadn't I reported it before now. I told them that I hadn't known it was going on until recently, and my daughter didn't want me to do this, but I had also recently discovered that my husband had abused his own daughters. And, much to my chagrin, I had to describe to them in great detail how I found out. I even had to show them Shanice's room. But, just like they said he would, George has already posted bail. They need concrete evidence in order to hold him, and unless Shanice agrees to be examined or is willing to be interviewed on videotape once she's home, George could be walking around loose on the streets for the rest of his life, free to do this to more little girls. They assured me that Shanice wouldn't have to go into a courtroom if she consented. As things now stand, all we have is a court order that prevents him from calling our house and he can't come within a hundred feet of me or Shanice when she does get home.

I don't know what else to do to convince her to undergo the examination or to get her to agree to testify against him. I explained all of this to her and Mama. I told them that a person called a child advocate—which means they're on Shanice's side—would ask her questions that would indict George. I told her that the whole interview might only take an hour. That it would be videotaped and used in court. Without doing both, they can't prosecute him. She still won't do it.

I don't know whether I'm coming or going. And my future is so up in the air at this point that I don't know what I'm doing from one day to the next. Not knowing is not a crime, and it's also one of the reasons why I came here to have my cards read. I've heard Zina is good. Very good. She's young. Can't be more than thirty-four or thirty-five. She's Indian. And pretty. There's a red dot between her eyes. I think this means she's married. She's dressed in a red-and-blue silk sari that looks like it wraps around her at least four or five times.

About fifteen or twenty candles are burning in this small white room, which has a window that looks out to a little court-yard. The smoke from the incense smells like jasmine. Zina has just unwrapped her cards from what looks like a Chinese silk pouch. It is purple and orange. The edges of the cards are quite bent, probably from so many readings. I'm sitting directly across a table from her. She shuffles for quite a few minutes.

"Take a few deep breaths and center yourself," she says. "Breathe and watch my hands while you think about the questions in your life, your hopes and dreams and aspirations and confusion, and try to focus, even as confusing and as difficult as it may be, and when you want me to stop shuffling the cards tell me to stop."

"Stop," I say.

She pushes them over for me to cut the deck, which I do. I've already told her why I'm here. I'm just waiting for her to lay down ten cards, which she is doing now. I watch closely. The first card is a Ten of Cups, reversed, which shows a happy couple with two children dancing under a rainbow. The second one is a Ten of Wands.

"All right, Janelle," Zina says, looking at the first two cards and then straight at me. "Clearly there's a lot of strife and difficulty here. You said you're already familiar with the cards, but if you don't mind, I'd like to tell you what they mean today, in this specific context, okay?"

"Okay." One thing I do know is that when a card is reversed it's somewhat messed up.

"The first card—the Ten of Cups, reversed here—indicates that something in your home life has gone very wrong, and there are some violent feelings here: anger and deceit. Would you say this is true?"

"Yes, I would."

"And card number two, the Ten of Wands, represents your obstacles. The figure on the card is carrying a heavy load: all the burdens of the situation, you might say. Conflicts and problems. What could this figure do?"

I know she's not waiting for my answer, so I just continue to sit still, and listen.

"Well, he could throw his burdens behind him and try a new direction. Or, on the other hand, if he does, if he throws the sticks down and tries to pass over them, he'll stumble over them all over again. We've got a negative situation in your past. Great strain from holding up all the things you have been trying to hold up. So—the question is: are you going to do things differently? As always with the Tarot, your own choice is bound up with what your destiny will become, so your choices are important."

I just nod as if I understand, and I think I might in fact be beginning to.

"I see some resistance, though. Look at the card below these two, which relates to the foundation or basis of the situation— the Two of Cups reversed. To me, this suggests a relationship that has gone bad, in which there never was equality, or a split between what you do and what you feel. Now, take a look at this card, which represents yourself as you see yourself: the

Five of Cups. There's a man in a cape, with his back turned. What do you think he's turned his back on?"

"I don't know."

"He's staring at what he's lost, not at what he still has."

"Well, I've lost my husband. I don't have a job. My daughter's been molested. And I don't know what's next for me."

"But what do you still have, Janelle? What two cups are you not looking at?"

"My daughter."

"But there are two cups there. What's in the other cup?"

"I don't know."

"Then that's the one thing you need to think about."

I think about it so much I hardly hear what she has to say for the next few cards. I'm waiting for her to get to that nine card. That's the one I want to hear, because it's the Hanged Man reversed, and this was the card I got the other time, and when I saw it I just had to get up and leave. When I see her finger touch it, I feel myself blink and my ears are at attention again.

". . . indicates being who you are even if everyone else thinks you have everything backwards. So is there some part of you, Janelle, that is not completely accepting of your reality right now? Are you just battling what you know is true?"

"I don't know."

"Well, the Hanged Man can lead you to the real source of your fear, and, whatever it is, deal with it and stop denying it."

All I can say is, "I'll try."

"Now, the tenth card is the Two of Wands reversed. This card speaks very strongly to someone who has lived in a very unsatisfying or unpleasant situation and decides to make a change. It's about leaving behind safe situations and entering into the unknown and the emotions and energy that are liberated when this happens, but the fact that the Hanged Man is reversed suggests that you're afraid to liberate that energy that's going to come about when you leave behind your old, unsafe safety net. It's going to mean being alone, like the Hermit—

which is your strongest card in this spread. You see, he's holding up the lamp, so he has something to light his way. We know that the Hermit is a wise man, so you are heading toward your own wisdom by leaving behind what was once secure but was really not secure at all."

And ain't that the truth, is all I'm thinking as I give her forty dollars even though her fee is thirty. In my heart, I think I already knew everything she just told me, but I needed to hear someone else say it.

"Thank you so much, Zina."

"My pleasure," she says. "And good luck."

I walk outside. I'd almost forgotten that I was on a quaint little street lined with all kinds of specialty stores, boutiques, and one-of-a-kind shops. I'm not even sure how I found this area, because it's not my usual place to shop. I pass a day spa, a small but packed exercise-equipment store, a pet-grooming place, a lingerie shop, a gorgeous leather-goods store, one of those new Starbucks coffeehouses, and then I come to a gourmet-sandwich-and-soup deli, but what really gets my attention is what's next to it. The store window alone looks like my own private fantasy. It's called Elegant Clutter and is full of colorful artifacts of all shapes and sizes, and I can't believe it when I walk in: there are candles and lamps and bookends and hand-blown goblets that swirl and twist and curve in purple and gold; and then I turn and see things bronze and brass, onyx and sandstone, oranges and purples; all kinds of hand-carved boxes and shelves of lotions and oils and aromatic mists and statues and stone fountains with real water trickling through them. And the walls. They're covered with a stunning selection of ethnically diverse paintings. This is great. I don't believe it when I see an entire glass case of black figurines like I have at home. And this place smells so good. I could stand in here forever.

"May I help you find something in particular?" a woman's voice asks.

I'm surprised to see a redheaded black woman about my age

standing behind me. She's just as beautiful as everything else. I want to ask her how long she's been working here, if she could use some help, and if so, how much they pay. But that would be tacky, and I don't have the nerve, so I just say, "I'm just looking. What a lovely shop. Everything in here is just perfect."

"Thank you," she says. "Let me know if I can help you find anything. We're technically closed, but I'll stay open as long as you like, and please don't feel obligated to buy anything. Take your time."

That was nice of her. I have my eye on something that has Mama's name all over it. It's a bunch of gold grapes sitting in a black lacquer dish. She loves this kind of stuff. I look at the price tag. I can actually afford it. I take it off the shelf, and as I pass another one, filled with lotions, a scent catches me. That's when the woman comes back over. "That's Fig Leaf. Isn't it wonderful?"

"It certainly is."

"It comes in a lotion, shower gel, and aromatic mist. There's also a candle."

I look at the price. Reasonable again. "I'll take the lotion, shower gel, and the candle."

"I'll wrap those right up for you. Are you new to the area?"

"No. I live about forty minutes from here."

"So do I."

"I live way out in Palmdale."

"So do I!"

"You can't be serious."

"I am."

"Where? What street or avenue?"

"Well, I live right up on the hill."

"Quartz Hill? It's nice up there. What street? I know a few people up there. Their kids go to school with my daughter."

"Well, right now I live in Goode Hill Estates."

"Oh, then you live in the upscale part of Quartz Hill for real. I know that's a gated community."

"I'm not exactly upscale by a long stretch, honey, and if I don't find a partner soon, I'll be moving into an apartment."

"A partner for what?"

"My shop."

"You mean this is *your* shop?"

"Yes. It surprises a lot of people. I don't even mention it to the white folks. Don't wanna scare them off!" She starts laughing, and I find myself joining her, even though my brain is clicking like ticker tape.

"Why do you need to find a partner?"

"Because I'm going through a divorce and I have to buy my husband out and I can't afford to run the shop alone. Know anybody?"

"I wish I could say me," I hear myself say. "But I'm probably going to be going through one, too, and right now I don't have anything to invest, but can we talk? I mean, can you give me a general idea how much it would take to become your partner? No, wait; don't tell me. I don't want to know right this minute. May I have your card? My name is Janelle Porter, I mean Janelle Price. I don't know if I'll get anything out of my divorce, but I'll get my name back at least."

"You always get something out of it, honey," she says. "But it's usually not enough to jump up and down about, believe me."

"And your name is?"

"Orange Blossom. And, yes, it's my real name. My mama was tripping, like so many others. But here's my card," she says as we take my things over to the counter and she wraps them in layers of orange-and-gold tissue paper and even puts some kind of little twigs with buds on the end inside the bag. I look at her card. Her last name is Snipes. Of course I wouldn't dare ask if she's any relation to Wesley. She doesn't look like she could be. Oh, who cares? She walks around the counter and gives me my bag. "You'll be hearing from me soon, Orange Blossom. Do you have a deadline or anything?"

"It's June now. I'll be okay until about October, November on the outside. By then I might have to start sending some of this stuff back."

I scrunch up my shoulders. "Okay. Give me a general idea of how much we're talking about? Just an approximate, vague idea?"

"Between sixty to seventy and you're in like Flynn."

My shoulders drop and I turn back to look at her. "Thousand?"

"Yes. It's a lot for most folks," she says.

"It is." However, I feel like saying that cliché, "I'll be back," but I don't. "Well, I hope we can talk more about this real soon."

"Whenever you're ready. In the meantime, do come back. Let's have lunch or dinner or something. Do you work out?"

"I do, although I haven't in weeks, but I'm dying to get back to the gym."

"Then let's do it. Regardless of what happens. Just so you know, my lawyer and accountant will be happy to show you our profit-and-loss statements for the last five years."

"You've been here for five years?"

"Been in business for five, but in this space three and a half years. We outgrew our other store. Business is good. I love what I do, which is another reason why I don't want to give it up. This store was my first baby."

"Did you ever have a second?"

"Nope. Probably too late for that now."

"You look like you're about my age."

"Which would be?"

"Thirty-five."

"Try forty-five."

"I want to go to your gym," I say, and we both laugh. I'm one step away from jumping up and down and kicking up my heels when I get outside. Just the thought of actually doing something like this is enough to get my adrenaline going. I do have about twenty to twenty-five thousand in stock, thanks to old Georgie Porgie, and depending on what kind of settlement I get, who knows? But I'm not going to take this too far. Not right now. Even still. I mean, what are the odds of me running into an opportunity like this? And why today of all days? I feel like running back down to Zina and giving her a big hug.

I don't feel like going home. It's only sixish, and I decide to do something I've never done before. Eat out alone. Which is exactly what I do. I go to an Italian restaurant and have lasagna and salad. Afterwards, I do one more thing I've never done before: go see a movie all by myself. In fact, I watch two. By the time I get home, I fall asleep so hard, I assume I'm dreaming when I hear the phone ring. But I'm not. The clock says three-forty-five. Something's wrong. I'm afraid to pick it up, but I know I should. "Hello," I say with so much fear and hesitation that it probably sounds more like a question.

"Ma, this is Shanice and they took Granny away in an ambulance to the hospital and I'm scared!"

"Shanice, slow down! Where are you?"

"At the hospital."

"How'd you get there?"

"I drove."

"Drove what?"

"Granny's car?"

"You did what?"

"They took her, and Miss Loretta was looking for Auntie Paris's number in London, and . . ."

"Where is Miss Loretta right now?"

"She's standing over there, outside that curtain where they have Granny. I'm scared, Mom. What if something happens to Granny? Can you please come now? Please?"

"Yes I will, baby. You just stay right there with Miss Loretta, you hear me? Can you ask her to come to the phone?"

"Miss Loretta, my mom wants to talk to you."

My heart is beating so hard I can't stand it. I'm already out of the bed. Standing up. Walking around. Wondering how fast can I get to Vegas at this time of night. There're no flights out of Burbank at this hour, and that's the closest . . .

"Hello, dear."

"Miss Loretta, how is Mama?"

"I don't know right now, sweetheart. I don't know."

"Okay, look, do me a favor. Get Shanice out of there, please. I don't want her there if anything happens, do you understand?"

"Yes, I do."

"Thank you. I'll be on the first plane out of here. Keep her with you, please, Miss Loretta."

"I will."

"Thank you. What hospital are you at?"

"Sunrise. And the doctor's name is Dr. Glover. Here's the number. . . ."

I write it down and get up and put my clothes on so fast that it seems as if the clock hasn't even moved. It'll take me fifty minutes to get to Burbank Airport, and what did I do with that piece of paper I just wrote the number down on? There it is. I run downstairs and push the garage-door opener and get in my car and start the engine. I decide to call the hospital now. I ask for Dr. Glover, and he comes on the line.

"Hello, Dr. Glover. My name is Janelle Price and I'm Viola Price's daughter and I'm on my way to Burbank Airport because I'm trying to get there as soon as I can, and I wonder if you can tell me how my mother's doing? I mean, I know she's in ICU, but can you tell how long she might have to be in there this time?"

There's total silence on the other end, so I back the car all the way out of the garage, thinking that maybe I've been disconnected or I'm just not getting a good signal, but then I hear a man's voice say, "I'm sorry, but your mother didn't survive."

"What? Wait a minute. Let me back up a little more." And I

do. I back this car all the way out into the fucking street. "Now, could you repeat that, and please speak a little louder?"

"I said your mother didn't survive. She's passed on."

I heard him the first time. But. I was hoping that in between that sentence and the next, maybe she might've been strong enough to fool them by taking one more breath. Mama's good at that. Not giving up. I wonder if they checked her carefully, because she could be napping. These asthma attacks wear her out. She's told me that a million times. She could just be asleep. Somebody should check. I open my mouth to tell the doctor this, but no sound comes out. Absolutely nothing. And then I pound the steering wheel with my fists until I have no energy left. The phone falls to the floor of the passenger's side and my head drops against the steering wheel. But I have to wait. Right here. In this driveway. In this car. Until I can move. Until I can figure out how to get through this thick loud silence.

One Entrance to Another

"It's moving right now, Cecil. Put your hands here and feel," Brenda say.

She's next to me, laying on her back. At first, I'm scared—I ain't felt no baby move inside nobody's stomach in thirty-five years—but the next thang I know she taking my hand and putting it against her warm smooth skin and my fingers is spread out wide as they can go and she slides it around and then I feel a little hump and it gets higher and then moves right under my hand and I jump. "Hey!"

Brenda laughs. "Wait, I think he's over here now."

"He?"

"He or she. It can't be but one or the other, Cecil."

And, sure enough, here he come again! This feels weird. I can't even imagine what it must be like for Brenda, being that it's swimming around inside her and all. "Seem like it would kinda hurt," I say.

"It feels good, to be honest with you. But it sure don't hurt. Sometimes it tickles. Praise God."

I slide my hand around her big belly some more and wait and wait and don't nothing happen for the next five or ten minutes.

"She sleep. Show's over," Brenda say, but don't move my hand. "I'm sleep, too," she says, and I just lay right here listening to her breathe till it sound like a light whistle, and then I roll over and do the same until that alarm clock whistle a little louder and I know it's 3:30 A.M., time to get up and go to work.

I don't know why I took this job. Sometime I stand here for hours and just walk back and forth from one entrance to another, watching for anythang that don't look right. I help people out when they can't find the bathroom or they drunk and can't remember where they parked they car or can't remember what casino they in. That kinda stuff. Don't nothing exciting ever happen in here. That's why I ain't got no gun, just this uniform. But anybody looking at me should know I couldn't catch 'em if I had to. I mean, I'm still walking every day and starting to enjoy lifting a few of them barbells, but I couldn't do no sprinting if you paid me. I'm only bench-pressing a hundred pounds. I seen girls in there lift more than that. The way I figure it, something is better than nothing.

Is that my name I hear over the paging system? Naw. Who in the world would be paging me? I start staring at the roulette wheel for the hundredth time and try to guess a number which don't come up. In all the months I been working here, I only got one number right. It's hard to win when you gamble. I done finally figured that out. I done lost too much of they money and mine, and it ain't even fun no more. Matter of fact, I'm seriously thanking about trying to reopen one of the Shacks, depending on how much we get for the house.

"Would Cecil Price please report to the security office? Cecil Price to the security office."

I heard it that time. That *was* my name. I ain't never heard it announced that loud before. It kinda make you feel important. Like everybody should stop doing what they doing and look around to see who Cecil Price is. I hope they ain't fixing to tell me that the IRS is taking my check. I hope that ain't what this is about.

I open the glass door and see Billy, the head guy, sitting behind a desk. "Somebody was paging me?"

"Yeah, Cecil, you got a call from a Loretta. She asked you to call her as soon as you came in. Here's her number."

"Did she say what it was about?"

"Nope. She just said it was important and to call as soon as you can. She didn't sound too happy, if that's any help to you."

It's Viola. I know it is. I can't thank of no other reason why that woman would be calling me at my job. When was the last time Loretta called me anywhere? I look down and he still holding that pink message slip. I thought I took it from him already. "Thanks, Billy."

"Hope everything's all right, Cecil."

"Me, too."

"You can use that phone over there if you want to, or go on into that empty office, if you think you might need some privacy."

"I thank I will." I don't know why I don't turn the light on, and by the time I press the last digit of that telephone number, something tell me that Viola's gone. And if she is, it's my fault. I shouldn'ta sent them damn divorce papers over there the way I did. I shoulda known they would upset her, and when she get real upset she can work herself right into a attack. I pray to God that that ain't what's happened. Please let me be wrong.

"Hello," I hear Loretta's little voice say. She sound tired, and I can tell it ain't 'cause I woke her up.

"Loretta, this Cecil. Have something happened to Viola?"

When she don't say nothing, that's how I know. "Where is she?"

"At Sunrise. They said she didn't help them this time, Cecil."

"What you mean?"

"The paramedics said they'd been out here before and Vy always did what they asked her to, but this time, they said, she didn't help them. That she didn't fight that hard."

"She didn't fight that hard," I say, and right then is when I feel my whole body sink in this chair and drop over this desk.

I wanna sit up straight and talk to Loretta, I do, but I can't find the strength. I wonder if this is how Viola felt. Like she wanted to, but couldn't. This my wife she talking about. My wife of almost thirty-nine years. The woman who had my babies. The woman who raised 'em. The woman who tried to help me to be a better man but I was just too damn hardheaded and too lazy and, later on, just too proud to listen. Didn't wanna admit that she knew what was best for me, when I knew all along she did. This is the same woman who snatched my heart right out my chest and put it on top a hers and then pressed down hard. So hard it felt soft. I loved Viola more than she ever knew. But I never knew how to show a woman how much you loved her. Nobody ever showed me how to be tender. Nobody ever taught me how to relax, and then, just surrender. Is it too late to ask, "How you do that, Vy?" I wanted to take you to Paris, but back then we didn't have no France money, and later on, when we did get a few extra dollars, we had kids and then a house note and then the Shacks, and nobody had no time to do nothing but work. I'm so sorry, Vy. I didn't mean to mess up all your dreams. I swear, I didn't.

"Cecil?" Loretta say.

"I shouldn'ta never sent them papers over there yesterday. This is all my fault!"

"Hold it! It is not your fault. As a matter of fact, she signed them and they're in the mail. Cecil, can I tell you something, even though I know this isn't the best time?"

I wipe my nose and eyes on my sleeve. "Go 'head."

"Viola loved you. I don't have to tell you that. But she also told me that she was glad you left."

"What?"

"She said you needed to be with somebody who could still appreciate you, because she couldn't."

"But she used to, Loretta. She did."

"Cecil, when women get older, sometimes our minds and bodies and hearts go through all kinds of stressful and even

traumatic changes and we are not our old selves, and it hurts
when we don't know how to get our old selves back. We look
around and everything's changed. Our kids are grown and don't
need us anymore—at least they don't think they do. Our bodies
are old and look nothing like we think they should. And in
some ways all these things make you feel a sense of hopeless-
ness, a sense of loss on top of loss, and you don't even know
you're grieving, but we are indeed grieving. I've been doing it
for quite some time. And your wife: your outspoken, big-
mouthed, cuss-like-a-goddamn-sailor of a wife, Viola Price,
who was my best friend, helped bring me back to life after
Robert died. We were going on a cruise next week, and, Cecil,
I know you're hurting, but I'm going to miss her something
fierce, too."

I make myself sit up, 'cause I realize that I ain't the only one
who losing Viola. What about the kids? Lord, how they gon'
handle this?

"Cecil?"

"I'm still here, Loretta."

"I have something for you."

"What you mean?"

"Viola gave me something yesterday afternoon to give to
you."

"Wait a minute. When did this happen, Loretta?"

"About two hours ago."

Two hours ago I was rubbing Brenda's stomach.

"She told me to give you this envelope if anything ever happened to her."

"What?"

"I have it right here. She just asked me to tell you that she
would appreciate your waiting until the first Thanksgiving after
she's gone to open it."

"A envelope? Thanksgiving?"

"Uh-huh. Viola also hoped you would spend it with your bi-
ological children, just this once. If you can't, then she doesn't

want you to read this until you can. Shall I hold on to it, mail it, or what?"

"I don't know, Loretta. I can't thank right now. Let me thank. I wonder why Viola had to write something to me. . . . Do the kids know?"

"I'm sure they do by now. I'm sure they do."

"What about Shanice? Where she at?"

"She's right here with me, sleeping. Janelle's trying to get on the first flight out this morning. They're both taking it pretty hard."

"I know. I'll be over there in a little while, but I gotta be still for a minute or two."

"I understand, Cecil. I understand. Just let me know what I can do to help."

I sit here for a long time. Until some fella turn the lights on and ask if I wouldn't mind going into a different office to finish blowing off steam. He said women ain't worth half the tears they generate and for me not to worry, 'cause, after his wife called him on this very same phone to tell him she was leaving, it didn't take him no time to find a replacement.

Old Purses

I don't even remember the plane ride. I know it took almost twenty-four hours to get home. Dingus met me at San Francisco Airport and drove me home. I remember his face when I told him. I still hear Charlotte and Lewis's voices when I had to tell them over the telephone. And Daddy. He's suffering from guilt when he shouldn't be. All of this feels like it's been a bad dream, a very bad dream, and I don't think I truly woke up and accepted the reality until I walked in here—into Mama and Daddy's house—and she still wasn't here. She wasn't anywhere. And there was nowhere I could call to talk to her to get her to come home.

Dingus is a mess. Shanice is so broken up there doesn't seem to be anything anybody can say to console her. Janelle even slept in Mama's bed. I'm not that strong. I'm afraid if I smelled her sheets I'd lose it completely. I can't afford to be out of control right now, because I'm the one who's been asked to make the arrangements for her funeral, which is going to be in Chicago, where she was born. Where we were all born. Imagine that: a funeral. And Mama's going to be the star attraction. Everyone's going to come out to see her: Viola Price. I wish they didn't have to. I wish everyone could've come and seen her live and in color, right here in stupid Las Vegas. I wish those paramedics had worked harder, or not tried to be such fucking heroes and gotten her to the hospital sooner. I wish Mama had called them five minutes earlier. I wish she hadn't eaten that greasy spaghetti before she went to sleep. Wish she hadn't inhaled paint and carpet and gas fumes all in one day.

But she did. And no matter how much I—or any of us—wish, she's not even here for us to chastise. As the oldest, I got away with telling her off, and if she were here, it would give her an excuse to cuss me back out. She always accused me of thinking I'm "so damn smart and know every-damn-thang." But I don't, Mama. I don't know anything except that I want the calendar to flip back a day, the clock to tick in reverse for forty-eight hours so we can go back and do this shit differently, do this right, so that Viola Price will be able to breathe on her own. So that there will be no funeral in three days.

None of us are actually talking. We're just moving through this house like zombies. Charlotte's not here. She said she's got too much to do trying to get things ready for friends and relatives coming in from all over, and did we forget about Quiet Hour? When everybody comes to her house after the services?

We're still waiting to find out if they're going to let Lewis out for the funeral. Daddy called and said he's coming by later. He sounded old. Tired. Like he might not survive this. I feel sorry for him. Even if he'd been thinking about coming back home, it's too late now.

Janelle and I have to go through Mama's things all by ourselves. I've never gone through her things before. Never gone through anybody's *things*. We haven't started, because Miss Loretta's on her way over here. She said she has to tell us something. Something important. I've just been opening and closing the kitchen drawers, wondering what we're going to do with all these forks and knives and spoons. When I looked in Mama's linen closet, there were tons of sheets and pillowcases, all of which had been starched and ironed and stacked flat. She even had a separate pile of handkerchiefs. I never once saw Mama with a handkerchief in her hand.

"Paris, wake up! Miss Loretta's here," I hear Janelle say.

She's shaking me. I didn't even realize I'd fallen asleep on the couch.

"Okay!" I yell, sitting up, but feel a crick in my neck.

"I'm sorry, dear."

"It's all right, Miss Loretta. How are you?"

"I'm probably feeling pretty much like you all, if you can understand that."

"We do," Janelle says. "We do."

"Mind if I sit?"

"No," I say, sliding over. "Dingus! Shanice!"

"Yes, Ma?"

"What are you two doing out there?"

"Nothing much. Looking at Granny's little garden. It's tight. She's got a bunch of stuff growing out here."

"Please stay out there until I say it's okay to come in, can you do that?"

"Yes, we can."

"Now," I say, turning to Miss Loretta, "what did you want to tell us?"

"Where's your brother and other sister?"

"He's been detained. We're hoping he'll be in Chicago for the service. And Charlotte lives there, so she's trying to make sure everything's organized."

"I see." Her white hair looks lavender. I just realized that. I never noticed much about her except that she was white and old. And for the first time, I realize that Miss Loretta is pretty. I'd bet she was a knockout when she was younger. It's written all over her face. I wonder if she has any other close friends. But she plays bridge, she should. I'm also wondering if Mama ever actually got the hang of it. She said Miss Loretta was trying to teach her.

"Do they need to be here?" Janelle asks.

"It's all right. You two can share this with them."

Janelle sits in one of Mama's gold chairs. What are we supposed to do with them? What about all of this stuff in here?

What do you do with someone's personal belongings when they die? I don't want to think about it right now. "What exactly is it we need to share, Miss Loretta?"

"Well," she says, clasping her hands together, "first of all, your mother and I talked about this quite some time ago."

"Talked about what?" Janelle asks.

"About what to do if she passed away suddenly."

"What?" I say.

"She knew it might happen, with her asthma and all."

"Okay," Janelle says, paying extra-close attention.

"Anyway, Paris, as the oldest, she wanted me to tell you a few things. First, she wants you to go through all of her old purses."

"Her old purses? For what?" I say. "Why?"

"I'm not sure. She just asked me to tell you that."

"That's kind of a strange request," Janelle says. "It sounds like she knew this was going to happen."

"Well, after the last attack, Vy told me that she didn't think she could go through it again. That she was tired of fighting, and if she ever had another one even close to one like that, she probably wouldn't be able to handle it."

"Really? She told you that?" I ask.

"Yes, she did."

"When?" Janelle says.

"Right after you all left back in March." Now she's reaching into her purse, pulling out what looks like a bunch of white envelopes. I forgot about Mama's mail. What do we do about her mail? Do we just open it and read it? And what if it's personal? What if it's something we shouldn't know? I never thought about any of this stuff before.

When Miss Loretta presses the envelopes to her chest, something tells me they're not bills or anything close to it. "Your mother wrote each of you a letter," she says, trying not to cry, but neither she, nor I, nor Janelle can help it.

"Mama wrote us all letters?"

"Yes, she did. And they're right here."

"May I have mine?" Janelle says, holding out her hand.

"No."

"Why not?"

"Because that's not how Vy wants it done."

"What does Mama want done?" I ask.

"She asked me to tell you that she doesn't want any of you to read them until the first Thanksgiving after she passes, and only if all four of you can manage to spend it together. At that time, she wants each of you to read the letter out loud and in front of each other, but you can't read your own."

"What?" Janelle says, obviously confused about this.

"Paris, she wants you to read Charlotte's."

"But why?"

"I'm not sure. And she wants Charlotte to read yours."

"So that means I have to read Lewis's and vice versa. But I wonder why?"

I sink back against the couch and drop my head. What could she say to us in a letter that she couldn't say or hasn't already said to us before? "Do you know when she wrote them, Miss Loretta?"

"No, I don't. But I already gave your father his."

"She wrote one to him, too?" Janelle says.

"Yes, she did."

"Does he have to wait until Thanksgiving?"

"Yes. And Vy hoped he'd spend this one with you all."

"What if we snuck and read them?" Janelle asks.

"Are you fucking crazy?" I say. "Oh, I'm sorry, Miss Loretta. I mean, are you crazy? Is that how you think we should honor Mama's wishes, by disrespecting them?"

"I'm sorry. I just asked. November's a long way off."

"Who should keep the letters?" I ask.

"You, because, and I'm quoting her, 'as the oldest, you're going to have to be the mama now.' Vy also suggested—or, I should say, insisted—that you children make every effort to spend at least one holiday together each year, because she was really worried that you all are missing out on being a family."

"But we are a family. We just live in different cities," Janelle says.

"You know, Vy told me that when she was a youngster they had family reunions every year, and since most folks didn't move away from home like they do now, everybody usually came. She said her cousins were just like sisters and brothers. That's how close they were. But nowadays, she said, too many families are like strangers. And I agree. I have two sisters I haven't seen in going on eighteen years. Vy just doesn't want you all to wait until you're all old and your kids are grown before they get to know each other. Do it now, while they're young. And she wants you all to try to spend some time doing things together, too."

"But we try to, Miss Loretta, it's just so hard with everybody's schedules," I say.

"Try harder," she says. "Vy said kinfolk should know kinfolk. Friends come and go, but family is forever. She said you don't have to like your kinfolk, but accept them—faults and all—because they're your flesh and blood."

"That's true," I say.

"Your mother was smart and wise, you know. I wrote down so many things she said, because they were just so helpful to me."

"She's right," Janelle says. "Shanice doesn't know Tiffany or Monique at all, and they're about the same age. They should have something to talk about, but they don't."

"I know," I say, agreeing. I realize Dingus doesn't really know my brother's son—or his aunts and uncles, for that matter. I never actually thought about this except as a passing thought. It's one of those things you hope to do one day, right up there with going to church every Sunday, reading the paper every day, or a book a week, or exercise, and thank-you notes.

"I'm not through," Miss Loretta says. "Paris, Vy wanted this first Thanksgiving to be at your house, since you like to cook, and that, every year thereafter, you children vote to see whose home you'll spend it at next."

"Well, we can just skip Lewis," Janelle says.

"Why?" Miss Loretta asks.

"It's a long story," I say. "A very long story."

"I'm not doing anything," she says.

"No, Miss Loretta. We don't want to bore you with it. But tell me something. Are you still going to go on the cruise?"

"Oh, no. I couldn't go now. There's no way I could step foot on that cruise ship without Vy."

"That's sweet," Janelle says.

"So does that mean you're coming to the funeral?"

"Absolutely. Vy begged me not to get sentimental. But I never listened to her when she tried to boss me around, I'm certainly not going to start now. If there's anything I can help you girls do, please yell right out that window."

"We will," I say, as we both give her a hug. "And thanks for being Mama's friend all these years."

Janelle is nodding when I blurt out: "Miss Loretta, did Mama ever learn to play bridge?"

"Goodness, no! Vy was terrible at it. Just terrible," she says, and is laughing as she walks out the front door.

———————

Janelle and I are sitting in the kitchen, drinking coffee and sifting through Mama's "junk drawer," which is full of every possible receipt for every possible thing she has ever bought. But when I come across a layaway slip for none other than Thomasville furniture, I pull this out from the stack. "Janelle! Look at this! Mama has a five-thousand-dollar dining-room set in layaway!"

"You have got to be kidding!" She takes the slip from my hand, and just as she does, the phone rings.

It's a collect call. And I know whom from. "Yes, I will," I say. "Hi, Lewis."

"Hi, Paris. How's everybody doing?"

"We're hanging in here, I guess. Can you come?"

"Yeah, they're letting me out, but my lawyer's gotta escort me. It's for security reasons. But at least I get to be there with y'all. That's how I see it, anyway."

"He can come," I whisper to Janelle.

"Good! We need you here, Lewis!" she yells.

"All right, then. I'ma hang up. That's all I wanted to tell you."

"You have to hang up so soon?"

"Yeah. We just came from court. But don't worry. I'll be there."

"We love you, Lewis."

"Yeah, me, too," he says. He's spent, too. All of us have been running on fumes these past few days. But now I need to perk back up. I get two pills out of my purse and down them with my coffee.

"What's that you're taking?" Janelle asks.

"Just something for tension headaches."

"Let me have one," she says.

"I can't. They're prescription."

"So? If they work for you they should work for me."

"Okay. But only take one, because they're strong."

"Then why are you taking two?"

"Because I need two. Now shut up," I say, and dial the store number. "Yes, hello, my name is Paris Price and I'm calling on behalf of Viola Price, she's my mother, and I understand she has a dining-room set on layaway."

"Yes, I waited on Viola. She practically lived in our store. She's such a character! We just adore her. Is someone coming to pick her set up, or is she ready to arrange for delivery?"

"I wish I could say yes to one of those, but my mother just passed away, and my sister and I are going through her things and we found the receipt, and we're not sure what to do about it."

"Oh my. I'm terribly sorry to hear this. The other salespeople are going to be just crushed when I tell them. She even brought us some sweet-potato pie once because we'd never tasted it. What happened?"

"She had an asthma attack."

"I'm so sorry. Please let us know where her service is being held so we can send flowers—or if she had a favorite charity, or if there's anything else your family needs, do let us know. She was our friend."

"Thank you."

"And as far as the furniture is concerned, whatever you want us to do, we'll do. We can refund the money. It wouldn't be a problem."

"I hadn't thought that far ahead yet."

"Well, I'm Nolene. I can get a refund check out to you in three or four days if you like."

"That would be fine. And thank you. Thank you very much."

I hang up the phone and look at Janelle. "They're giving Mama her money back."

"But Mama's not here, Paris, and it was your money."

"Whatever. We can use it to help pay for her . . ." and the phone rings again.

"I'll get it," Janelle says. "Hello. Oh, hi, Charlotte. Yeah. Paris and I are here. Yes, Lewis will be there. Yes. Everything's going fine. What about there? Well, we just looked in Mama's junk drawer and found out she had a cherrywood dining-room set on layaway at Thomasville and had put two thousand dollars on it and owes a little more than three. . . . What? They're refunding the money. What? Wait. Hold on a minute." Janelle covers the mouthpiece with her hand. "Charlotte says she wants the dining-room set."

"What?"

"You heard me."

"She can't have it."

"Paris said you can't have it. Hold on a minute." She covers the phone again. "She wants to talk to you."

I take the phone. "Charlotte, what would make you think you should get this dining-room set?"

" 'Cause it was Mama's, that's why."

"It isn't Mama's. It's not even paid for."

"She was paying for it."

"But it's not paid for, Charlotte. It's still at the store. It's not even in the house."

"Me and Mama had the same taste, and I don't see why I can't have something to remind me of her. If I wanna finish paying for it, that's my business, not yours!"

"Look, I'm the one who gave her the two thousand dollars to put it in layaway, and I'm getting the money back to help pay for the funeral."

"You just always have to be in control of every-fucking-thing, don't you, Paris? You make me sick, you know that! You're so fucking manipulative, you think everybody's too dumb to see it, but I see right through you! Bitch!"

And here we go again. Click. "She never ceases to amaze me."

"But it's not right, Paris. She shouldn't feel entitled to anything. None of us should. How could she think that furniture belonged to Mama when it's on layaway with your money? And, besides, there's a whole lot of things in here she could have. If she was here to see it."

"Yeah, but, as usual, she's not," I say, and leave it at that.

———

I ask Janelle to go into Mama's big closet first, and then I go in. After pulling them from every shelf and box we open, we sit on the floor, surrounded by purses. Most of them are black and dark-brown leather; but I see one navy, burgundy, and cream Dooney & Bourke; a cherry-red shoulder-strap bag; and an occasional small yellow, fuchsia, or mint-green silk or linen handbag emerges, and we know these were for Easter or Mother's

Day. What are we going to do for Mother's Day? Do not think about this right now, I say to myself, as I open a green Coach bag I know Charlotte sent Mama last year, although it looks like she never carried it. It's empty, as are the next six or seven we go through. Janelle is steadily zipping and unzipping, snapping and unsnapping them. She's not exactly rising to the occasion, and I didn't really expect her to. I just wanted her here for warmth.

I pick up a dilapidated, ugly brown purse with those puzzle pieces of leather shaped like cities on a map sewn together with zigzag stitching, and I get a smile on my face, because I've been hounding Mama since the late eighties to get rid of this sucker, but she wouldn't do it. I slide my hands inside, and when I feel something, Janelle sees it all over my face.

"What is it?"

"I don't know! Damn. Give me a minute," I say, slowly easing out what feels like a bunch of papers or envelopes. When I take my hand out, that's exactly what they are. I pull the rubber bands off and start sorting through them one by one.

"What are they?" Janelle asks again.

"Wait a minute! Here's Mama's birth certificate. Look at her little footprints!"

She reaches out to take it and both of us stare at it and freeze, and then we try our damnedest to sit up straight and not fall apart in this closet. I wipe my eyes. Janelle wipes hers. She kisses the birth certificate, then hands it to me, and I inhale it, and press it against my heart. I take a few deep breaths and then continue. "These are all of our birth certificates. Wait a minute, what are these? Insurance policies. Two of them."

"Why would she have two?"

"I don't know," I say, removing more rubber bands. "Whoa, you won't believe this."

"What?"

"Mama's got two life-insurance policies. Daddy's the beneficiary on one, and all of us are on the other."

"What?"

"Would you stop saying that? Damn! I don't believe this woman. Daddy's is for twenty thousand and the other is for fifty."

"Thousand?"

"What do you think, Janelle? Mama's had the one for us for . . . almost fourteen years."

"You mean she's been paying these big premiums all this time? I bet Daddy doesn't know about ours."

"Looks like she's been paying about sixty or seventy dollars a month. Mama. You are too much," I say, folding the policies back. "I don't want my part, I can tell you that much right now. I don't need it."

"Well, I do," she says. "And you know Lewis does. I don't know about Miss Lottery Winner, but what are these?" she asks, holding up another bunch of dingy white envelopes that I have to scrunch to read what's written on them because it's in pencil and obviously a long time ago. "This one says 'Paris's first tooth.' And this one 'Lewis's first tooth.' 'Charlotte's . . .' 'Janelle's . . .' And Lewis's braid from his first haircut!"

"Can we open them?" Janelle asks.

"No! We still have quite a few purses to go. So keep looking."

And she does.

"Check this out!" Janelle screams.

"What what what?" I ask, leaning way over and dropping Mama's black straw clutch—which feels empty anyway—into my lap.

"All of our report cards! Since kindergarten, Paris. Since kindergarten," she groans, and we're crying again, but for some reason these tears feel good. Very good. And we keep looking. When I pick up a manila envelope, it slips from my grip and out comes a slew of mostly black-and-white baby pictures of Charlotte, and then when she's in school, and they're in color up until she graduated. She was always the prettiest. No doubt about it. And so smart. She could've done anything she wanted to with her life. I don't know why she hates working at the post office so much. What she does is important.

There are four more envelopes like this one, and I assume they're more about us kids. I peek inside each one until I see pictures of Mama. I shake them out onto the carpet, and there she is in all her facets. One shot is a black-and-white photo with a group of other black girls; Mama's standing out front, leaning on a baseball bat with both hands, her head is cocked to the side. Her hair is parted down the middle with two thick braids sticking out on the sides. She must be fourteen, fifteen, maybe.

"She looks like you, Paris."

"She looks like Charlotte," I say.

"Look! Here's Mama and Daddy when they got married!"

The two of us just stare at them. They look like they're really in love. Mama's lips are red. Her hair is auburn, pulled back in a French twist. She's wearing something that's navy-and-white polka dots. Even Daddy looks sexier than I ever imagined, with a genuine grin on his face. As he looks down at Mama with his arm draped softly over her shoulder, I can almost see why she loved him. I've never seen them look this soft together. Wow. There are no more pictures of them together. Just of her pregnant, and one of her bowling. That one looks recent. Like it was taken on her birthday. It was, because here's her and Shanice eating cake. "Keep looking," I say to Janelle.

And she does. But we don't find anything else. Nothing. We are somewhat disappointed, but mostly relieved at what we have found: our history, our lives together as a family; and after looking at our mother and father, I think we both realize where we came from and who we are.

"Let's get out of here and get some air," Janelle says.

When I try to get up, my legs are asleep and starting to feel like electricity is shooting through them. I kick and shake them until I'm able to stand. As I'm about to turn off the light, Mama's clothes are just hanging there. I pull out a dress. It's a size fourteen and still has the price tag on it: $59.99 from Marshall's, marked down again to $25.00. She always loved a bargain, but when was the last time Mama wore a fourteen? I smile as I walk out into the bedroom and feel the fresh evening air coming through her window. I sit down on the bed. I'm crying again. I see Dingus standing in the doorway.

"Can I do anything, Ma?"

I just shake my head.

"You sure?"

I nod, and then it occurs to me that I'm not the only one feeling her loss. Not by a long shot. "How about you, Dingus? How're you holding up?"

"I'm all right," he says. "I just can't believe I'm in Granny's house and she's not here. I wanted her to watch me play college ball. She wanted to watch me. I *really* wanted her to watch me." He comes over and sits next to me, puts his head next to mine, and I hug him until I hear Daddy's voice in the living room.

I was right: Daddy has aged. His gray roots are inching in, and his eyes are red and glassy, with deep circles underneath. He looks like he's hurting everywhere, like he's lost. We don't say anything. Not even Janelle and Shanice when they come from the back bedroom. We just take each other's hands and squeeze until we lose our grip.

Sock-It-to-Me Cake

They almost had to carry me outta that church. I ain't never liked going to funerals, 'cause I guess I take loss too personal. I do everything in my power to avoid 'em, but this time I couldn't. I stared at that big mahogany casket for the longest time, trying to make myself not believe that my mama was inside it. But it didn't work. And all them gigantic floral arrangements started closing in on me and made me nauseous. For a while I just sat there till I felt my body jerking and I couldn't stop it and I guess I musta slid off that bench and was headed up there to save Mama from eternity when somebody grabbed me and sat me back down. I screamed and hollered so long that my head went cold, until it felt like I was the only one sitting in the front row during the whole eulogy.

But I wasn't. Lewis locked his arm through mine, and I couldn't tell if it was to keep me close or to stop me from getting up again. But I felt purged, like I had passed through something that had lightened the load I brought here. By the time I stopped shivering and was able to appreciate the breeze from Janelle's fan, I guess it was Lewis's turn to drop. All he did was be his usual pitiful self, 'cause he leaned forward while his eyes was glued up toward that plastic Jesus and started shaking his head back and forth, slower and slower, until he finally said, "What we gon' do now?" What a stupid-ass question. What we been doing? But since I had just barely pulled myself together and this didn't seem like the time or place to be criticizing, I kept my thoughts to myself.

And Miss Keep-Her-Cool Paris shed a lotta tears, but it looked like she was controlling them, too. I ain't said one word to her since she got here, and she ain't uttered a single syllable to me neither. She got a lotta nerve, is all I can say. Of course she staying in a hotel, but Janelle and Shanice is sleeping in the girls' room with them. Through most of the service Janelle squeezed my hand and smudged the left shoulder of my navy-blue dress chocolate brown and red from her makeup, but I didn't mind.

Al sat right behind us. Next to him was Lewis's lawyer. Paris almost had a stroke when her ex-husband showed up. Everybody, including Nathan, knew Mama couldn't stand him. Dingus was the one who called him. But then Nathan turned around and asked if I thought it would be okay for him to come. I told him I didn't see no reason why he shouldn't at least be there for his son. I have to be honest, the only real pleasure I done felt all day was watching Paris grinding her teeth and reaching in her ·purse to pop whatever kinda pills she taking, after she saw him.

. So many folks wanted to say goodbye to Mama that at the last minute we had to switch to a bigger church. Paris had a hissy-fit about that, too. But I took care of it. And everything went good. The choir sang some of the worst songs I done heard in a long time, but mostly by friends who ain't seen her in at least thirty years, since she left Chicago, but they wanted to honor her by doing solos. That white lady Miss Loretta even came. She gave us all the biggest hug and she smelled good, like Shower-to-Shower powder, and when she told me how much I looked like Mama, her smile was just as warm as when she squeezed my arms. Now I see why she was Mama's friend. A few of her old boyfriends had some kind words to say. Daddy kept a frozen smile on his face and didn't blink once when they got up and started reminiscing about what it was about Mama that got their attention forty-some-odd years ago: Her pretty legs. Her deep smile. Her take-no-prisoners attitude. How far she could hit a ball. How fast she could run. How clean and fresh she always smelled. And one man thanked her for teaching him how to dream. Said he was a surgeon in D.C. After fifteen or twenty minutes, wasn't nobody listening to them. We even had to cut some of her close friends' speeches short, 'cause it's obvious when folks get dressed up and got a audience they get long-winded and you can't hardly get the microphone outta their hand.

It had been raining for three days straight, so it was hot and sticky as I don't know what at the cemetery, and I couldn't watch 'em lower Mama into that damp ground. I didn't care how pretty everybody said that casket was. All I kept thinking was, How in the world is she gon' breathe in that thing down there? Deep down, I guess I been playing a game with myself. That I'll see her on her next trip to Chicago. That she's just going on a underground cruise instead of one on water. That she'll still get to see them islands and I can't wait for her to tell me all about it when she get back.

I left everybody out there and went on back to the house to make sure everything was ready when the folks got there. Aunt Suzie didn't go to the funeral, but since she belonged to a Circle Group—which ain't nothing but a bunch of churchgoing old women who love going to funerals and don't care who died—she pretended like it was a stranger who had passed and stopped by to help out. They claim their whole purpose is to honor the dead, but it seemed like they really just came for the free food, 'cause they sure was killing it.

I didn't know half the people that showed up. It musta been at least a hundred folks. It's times like this when I wished we had central air conditioning. Next house. She wasn't in here fifteen minutes when I heard Paris tell Al she might run to the store to buy some more fans, since everybody kept saying how hot it was. She love testing me. Everybody did look hot, but what the hell they expect? It's ninety degrees outside. It's Chicago. And it's June. I told Al to tell her to keep her American Express in her wallet, that we didn't need her charity. He just told her maybe they wouldn't stay as long; that they could cool off at home.

I wished there was somewhere I coulda hid from all the kissy-huggy-too-much-makeup-and-perfume-wearing relatives I didn't remember, but Janelle seemed to. For the past two hours, all I been doing is watching folks eat and in between bites listening to 'em trying to get us to remember how much they remember about us: how many of our shitty diapers they changed; who was there when we took our first step; who burnt our ears and necks with smoking straightening combs and big bumper curlers; who saved us when we almost drowned in Lake Michigan. After a while, I did hide upstairs in my room, but Al found me and made me go back. A lot of people started leaving, 'cause the food was almost gone, and then some folks still begged for aluminum foil and paper plates. Janelle was running back and forth to the kitchen. Aunt Suzie Mae's friends was the last ones to go, 'cause I just came out and told 'em to please leave so family could be with family. Aunt Suzie, she went with 'em.

Last night, relatives and friends who know our family tree stopped by to drop off all kinds of food. I'd spent the past two days cooking and cleaning myself. Had to—to stay busy and keep my mind off why I was doing all this in the first place. A little while ago, the dining-room table, kitchen counters, and all them rented tables was full of Tupperware bowls, roasters, and platters. You couldn't even see the nice lace tablecloths I had put on 'em. It musta been at least four or five hams over there, pots of collard greens, and fried chicken galore. I counted three bowls of potato salad, one coleslaw, and three twenty-pound turkeys, but somebody's dressing wasn't hitting on nothing, 'cause didn't nobody touch it. Some of them Pyrex dishes was still bubbling with macaroni-and-cheese and baked beans when we first set 'em out. I made two big pots of string beans: one with potatoes and one with ham hocks and okra. I even put out my good silver trays for hors d'ouevres: carrot and celery sticks, broccoli and cauliflower spears that nobody touched even though I put some Thousand Island dressing right next to it. Target had a special on white dish towels, which I used to hang over the edges of the bowls for the dinner rolls and corn-bread squares. They been gone.

We had two of every kind of cake you can think of: coconut cake; Seven-Up cake; red velvet cake; four pound cakes—one lemon, one almond; a nasty German-chocolate and a serious Sock-It-to-Me cake, which I cut in half and hid in the breadbox, 'cause it taste just the way Mama always make—I mean made—hers. A lotta people don't bother using a bundt pan or take the time to make the cinnamon, chopped-pecan, and brown-sugar filling, but whoever made this one knew what they was doing. The glaze dripping down the sides was pitch-perfect. I cut myself a thick slice, put it on a little paper plate, and put a napkin over it, hoping nobody would touch it. So far so good.

The only thing we put out to drink was punch, 'cause people turn into alcoholics after funerals. I even used my good crystal and sterling bowls with a ladle and set out two extra cups for dipping. I dropped a mound of orange sherbet in one. Everybody was just sipping away, but I couldn't help but notice how many of them glasses landed on top of the bar so Al could add something to give that punch some punch. I sure need one now, which is why I pick my cake up and walk straight over to the bar. Al over there sleep in the recliner. I hope he spend the night. I don't want him to do nothing but hold me, and then he can leave when it's daylight, 'cause death is easier to deal with in the daytime. We ain't back together, but we ain't talked about the divorce since this happened. It's amazing how two tragic things can cancel one out. But I ain't forgot.

Right now I'm swiveling on this bar stool, pouring myself a

double shot of scotch, nibbling on my cake, and watching the last of the folks leave. Janelle is at the front door playing hostess, thank God. The kids is still pretending like they know each other, but as soon as our eyes locked, they got that look of mourning in theirs even though they was horsing around. Dingus is standing over by the garage door talking to his daddy. Nathan look the same. Something good done happened to him, 'cause that's a Armani suit or my name ain't Charlotte. Dingus is taller than he is, and look just like him. How could he not be a daddy to this boy all this time? When I hear a voice I know belong to my sister say, "And what exactly are you doing here, Nathan?" I swirl this stool all the way around to be nosy. They ain't paying no attention to me.

"Dag, Ma. He came to offer his condolences like everybody else."

"It's true, Paris. I came to show my respect. And I come in peace. Truly, I do." He bends over to give her a hug and her body twist and lock up like a piece a rope.

"Who told you about Mama?"

"I did," Dingus says.

"I cannot believe that after all these years of not hearing from you that you would have the nerve to show up at my mother's funeral."

Now I turn my back away from 'em and take my fork and cut another little slice off my Sock-It-to-Me cake. I guess she must be walking away, 'cause then Nathan say, "Wait a minute."

"What?" Paris say, real nasty.

"Will I get a chance to spend some time with you and Dingus while I'm here?"

"With me and Dingus? You can spend as much time with Dingus as you want to in the next twenty-four hours, because that's when we're going home."

"Well, the good news is I'm flying out to San Francisco for a week when I leave here to look for office space."

I gotta see this, so I turn around again. She done stopped dead in her tracks and then she turns around to look him in the face. This is getting good.

"Things have worked out well for me, Paris. I miss the Bay Area, and quite a few of my athletes are from California, so I thought this would be an opportune time to come back home to recruit and practice."

"Home?"

"Look, Paris. No need to jump up and down with joy right now, and under the circumstances I can see why you wouldn't be too keen to hear my good news, but there are a lot of things about me that have changed. For starters: I've grown up. My practice is booming. I'm an inch from making seven figures. I've even done the therapy thing. I'm a new man. A different man, but the same man you fell in love with."

"Word up," Dingus says, and Paris hauls off and kicks his young stupid ass. I just pretend to be eating, but I ain't been able to swallow the last two bites.

"If you so much as dial my number when you get to San Francisco, I will hire someone to blow your fucking brains out."

"Ma?"

"Shut up, Dingus!"

"Well, it was worth a shot."

"And Dingus," she say pointing to him, "you can love the one you're with if you want to, but just make sure you tell him that he'll have to buy a season pass to your games, and if he does, they better not be within spitting distance of mine."

After she do her movie-star thing and storm off like she got the last say in the matter, Dingus and his daddy go on out to the garage. I'm about sick of her and her high-and-mighty role, like whatever Paris say is law. Like what she say is final. I've had it with her thinking she Queen of Sheba. Well, she don't run me. And since we ain't got no audience except for a few strag-glers, and most of them is drunk anyway, and since don't nobody else seem to never have the nerve to tell her, I think it's time somebody put this bitch in her place. She walks right behind me to the kitchen, where she act like she getting ready to start cleaning up. I hop off this stool and follow her and set my little paper saucer down on the counter. "That was cold," I say.

She do that Linda Blair thing from *The Exorcist* with her neck and says, "Who the hell do you think you're talking to, Charlotte?"

"I'm looking at you."

"No, you're not looking at me, you're gawking. And what I say to my ex-husband is my business, not yours."

"That's true, but you ain't got no right telling Dingus how to deal with him. That's all I'm saying."

"You've got some nerve. You haven't spoken to me since I got here and these are the first words you open your little monologue with? Spare me."

"You just always gotta be dramatic, don't you, Paris?"

"Dramatic? Hah! First of all, who was it that put on a show at the funeral?"

"That wasn't no damn show."

"Yeah, well, you know what the old folks say, don't you?"

"No, you tell me."

"They say whoever yells the loudest is the one who feels the most guilt. And the reason you couldn't look at Mama was 'cause she'd be looking back at you, and you know you did some nasty shit to her that you never quite fixed, am I right?"

"Fuck you, Paris. First of all, I ain't got nothing to feel guilty about. I loved Mama just as much as you and everybody else."

"Nobody's doubting that, but I beg to differ with you on the guilt issue, little sis. First of all, you weren't even speaking to Mama when she died. You didn't bother to come out to see her when she was sick. You couldn't even manage to come out and help me and Janelle go through her things. And then you seem to have had this sense of entitlement when it came to her furniture. Seems like all Charlotte really thinks about is Charlotte."

"That's bullshit. First of all, I *was* speaking to Mama. I called her a couple of times but got her machine. So there, Miss Know-It-All. And Mama didn't need me out there because you always Johnny-on-the-spot, running to rescue her and every-fucking-body, so why should I break my neck when you do everything anyway?"

"I *do* everything because I can't fucking depend on anybody else to do it. That's why."

"You don't give nobody a chance."

"Oh, stop feeling sorry for yourself, would you? I'm so tired of this woe-is-me and Mama-didn't-love-me-as-much-as-she-did-you bullshit, I don't know what to do."

"It's not bullshit. It's true. Mama always favored you."

"Favored and loved are two different things."

"Not in my book."

"Okay, since we're telling it, I'll just say this. Who had to put all of you little son-of-a-bitches' needs first, before I was even twelve years old? I was a goddamn mother before I even had my period! Mama showed me how to get things done and I got good at it. And . . ."

"Just wait one . . ."

"No, shut the hell up, Charlotte. I'm not finished, and this time you can't hang up in my face. I can't help it if you decided to get married and have kids and skip college and I didn't. Why do you hate me because I did what Mama wanted all of us to do? It's not my fucking fault you took a route that didn't manage to upstage me or any of us. It was never a contest, Charlotte. In case you didn't know that. So—you're pissed at the wrong people. You should be pissed at yourself."

"Ain't nobody jealous of your ass. Don't give yourself that much credit."

"Then why do you always make it seem like everything I do in my life is meant to outshine you? Huh? I want you to be just as happy and successful as me and every-fucking-body else! Why wouldn't I? All I'm trying to do is live my life. I mean, I used to sleep in the same bed with you. Bathe you. Comb your hair. Keep you warm at night. And now you talk to me with so much hostility in your voice that I can't believe we grew up together. You act like you're the one who always got the short end of the stick when you know damn well Mama loved you, and I love your stupid ass, too, even though you keep hanging up in my face every time we have a disagreement. Do you know how humiliating it is to have a misunderstanding with your own fucking sister and she always hangs up in your face after she says what she has to say, but is never interested in hearing your side? It's such a cop-out. It's so unfair. And childish as hell. But it's also a very safe place to be."

"Yeah, well, how safe is it running around trying to act like you perfect, like you ain't got no problems, like you got everything under control? And then you got that perfect son, too."

"I have never tried to act like I'm perfect, or that my son is. Mama's the guilty party there, and I wish you would understand that."

"Yeah, well, she sure did a good job of it."

"I'm not Mama, Charlotte! And stop acting like she did it on purpose, because she didn't!"

"Well, how come we don't never hear about your problems?"

"Because I don't blab 'em all over the place."

"I'm your fucking sister, bitch. If you can't tell 'em to me and Janelle, then who can you talk to?"

"Maybe . . ."

"Now you shut the hell up. The real deal is, you want everybody to think you so together 'cause you make all that fucking money, which you good at throwing in our face every chance you get, just 'cause you can take trips and buy a Mercedes or a Lexus or whatever the fuck you drive, and your son gets letters from all kinds of universities, but, hey, Paris, you ain't got everything under control, 'cause you ain't fooling me. Exactly what kinda pills is them you been popping all day anyway?

Huh? They damn sure ain't no Advil or no Tylenol. Janelle told me they was prescription. You got a problem with pain? Or just pills? Stressed out about something, Paris? Why don't you tell your little sister what it is? You lonely? Wish you had a husband? Is it something your money can't fix, is that it?"

"Fuck you, Charlotte. What kind of pills I take is my business, and, for your information, I'm not lonely and, whatever the reasons, it's nothing I can't handle."

"Yeah, well, we'll see, won't we? Miss Fucking Perfect!"

"I wish you would stop calling me that!"

"Mama always thought you was perfect, and you think you know everything and go around acting like can't nobody do nothing right except you. That's how you always been, Paris. You just gotta run the whole goddamn show, and you don't give nobody credit for nothing they do."

"I told you: I know I'm not perfect, and I don't always feel like I have to be in control."

On that note, I grab my Sock-It-to-Me cake and throw it at her, but it hits her in the face. I didn't mean for it to get her there. "I'm sorry. I didn't mean to do that."

"Yes you did!" She's crying.

"What you crying about, Paris? It didn't hurt. But if it'll make you feel better, go get another piece and throw it back in mine."

"I don't want to do anything to hurt you, Charlotte. I never have and never will. But I'm so out of here it's not funny. I was trying to help clean up, but just fuck it!"

"Fine, then, leave. I don't need your help. And by the way: don't look for me at Thanksgiving."

And then, out of nowhere, I hear Janelle say, "You'll be there or I'll throw more than some goddamn cake in your face, Charlotte. And, Miss Leaning Tower of Pisa, you better lay out the red carpet when she gets there."

"Shut up, Janelle. This has nothing to do with you," Paris says.

"Oh, really? Have you both already forgotten about our mother's request, or are you going to ignore all rationality and that little thing called respect and let your anger decide what you should do? And you've both got the nerve to talk about being in control? Where's yours? Do you two think this is how we should be behaving on the same damn day we bury our mother?"

"She started it."

"You started it," Paris snaps. "Criticizing me about something that didn't even concern you!"

"Stop it!" Janelle screams.

"Okay, but one last thing. From the sound of things, Charlotte, it seems like this shit started a long time ago," Paris says. "I don't know what I've done to you to cause you to dislike me so, but I wish you'd tell me what it is."

But I can't think of nothing right now. I need some time to remember. And besides, I don't like being put on the spot like this. "I don't feel like getting into it right now."

"Well, what breaks my heart more than anything is that you seem to have convinced yourself that I'm out to get you, when I'm not. I love you, Charlotte, but you're making it awfully hard to like you."

"Yeah, well, the feeling is mutual."

And on that note Paris throws the dishrag in the sink and walks right past me and Janelle and heads out to the garage, where I hear her rental car start up. Janelle is just standing there with her hands on her hips. The house is damn near empty now, and it's a mess. Paris did say she loved me, didn't she? I feel kinda bad but relieved at the same time.

"I hope you're satisfied now, Charlotte."

"What you mean by that?"

"Nothing," she says. "Let's just get this place cleaned up so we can all get some sleep. It's been a long day, and you must have confused it with the Fourth of July, because these grand-finale fireworks were truly magnificent." She bends down to pick up my Sock-It-to-Me cake saucer, but then stops herself. "Why don't you pick this up?"

"I will."

"Good. Mama's probably turning over in her grave already if she was watching you two act like two bitches on a side street. It's a damn shame."

"I said I'm sorry!"

"Sometimes that's not enough, Charlotte. Sometimes that's just not enough. As a matter of fact, you clean up. I'm tired, and I'm going to bed. I'll get up early and help. But I can't right now."

She's crying. And as soon as she leave, I pick that plate up off the floor and slide my index finger through the frosting and lick it. But it taste terrible mixed with tears.

What I'm
Fighting for

"Hey, get away from that car," I yell.

"We ain't doing nothing to this fucking car," one of the Mexican dudes says. It looks like there's about four of 'em, but I can't be sure. I'm kinda fucked up. I've been kicking it with Silas all day, 'cause he just had a baby and we were celebrating the birth of his son. He left a few hours ago, and I guess I kept the celebration going.

"Look, I asked you nice once. That's my car and I don't want you guys sitting on it."

"This piece of shit!" one says.

"Yeah, but it's my piece a shit! Now, get off of it or I'ma have to go call the police, 'cause it's my personal fucking property and I don't want your drunk asses on it!"

"Fuck you!"

The next thing I know, one of 'em picks up a jack and is running towards me with it, but before I can even do anything, two of the other dudes are pulling my arms behind my back and I feel that hot steel hit my head and see blood gushing down my face, in my eyes, but because I got so much malt liquor in my system, the full extent of the pain ain't registering. It's this fucking alcohol that gave me all this goddamn courage to come storming out to this parking lot when I heard these motherfuckers out here partying, drinking beer, and blasting their loud-ass Mexican music.

But now that jack is landing in my chest and, fuck, I can't

breathe. Somebody else is kicking me in my back and on my side, and when I fall forward my face hits this pavement. When I roll over I see some guy swing that fucking jack like a golf club and I feel it slice the skin over my right eye off. I know it's supposed to hurt more than it is, but all I see is blood and more blood. Blood and more blood. That's all.

———

When I open my eyes, I can't believe I'm in a hospital. I know these dudes didn't hit me this bad. But I feel like 165 pounds of crushed ice and hot coals all at the same time. I can't wait to find the motherfuckers when I get outta here. I remember exactly what they look like. I think.

"Hi, Lewis," I hear Janelle say.

"What are you doing here?"

"That's a stupid thing for you to ask under the circumstances."

"Under what circumstances?"

"You almost died, Lewis."

"What the hell are you talking about, Janelle? Some dudes jumped me. I was trying to protect my property, and . . ."

"Lewis, you were so drunk when the paramedics got there that, in addition to your head injuries, your nose wouldn't stop bleeding."

"They hit me in the head with a goddamn jack and I fell face-flat on the concrete!"

"I know they did."

"How do you know?"

"Because they were caught."

"Really? How?"

"Don't worry about it right now. Listen to me, Lewis, this is serious."

"I know it is."

"No, I'm talking about your health. You didn't just bleed where they hit you. You bled from your eyes and ears, and take a look at your goddamn fingernails."

I'm almost too scared to, because Janelle is too shook up and I have never heard her swear. But she's right, 'cause when I look down I see dried blood around my cracked cuticles. "What the hell do you mean, I bled from my eyes and ears? And how does a person bleed from their fingernails?"

"You want the truth?"

"Of course I do, Janelle."

"You've been drinking so much for so long, Lewis. . . . Do you realize you've been in this hospital for four days?"

I just look at her. Four days? That's impossible. I got here last night. Didn't I? But my sister wouldn't lie to me, and all I can do is shake my head.

"Anyway, the alcohol you've been consuming all these years has finally caught up with you. The doctor said it's destroyed your platelets—the stuff that clots your blood—and when you came in here your level dropped all the way down to forty in just a few hours."

"So what does that mean?"

"Well, I'll put it this way: they said a normal level is about a hundred and forty to four hundred."

"Oh," I say. "So I fucked up."

"No, you didn't just fuck up. You almost died."

"You serious, Janelle?"

"You want me to go get the doctor and have him repeat it?"

"No. Don't."

"You've got twenty-two stitches in your head and six across your eyebrow, and your right shoulder's been fractured."

I know my head feels like a watermelon full of boiling seeds and my eye like it's being stretched; I can't lift my right arm, but I still say, "Is that it?"

"No, Lewis, that's not 'it.' You better take your ass to AA every single day for the rest of your life or you're going to die, for real. And it's no joke. We just lost our mother, we don't want to lose you, too."

"We?"

"Your sisters. Your family."

"Don't worry. But, Janelle, please don't tell me you told Paris and Charlotte and especially Daddy?"

"I just got the call a few hours ago myself. From some girl named Luisa. She said she's the one who called the paramedics, because she was dropping off some homemade tamales for you and she said when she saw those guys running and everything, she recognized one as her brother, but then she said, when she saw you down on the ground like that, she was so scared she ran and called 911, but didn't know what else to do until today, when she went over and got your key and looked around your apartment and found my number. She said she remembered me because she saw the note I left on your door about Mama way back in the spring."

I just stare at the light-blue wall behind my sister. And then, just for the record, I say, "I almost died for real, Janelle?"

"You could have. Yes."

"And Mama's dead," I hear myself say.

"Yes, she is, Lewis. She's been dead for almost two months. Two long months."

"I need to talk to her, Janelle."

"We all need to talk to her, Lewis, but we can't, all right? So get over it."

"Get over it, huh?"

"You know what I mean. Look. I've gotta go look at an apartment today, and if all goes well, my daughter can come home in a few days."

"What exactly is going on with the George situation?"

"He's out."

"Yeah, but is he going to prison?"

"Not unless Shanice agrees to take that test and testify on tape, like I told you." .

"But I thought you said he did this to his other daughters, too."

"He did. One was his stepdaughter."

"Can't they testify against him?"

It looks like a lightbulb just went off in her head or something. "I never thought about asking them. It never even crossed my mind. If they did, I wonder . . . ? I'm going to call and find out. Lewis?"

"Yeah," I say, kinda grateful that I finally offered a member of my family something that was helpful.

"Thank you," she says.

"You're welcome. Can I ask you something, Janelle?"

"Sure, Lewis. What?"

"Sometimes, don't you ever wonder what you're fighting for? I mean, doesn't it ever seem like you mighta missed the point?"

"Yeah, but sometimes things happen to make you wake up, and if you don't, then that makes you a fool. I'm tired of being a fool, Lewis. And what am I fighting for? Me and my daughter's happiness and sense of well-being. If I can manage that, as far as I'm concerned I've done a lot."

"I agree."

"What about you? Do you know what you're fighting for?"

"My sanity. Some dignity. Sobriety. Self-control. But I'll stop there."

"Then let's just keep fighting," she says, and bends over and gives me a kiss on the good side of my forehead and then leaves. I lay here and just stare at that blank blue wall for so long that it becomes a movie screen like the kind we used to go to when we were little: at the drive-in. I see myself. Cutting grass with a power lawnmower in front of a nice little ranch-style house. It's my house. And in the driveway is a brand-new burgundy Ford 250 pickup. It's mine. On the visor is my burgundy leather garage-door opener I invented, with Jamil's picture under the plastic, right next to it. My hands and wrists are still deformed, but I'm finally taking the right kinda medication, and it's helping the pain. When I finish, I walk inside my garage and look at all these cans stacked high on the shelf. My name is on the labels. I've got a workstation that takes up a whole wall. I've got every kinda tool I ever wanted. I even got a TV and stereo out here. A little refrigerator that I keep stocked with water and every now and then a Pepsi, but nothing stronger than that. I hear a car pull up behind my truck. It's Donnetta and Todd dropping Jamil off for the weekend. We ain't best friends, but I remembered one of the Steps in AA and made amends and apologized to both of them and they accepted it because they're decent. I stand there and smile, waving goodbye, and when I hear the door to the kitchen open I turn to see who it is, but all I see is the tip of a woman's sneaker sticking out between the wall and the screen door. When I blink, I'm waiting for her to come out, but the movie is over. The screen goes blank. The wall is blue again. And I'm glad I ain't dead.

As a matter of fact, I'm crying. I'm crying because I wish my life was like that movie. Mama would be ashamed if she saw me like this. And so would my son. So would the rest of my family. Hell, I'm ashamed. But I also don't wanna die no time soon. I know I'm fucked up. And I'm an alcoholic. But at least I'm finally admitting it to myself. And maybe this knowledge and acceptance can make me stronger instead of weak. I'm the one who's been letting all this bullshit break me down to nothing. But I ain't gotta accept being fucked up—'cause basically everybody is, when you get right down to it—but it's what I do with this insight that can help me walk through, around, and over the hard stuff. I need to see this as an opportunity to learn how to live. The only way I'll stand a chance is sober. I should've known this a long time ago. But, hell, fuck the past.

Right now all I want is my family, and especially my mama, to be proud of me. I want them to know that I'm a good person, that I'm a strong black man. That I can be responsible. Can take care of my son. That I can be a good father. That I'm smarter than they think. I just want to feel necessary and needed. Want to feel important to somebody. I don't have to *be* important, I just want to *feel* important. Up to now I've been in love with the wrong thing, 'cause alcohol ain't my buddy or my girlfriend. It sure ain't my wife. All this love been killing me. And I'm tired. Tired of not thinking clear. Tired of not remembering. Tired of falling down and not being able to get back up. I guess I been dead, Mama, but I think it's time for me to stand up straight and tall like you taught us to. It's gotta be a whole lot easier than this.

Loosening the Knots

It's ten o'clock at night and I'm putting groceries in the trunk of my car. As I lift another bag out of the metal cart, I bang my knee into the back bumper. "Shit!" I scream, but there's hardly a soul out here at this time of night, so no one even hears me. "Fuck!" I say even louder, and then kick the car. I throw the last bag in, not even thinking that it could be the one with the eggs or something breakable in it, but I could care less right now, because that bumper shouldn't have been in my fucking way.

When I get in the car I start it up, but I don't put it in reverse. I just sit here, because I realize that I just got mad at a bumper. Now that I think about it, I've been mad about a lot of things lately. I've got a sister who hates me, a cookbook that's not even close to being finished, an ex-husband who has resurfaced and suddenly wants to be a father again, and basically everything and everybody seems to get on my nerves in no time flat. I'm always running into or tripping over things and have gotten more cuts and bruises on my body this past year than I have in my whole life.

"You are out of control, Paris," the Smart Side of Me says out loud. "You've been taking these stupid pills for so long now that they've become a part of your daily routine. They're affecting your whole demeanor. Your personality, even your thoughts."

"But that's not completely true," the Dumb Side of Me says.

"Bullshit. You can't even start your day without figuring them into the equation."

"That is not true."

"Bullshit. You can't *get* through a day without them."

"Wanna bet?"

"Yes. I'll bet you can't do it."

"Watch this," the Smart Side of Me says, as I reach into my purse and get out my brand-new full-to-the-top bottle of sixty extra-strength Vicodin (the Dumb Side has not only moved up in the world, but found a new doctor, who was even more gullible than the others), untwist the top, and toss every single one of them as far as they'll go out into that parking lot. "There!"

And as soon as I do it, I panic. But the Smart Me refuses to succumb to the sudden pang of being left out in the middle of an empty lake in a paddleboat with no oar, and I back the car out and drive home. When I get inside the garage, I push the bottle inside an empty milk carton in the recycle bin.

"I can do this," I say as I walk in the house, where Dingus is sitting with a long face. We've both been so blue since Mama died that it has become our manner: sadness. I've been told that we're just grieving, that it's normal, and as time passes it'll get easier. But it's been three months, and I feel exactly the same way. I miss her and want her to come back. I can't imagine not feeling like this. Ever.

But I'm trying. In fact, I actually have a real-live date tomorrow with Randall. Finally. After I got back from London, I called him to tell him what had happened to my mother. He completely understood when I said I wanted to hold off finishing the yard because it didn't seem that important at that time. Now I feel a need for motion, activity, company. Someone to talk to besides my family.

"Ma, you got a minute?" Dingus asks.

"The question is, do *you* have a minute? Can you get the

groceries out of the car first, or is this something that can't wait?"

"I guess it can wait," he says, and saunters out to the garage and comes right back, carrying all six bags. How does he do that?

"You want me to put this stuff away?"

"No, I can do it. What's going on?"

"Have a seat," he says.

"Why do I need to have a seat?"

"Just because."

"Get to the point, would you, Dingus?"

He takes a few deep breaths. "Jade's pregnant."

"Who?"

"Jade."

"That's impossible."

"No, it's not impossible, Ma."

"How did that girl get pregnant, Dingus?"

"We had an accident, is all."

"You seem to be big on sexual accidents, aren't you?"

"No."

"Does the name Meagan ring a bell?"

"She doesn't count."

"I don't see why not. But that's beside the point. I thought Jade was a nice girl."

"She *is* a nice girl. I love her. And just because she slept with me doesn't make her a slut."

"Did you hear me call her a slut?"

"No, but you're implying it by your tone."

"Don't tell me what my tone implies. And don't try to put words in my mouth either. Where's my purse?"

"Right in front of you, Ma."

When I pick it up, that's when I remember that what I'm looking for isn't in it. Which means I have nothing to rescue me from this bullshit going on in front me. Nothing. I'm waiting for the Smart Side of Me to step up to the plate and deal with this, but she must be dozing or something, because, the next thing I know, I hear myself say, "I forgot my wallet at the store. We have to finish this conversation when I get back."

"I can go get it for you."

"No! I'll get it myself," I say, and fly out the door. Before I even know it, I'm back in the parking lot. With the engine running, I turn my brights on and try to look nonchalant as I search the pavement for white pills. I don't see any. This is impossible, because I just tossed them out here! I walk around in circles and then stand in the spot where I parked before and try to imagine every possible direction they could've rolled in, and that's when I notice that parts of the pavement are wet. The sprinkler system has been watering these fucking little trees, and when I go over and stand next to one, I finally see something white. I bend down and with one fingernail, scoop up what is now apparently a pile of gooey white paste. I can't. I won't. And I don't.

When I get home, Dingus is in his room. I knock on his door and don't wait for him to tell me to come in. I sit down on the edge of his bed. It's hot in here. Very hot. "Talk to me," I say.

"I don't know what to say, except she's pregnant."

"And? When is she going to get the abortion?"

"Who said anything about an abortion?"

I know he didn't just say what I thought he said. "Have you gone and lost your fucking mind, boy?"

"Ma, please don't swear at me. I don't like it. And you promised you would never use that word and you just used it."

"Fuck you, Dingus!"

He puts his head in his hands and covers his ears. "Look, Ma. I messed up. We messed up. But I'm willing to accept responsibility for this."

"So—does this mean that you just want to throw away your chances for a scholarship and forfeit college because of a girl?"

"No."

"You mean you're not planning on making me proud by becoming a high-school dropout? I mean, it's what we've worked so hard for, isn't it, Dingus?"

"Who said anything about not going to college? And I wouldn't dream of dropping out of school."

"Are you going to take Jade and the baby with you?"

"If I have to, yes."

"This is sweet. What about her parents? How do they feel about this? I betcha her father won't have to search for a topic for this Sunday's sermon, you think?"

"They don't know yet."

I slap him upside his head so hard it stings my hand. "Oh, but they will. And you're going over there first thing tomorrow morning to tell them."

"Ma, will you come with me?"

"Not this time, buddy. You're on your own. Wait. I forgot. Ask your father for advice, since you two are so chummy-chummy these days."

"I don't know if I trust his judgment all that much."

"Really? And why is that?"

"He's kind of phony and too hung up on his image."

"Surprise, surprise. Well, whatever you and your in-laws decide to do, I'll just go along with the program. Especially since you and the missus already have it all figured out. Good night."

"Ma, don't leave! I don't know what to say to her mother, and especially her dad. Help me out here."

"You should've thought about that when you didn't slide that condom on. Sleep tight, Dingus."

I slam the door behind me. I'd like to strangle his stupid ass right now. Like to knock every single one of those trophies off the shelves and throw them out the window so they land in the trash, because I wonder if he'll be reminded where he was headed while he's changing Pampers, searching through the classifieds for a job that pays more than minimum wage, and trying to watch *Monday Night Football* all at the same time?

In the morning, I'm surprised I don't have the shakes like alcoholics get when they can't get a drink. But I don't. When I check to make sure Dingus is up, he's already gone. I decide to do exactly what I'd planned to do today, before I found out I might be a grandmother. And I'll do it without pills.

I'm going to walk that reservoir in Lafayette, which is about three miles around. I don't care how long it takes. I'm going to a place to detoxify my body. A year ago, one of my clients gave me a gift certificate for a week at a luxury spa in Arizona that they swear is like ordering room service for the soul. They go twice a year to regroup, to clean out their bodies and minds, but mostly to prevent what they call "major burnout." I've read the brochure at least a hundred times but never felt like I deserved or earned the right to blow off an entire week doing nothing. But, then again, I've never felt a need to learn how to manage the pressures of daily living until now. Never thought I could get any real benefits doing yoga or tai chi or even meditation. Never knew I needed to be still. Never knew I didn't know how. I've never even heard of the term "mindful" before, but I like the idea of living in the present instead of always projecting and stressing about tomorrow or next year. And the thought of having my body polished and scrubbed and wrapped in seaweed or soaking in a tub of hot water with 109 jets going sounds almost too good to be true. I would certainly be willing to try a deep-tissue or hot-stone or cranial-sacral massage.

And of course I've never thought anyone knew me better than I did. So why would I need anything to promote "self-discovery"? What's left to discover? Wait a minute. Charlotte accused me of being a control freak. And maybe she's right. She basically said I was a manipulator, which I disagree with, but I do know how to get what I want. She said I'm bossy. And I can be. That I think I'm always right. Not true. I can admit when I'm wrong. That I feel I'm the only one who can get things done. I do not. In all honesty, by the time I explain the shit and wait to see if it's done right and in a timely manner, half the time I could've done it faster and better myself. That's just the way it is. But maybe I get on other peoples nerves, too. And not just hers. I'd also like to learn how not to care so much. So—the Smart Me understands that it wouldn't hurt to find out why the Vulnerable-Scared-Lonely-Has-to-Be-Perfect-at-Everything Side of Me has been hiding with the swallow of every pill. I do want to return to my senses. I want to feel a sense of balance. I want to not have to be everything to everybody, and I also want to forgive myself for not being perfect. I just wonder if any of this stuff can really happen at a place like this. We'll see.

When I hear a tap tap tap on my door, I'm wondering what Dingus is doing back so soon. It's only nine-thirty. "Come in."

He's wearing his school colors: purple and gold. He walks over and kisses my forehead. "Are you feeling any better this morning?" he asks.

"As a matter of fact, I'm not."

"I'm totally sorry, Ma. I couldn't sleep, so I went over there early."

"So what happened?"

"Her parents are pissed at both of us. They asked Jade if she was ready to be a mother."

"And what did she say?"

"She said no, but it's a price she's willing to pay for making a mistake."

"And what'd you say when they asked if you were ready to be a father, which I'm sure they did?"

"Her dad did. I basically said the same thing."

"And?"

"And we talked about our college plans, our goals and stuff, like once we're out in the real world, and . . ."

"And what?"

"She's not having it."

"You mean to tell me that a preacher's daughter is going to have an abortion?"

"Yes."

"How is that possible?"

"Because her parents said that times have changed. And, plus, they said Jade has plans. She's got a three-point-eight-seven GPA."

"So do you, dummy!"

"I know. And she's been getting scholarship offers. She's a very good writer. And wants to major in journalism."

"Did you tell them what you want to do besides play football?"

"Yes."

"And?"

"I told them I'm planning to go to med school. That I'm majoring in biology and chemistry."

"Thank you very much. What else?"

"Well, they asked us, if we could do this all over, would we do it differently, and we both said yes. And they asked if we wanted another chance, and of course we both said yes again."

"And that's it?"

"Yep. But I have to pay for it."

"You certainly should."

"That, plus we both promised to go to these teenage church groups to talk to them about the dangers of having unprotected sex. Once a week for the next nine months."

"Good. Do you still plan on dating this girl?"

"I think we're going to chill for a little while."

"And you're sure about this?"

"Ma, I know I messed up big-time. I was major scared, and then, when you made me deal with this by myself, it became crystal-clear just how much was at stake. So—don't *even* worry about this anymore. And thank you." He turns to leave.

"Wait, I have something to tell you, too."

"Yeah?"

"Well, you know how testy and mean I've been lately?"

"Sort of."

"Anyway, Dingus, let me just be honest. A little over a year ago I had some dental work done and then ... I know you know I had my breasts done, don't you?"

"I kinda noticed, yeah."

"Anyway, I was prescribed some pain medication that at first I took for pain, but later on, whenever I'd get a little stressed about something, I'd take one, and then two, because they took the edge off and I thought they helped me think clearer. But, well, fast-forward the film and here I am."

"You mean you got strung out on the medicine?"

This is a hard one for me to answer, but I say, "Yes."

"What's the name of it?"

"Vicodin."

"I heard of that. I think I have some."

"Had."

"Word."

The next thing I know, tears are rolling down my face, and I don't know how this happened, because I didn't mean to cry, and I don't even know why I'm crying. Yes I do. I'm embarrassed, because I've finally admitted one of my many weaknesses to my son, and it feels weird.

"It's all right, Ma. You always have so much stuff on your plate, it's understandable how it might get a little tough to deal with sometimes. You don't have to feel bad. Is there anything I can do to help?"

I just shake my head as he puts his arms around me like I'm his child. "I guess I picked the wrong time to lay my craziness on you. I'm sorry, Ma."

"Dingus, it could've been next week or next year—this has nothing to do with you. It's me, and how I handle things. I should know better."

"Come on, Ma. Dag. So you made a mistake. It just proves that you're human like the rest of us. Thank the Lord."

"What's that supposed to mean?"

"I had my doubts."

I slap him softly. "Anyway, I'm going to try to go to this place in Arizona where I can do some soul-searching and maybe cleanse my body and mind some, too."

"Cool. I told you to get some running shoes and hang with me. I guarantee no pill can touch these endorphins."

"I'll take you up on that, as soon as I master walking."

"Word up," he says.

"Word up," I say back.

As soon as he leaves, I put on a sweatsuit I've always wanted to wear, stop by Forward Motion Sports and buy a good pair of running shoes, and head to Lafayette, where I manage to walk around that reservoir in less than forty minutes. I even perspired. It felt good.

But I spoke too soon. All of a sudden I felt hot. And then I started sneezing and then I was freezing. I guess this is what withdrawal feels like.

I go straight home and get under the covers and wake myself up snoring. It's been fourteen whole hours since I had a pill. I almost want to congratulate myself, but, then, I'm the one who did this to myself in the first place, so it doesn't seem practical or logical to even celebrate on a mental level.

I sleep for three whole hours, and when I get up, even though I'm excited about my dinner date with Randall, my body has its own agenda. It's screaming for just one pill. I'm feeling agitated, jumpy, and I'm surprised when I find myself ransacking all my desk drawers, old purses, jewelry boxes, sunglass cases, every suit and coat pocket, even the ashtray in my car, where I usually keep two dollars for the bridge toll—all the places I've hidden pills from myself in the past, in hopes of finding them one day by accident, or like now, when all I need is one or two. The Smart Side of Me says, "You're being stupid again! You're acting like these things are some kind of fucking reward or hidden treasure. You better be glad nobody can see you doing this."

I'm embarrassed, and it feels like I'm being watched. But this is so hard, pretending I don't want one when I do, pretending I'm not craving one when I am. I mean, I know one pill isn't going to change anything. They never do. Everything is exactly the same before I take one as it is after it takes effect. I wish I understood why they make me feel like they're compensation for my good behavior, for not falling apart, for functioning well, being able to connect the dots without anybody's help, for running my world in what looks to be effortless fashion when in fact it often weighs a ton. But, then again, that's part of the game, too, making it look easy when it really isn't.

A pill is a very small prize for what I do. In fact, the Smart Side of Me knows all this shit but the Dumb Side seems to have the most power. After exhausting my search, and I don't find a single pill, I just say fuck it and take my shower. When I open my bra-and-panty drawer and start moving them around to see if I can find a match—whamo!—a plastic sandwich bag with about twenty pills in it is stuck in the back corner.

I dump them all on top of the bed and watch each white pill roll toward the middle of the purple comforter. I want to put one in my mouth, but I'm afraid if I do that I'll have to do it again in two hours, and then the next two and the next, and then I'd just be right back where I started.

I decide to play the waiting game. To see just how long I can really go. It's almost seven o'clock, and Randall's not due for another hour. I'm thinking: What am I going to do to kill a whole hour? Can't eat. If I start doing something, won't be able to finish. Could call Janelle, but all she'll want to talk about is her new townhouse or her new job at Elegant Clutter, and since George's daughters testified against him, when she gets her settlement most likely she'll be able to go into partnership with the Orange Blossom lady. She'd probably tell me again how she's going to put George's ex-wife's name on the deed to that duplex she's been living in all these years, and how much she and Shanice are getting out of the support group they're going to for incest survivors. And even though I'm happy for them, I just don't think I can be engaged right now. I always do the listening, and this time I need someone to listen to me.

The miracle of miracles is that I can finally call my brother, who actually has a phone in his own name, but all he wants to talk about these days is his sobriety and how he's started filing patent applications for his many inventions and how he's even getting prototypes made for some of them. He's so excited about being productive that you can't shut him up, except when he switches to the subject of his kid and how he took some of Mama's insurance money and cleared up his back child support. He's been working on the Twelve Steps of AA and even apologized to Donnetta and her husband for hitting him with that mop, and they forgave him and are letting Jamil spend a weekend with Lewis. He's so excited to be alive and feeling good that I doubt if he'd be able to hear my plea for a receptive ear.

And last but not least is Charlotte, who actually left me a message a while back explaining that she may or may not be ready to talk to me by Thanksgiving, because she and Al might start going to couples therapy, but first she's thinking about going by herself. She said she can't deal with him and her, me and my bullshit, Mama being gone, her son being gay, and now both daughters bleeding, all at the same time. She said we've still got issues, so I guess I have to wait for her to come around.

Since I didn't get my hair done like I'd originally planned, I stand in front of the mirror and pull my ponytail on top of my head and twist it into a knot. But the knot is too tight, so I loosen it and make a tornado bun in the same spot. I wonder what Randall and I will talk about over dinner. We're going to Sausalito. I look down at the pills. We might have to cross two long bridges. Maybe one wouldn't hurt. The restaurant will probably be on the water. My head is starting to throb. I'll eat lobster. Maybe I'm getting a headache. I wonder, will he be as interesting with his hands out of dirt? Maybe I just need one. To take the edge off. How much fun will I be like this? I want to ask him more about his daughter. Tell him about my son. How does he handle being a parent? Now my temples are throbbing. This feels like a migraine. But I've never had one before. Why now, Paris? What is your problem? My hands are clammy. And then I sneeze. I wonder if I'm catching a cold? Damn it. I can't go out if I'm getting sick. I wouldn't want to give this to him. Stop it, Paris. I know I'm not catching any cold. And my head isn't really hurting either. I *want* it to hurt. I *want* to be sick, so I won't have to face the music. And just what music might that be, Paris? Is it blues or jazz or light rock? Is it rap or classical or R&B? What's so hard about facing the fucking music, Paris? Huh?

I fall back on the bed, and as soon as I do I feel those pills pressing against my damp skin. I roll over and snatch them up by ones, twos, threes, until they're all in my right hand, and then I march into the bathroom and flush every single one of them down the toilet. When I hear the doorbell I feel a sudden surge of energy. In fact, I feel as if I've been given some kind of emotional charge. I press the intercom and tell Randall to come on in, that I'll be right out. As I slide into the pretty peach slip dress I bought in London, for some strange reason I imagine myself telling him the truth about what I'm going through, and by the time I pull the straps on my slingbacks, I'm pretty certain I will. What's the point of starting any relationship with a lie, even if all we end up being is friends? Besides, he was honest with me about his situation, and if the truth doesn't scare him off, and he's still as interesting to me as I am to him, hopefully we'll have a whole lot more to talk about on the ride home and I won't mind how many bridges we have to cross.

Help

"How do this work?" I ask.

"Well, it's up to you, Charlotte. There are no set rules or strict guidelines we have to follow. But the things that are causing you the most trouble would be a good place to begin."

"Oh," I say, and find myself looking around this light-gray office. It ain't quite *Cuckoo's Nest*, but you can tell a white person work in here. Everything is so nice and neat. Too nice. Ain't no papers on her big maple desk, except for that questionnaire I gave her that she's reading over right now. There's one of them black blotter things, a fancy gold pen sticking up out of a marble holder that I bet ain't got no ink in it, a burgundy stapler and Scotch-tape dispenser, and a yellow pad with lines on it right next to a sharpened number-two pencil like my kids use at school. Things is just a little too perfect in here for my taste. I can't even smell nothing.

And where's the couch? I don't see no couch. Just a window seat, and it's full of stuffed animals. The walls is lined with all these weird pictures that look like some kids just scribbled crayons or markers on some paper, and since they probably her kids, she felt obligated to frame 'em and hang 'em here instead of at home, where nobody she know gotta look at 'em, just people like me: complete strangers. Wait a minute. She ain't wearing no wedding ring, so I betcha she ain't even got no kids. I'll tell the truth: if I was a man and I passed her on the street, she ain't nothing I'd do a double take for. But if somebody was to do her makeup—at least put some on her—and if she got rid of that mousy brown hair and maybe highlighted it or at least added some blond streaks, she could maybe halfway pass for attractive.

But she's a psychologist. She should know this shit already. Maybe she like the way she look. And, plus, I know she's rich, so I wouldn't be surprised if these pictures wasn't painted by some famous artists and she probably spent a fortune on this shit. White people sure know how to waste money.

But. Belinda, the very nice white girl I still work with at the post office (since I found out just how fast a hundred thousand dollars can last), told me that last year, after a divorce and losing custody of her kids, she took a three-month leave of absence and spent quite a bit of time with a psychologist who helped her get her head back on straight. She found some confidence, too, which Belinda said she never really had much of in the first place. I could relate to that, 'cause you can fake having confidence. I'm real good at it.

Last week I just came out and told her that ever since my mama passed away I got too much on my mind these days, and could I get that woman's number. I didn't feel like telling her all the details when I knew I'd just have to repeat the shit to the doctor. So. I saved it all for this white lady in this navy-blue suit that look like it could be Ellen Tracy, but with the kind of money she making, she wouldn't be wearing Ellen, but, then again, some rich white people is stingy and spend all their money on silly art and drive cheap cars but got investments all over the world, so it could even be a knock-off. She coulda got it at Loehmann's, Marshall's, or even Ross, but, hell, who cares?

This is exactly why I'm here. My mind be zigzagging all over the damn place. Everybody said that the grieving process takes a long time, but I was feeling like this even before Mama died. It just got worse. I really don't know where to start or what to say. I done already answered a million questions on that form she still flipping through, so she should know my whole history up to this very minute. Some of them questions was a little too personal and none of her fucking business, so I either left 'em blank or just lied.

They say you should always get two opinions, which is why, right after I leave here, I'm going to see another doctor. This one's a psychiatrist, and she's black. Last Sunday, right after church, Smitty's wife, Lela, told me ever since she accused him of cheating on her it was 'cause she had forgot he had told her he was going fishing, and she said she had to admit that there was a whole lotta loose ends just hanging and not connecting to stuff like they used to, and she was worried that maybe she was going nuts, so the pastor's wife gave her the name of a psychiatrist who she went to see, and Lela said that doctor told her right off the bat that she wasn't crazy, and she said the doctor—who didn't even seem like a doctor, but just a woman you would want to be your friend—made her feel comfortable. Lela said she didn't want to sound like no racist, but she thinks it's 'cause they was both black and it was just some things this doctor already understood and she didn't have to explain. Lela said she done got to the heart of quite a few of her problems and her thinking is getting clearer.

When Dr. Simpson looks at me, I feel kinda weird. I'm scared of what's about to come outta her mouth, but when she opens it, she just says, "You've got a number of stressful things going on in your life right now, especially with the recent loss of your mother, don't you, Charlotte?"

"Yes, I do."

"Which of these do you feel is occupying your mind most?"

"All of 'em."

"Wow, all of them are preoccupying you."

"Yeah."

She just sits there like she's waiting for me to say something, but I'm waiting for her to say something first. Finally, she says: "You said your son might be gay?"

"Is."

"That must really be hard to digest."

"It certainly was. Don't you think it's sick?"

"Doesn't matter what I think. It's what you think about it."

I just look at this bitch. She probably from California. They all think like this in California. I get more comfortable in this chair and then I say, "I don't like it. It ain't normal. He should be liking girls."

"But if he doesn't like girls, does that cause you to have ill feelings toward him?"

"I don't know. I love my son, but I just can't accept the thought of him kissing no boys, and Lord only knows what else they do. It's weird, I don't care what you say."

"Okay," she says. "We can come back to this issue another time, if you don't mind?"

"No, I don't mind. But what about my husband? And my sister who don't like me and always accusing me of being jealous of her, which is not true? And then, before my mama passed, she asked that all her kids spend Thanksgiving together, and I'm supposed to go to my sister's fancy big house when deep down I don't want to, but if I don't, I'll be labeled the wicked witch, and I don't want no more friction if it can be avoided. So what you think about this?"

"Wow. That's a mouthful. How about we start by talking about your situation with your husband?"

"I'm listening."

"What do you think about it?"

"He's a liar and I don't trust him."

"I think that makes a lot of sense. Given what you've said here about him, it would be hard to trust him."

"So you think I should go on and divorce him?"

"I think we have to figure out what you really want to do about this. I imagine you have mixed feelings and are conflicted about some of this."

"Yeah, but so what?"

"What kinds of things does he lie about?"

"I only caught him in two. But they was two big ones."

"Can you tell me what they were?"

"Yeah. Ten years ago he had a affair with some woman and I busted him on it, and now I just find out that she had his baby and he been taking care of it all these years."

"And?"

"And that's it."

"That's why you want to divorce him?"

"Yeah, wouldn't you?"

"I can't say what I'd do in this situation. I'm more interested in what you're feeling."

"I'm pissed off. I hate his guts. I don't trust him. Don't believe a word he say."

"Do you still love him?"

"That's beside the point."

"That's beside the point?" the doctor says. Is she a echo doctor or what?

"What's love got to do with it? Like Tina said."

"Charlotte," she says, folding her hands.

"Yeah."

"Tell me why you're here. What you want me to help you do."

"I told you on the questionnaire. I want to make some changes in my life, and it's so much stuff going on I just don't know where to start. I need to sort some of it out."

"Well, you are starting. You're here, today." She takes a quick peek at her watch.

"Is my time up already?"

"Not quite. About ten more minutes. We stop at ten to the hour."

"Okay," I say, trying to hurry up. "I also wanna talk about my job."

"What about your job?"

"I hate it. I wanna quit. I work for the post office, but I

wanna start my own business and stop punching in and punching out. I'm tired of getting up at the crack of dawn five days a week and still ain't making no money. I wanna do something on my own. I forgot to mention that I hit Little Lotto for a hundred thousand."

"Wow, that should've come in handy."

"It'll be gone before Christmas at the rate I'm spending it."

"So—do you have any entrepreneurial ideas?"

"A few."

"Tell me."

Why she have to put me on the spot like this? Shit. I don't know, but I hear myself say, "I wouldn't mind starting my own catering business, 'cause I'm a good cook and I know all kinds of rich people from the routes my carriers deliver to, and a lot of 'em been knowing me for years, when I used to do the same routes. That would be one."

"Do you know much about this business?"

"I could learn. My sister does something like this out in California."

"Perhaps you could ask her for advice?"

"No. I wouldn't wanna do that."

"Why not?"

"I don't wanna get into that right now."

"Okay. Any other ideas?"

"I can sew. I was thinking of maybe doing some upholstering or making drapes, or maybe learning how to do interior decorating, or refinishing furniture, I don't know."

"These all sound like great ideas. And fun, creative things to do. A lot of successful people in these areas."

"Yeah, I just want one that's gon' be the most profitable."

She looks up at me like I just said the wrong thing. "What's wrong?"

"Nothing," she says. "Money is really important to you, then?"

"Ain't it it to you?"

"Yes. But I'm more curious as to how vital it is. I mean, would you choose to do something you didn't feel passionate about because it made you more money, versus something you felt passionate about that didn't make quite as much?"

"I can learn to like a lotta things. I been at the post office for eighteen years and it's just starting to get on my nerves. I just need a bigger payoff."

"Okay," she says, in a singsong voice.

She's getting on my nerves. We ain't solved nothing in all this time, and I thought I'd be able to walk outta here with some solutions. "What about my husband? What should I do about him?"

"Oh, Charlotte. I can't answer a question like that for you."

"Why not?"

"First of all, I don't tell my patients what to do, I try to ask questions so that you discover the best way to resolve a situation, and sometimes that requires more than one session. I mean, you have a history with this man. There are so many issues that come into play, and we haven't even begun to discuss them yet. Would you like to start there next time?"

"I guess so. But just tell me. Based on what you do know, do you or do you not think I should divorce him?"

She picks up her yellow pencil and then puts it back down, real slow. "I can't answer that question, Charlotte, and it would be totally unprofessional for me to even try. Let's talk about this further next time. When can you come back to see me?"

"I don't know," I say, getting up.

"I'm open this time next week."

"Let me check my schedule and I'll call you, okay?"

"Okay," she says, and stands up and comes from around her desk. Damn. She must be about six feet tall. No wonder she ain't got no husband. I shake her hand and tell her I'm looking forward to seeing her next week, but as soon as I get outside, I take that little business card she gave me and throw it in the first trash can I come to.

Well, this is a switch. First of all, Dr. Cecily Greene's office ain't even in no office building. It's in a brownstone. When I walk in, there's a little rock fountain in the hallway with water trickling through it. It's pretty. I smell incense burning. Whatever kind it is, I like it. And is that jazz I hear playing in the background? Before I get a chance to sit down, a handsome woman in her early forties with a short curly afro and great makeup application opens the door and smiles at me.

"Hello, Charlotte. I'm Dr. Greene, but please feel free to call me Cecily."

"Okay," I say. She smells good, too. What is that she's wearing? If I get a little closer, maybe it'll hit me. When she turns around, I'm almost staring her in the face. I feel like a damn fool. "What's that perfume you wearing?"

"It's a combination of essential oils."

"What kinda oils?"

"Jasmine, ylang-ylang, and geranium."

"Never heard of 'em."

"I've got an extra little bottle I keep here in my office you can have."

"No, I wouldn't want you to do that."

"I mix them myself. It's no problem."

"Thanks."

"So—sit anywhere you like," she says, pointing to two big thick oversized velour chairs. Purple with orange piping. Nice. Across from them is a loveseat, and this is a deep-tangerine color with purple piping. I sit in one of the chairs. She got a few books and what looks like medical journals stacked on one side of her desk, which looks like a antique. I see a *Essence* magazine and *Black Enterprise* and a crossword puzzle and a coffee cup with a teabag hanging over it that's sitting on one of them little cup-warmers. There's a purple glass dish sitting on the corner of the desk and it's full of hard candy and mints. I want one, but I ain't gon' take one.

"Can I get you something to drink? Water, juice?"

"Nope. I'm fine."

She walks over and turns the music off and then comes and sits across from me. I don't know why I ain't nervous.

"So—Lela referred you to me."

"Yep."

"Good. She's nice. A very smart sister. So, tell me, Charlotte, what can I do for you?"

She used the term "sister"? I can't believe a doctor would say that, but I like it. "I don't know, Cecily," I say. "Where's your questionnaire?"

"I don't use one."

"Why not?"

"Because they don't really tell me anything about you as an individual. It just puts you in a yes-or-no square box, you feel me?"

Did she just say, "You feel me?" She did. Yes she did. I like this, too. "Yeah, I do," I say, and just look at her.

"Let me tell you how I work. First of all, most of my patients come to me because they've had some kind of trauma or negative experience and they're suffering. One of my goals is to help relieve some of your suffering and help you to learn something about yourself. But it's something we do together."

"Okay, but I don't really feel like I'm suffering, except over the death of my mama, but when it comes to everything else, I'm just pissed off."

"I'm sorry to hear about your mother."

"Thank you."

"Who are you pissed off at?"

"At my husband, my older sister, and my son. Some days my daughters is on the list, but not today. That's it for right now."

"Well, let me tell you how we can start. If you feel comfortable with me, during our first three sessions my hope is to begin to get a clearer picture of you and your background. This includes everything from what you believe in to any traumatic experiences you may have had, such as the loss of your mother—and that's a biggie for most of us. As time goes on, when we're really getting somewhere, these will probably be the times when you're going to feel a little uncomfortable because I may say something that stirs something up. This is when you might not want to come back, but this is when we're getting beneath the surface. This is when many of my patients start to cancel appointments and become angry with me to some degree, because they want to blame me for their discomfort."

"I won't do that," I hear myself say.

"Let's hope not. So—you have one sister for sure; do you have other siblings, Charlotte?"

"I have a older sister and a younger brother and sister."

"So you're in the middle."

"I guess. But can I just tell you what my husband did, and then, if we have time, I wanna tell you about the fight me and my sister had right after Mama's funeral—well, actually, it was the day of the funeral—and this is the oldest sister, who was Mama's favorite, and she thinks everybody jealous of her 'cause she got money, but I ain't, and she thinks her shit don't stink—forgive my French—and she gets on my last nerve, and even though I love her I can't stand her ass half the time, but because Mama made us promise, I'm supposed to spend Thanksgiving at her damn house, and I'm trying to get myself mentally prepared for more bullshit or else figure out how to just get along with the huzzy once and for all and be done with it. Should I start with my husband first?"

She kinda leaned back in her chair, but she got a smirk on her face like she already know what the deal is. Or—maybe I'm just a complicated case. Hell, I don't know. "You certainly may."

And then I tell her the whole thing. Afterwards, my throat is dry, so I ask for some water and she gets it for me and comes and sit back down. She looks dead in my eyes and says: "Let me get this straight. This is something that he did ten years ago and you're going to leave him now?"

"Yeah."

"Well, what's happened over the last ten years? Have there been other affairs?"

"I don't think so. No."

"Does he have a gambling or drinking problem?"

"No."

"Has he been a good husband?"

"Yeah, but I can't trust him no more. I already filed for divorce."

"How does that make you feel? I mean, do you feel better now that you've done that?"

"No. That's why I'm here. I feel confused."

"Well, you know what this feels like to me?"

"No, what?"

"It feels like you're applying suntan oil today for a burn you got last summer."

"What?"

"Think about that for a minute."

I do, but, shit, a sunburn ain't the same as a lying husband, so I say, "But he still lied. They took our income tax and everything."

"Okay. But what if he had told you the truth, what would you have done?"

"Probably divorced him."

"Then I can understand why he didn't tell you."

I sorta feel like slapping her, but then I remember what she said a few minutes ago, and I ain't falling for that trap, so I just take another sip of my water and don't say nothing but act like I'm all ears, which I am.

"Are you leaving him as a statement to society, or because you really don't love him and don't want to be married to him anymore?"

"It's about my pride. I don't want him to feel like he can walk all over me. He should tell me the truth."

"This is just one incident that happens to be quite emotionally loaded. But trust is a very fragile bond that's been woven between two people, Charlotte, one that sometimes has to be rewoven, and when it is, that reweaving can even be stronger."

"Okay, but I gotta go."

"Okay, but let me say this. If after almost twenty years of marriage you don't think there's going to be some secrets, or that your partner isn't going to keep something from you, then your expectations are unrealistic."

"You saying that everybody do this?"

She smiles at me, and now, for some reason, I don't feel like slapping her and wanna take back the one I was gon' give her. "What I'm saying is that sometimes people keep secrets to avoid causing pain to someone they love. That's all."

"Well, I guess that make some sense, but it don't feel good when you find out the truth, that's all I gotta say."

"I know."

"When can I come back?"

"You want to come back?"

"You know I wanna come back. I wanna get my sister's stuff out the way, 'cause Thanksgiving is right around the corner."

"Then why don't you check your schedule, and let's try to meet a week from now, and from there we can decide how often. How does that sound?"

"It sounds good," I say. "It sounds real good."

When I stand up, she gives me a hug. A soft, warm hug. One like a mama or a sister would give you. One like I ain't felt in years. I really ain't gotta go nowhere right now, 'cause I took a sick day. But Cecily was right, she was already starting to tap into something that was making me feel ridiculous, and now I wish I'da kept my big mouth shut, 'cause I really felt like curling up in that chair with a blanket and drinking some hot tea with her and rubbing some of her oil on my wrists and behind my ears while I explained why I wasn't speaking to my mama when she died and how bad I feel about it and why I don't confide in my sisters no more. Because I don't really think they like me. And it hurts. I want to tell Cecily the truth. That I miss my sisters and brother and Mama, and how tired I am of living like I'm out in the middle of nowhere and don't nobody seem to hear me begging to be rescued.

Thanksgiving

"Daddy, I think we should go ahead and eat without them," Paris says. "The food is getting cold."

"I agree. She knew what time dinner was being served," Janelle says.

"Maybe they got lost. They ain't never drove way out here to California before."

"She probably just wants us to wait so she can make a melodramatic entrance," Paris say, moving Janelle's little plastic turkeys with everybody's name on 'em around the table so nobody a be sitting next to somebody they gave birth to, fathered, or live in the same house with. Janelle thought this would give everybody a chance to get to know each other better. Look like I'ma be sitting next to Randall, Paris's new boyfriend, and the same one who fixed up her yard all fancy.

"Let's all try to think positive," Lewis say, putting ice cubes in our glasses for the second time. He look good, but it's written all over his face that he wish it was a turkey with Jamil's name on it. For sure, next year, he said. One good thang is he been sober for ninety days and'll probably get his driver's license back early next year.

"It's not like she doesn't have my number. She could've called us one way or the other."

"Daddy, are you sure she said she was coming?" Janelle ask.

"I said I'm *hoping* she'll be here. That's all I said. Look, I'm going on out in the backyard for a few minutes. Somebody let me know if and when they get here."

"We're giving her another fifteen minutes, and then let's eat," Paris says.

All I can say is, Charlotte is just as stubborn as Viola. My long-distance bill gon' be sky-high from listening to her go on and on about her and Paris's differences. At first, I thought I was doing a good job convincing her that everybody can't see eye to eye all the time. That folks ain't gon' always agree about the way thangs is, was, or should be. But regardless of everythang, when you blood relatives, somehow you need to figure out a way to overcome all these differences and remind yourself that you part of a family. You ain't gon' never have but one. In this case: y'all sisters. And all this not-speaking mess is ridiculous. I told Charlotte this, and I sat in that kitchen all morning with Paris and repeated the same thang.

Charlotte swore I just didn't know what it felt like always being made to feel like a outsider in your own family. I said ain't nobody taking sides. We ain't laying blame. This is why thangs don't get put right. Everybody wanna blame somebody else. Do you wanna be sisters again, or do you just wanna be right? Paris said she wanted her sister back. Charlotte didn't answer me, so I said, Somehow, some way, everybody gon' have to step up to the plate and accept responsibility for this nonsense. It might not never get solved, but so what? Get the hell over it and let's move on. She kept on ranting, so finally I just said, outta all the times she need to put her pride aside, this is one of 'em. It wouldn't kill her to try it. Plus, I told her to show some respect for her mama, me, and the other kids, and have her black ass sitting at this table with the rest of the family come Thanksgiving Day. I cursed her. Sure did. And I told her I didn't care how she got here either. I was steaming mad. 'Cause this don't make no kinda sense whatsoever, which is why I did something that probably shocked the heck outta her—something I understand she very good at doing: I hung that phone up before she had a chance to say another word. Even still, I been sneaking and calling the house for the past three days and ain't got no answer. Suzie Mae said she ain't seen 'em or talked to Charlotte in going over a week.

And even though it's gon' hurt everybody if she don't show up, one monkey don't stop no show.

———————

It's nice out here. I been watching these orange fish just a-swimming away in they own pond. I ain't never been in no house quite this grand before, and Brenda is sho' 'nough impressed. At first she didn't thank her and the kids—and especially our new baby girl, Chanterella—would be welcome, but Paris set her straight real quick and told Brenda that since her and the kids is part of my life now, that makes 'em part of our family.

I decide to smoke one of them expensive cigars she brought me back from London. This only the second one I even lit. I tasted the first one on my birthday and finished it when Chanterella got here a few hours later. Howie say she look like me even if she ain't mine. But it don't make no difference one way or the other, she my daughter, my brand-new baby girl. And, speaking of Howie, here he come. Just can't let a man have no peace.

"Cecil, you missing the last quarter of the game, man. It's Detroit thirty-five, Buffalo twenty-one."

"I'll be in there in a few minutes, Howie."

"All right," he say. He clean up good. Howie woulda been spending the holiday by hisself, so I asked Paris if he could come with us, since we got plenty room in our new Dodge van, and she said no problem. She a whole lot nicer than I remember. Maybe it's this Randall fella who done put the sparkle back in her eyes. He is a nice young man, no doubt about it. During the first quarter, he told me straight out that not only did he love my daughter, but why he loved her. I ain't used to hearing no man be so honest with his feelings like that, and I'ma see if I can try it. The one thang he said that I truly prized was how much respect he had for her. "Respect" is a strong word. If I didn't know no different, I'd swear Paris gave birth to his little girl, Summer, 'cause, first off, they downright favor each other, and, plus, she been all up under Paris since they got here. Paris been stroking that girl's head, and seem like, the longer she did it, the closer Summer leaned in. She must need a woman to touch her soft like that. I don't know what her own mama's up to, but it ain't none of my business.

They say ain't no accidents in life. Chanterella was born on my birthday and Paris was on her way back from some health club in Arizona and drove all the way to Vegas just to see her. Then Janelle and Shanice turned right around and drove up the next day, and to top it all off, Charlotte went and did something that almost gave all of us a heart attack: took a train to Vegas to give me Viola's half of that lottery money and helped me finish sorting the rest of Viola's belongings since the house finally sold. I took her down to Thomasville and she went and bought the very same dining-room set Vy had on layaway and shipped it back to Chicago.

Charlotte asked me to use some of that money to reopen my barbecue joint so I could stop working at the casino. I told her the only way I'd even thank about doing that was if she was to be my partner. She said that would be kinda hard, living all the way in Chicago, but I told her that weren't necessarily the truth, 'cause this time around I'd be getting me a certified accountant and a real bookkeeper so we can keep track of the money the way them IRS like folks to do. I told Charlotte she could trust me. That I would send her her cut as long as there was some-thing *to* cut. She said she'd trust me. I liked hearing that.

She even told me she learning how to sell and market food, and can show me how to sell my barbecue sauce in them fancy upscale type a stores. That I can get my picture on the bottle if I want to. Hell, I mean, heck, I can't take so much excitement at one time, but I'm trying to get used to a whole lotta thangs, including missing Viola. I thank she knew exactly what she was doing when she passed, 'cause she done caused a whole lotta good for all of us.

With that insurance money she left me, I took it and bought her a beautiful headstone and had her picture put on it—the one I got from the kids, with her new teeth and slim body. She'd get a chuckle outta that, I know she would. Me and the kids chipped in and gave the church where she was baptized some money to start a memorial fund in her name that's gon' send a bunch of little ones to sleepaway camp in the summer. Viola'd get a kick outta knowing something was being done in her honor. The rest of the money I used to put a down payment on a nice four-bedroom tract house in a neighborhood where the kids can go to a good school. They don't need to catch no buses. It ain't but four or five black families in our subdivision, but it don't make me no difference. It's still a whole lotta vacant lots and seem like they finish a new house every other week, so it should be some more folks moving in real soon.

And as soon as Chanterella get weaned off breast milk, Brenda say, as long as she ain't gotta give up going to choir practice on Tuesdays and Thursdays, she be more than happy to help run the Shack, 'cause she said she got skills she ain't never had a chance to use. I told her one thang we doing is changing the name to something a little classier. It ain't gon' be no shack, that much we already know. We found a nice spot about ten minutes from where we live, but Brenda worried that black folks won't drive all the way out there for no barbecue. I told her black people will drive as far as they have to for a good bone to suck on, and, besides, white folks like barbecue, too. Our food ain't prejudiced, and this time around I ain't hiring nobody that can't be bonded, or operating nowhere we gots to keep a gun hid underneath the counter.

I could probably sit out here all day, 'cause it smell just like I imagine a rain forest would. It's getting nice and cool, too. Just the way I like it. I guess I feel brave enough to do this now, so I take Vy's letter from inside my jacket pocket, unfold it, and start reading to myself:

June 9, 1994

Dear Cecil:

First of all, I want you to know right now that I ain't been feeling good all day so if for some reason I don't make it to tomorrow don't go blaming yourself cause I got your papers today. That ain't what did it, baby. It was paint and gas and smoke or maybe just pure excitement at the thought of moving into my new place. But then again, I guess I can tell you that even though I was real happy about my new condo, deep down inside I was scared. Scared to leave this house we been living in all these years, and scared to go somewhere else by myself thinking I'm starting over. I didn't want to start over. I liked it the way it was. But that ain't true either. I wanted you to know that I understand why you left, Cecil. I do. And I know you ain't no low-down dirty adultururous or however you say it. You ain't never done nothing deliberate to hurt me and I appreciate that. I know I turned into a first-class bitch over these past five or ten years and I do believe that the change of life had a lot to do with it, but I didn't know it at the time, and of course now, I know that they got medicine you can take to make you feel like your old self again. I do believe this was when I started turning against you and I guess you started turning to somebody else for comfort. I don't blame you. I just want you to know how much joy you brought me over the years and how grateful I am to you for giving me four beautiful kids and that I loved you like you was a delicious apple, Cecil. You remember when we used to be nice to each other? Couldn't get enough of each other? When we made each other laugh and smile? Well, I'm smiling now, Cecil. I'm smiling cause I hope you find some kinda happiness with that young woman and them kids. Don't let Howie talk you outta enjoying her cause he ain't got nobody. Our kids may not warm up to her at first, but give them some time and they'll come around. If they don't, to hell with them too. You do

*what makes Cecil feel good and help that girl with them kids. I
didn't give you a whole lotta credit or time the first time around
but now you got another chance. So enjoy it. I'll be honest with
you, I hope you don't love her with the same hot torch you had
for me, but give her a low steady flame, the best part of you,
and she'll be happy. I hope you use some of the insurance
money to get at least one of the Shacks back open, and if you
can, change that stupid-ass name to something classy like
"Cecil's House of Barbecue" or "The Best BBQ in Vegas."
And try to open it in a decent neighborhood. White folks love
barbeque too and you can trick them into thinking it's gourmet
food (the same way they do us when we spend a fortune on that
mess they make that don't taste like nothing), and black folks
will drive to hell and back for some good barbecue, some collard greens and potato salad and peach cobbler. Can that girl
cook? Ain't her people from Texas? If they are then she should
know how to make a decent cobbler and at least a respectable
sweet potato pie. And sell your sauce. Ask Paris to tell you how
to do it. Let it sit right up there on the shelves at one of them
gourmet grocery stores next to all them marinades you scared
to try. And do me a few favors, Cecil. Try to see your own kids
every now and then. Talk to them on the telephone. Let them get
to know you so when you gone, you'll be missed too. And you
be happy. Would you do that for me, Cecil? For old times sake?*

Always, Your wife, Viola

*(P.S. If you plan on keeping that young woman, please get
rid of that Jheri Curl, and buy some modern clothes. Throw
every last one of them pastel shirts and polyester pants in the
trash or give them to the Goodwill!)*

"Cecil! What you out here laughing so hard about? It was
Detroit, and kick-off for the Dallas–Green Bay game be on in a
few more minutes!"

"I'll be in there in a minute, Howie," I say, and fold up my
letter and put it back in my jacket pocket.

Viola. Viola. Had it all figured out, didn't you, baby? I don't know why I ain't surprised. "Thank you, Vy," I say, and take a nice long drag off my cigar. Was that a car door I just heard slam? I walk along the path leading to the side of the house, and when I flip the latch and crack that gate open wide enough to see, Charlotte, Al, and the kids is getting out of a silver Lincoln Town Car I know ain't theirs.

I go on back inside, where the whole family's standing in the entrance saying hellos and glad-you-made-its, and after kissing all my grandkids and they disappear faster than I don't know what, the air suddenly feel a little thick in here, so I walk over and give Charlotte a big hug. "Hi, Daddy."

"Did y'all have any trouble finding it?" I ask. Al is just now coming in with a coupla suitcases.

"Naw," she say, looking around like she getting ready to do some kinda inspection. "All these houses out here look so much alike we drove right past it. A few times."

"How you doing, Al?" I ask, hoping to lighten things up.

"Hey there, old man. You looking good. Hey, Lewis. Good to see you, too, dude."

"The address is right on the front," Paris snaps.

"Thanks," I say to Al, trying to figure out how I'ma stop this before it get started. "Well, we just glad you all made it here all right."

"Would you like me to show you where the guest room is, Charlotte, so you guys can put your bags in there?"

"We staying at a hotel. But thanks. Nice house. Just tell me where a bathroom is so we can freshen up."

"Then why'd Al bring the . . ."

"I'll show you," Janelle say.

"How many days did it take y'all to drive all the way from Chicago?" I ask.

"We didn't drive," Charlotte say before walking down the hall. "Our plane was late."

"You mean you got on a plane?" Paris asks.

Charlotte stop dead in her tracks. "Yes, I did."

"Go on and tell the whole truth, Charlotte," Al says.

"All right, Al! First of all, the plane was late and we did get a little lost . . ."

"No we didn't, Mama," Tiffany says, coming outta nowhere and just a-giggling away.

"Okay! The truth is, I made Al drive around this block I don't know how many times till I could get the nerve up to come in here."

"Well, you're here," Paris says. "And now that we're all under one roof, can we please hurry up so we can sit down and eat?"

Everybody seem to be in agreement, and after all the introductions is out the way and we finally sitting at the table, Paris looks up and say, "Who's going to say grace?"

Everybody look around at somebody else.

"I will." And I do. And we eat. And it's good. And afterwards I get a little upset stomach from eating too much of everything, and by the time I come out the bathroom, everybody done left to go see *The Lion King* except for my kids, Brenda, and the baby.

"You all right, Cecil?" Brenda ask when I come out.

"I'm fine, sugar. Just fine."

"All right, me and Baby Girl going upstairs to take a nap, so y'all go on and do what you gotta do."

"Where is everybody?"

"They all down there in the family room—or whatever room that is—waiting for you. Praise God."

I give her a kiss on the lips and then give Baby Girl one, too. She ain't no fussy baby, thank goodness. I walk on down the hall, and they all sitting on the floor in front of a big fire going strong.

"Hi, Daddy," they say at one time.

"Hi. Y'all all right in here?"

"Yep. We're fine. But we want to hurry up and do this because it's driving us crazy," Paris says.

"Speak for yourself," Charlotte says.

"I'm perfectly fine," Lewis says.

He sure look hot in that brown sweater, 'cause his forehead is full a sweat beads. I sit on a black leather couch.

"What was yours like, Daddy?" Janelle is asking.

"Don't be so nosy," Charlotte say.

"She was just curious," Paris say back.

My big Baby Girl sho' look pretty in yellow. "You know what, Janelle, you sho' look pretty in yellow."

She look surprised to hear me say this.

"As a matter of fact, all three of you girls look lovely. And, son, you looking healthy, and I'm proud of what you doing with yourself these days. That's all I wanna say. No it ain't. Paris. I want you to know how much I respect what you doing with my grandson and with your own life. And you, too, Charlotte. 'Cause if it wasn't for you people wouldn't be able to get they mail. You been through a lot, Baby Girl, and I'm proud of the way you handling it. Vy always said you kids was as smart as they come. I feel blessed to be y'all's daddy and I'm sorry I wasn't able to spend as much time with you as I wanted to when y'all was little, but I'm here now. Is that all right?"

"It's all right, Daddy," each one of 'em say together. It's all right.

"Now, why don't y'all go on and read your letters?"

Nobody don't say nothing.

"Okay, see what I mean? Now, I'm trying *not* to run the show here, but nobody's opening their mouth. So who wants to go first?" Paris asks, looking at Charlotte. Everybody's holding a letter.

Don't nobody say nothing again until Charlotte point to Paris. "Since you the oldest, why don't you go first?"

"Okay, I will," Paris say, and put on some glasses. I didn't know she wore glasses.

"Dear Charlotte:

"I hope you ain't still mad at me cause I ain't mad at you. It

ain't gon' take me all day to say what I gotta say, so please pay attention. All my life I tried to show each one of you that I loved you. I did it the best way I knew how but sometimes as a parent it's hard to tell when one child might need a little more atten- tion and affection than the other ones. Trying to keep four kids and a husband happy, warm, full and clean, sometimes you don't notice which one that is. That's what happened to you. I didn't notice, and it just dawned on me that that's all you been trying to do with all your theatrics and what have you, is to get me to notice. I understand it now, and hope it ain't too late to say I always noticed everything about you, and I'm just sorry for not letting you know it, and just how much joy you brought me. Charlotte, I'm sorry if I didn't make you feel like you was something special, cause you was. Your light always shined bright but I guess since we had 'four' lights glowing at the same time, sometimes it felt like y'all was just one big bulb. But do me a favor, don't take it out on your sisters and brother, cause it ain't they fault. And especially Paris. It was me who put her on that pedestal, but it was pure selfishness on my part cause I needed her to help me with y'all littler ones. I'm sorry if doing this made you feel like you didn't measure up to her but you did, Charlotte. And still do. If I could go back and do this all over again I would hug you a little more, kiss you more, let you sit on my lap as long as you wanted to and pay attention to every word of your long boring book reports. (smile) I'd listen to you take all day to memorize your five-line Easter piece. I'd watch you do the hop-skip-and-jump a million times if that's what it would take for you to know what a amazing child you was. But I can't go back, Charlotte. So for now on please try to understand that you been getting mad at the wrong folks. Ain't nobody in this family trying to hurt you. Nobody. So soften up a little bit. Let the sweet part of you come back out and share it. Please stop cussing so much. Of course you got it from me but it don't become you and it didn't become me. I also wanna apologize for talking like I wasn't educated, but I wasn't.

*Please teach my granddaughters how to act like young ladies
and make them go to college. And get Monique off that damn
medicine cause that stuff ain't doing nothing but messing—"*

"I did, Mama," Charlotte blurt right out. "And you right.
She's been getting all A's and B's since I took her off that mess,
and even her teachers notice how much more alert she is." And
then it's like she catch herself or something, and she say,
"Sorry, y'all. Didn't mean to interrupt."

"Way to go, Monique," Paris says.

"Right on," Janelle says.

"All our kids is smart, if y'all ain't noticed," Lewis say to
the fire, and then throw another log in it.

"Okay. Quiet, please! We're only on the first letter. May I
continue?" But Paris don't wait for no answer.

*". . . doing nothing but messing up her young brain. Please
make them read books and not just magazines. Take them to the
library and make them stay out that damn mirror so much.
They can't get no prettier. And pretty ain't enough no more.
Make sure they know that. And please try a little harder to accept the fact that your son is gay and don't make him feel bad
about it. We all have to learn to accept people for who they are
and not who we want them to be, Charlotte. Just think about
what other people might be feeling before you criticize them,
and forgive them when they make mistakes. Because everybody
do. Including you. So forgive your husband. Forgive everybody
that don't do exactly what you think they should do when you
think they should be doing it. Ain't nobody perfect. And, Charlotte, learn how to be happy. And then get used to it. I don't care
if you work at the post office for the rest of your life. Be proud
of yourself for doing something constructive. The only person
you need to impress and compete with is Charlotte. I been impressed. Kiss my grandkids for me, and try using a speaker
phone so you won't be able to hang up in nobody's face no
more! (smile) I'm gon' miss you, Miss Black America, cause
that's what me and Paris used to call you when you was little.*

We always knew you had what it took. Why you think Paris used to love combing your hair? Telling you how to act. And who you think was showing her? Even when you was a baby and fell off the kitchen counter, who you think it was that ran to pick you up and rubbed cocoa butter on your scar which is why you ain't got one on your forehead to this day? We had dreams of you being on TV, wearing a crown, cause Paris always said she wished she was as pretty as you, and she wasn't jealous, she was just proud to be your sister. I love you, and don't forget it. Now put that in your pipe and smoke it!

"Love,

"Your Mother

"(P.S. If you ever hit that damn lottery please give my share to your daddy. He could probably use it. A few dollars to your brother would be nice, but only if he ain't drinking.)"

Charlotte's a goner. But I don't thank we should say nothing to her right now. She need to feel this. All of it. I just hope she can tell by how quiet it is in here that we all on her side. All of us is wiping our eyes on our sleeves, so I go grab a handful of napkins off the bar and hand one to everybody. I keep one for myself.

"I can't read mine right now. Lewis, can you go? Please?" Charlotte say this with a softness I ain't heard since she was a little girl. When I look at her, I'm wondering if I wasn't too harsh with her on the phone. I was mean. And I know it. Now I'm thanking maybe it felt like I was just one more person who didn't care or didn't understand how she felt.

"All right, then," Lewis say, "I'll go."

"May 3, 1994

"Dear Janelle:

"I know you probably think I'ma light into your ass about George but you done been through enough over that sorry son-of-a-bitch, and I'm hoping that by the time you read this he'll be sucking lifesavers in a cell. He gon' get his. God will see to it, but I don't wanna waste another drop of my precious energy

talking about him, so I'm skipping the subject. I want you to know how proud I am that you finally took a stand. You always been so wishy-washy, Janelle, and I ain't ashamed to say it, cause it's true and you know it. You different. And even though all of us kinda make fun of some of the shit you do I hope you know we don't mean no harm by it. I just don't know no black people that go to psychics and get people to deal some cards to tell you shit you already know. What really baffles me is why you keep going back. And how much do this mess cost? Do you ever get any answers to your problems or do they just generalize? I also don't know too many folks who celebrate every single holiday by putting all kinda shit out in they yard like you do, but the one thing I have always liked and loved about you, Janelle, is that you did the shit anyway. You didn't really give a damn who laughed at your big bunnies or your groundhogs or even them inflatable secretaries sitting at a real typewriter on your front porch, which was pushing it, but I didn't wanna say nothing, not to mention all them flags flapping in the wind and folks not knowing which country you from, but you didn't care, did you, baby? You did it cause you enjoyed doing it and because it was your way of being creative. The same goes for all them college classes you been taking for the last fifteen years. You speak like you educated even if you ain't got no degree and I love hearing you and Shanice talk cause y'all speak English the way it was meant to be spoke. I want you to know that everybody that graduate from college ain't smart, so please don't feel bad about that, Janelle. It's some very stupid educated people in the world, cause if it wasn't, don't you think the world would be in better shape than it is? Think about it. But not right now. The point I'm trying to make is this: all these years you been trying to figure out where your place is, where you fit in, what you can do that's gon' make you successful, I don't think you realize you probably already found it. Look in your garage! It's full of all kinda stuff. Look in your house. All them ruffles and ridges and shit should tell you a thing or two,

*like maybe you should be doïng something where you can putz
around and make things pretty, as corny as some of it is, but
hell, it's a lotta people out here just like you who love corny
stuff. Plus, some of the things you make are downright pretty.
So think about it. And stop judging your success by everybody
else's. Appreciate the talent you got and work from there. Make
a good living, don't live to make it big. Happiness ain't got no
Ph.D. or no certain amount of zeroes behind it. Have some fun.
Pretend like the rest of your life is a emergency and you might
find a whole lotta happiness right now, which is all I want for
you and your sisters and brother. I ain't got too much else to
say, other than please don't run and try to find a replacement
for George. You can survive without a man, baby, believe me.
And let one pick you this time. And be picky. Do a background
check if you have to. Please take good care of my granddaughter cause she gon' have some problems. She gon' have some
rough times and I hope you know she gon' need somebody who
specialize in this problem but try to make sure you get somebody that's been through it theyself and didn't learn how to
cope from no book. Help her learn to be comfortable with herself. Help her understand that this was not her fault and try to
get her to realize that George was just one sick man, that most
men ain't like him. Tell her there's some Cecils in the world,
cause your daddy is a good man. Oh yeah, and y'all try to accept Brenda. She ain't taking my place, she just picking up
where I left off, and ain't nothing wrong with that. Anyway, I'm
cooking some chili for me and Shanice and I think it might be
sticking. Hey! Maybe you should learn how to become a psychic? I saw a few ads in the back of my Star or Globe, where
you can go to school to learn this stuff. Even shuffling them
tarak cards. Seem like they make damn good money and pick
they own hours. I don't know about benefits but think about it.
Hell, this way you can predict your own damn future. How
about that?*

"*Love,*

"Mom

"(P.S. Janelle, I been meaning to tell you this for years. Get a new hairstyle cause the one you been wearing for the past five years done played out.)"

Now everybody is cracking up. Even Charlotte. This is good. This is real good.

"Thank you, Mama!" Janelle yell at the top of her lungs.

"Okay, I'm ready now," Charlotte say. "And Mama's right about the hair, Janelle."

"Shut up, I heard her. It seems only fair that I should read Lewis's letter to him now. What do you think, Daddy?"

"I ain't in it. I'm loving every minute of this. Hell, it seem like Viola right in here with us. Maybe we should just ask her."

"WHO SHOULD GO NEXT, MAMA?!" Janelle scream while pushing Charlotte against the couch, and she starts reading anyway.

"April 15, 1994

"Dear Lewis:

"I hope you outta jail if you reading this the way I asked y'all to read it, but I ain't heard from you all day and you know damn well it's my birthday. I know what this mean if I ain't heard from you. Was you in jail today, Lewis? I hope you ain't done finally killed somebody driving drunk. I pray that ain't the case. You been lucky so far. Well, maybe not lucky. But anyway, Lewis, even though you done had problems dealing with your problems these past ten or fifteen years, I still wish I woulda had two more of you cause you got a heart of gold, and you ain't got no qualms when it come to showing your feelings like a lotta men do. More women should love you, but that ain't what I wanted to say. I wanted to tell you that I know why you didn't wanna go to Squirrel and Boogar's funeral. That it's been bothering you all these years, but let me tell you something: they probably in hell for what they did. But it's okay. Folks do terrible things to other folks and then you the one who *suffer while they off dead somewhere. That ain't meant to be no joke, even though I'm chuckling—"*

"Excuse me for interrupting, Baby Girl, but what did your cousins do to you, Lewis?"

"We know," Paris says.

"We've known for years," Janelle says.

"How come y'all never let me know you knew?" Lewis say.

" 'Cause we didn't want you to feel uncomfortable or feel any shame or embarrassment about us having this knowledge. Plus, at the time Mama found out, she went straight to Aunt Priscilla and Uncle Julian, but of course they didn't believe her, so she told the police and they kept an eye on them both until they finally got caught doing more wrong. Karma is Law. So— may I finish?"

"Wait," Paris says. "There's nothing for you to be ashamed of, Lewis, and we don't ever have to mention this again if you don't want us to."

"Thanks, sisters. And if you ain't figured it out by now, Daddy, I'll tell you later."

"That won't be necessary. But I'm here, if you wanna talk to me about it."

"Okay!" And Janelle start reading again:

"I left here worrying about you cause I don't want you to spend the rest of your life in pain, trying to drink your way to happiness. You ain't gon' find it that way, baby, and you know it. Have it worked so far? Hell no. That's why your ass always end up in jail. You got a disease and you act like you don't know it which is why you do dumb shit when everybody know you smart. Don't you remember what your IQ is, or was? They was genius numbers, boy. I raised you to know the difference be-tween shit and shinola so grow up, be a man, and do whatever it take to get yourself together. Stop drinking altogether. Not even a beer every now and then cause beer is still booze. Go to AA on a regular basis. Going to church wouldn't hurt either. I didn't write this letter to preach. But. Do something with your

son. *I don't care if you ain't got a thousand dollars to send out there, just send something and do something before he grown and don't give a flying fuck if you live or die. That's how it happen, Lewis, believe me. You had a daddy but you don't even know Cecil, do you? Try to get to know him before he join me. It ain't too late, you know. And watch over your sisters. You they* only *brother. Be strong for them, like they been trying to be for you. And I want you to know that the only reason they be pissed off at you all the time is cause they love you and know how smart you are too. They always wanted more for you. Not the life you got. They want to see you live better. They want to see you happy, and the shit you been doing disappoints them, but probably not nobody more than it do you. Don't kill yourself trying to do everything at once. Take your time. Take one step at a time. Do something with them inventions you been telling me about for years. Put your fucking money where your mouth is. And find yourself a good woman. Not them ones you meet in bars. Leave them whores right there on them bar stools. Or, learn how to be by your goddamn self till you got something good to offer a woman besides what's between your legs. Men always think that's enough, but believe me, baby, it ain't. I'ma be watching you and I want you to know that I'ma be your biggest cheerleader. Know that. So Sis-boom-ba!*

"Love,

"Mom

"(P.S. *Please don't drive until you get your license back and go to the doctor and get some real medicine for your arthritis or you gon' be cripple by the time you forty. And a little exercise, like walking, wouldn't kill you. Of course I tried it, but just cause it didn't work for me don't mean it won't do you no good. Oh! Watch Oprah Winfrey sometime. She'll make you feel good even when you depressed. Four o'clock on Channel 4. Tape it if you ain't gon' be home. You do have a VCR, don't you?*)"

Janelle fold up his letter and then get up and hand it to him, but Lewis got his head down. She put her hand on his shoulder and then kiss the top of his head. "It's okay, Lewis," she say.

And he just nod his head up and down and say, "I know. I know."

"It's on me now," Charlotte says, "so sit your butt back down and listen. Wait. Y'all is . . . I mean, has everybody been paying attention to the dates on Mama's letters?"

"Yep," Lewis say. "Mine was pretty obvious."

"She wrote mine right after we left Vegas," Janelle say.

"Well, mine is dated the day she left," I say.

"The day she left to go where?" Janelle ask, and then, I guess before somebody get a chance to say a word, she say, "Strike that. I didn't mean it. I know exactly what you meant, Daddy. Sorry. Go ahead, Charlotte. When was Paris's written?"

Charlotte looks down. "Hers got two dates on it. Just the months March and April 1994. Okay, can I start today?"

"Wait a minute. I wanna take this sweater off," Lewis say. "I'm burning up."

Everybody watch him, and I just wanna see if he got on a undershirt or not. He do. But if Vy was here I know she would snatch it off his back and go soak it in some light bleach water, 'cause that thang so dingy it look light gray. "Okay," he say.

"Wait a minute!" Now Janelle got two cents to throw in. "I forgot to tell you that when we finish we're going to draw names."

"Oh, yeah," Paris say.

"For Christmas. The four of us will draw a name and we have to make each other a handmade gift. The kids'll do the same thing, except they can buy theirs, but they can't spend more than ten dollars. Tops. And they absolutely positively have to reach the person on or before Christmas Eve—got that, Charlotte?"

"I heard you! And don't worry. Mine will be on time."

"One more thing," Lewis say like he deep in thought again. "This may sound stupid to y'all, but, speaking of Christmas, this will be the first one we can't send our mama a card, but I was thinking that maybe we still should."

"What?" Janelle ask.

"What I'm saying is, we can still send her cards for Christmas, her birthday, and Mother's Day, like we always did."

"And send 'em where?" Charlotte ask.

"To heaven, where else? Just don't put our return address on the envelope. This way we can keep her posted on what's going on in our life."

"I like that idea," Paris says.

"Me, too," Janelle says, now that it sunk in.

"I couldn't agree more," Charlotte says. "Right on, Lewis. Brilliant idea. Now, sit your behinds down so I can read this. I wanna hurry up, 'cause it feels like it's almost time for round two for the grub. I'm reading right now, so everybody shut up.

"March 1994, April, 1994

"Dear Paris:

"I don't know who told you that you had to be perfect when you grew up. It wasn't me was it? I hope to hell not, cause if I did, I'm sorry. I'm so sorry. Or maybe it's just cause you was the oldest you just felt like you had to set a good example for everybody else, was that it? My heart been breaking watching you trying to do everything right, trying to get everything just so. You do a damn good job of it, but it's a hard act to keep up, ain't it? I see the answer when I look at you. It's the reason why you sneak and take them pills that I know damn well ain't no Advil. I remember Liz Taylor got addicted to some pills, too, and I betcha that's what's happening to you. I betcha you don't believe it though, do you? I betcha you think you too damn smart to get strung out on some pills, don't you?

"Hold it. Wait a minute here," Charlotte says. "What she mean, strung out? I *know* you ain't strung out on no pills, are you, Paris?"

"To put it bluntly, yes. Was. I got addicted to painkillers and just got off of them a couple of months ago."

"Is that what you've been popping all this time?" Janelle say. "I didn't know those things were addicting."

"It ain't no crime," Lewis butt in. "She human just like everybody else."

"Well, did that spa help you, baby?" I ask.

"It was rehab, Daddy. I only told you guys about the spa because it was right next door. I spent four days at both places."

"How'd this happen?" Charlotte's asking. "And how come you didn't tell us?"

"There's a whole lot of reasons."

"We listening," Charlotte say.

"I don't want to get into it now. . . ."

"Get into it," Charlotte says.

"Yes, do," Janelle says. "Your letter's right here and it'll wait a minute or two."

"Okay, well, this is just how I feel, I'm not saying it's true, but, being the oldest, I've always felt like everybody was always looking up to me, and I don't think I ever really felt entitled to make mistakes. And when I did, I kept them to myself, because it was embarrassing. And I didn't want you guys to think of me as a failure or not being able to hack it. Everybody expected me to be in control, even Mama, so I just got good at faking it. A few trips to the dentist later, I got something that made it easier to cope. I got tired of always being asked to do everything. Tired of coming up with all the answers. And I got tired trying to help solve everybody else's problems but didn't know where to turn when I needed help solving mine."

"What you think we here for?" Charlotte says.

"You haven't 'been' here for a long time, Charlotte, and that's the reason I'm glad we're here now. We used to all be tight. Close. Like sisters. And brother. But somewhere along the line we all went our separate ways and became estranged—not strangers, but distant. I feel like I've been out on an island with no boat. I mean, my son got a girl pregnant and I was scared to tell you guys because Dingus is supposed to be such a good kid, and he is, but he's not perfect, and neither am I."

"Who's pregnant?" Janelle asks.

"Nobody now. It was Jade."

"That preacher's daughter?" Charlotte ask.

"Yes."

"Them's the one who give it up the most after being in church all day and locked up in the house all night," Charlotte say. "But, anyway, you can call me from now on, you got that?"

"I got it."

"I got a phone," Lewis say. "And it won't be getting cut off any time soon."

"Okay," Janelle says. "But I want to know if you still crave those things."

"I have my moments."

"Don't give in to it," Lewis says. "It's just a trick, believe me."

"I won't," Paris say, and she look so relieved. That same softness seem to done spread across her face, too. When she lean back against the couch, her shoulders look like they just drop.

"Okay, I'm reading again!" Charlotte yell.

"I betcha you think you too smart for a whole lotta shit, don't you, Paris? But let me tell you something you should know by now: ain't no pill in the world can make you feel better from the inside. Ain't no pill gon' make you hurry up and live. Ain't no pill gon' stop you from feeling lonely or take the place of a good fucking orgasm neither. Yeah, I said it. And meant it. So stop fooling yourself. If you can't throw them things in the trash and go on about your business, then go somewhere and let somebody help you get off 'em. And don't be too proud. You ain't done nothing wrong except be human. You are human, Paris, in case you don't know it. I pray to God that you stop trying to be Superwoman. You can't be everything to everybody. Can't always be a perfect mother and perfect wife

and perfect cook and perfect caterer and a perfect woman. This is something I been wanting to tell you for years: you ain't gotta be perfect at every-damn-thing. Do something half-ass. Let the shit stick to the pan and burn. Being mediocre ain't no crime. I been mediocre all my damn life and I think I did all right. Stop thinking you gotta save the whole goddamn world. Save your-damn-self. Lord knows I apologize for begging you to do that TV show. To hell with cooking meals on television can't nobody but you make, no way. I just wanted to see you on TV, that's all. Anyway, I'm sorry for expecting so much from you. You done did so much for me and right this minute I'm clicking my teeth together cause they fit perfect. Thank you for these dentures. Thank you for my condo and my car and my cruise. Did I get to go on my cruise? Even if I didn't, I'm cruising now, baby, believe me. Oh! Do this for me. Sleep with somebody just cause the spirit move you. You ain't gotta wait till you in love. Otherwise, you might dry up. Them days of waiting for the phone to ring is long gone. Act like a man. You see somebody you like, talk to him. Ask him out on a date, and even if he reject you, fuck him. Ask somebody else. And keep on asking. As for my grandson? Tell him my choice is USC or Stanford. But he can go wherever he wants to go, just as long as it's a university. And when he throw that first touchdown pass on nationwide TV, tell him to look directly at that camera and blow his granny a big sloppy kiss and I'll get it. Yes indeedy. I love you back to back. Know that.

"Your Foxy Mom

"(P.S. I forgot. I bet money that if Nathan show up at my funeral, it'll be cause his shit ain't raggedy no more and he gon' try to weasel his way back into you and his son's life. If and when he do, slap him for me and tell him to keep stepping. He had his chance to be a daddy and he blew it. So fuck him and the horse he ride in on. Unless of course Dingus feel like being bothered with him. What else? Oh yeah. If Lewis ever get his driver's license back, let him have my car, but tell *him don't take my little felt dog whose head shakes back and forth out the back window. I like that dog. Oh. And one more thing. It wouldn't kill you to join a health club or start jogging. I know you think you cute, but you ain't that cute. You was looking like you was in your first trimester the last time I saw you and your ass was on its way somewhere else. All three of you girls ain't nothing but younger versions of me, except I was sexier and better looking, but you didn't hear that from me, now did you?)"*

Now Paris the one who done lost it. Everybody have. Including me, again. I'm surprised when Charlotte walk over to Paris, grab both her hands and pull her to her feet, give her a big hug, then push her away and hauls off and slap the taste outta her, but Paris look like she was waiting for it, 'cause then she turn right around and slap the living daylights right back outta Charlotte, and then they put they arms around each other again and cry till they lips is trembling and they turn into smiles, and then the other kids join in, and the next thang I know, everybody laughing like somebody just told a good joke. I join all four of 'em.

My babies. My kids. My grown-up children.

I hear Chanterella crying through the door.

"Come on in, Brenda, since you're family now, too!" Paris yell out.

But that door don't open.

"I want to ask whose house will Thanksgiving be at next year, but I won't, because I'm trying not to be pushy and controlling, which is why I'll just sit here and chill and wait for somebody else to ask."

She look around the room and don't nobody say nothing, 'cause everybody acting like they don't hear her.

"Okay, I'm taking one step at a time trying to change my evil ways, but I guess I'll just have to start again tomorrow. . . ."

"No, you won't," I say. "Have a seat, Paris. And relax."

"Right on, Daddy!" Janelle say.

Paris sits on down and crosses her legs like them people do who meditate.

"For your mama's sake, and mine, which of y'all kids will have Thanksgiving dinner at they house next year?"

Charlotte say: "Well, me and Al is, are, thinking about building a house big enough for all y'all, but we positive the foundation won't be dug by next November, and, plus, it's too damn—I mean, it's just too doggone cold in Chicago."

"How big do a house have to be to eat in it?" I ask.

"Bigger than our little duplex, I'll tell you that much," Janelle says. "Our place is so small, Shanice and I bump knees under the table. But, if all goes well, and Orange Blossom and I manage to branch out in two years' time, hopefully it won't be."

"That said, I wish you the best of luck in your new career, Janelle. Now, your mama had asked that y'all meet at each other's house, but since everybody seem to have a reason why they might not be able to, me and Brenda is buying us a nice spread in Vegas and it'll be ready in six weeks, and since we never did have the family reunion like we was supposed to, we wouldn't mind if everybody was to come spend it with us, would we, Brenda?"

"No, we wouldn't mind one bit," she say through the door.

"We can have it at my house next year," Lewis say.

Everybody turn and look at him like he some kinda alien or something. But not me, I'm smiling.

"What house?" Charlotte asks.

"Yeah, what house?" Paris say.

"The one I'll have by next Thanksgiving," my son say, and we all know he mean it. "And, Daddy, thanks for the gesture, but I think there's quite a few other weekends we'll find to come visit you. Is that all right?"

"That's all right," I say, and his sisters walk over and give him a high five, and then he come over to me and we look each other in the eye and smile for the first time in years, and I give him some skin, too, but on the black-hand side.

Please turn the page for an excerpt from
Terry McMillan's unforgettable novel of
love, yearning, and self-preservation

DISAPPEARING ACTS

Coming from Signet in April 2002

Zora

I've got two major weaknesses: tall black men and food. But not necessarily in that order.

When I'm lonely, I eat. When I'm bored, I eat. When I'm horny (and can't resolve it), I eat. When I get excited, I eat. When I'm depressed, I eat. When I just feel like it, I eat. When I smoked, I didn't eat as much, but smoking wasn't half as satisfying as eating, so I made a choice. I chose food. I had migrated up to a size sixteen, and that's when I looked at myself in the mirror and couldn't stand it. I said, "Just wait one damn minute here, Zora!" and, along with some of the other flabby teachers at the junior high school where I teach, joined Weight Watchers. I lasted about a year and am now down to a slender size twelve—well, it's slender enough, considering I'm almost five foot eight. Of course I've still got this damn cellulite, which drives me crazy. I can feel the ripples other people can't see. Which is precisely why I went out and bought Jane Fonda. Now, when I wake up, before I have my coffee, I work out with Jane. I've been doing it with her for a few weeks now, but so far I can't see a bit of difference.

Weight Watchers turned out to be a drag. It was just like going to the fit doctor, aka neurologist. One thing I can't stand is people telling me what to do—after all the years I'd been told what not to eat, drink, and think—so I quit when I thought I looked halfway decent in my favorite Betsey John-son dress.

Yes, I used to have fits. And not the kind kids have when they can't get their way. Real fits. Seizures. When I was little, I fell off a sliding board and hit my head on the cement, and I guess that's what did it. But it's been almost four years since I've had one. The neurologist calls it a remission, but that's not true. I stopped taking those stupid pills is what I did, and started picturing myself fit-free. No one really believes in the power of this stuff, but I don't care, it's worked for me—so far. As a matter of fact, when I started visualizing myself less abundant, and desirable again, that's how I think I was able to get here—to 139 pounds. And no, I am not from California. I just taught myself how to say no.

I cannot lie. There are times when I have to say yes to chocolate, but I try to minimize my intake. And Lord knows I make the best peach cobbler and sweet potato pie in the world, but I've not only learned to share, but also how to freeze things that beg to be consumed in one sitting.

Except when it comes to men. I've got a history of jumping right into the fire, mistaking desire for love, lust for love, and, the records show, on occasion, a good lay for love. But those days are over. I mean it. Shit, I'm almost thirty years old, and every time I look up, I'm back at the starting gate. So yes. I would like a man to become a permanent fixture in my life for once. But don't get me wrong. I'm not out here cruising with lasers and aiming it at hopefuls. My Daddy always said, "Sometimes you can't see for looking," so what I'm saying is that from now on, no more hunting, no more rushing to discos with Portia on a Saturday night, standing around, trying to look necessary. I made up my mind that the next time I'm "out here"—which just so happens to be right now—it'll have to start with dinner (which won't be me) and at least one or two movies and quite a few hand-holding walks before I slide under the covers and scream out his name like I've known him all my life. Some flowers wouldn't hurt either.

And just why do I feel like this? Because some of 'em don't last as long as a Duracell, no matter how much you keep recharging 'em. And I've been tricked too many times. Maybe misled would be a better word. No, maybe falsely impressed would be even more accurate. Then again, I'm really too damn gullible. I believe what I want to believe. One of my best girlfriends, Claudette, told me that my biggest problem was that I didn't do my homework. "Find out the most vital things first," she said.

"Like what?" I asked, even though I knew exactly what she meant.

"Has he been to college? Does he have a drug problem? Interested in personal hygiene? Does he believe in God, and if so, when was the last time he set foot inside a church? Does he know that respect is a verb? Does he love his mother and father? What's his family like? His friends? How does he feel about children and marriage? Has he ever been married? Does he have any idea what he'll be doing ten or twenty years from now? Is it remotely close to what he's doing now? That kind of shit."

But I'm not into interrogation. I prefer to wait and see if the image he projects lives up to the man. And vice versa. Let's face it: All men are not husband material. Some of 'em are only worth a few nights of pleasure. But some of 'em make you get on your knees at night and pray that they choose Door Number One, which is the one you happen to be standing behind. And it's not that I haven't been picked before. Because I have. They turned out to be a major disappointment. Said one thing and did another. Couldn't back up half of what they'd led me to believe. Then begged me to be patient. And like a fool, I tried it, until I got tired of idling, and the needle fell on empty. Some of 'em just weren't ready. They wanted to play house. Or The Dating Game. Or Guess Where I'm Coming From? or Show Me How Much You Love Me Then I'll Show You. And then there're the ones who got scared when they realized I wasn't playing. "You're too intense," one said. "Too serious," said another one. "You take them lyrics you write to heart, don't you, Miss Z?" I told them that this wasn't high school or college, but the grown-up edition of life. They were still more comfortable not having a care in the world, so I let 'em run and hide, especially the ones that needed professional help. So now I'm taking off the blindfolds and doing the bidding myself. After a while, even a fool would get tired of bringing home the TV and finding out it only gets two or three channels.

None of this is to say I'm perfect. I just know what I've got to offer—and it's worth millions. Hell, I'm a strong, smart, sexy, good-hearted black woman, and one day I want to make some man so happy he'll think he hit the lottery. I don't care what anybody says—love is a two-way street. So yes, I want my heart oiled. I don't want to participate in any more of these transient romances—I'm interested in longevity. Let's face it: Some men take more interest in their pets than they do in their women. And even though I wish loving a man could be as easy for me as it was for Cinderella, I know it's not that simple. But it can be. And it should be. All you need is two people who are willing to expend the energy so that their hearts don't rust.

Which is one reason why I envy Claudette. She is so normal. She's a lawyer, married, has a daughter, and she's happy. She loves her husband. Her husband loves her. They are buying their house. They have lawn furniture. They ski in the winter and spend weeks in the Caribbean. He brushes her hair at night. She rubs his feet. And after seven years of marriage, they still unplug their phone.

On the other hand, Portia, who Claudette can't stand but I love, has an entirely different set of standards. "He's gotta have hair on his chest and no skinny legs. And he's gotta have some money. I don't care what color he is, but ain't no getting around no empty bank account."

"*Money isn't everything,*" I said.

"*Since when?*"

Portia thinks her pussy is gold. She's not all that educated—she got as far as court reporting school—but I don't care. I refuse to discriminate when it comes to my friends. I'm more interested in the quality of their character than I am with credentials. Besides, I know plenty of folks with degrees that are stupid. They lack the one essential thing you need to get by in this world: common sense.

I can't lie: Sometimes I fall into that category myself. Because I still don't know what it is about deep-black skin and long legs that turns me on, but some things aren't worth analyzing. It's taken me years to realize what I like and what I don't like. For instance, short men simply do not appeal to me, at least none have so far. And men who could stand a few trips to the dentist will never kiss me. Men who are afraid of deodorant knock me out. Men who roll over, stick it in, and think they've done something miraculous make me want to slap 'em instead of shudder. I can't stand vulgar men. Dumb men. Lazy men. Men who think the word respect means expect. Men who are so pretty they spend more time in front of the mirror than I do. Men whose brains can be measured by the size of their dicks. Selfish men. Men who don't vote. Who think all the news that's fit to print is on the sports page. Liars. Men who think that the world owes them something. Men who care more about the cushion between my legs than they do about the rest of me. Men who don't stand for anything in particular. Who think passion is synonymous only with fucking. And men who don't take chances—who are too afraid to stick their damn necks out for fear that they're going to drown.

So I guess you could say that the kind of man I like is just the opposite of these. Which means I like a clean, tall, smart, honest, sensuous, spontaneous, energetic, aggressive man with white teeth who smells good and reads a good book every now and then, who votes and wants to make a contribution to the world instead of holding his hands out. A man who stands for something. Who feels passion for more than just women. And a man who appreciates that my pussy is good but also respects the fact that I have a working brain. And last but not least, a man who knows how to make love.

I have not run into him lately.

Every man I've ever loved—and there've been three and a half—or that I've cared substantially about, brought me to these conclusions in a haphazard way, but I'm grateful to all of 'em, because had I not experienced them, I wouldn't have had any.

When I was sixteen, there was Bookie Cooper, whose skin shone like india ink and whose fingernails were yellow. He had muscles. He fixed the chain on my bike when it broke, then walked me home through the woods the long way and gave me my first kiss. Bookie used to whisper in my ear. He had such a soft voice that I often had to stare at his lips in order to figure out what he was saying. He was the first boy that made me tingle. And he taught me the power of kissing—just how serious it can be. But Bookie got killed. He was crossing the street on his bicycle when an ambulance hit him. For months, I couldn't believe it. I slept with that orange elephant he'd won for me at the state fair so I would still feel close to him. I even walked by his house and waited for him to come out, but another family had moved in, and this white woman with pink sponge rollers in her hair kept peeking through the curtains suspiciously. It took a long time for it to register that Bookie's absence was permanent. But I can't lie: I had to teach myself to forget him.

There was Champagne, the college basketball star who held my hand and stroked my hair while he talked, and forever smelled like British Sterling. Even though I was just a junior in high school, he made me feel like a woman. After my senior prom, with my very first glass of rum and Coke exaggerting everything, he talked me into giving up my virginity, and I did it because I was tired of saying no and figured if I got pregnant at least I'd be out of high school by the time it was born. And it hurt. I was grateful when it was finally over, and couldn't understand why everybody had made such a big deal about sex if this was supposed to be the thrill of a lifetime. I never did feel electric. But I didn't care; I still wanted Champagne. Being wrapped inside his strong arms was warm enough for me. As a matter of fact, I used to lie beside him and dream about him. Play every sad, slow song by Aretha and Smokey Robinson I could get my hands on and dig my face in the pillow and cry. Which is how I knew I was in love. We agreed to get married once we both finished college and he was playing in the pros. But what happened? I won a music scholarship to Ohio State, and he went to a Big Ten university in Indiana and never wrote so much as a word, not to mention the fact that his fingers must've been stricken with arthritis, because he never called either.

"To hell with Champagne," is what I said when I met David, who was bowlegged, walked like Clint Eastwood, drove a Harley-Davidson, and boxed. He was so black he was purple, and I swear I could've eaten him alive. Especially after he lifted me up on top of him and let me move any way I wanted to, as long as I wanted to. And I liked it. Loved it, really. He taught me that there were no limits to passion if you didn't impose any. So every time I felt like doing it I would dial his number. Tell him I needed to see him. David's body was my very first addiction. It was so cooperative. And he would take me for long motorcycle rides—in the rain, at night, in freezing weather, it didn't matter. This was the first time I experienced real adventure and understood what freedom felt like. But we hardly ever talked. So by the time David asked me to marry him, I realized two things: that he was boring except in bed and that there was *a big difference between wanting to spend the rest of your life with someone and wanting to experience continuous moments of ecstasy. I said no and told him I was moving to New York City to launch my singing career. I told him I wanted to live a bold and daring life, not a safe little cozy one in Toledo. He said he would make it exciting, but I told him I'd rather not try.*

By the time I got here, I decided to take a short sabbatical from men. But not all that short. It lasted about four months. Sometimes men can be more of a distraction than anything. Marie—she's my comedienne friend—says that I not only take them too seriously but I put too much emphasis on their worth. But I can't help it. As corny as it may sound—considering this is the eighties and everything— there's nothing better than feeling loved and needed. And until God comes up with a better substitute, I'll keep my fingers crossed that one day I'll meet someone with my name stamped on his back.